I0575256

Alexander Earl of Crawford and Balcarres

Argo

Or, The Quest of the Golden Fleece

Alexander Earl of Crawford and Balcarres

Argo
Or, The Quest of the Golden Fleece

ISBN/EAN: 9783337079116

Printed in Europe, USA, Canada, Australia, Japan

Cover: Foto ©Andreas Hilbeck / pixelio.de

More available books at **www.hansebooks.com**

A R G O:

OR,

THE QUEST OF THE GOLDEN FLEECE.

ARGO:

OR,

THE QUEST OF THE GOLDEN FLEECE.

A Metrical Tale,

IN TEN BOOKS.

BY

ALEXANDER, EARL OF CRAWFORD AND BALCARRES,

LORD LINDSAY, ETC.

LONDON:

JOHN MURRAY, ALBEMARLE STREET.

1876.

LONDON:
PRINTED BY WILLIAM CLOWES AND SONS,
STAMFORD STREET AND CHARING CROSS.

CONTENTS.

PROPYLÆUM.

'AYE, born a Poet!   All my boyhood's dreams,
'My manhood's visions, bright and wild, yet each
'Seal'd at my will with immortality—
'Think ye I know it not?   A child, I read
'In Nature's page my mission,—angels' hymns
'Dwelt in mine ears; and, 'mid the flow'rs and trees,
'Murmuring alternate verse and prayer, I walk'd
'With God, a Poet in my Paradise.
'Youth hath its anguish,—boys may bleed like men,
'Like men endure, like men subdue themselves,
'And, slaves without, rule o'er the world within :—
'And thus rul'd I, crown'd with no earthly crown,
'My mind my empire ; where I would I roved,
'Flowers as I pleas'd I gather'd ; garlands wove
'For Homer's shrine, my sculpture, and for his
'Who sang of Danaé, wise Simonides.
'And what car'd I for worldlings?   Could their scoff
'Blight the fair visions, taint the breath of heav'n
'That robes as with a veil young Poesy?
'Ah no!   I lov'd not whom I mingled with,
'Kept my own lonely path, conscious within
'Of powers I watch'd with awe, yet immature,
'But struggling into life—in silence watch'd,
'Nor sigh'd for other converse than mine own.
'Then rose thy sun, Italia! on my soul,
'Revealing beauty, harmony, and power,
'Till then unseen, though not unfelt, nor yet
'Seen fully till my noon of song be nigh,
'When utt'rance meet no more shall be denied.

'Till then—probation!   Yet e'en now I strike
'With fearless hand the chords, that then shall answer—
'True as old Ocean's mirror to the flash,
'Or Echo to the storm!'

               Thus sang I years—
Long years ago, in heat of youth; and dream'd
Of a great song, 'Jerusalem Destroyed,'
Should crown me 'mong the poets of all time,—
But, ere such venture, went on pilgrimage
To ancient Egypt and the Eastern land,
And learn'd unlook'd for lessons.   'Mong the wreck
Of empires, on a broken obelisk
In Carnac's temple resting, Thoth unroll'd
The map of ages, large, before my eyes;
And show'd me that Jerusalem, though dower'd
With gifts of promise, and her fall the knell
Of superstition, doom'd, those gifts mispriz'd,
Was but a part of a vast whole, of God
Plann'd, meted out, develop'd, and combin'd;
Which, to sing worthily, I must understand,—
Himself would teach me.   And once more I dream'd
Of a great Hist'ry, told how Providence
Works out the mighty epos of mankind.
But then I ask'd, 'What is the key unlocks
'Such secrets?   What the principle that rules
'Time's evolution, man's progressive march
'Controls and animates, and men with men
'Links through all ages, and mankind with God—
'The past, the present, with the world to come?'
And, as the evening shadows fell, I cross'd
The river, and in Thoth's still chamber pray'd,
Before the Tree, for guidance to such truth.
And from the Tree the answer came, that not
Through mystic ecstasy, but by the sweat
Of thought's knit brow and toil of the hard hand,
Delving among the ruins of the past,
Tapping the springs of time, and to both worlds
Of Faith and Knowledge free'd by Socrates,

And faith-inform'd by those who spake with tongues,
Bridging the gulf 'twixt God and man, inspir'd—
Such insight must be won.   And then I saw—
Dwarf'd in my self-esteem, humbled, and yet
In conscience of imparted power elate—
Wisdom how noble, Knowledge mean, compar'd;
And knew life worthless that subserves not truth,—
Beauty thenceforth less worthily esteem'd :—
Erring, for each to each is correlate.
Then cried I, 'Thou, Divine Philosophy!
'Thou, and none else, henceforth shalt be my Queen!'
And bright Urania came with all her stars,
And swore me vassal, and possess'd my soul.

Thus, toiling, pass'd my wealth of life away;
And when with siren voice across the sea
The Muse call'd on me, I or stopp'd mine ears,
Or answer'd but one instant, then was mute.
Like dogs that thrust their noses in the hand,
Craving for notice, longing for the life
Of sunny skies and uncoop'd liberty—
Oh! how I long'd to join them in the chace!
The bright ideas came; but brief caress,
Or rude rebuff, their sweet advance repell'd.
Yet oft I said, 'Some time perchance, not now!
'When but the heat of this long day is done,
'And I may ask my wages in repose.'

Meanwhile I found, or fancied found, the key
That loos'd Nile's sluices; and I sow'd a seed,
Which bore fruit upwards, and a harvest reap'd;
And sow'd and reap'd again; and now have sown
One last fond venture—if I see the end.
And some have recognis'd, but more have fed,
Unconscious whose the hand that turn'd the soil.

And now, the first time during all these years,
Came weariness, not of the head, but heart;
Weariness at the lagging march of truth;
Disheartenment, seen rather retrograde.
And I betook me to my Southern home,

The villa-palace and the garden fair
Where those bright youths and maidens whil'd the hours,
The Black Death raging, and Boccaccio told
Th' immortal tale of the Decameron.
And a great sadness fell on me—as falls
Sadness on eld'ring men, who think the world
Is aging with themselves, the younger race
Less gen'rous, less heroic than were their sires.
And certés, after each great tournament
In the world's progress, a reflux takes place,
And Doubt, and Fear, and Licence will prevail,
The many wearying of the fight prolong'd,
The few far-seeing tempted to despond,
When all that truth has conquer'd seems as lost.
Such flux of late years recognis'd, I felt
Hope's anchor loosen'd.   Europe's face I saw
Darken'd, the nations arm'd, and lovely Peace
Trembling betwixt the French and German scales,
And Red Democracy, repress'd, but coil'd
Ready to spring, and propagating foul
Her venomous offspring to pollute the world.
Nor less at home I watch'd with troubled eye
Much that I deem'd un-English rampant lewd.
The bonds that link the people with the throne
Relax'd, but for the personal rev'rence paid,
The office slighted, to a virtuous Queen ;
False teachers, welcom'd everywhere, abroad ;
Knowledge for Wisdom counted ; and the voice
Of numbers, erring witness, hail'd for truth :
Authority held cheap, and law defied ;
Dignities evil spok'n of,—all that most
Our sires rever'd—all holiest, noblest, best,
In Church and State, that stamp'd our England great,
Presum'd base metal, current only allow'd
By use and custom till new dies be struck
For cents and dollars, pounds to supersede,—
'What is' in all things held to need excuse :-
Vile teaching, viler credence, vilest most

The cow'rdice of the few that, wiser, know
Such teaching folly, but withhold their blame.
These things, grieving, I saw ; but, worse, miscem'd
That in life's higher spheres cold apathy,
A creeping palsy, everywhere gain'd ground,--
' Non-intervention,' ' peace at any price,'
' Our commerce is at stake,' the statesman's cry ;
And doubt of all that true our fathers held,
And we know truth, a fashion 'mong young men.
Indiff'rence gend'ring--reck'ning all as one
Falsehood and truth, a Christian and a Turk ;
Conviction's once strong will too weak to hate.
And Pyrrho's touch too paralys'd to love.

   Thus I desponded in that hour, and fear'd
The future's gath'ring vision dread, and cried,
' Where is the old enthusiasm that inspir'd
' Our sires, ourselves, the fathers of this time :
' Who own'd no law save honour and the voice
' Of duty, champions of humanity,
' Vassals of God, that Britain's sanguine cross
' Bore in the van of Europe's chivalry ?
' Then poor but, like the Hospitallers, free,
' Single in heart and strong of hand ; but now--
' Have we not, like the Templars, eat the fat
' And drunk the sweet of luxury and ease,
' And traffick'd with Mahound and Termagaunt,
' Till slight thing seems it that the paynim tread
' Jerus'lem and the Sepulchre defiles ?
' Would we do now as in this age's prime,
' When we withstood the world in arms 'gainst God,
' And Revolution cower'd and slunk away
' To the dark sewers and entrails of the earth ?
' Now hath the hydra rear'd her head again,
' And where the Heracles to crush her down ?
' Have we not bound our hearts, our wills, with chains
' Of adamant, of wealth--unduly priz'd,
' The curse of nations, nurse of low desire
' Till now we say, " Sufficient to ourselves

'" Our island home!   What though the strong oppress,
'" Or old friends bleed, or treaties be torn through,
'" And moral suasion unsupported by
'" The cannon's logic leads to light esteem--
'" What matters while our commerce rings the globe,
'" And neighbours pay meek homage while we preach ?
'" Let others fight, and welcome—we sit still."
' How chang'd from what it was when, in my youth,
' Each Briton walk'd o'er Europe as a king ;
' And Turk and Arab yielded me to pass,
' Known such, alone, respected and secure,
' Where now no Christian dares to show his face!
' Where is the prestige of old England gone ?
' And, England failing, who shall take her place,
' Undower'd with all these mercies which we sin,
' Heading th' undying war 'gainst Antichrist ?
' Are we then near the end, Typhœus' day,
' When Gods and men shall perish, time no more,
' And Argo come in clouds to save the just ?
' Where is religion, where philosophy ?
' Where is our faith in God and in ourselves ?
' For, as the whole, so each,—nations are but
' The individual on a larger scale.
' What can we hope when old worn fallacies
' Crop up as new, the wisdom of the past
' Flouted, God voted a nonentity,
' And man a brute, nay, animated clod.
' That blindly gropes its hour, and perishes ?
' Such are thy teachers now, O Israel !
' And we applaud, and love to have it so.
' O pristine Faith, how is thy fine gold dimm'd !
' O holy Rev'rence, where thine honour fled ?'
    Thus pond'ring, sad, depress'd, I sat and mused
In that old garden ; and I ask'd, what fruit
Of all my toil, of all the toils of those
My elders, who have taught since Socrates--
Save by myself, I deem'd, scarce understood
In fulness   'gainst the dragon's brood once sown

By Father Cadmus, but reviv'd in strength—
My arm now weak'ning, followers few to cheer,
Save those, too loving, who my nearest be,—
Beyond such, my poor name already rank'd.
Once honour'd a mere dreamer's, past his time :—
Why should I struggle more?   Why set forth this
Last argument for truth ?   Best, lay it by,—
Small chance to be found gold another day.
Philosophy seem'd lovelier less, her stars
Pal'd, in that access of discouragement.
—Fool! not remomb'ring this, that Truth is great,
And will prevail—that Time truth's harvest sows
In every cent'ry for the next to reap—
And that we toilers, not for time alone
Work, but for all eternity and heaven ;
There, on the lines reveal'd to us on earth,
To build Truth's perfect pyramid, and know
Beauty with Truth consistent, Harmony
Resulting thence, true music of the spheres —
And from that height sublime adoring hands
Stretch upward to the throne of ord'ring Love :—
Thoughts long familiar, nor for long obscur'd.
  For a soft dying breath of autumn's fall
Woke as I sat there, and refresh'd my brow ;
And the sweet bells swept down from Fiesolé.
And, long unseen, a presence came, on wings
Of beauty, and with smiles that mock'd the dawn ;
Young, as in those old days when Linus sang ;
Voice sweeter than the melodies of spring ;
Her virgin tresses dropping with the dews
Castalian, and Apollo's lute in hand,—
Truth in her eyes, and love in her accost.
I knew her, the bright presence, nor repell'd.
    " Thou hast," she whisper'd, " been unfaithful long.
" I claim my dues, if only for a time.
" Bound to the oar, yet slaves must rest awhile,
" Or little worth their labour.   Heracles,
" Sever'd from Iölé, must weep: but long

" Endurance brings the maiden to his side,
" Though but to greet and bid farewell.   The hour,
" By me long look'd for, now hath fall'n on thee.
" Not Thoth's dark cell, Parnassus is thy home.
" I was thy first love— come to me again !"
    Then, as I gaz'd enraptur'd, she went on :—
" Sing the old song of Argo, once in Greece
" Sung by Thymœtes   'tis a tale thou lov'st—
" Of Argo, great exemplar of the world,
" But in sparse fragments ill remember'd now,
" Distorted from its glory and debas'd.
" Thus shall thy early vows, thy debt, be paid."
    " Belov'd !" I answer'd, " I am weary-worn ;
" Thrice twenty-one long years have plac'd my foot
" On the third trembling stage of human life—
" Thou know'st how I have toil'd—how can I sing ?
" My voice is feeble, and the fire burnt low.
" Too happy have I liv'd ; nor, suff'ring, learnt
" Those lessons of the heart that teach in song.
" Nor would I spin the lighter measures led
" By thy mock sisters, slip-shod, that the slopes
" Haunt of the new Parnassus of this time—
" Bred in a sterner school now out of date.
" What audience could I, being such, expect ?"
    " True, thou art old," she said, " tho fire is low,—
" But debt thou ow'st ; and, if short reck'ning found,
" I am no usurer—pay me what thou canst.
" I know thee ever true to me in heart.
" Hast suff'red not ?   Thou hast.   'Tis not the dregs
" Of sated passion that give strength to song ;
" But sympathy, large, loving, for mankind ;
" And thou hast wept for others bitter tears.
" For measure—sing to me as did thy sires
" Ere Revolution dwarf'd the children's growth.
" There are that Chaucer, Dryden, Pope love still.
" Nor those despise that wake a lighter strain,—
" Greece had her Sappho, her Anacreon.
" The firefly shines as brightly as a star.

" If pure the fire, unsullied by the touch
" Of earth defiling, 'tis the gift of God,
" T' enlighten, purify, and cheer the time.
" There is no wisdom in exclusiveness.
" But doubt not. See this fountain, how it springs,
" Touch'd and set free, the stronger, long repress'd :
" How it springs up and sparkles in the sun !
" Doubt not, and trust me—I will sing with thee.
" For thou hast liv'd in the old days of Greece,
" And convers'd with the fathers of the world,
" Friendly, beneath their common patriarch's tent.
" Thou know'st their old songs and their mystery,
" Nearer Christ's faith than this learn'd age allows
" Old truths, forgotten long ere Homer sung.
" So shalt thou breathe a freshness on the brow,
" Fever'd with task-work, of this restless age ;
" So shalt, thyself refresh'd, to toil return.
" And if aught else be needed—if a touch
" Confess'd of such fond weakness—look at you
" Fair town, her dome, her tow'rs, where Dante dwelt ;
" And think how in this garden, in these halls,
" Thine own Boccaccio sang—his tongue is song—
" Legends as sweet as the Milesian Tales.
" Sing this tale too ; and make thy Tuscan home,
" Here singing, doubly famous to all time !"

So I obey'd the voice, the fount unseal'd,
And the sweet waters sprang up in my soul,—
But with less gen'rous freedom than of old.
And, as dead Fergus came to Senchan's son
By his tomb sitting, journeying to the south—
Sent to recover the old tale that told
Of Meva's and her husband's rivalry,
Lost heritage of Erin—to the tomb
Came in his shroud of mist, and the great song
Recited to the youth, and disappear'd ;
So old Thymœtes from Elysium came,
Sent by that fair one, pitying, as I deem,
My wreck of fancy ; and inform'd me how,

Not distant born from sage Æthalides,
That herald's soul liv'd on in him, and kept
Rememb'rance, Hermes' gift, of all had pass'd
In Argo's voyage to Æa and return,
Transmitted with that soul through all his race,
Hence true the record that his verse enshrin'd.
And he recited it, from first to last,
As sung by him in th' old Pelasgian tongue,
Which I had learnt in my long wanderings—
Now render'd thus by me in English speech.
And I have ended it this Whitsun-eve,
On the old garden-terrace sitting, where
That presence visited and sooth'd my heart,
And bade me of the future not despair.

The sun hath set beyond Carrara's hills,
And heav'n is all one blaze of purpled gold.
Fair Florence lies in loveliness below,
Each line of beauty pencill'd soft, distinct,
Set like a picture in her frame of hills,
With Arno rolling, though unseen, betwixt.
Villa, and tower, and cypresses afar
Mark the horizon, cut against the sky,
All soft'ning as the evening shades come down,
Light longest ling'ring on Fiesolé.
Sweet bells ring distant round—the nightingale
Trills from the copse ; the contadino's chant
Rises, and dies away in minor fall ;
The plashing fountain croons her lullaby ;
The orange-blossoms rich their perfume shed,—
Each several sense in ecstasy is lapp'd ;
Thought's busy visions slumber in repose.
My daughters' voices carolling I hear,—
And one comes forth, their mother, who hath been
My inspiration since her childhood's hour ;
The Beatricé of my life renew'd ;
My truest monitor 'tween earth and heav'n ;

Composing all harsh chords to harmony—
Beautiful more than even in her prime,
In womanhood's completest grace mature—
Comes forth, to crown the hour with sympathy,
With steps sedate and brow of heaven's serene.
Giotto's full ' O ' is rounded in my life.
If blessing lack I one, I know it not ;
God's hand is bounteous, and my cup is full.

    And she, that fair one, mistress of my youth,
So late a visitant, now pass'd away
And lost to view on Lycorcia's height—
Will she return ?   I know not, nor expect ;
For I am old in years, though not in heart ;
And I have paid the debt she claim'd of me.
I turn me now to life's hard work again,
Refresh'd,—more hopeful for the time to come.

                    VILLA PALMIERI.
                    May, 1875.

GENEALOGICAL TABLE OF THE PRINCIPAL DESCENDANTS OF ÆOLUS

WHO TOOK PART IN THE ARGONAUTIC EXPEDITION.

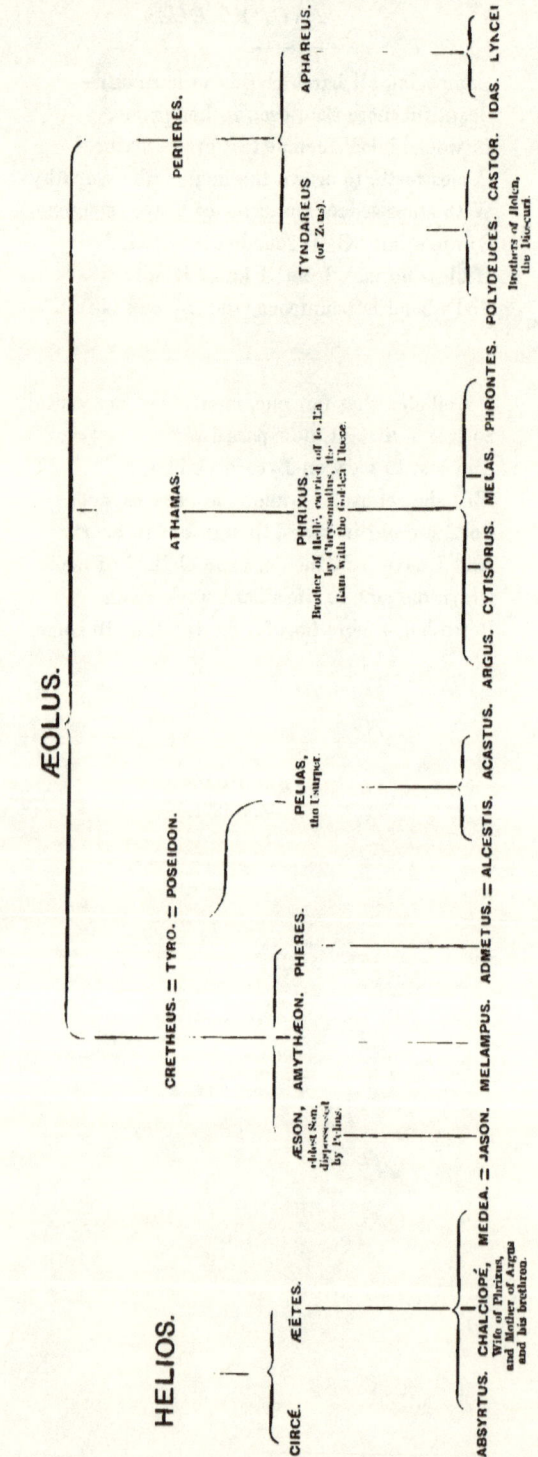

A R G O :

THE QUEST OF THE GOLDEN FLEECE.

Book I. Jason.

Chiron on Mount Pelion, vss. 1 sqq.—The Minyæ and Æolidæ, 39.—The
family of Æolus; Cretheus, father of Æson and Pelias; Athamas, father of
Phrixus and Hellé, 102.—Usurpation of Pelias, to the exclusion of Æson,
the rightful heir, and his son Jason, 118.—Alcimedé, mother of Jason,
123.—Prophecy of Delphi, 137.—Jason saved from the wrath of Pelias,
and educated by Chiron on Mount Pelion, 150.—Æson at his farm, 163.—
Market-day at Iòlcos; arrival of Jason; meeting with Pelias, 183.—
Family council of the house of Cretheus, 281.—The compromise with
Pelias, 359.—Summons of the heroes to the quest of the Golden Fleece,
409.—Building of Argo by Jason, 429.—Athena sends Jason to Dodona,
503; and engrafts a branch of the sacred oak within Argo, which endows
her with speech and immortality, 637.

On Pelion's brow the Centaur Chiron stood;
The west'ring sun was sinking in a flood
Of cloudless glory to his bourne of rest,
Behind the long-drawn wave of Pindus' crest.
Below broad-stretch'd the rich Æmonian plain,
Thessalia now, the old Pelasgians' reign,—
Once one vast lake till through cleft Tempé free
Poseidon loos'd its waters to the sea;
Yet still, in mem'ry of that distant day,
Marking their track, Peneius keeps his way.　　　　10
Northward, half-hid by Ossa, tower'd on high
Snow-crown'd Olympus, kindred with the sky,

B

Throne of the Gods; far to the South were seen
Parnassus' peaks, with many a range between;
But fogs hid Lake Copaïs and divine
Orchomenos, the Graces' early shrine,
Where Minyas built his treasury, to hold
The heaps uncounted of his hoarded gold.
Slowly his eye the wide horizon swept,
And, as he gaz'd, the princely Centaur wept,   20
Rememb'ring days long past, ere crime had birth,
When Gods and men in commerce dwelt on earth—
Dear friends departed, generations gone—
While he, their hoary teacher, stood alone,
Bow'd with the weight of immortality,
Longing for death, and yet he could not die.
A few short hours, and to that height sublime,
Fresh still in heart, untainted yet by crime,
Had Jason come, to bid the sage farewell,
And crave his blessing ; and, as his eye fell   30
Down on the shelt'ring Pagasæan Bay,
Where, radiant-glitt'ring, new-built Argo lay,
He saw him issue from the woods, and seek
His father's house, intent fond words to speak—
Words that might soothe his tender mother's sorrow—
One last night's converse ere they part the morrow.
Long linger'd Chiron o'er the dark'ning scene,
Pond'ring on what should be, and what had been.

From the far East the wealthy Minyæ came;
But they were men, not heroes,—the pure flame   40
Of honour burnt not in their bosoms,—pelf,
The lust of gain, idolatry of self,
Harden'd their hearts.   Not sluggards they in war,
But, still, defensive.   Gold from near and far

Their merchants brought, from Afric and from Ind;
Art's varied gauds and luxury refin'd
Adorn'd their ample dwellings; but—to fight
In some great cause for honour or for right,
Stake life and fortune on some high emprise,
Crown'd at the last by stern self-sacrifice—   50
This lay not in their thought.   Scant honour they
Paid to the Gods; but ever, day by day,
Wealth to create, and on themselves to spend,
Such was their being's object, hope, and end.
Still they were not without their better side,
To their engagements staunch—no touch of pride.—
Liberal—unless to debtors—now and then;
The women were far kindlier than the men.
      Not such the race of Æolus, the free,
The open-handed; prompt by land and sea   60
To seek out honour,—somewhat overbold
Towards the Gods, but their hearts never cold
To duty's call or generous impulse; still
Subduing circumstance to their strong will,
Save when they stoop'd, in pride of intellect,
To stratagem their purpose to effect—
Foolish! for, just and true, th' immortals love
Straightforward paths, nor devious craft approve;
But, though the issue work their counsels, blame
The means, and visit all such acts with shame.   70
Monarchs by birthright, haughty but sincere,
To all the Gods, most to Poseidon, dear
From age to age, whenever crime grew such
That heav'n's forbearing love was tax'd too much,
Off'ring themselves to bear their brothers' load,
And by self-sacrifice atone to God—

Such were the hero sons of early Greece,—
Fame be their guerdon—to their Manes peace !
   Men must to heroes yield.   'Twere hard to tell
How to the Greeks the Minyan empire fell.   80
Alliance first, then marriage—gifts t' attain
Protection, grants immunity to gain
From threaten'd vengeance—peace, in fact, did more
Thus to subject the weaker race than war.
Insensibly, as steals a mist upon
A smiling landscape, creeping slowly on
Till each fair feature disappears from sight,
Obscur'd and lost to view, though not by night,
So stole th' Æolid influence o'er the power
Of these their rivals, deep'ning hour by hour,   90
Till, peaceably, insensibly, the name
Of Minyæ lived—the same, yet not the same—
But in the mingled blood of those whose sires
Trac'd up to Æolus their natal fires,—
Those fires attemper'd, their rude strain improv'd
By the sweet Graces whom the Minyæ lov'd ;
While all their energy remain'd, though blent
With courtesy and chivalrous intent.
—These were, of course, the nobler of the race ;
The average man is always common-place ;   100
And mingled breeds oft yield, in Nature's plan,
Abnormal births, or more, or less than man.
   Three sons had Æolus—to name no more ;
Cretheus, his first-born ; Athamas, who bore
Sway over Thessaly, and there begot
Phrixus and Hellé,—Periëres' lot
Was Pylos.   Cretheus as his share obtain'd
Orchomenos, and o'er the Minyæ reign'd,—

Till, as the eagle soars to purer air,
Iölcos built, he fix'd his eyry there.   110
Æson, young Jason's sire, was Cretheus' son—
A true philosopher, if e'er was one—
By Tyro, daughter of Salmoneus,—she,
Forc'd by Enipeus, river-deity,
(Some say Poseidon's was the fond assault,
But all agree it was not Tyro's fault,)
Bore Pelias, Æson's brother. Cretheus dead,
Pelias usurp'd the throne. Disherited,
But affluent, easy Æson acquiesc'd,
And all contention 'tween them seem'd at rest.   120
He wedded fair Alcimedé, and, ere
A year was past, Jason was born, his heir.
    But Pelias much misdoubted of th' event,
And messengers forthwith to Delphi sent,
Thinking that, though the sire's cold blood consented,
The wife and mother might be less contented,
Excluded from her lawful rights as Queen,
Her son too Cretheus' heir, or should have been.
But she, sweet simple soul! a Minyan born—
Such words as jealousy, resentment, scorn,   130
Were not in her vocabulary,—how
Her bees came on, the purchase of a cow,
The last new charm to make the butter come,
Choice of quaint knickknacks to adorn her home,
Fulfill'd her days—a happy round of cares,—
She troubled not herself with state affairs.
    Meanwhile the messengers came back, and brought
To Pelias answer other than he sought:—
" Thou cuckoo, planted in an eagle's nest!
" Tremble, and mark the Pythia's behest.   140

" Thy fate is by Æolid hands to die.

" But most beware when, fall'n as from the sky,

" With one foot sandall'd, t'other bare, a man

" Shall come to fair Iölcos,—then thy span

" Dwines to its ending."   Cold broke out the sweat

On Pelias' brow ; and fierce his heart he set

To extirpate all of Æolid blood,

Jason the foremost ; but his evil mood

Hera reveal'd to Æson and his wife ;

And they, in terror for the infant's life,   150

Acted for once with common sense ; gave out

The child was ill—then dead ; and went about

Mourning ; and buried—what, I know not—in

A stately sepulchre, a grove within ;

And on—what truly was a cenotaph—

Carv'd, boustrophedon-wise, an epigraph.

Meanwhile, their friends bore off the babe, and gave

To Chiron's keeping, in his mountain cave

High on Mount Pelion ; where he grew to man,

A son suppos'd of the Magnesian clan,   160

And there receiv'd a hero's education,

Fit for the future ruler of the nation.

   Æson liv'd on untroubled at his farm,—

Pelias despis'd and would not do him harm.

He pass'd his days calm and contentedly,

Trying experiments in husbandry ;

Improv'd the plough,—till then a horse's tail

Drew it attach'd ; he bade two oxen trail

By straps, tied to a yoke, th' unwieldy mass

Of sharpen'd ilex,—but the stubborn, crass   170

Bucolic mind view'd it with strong objection ;

It almost rais'd a servile insurrection ;

They broke the model—it nigh broke his heart;
But bumpkin nature ever scorns at art.
Learn'd on manures he was, and weather-wise.
Fast, as the yearly constellations rise,
And set, he fix'd the calendar of toil.
He wrote a book on various kinds of soil
To various plants best suited,—'tis with praise
Cited by Perses in his ' Rustic Days.'   180
He liv'd life and enjoy'd, the Gods rever'd,
And, kind to all men, was to all endear'd.

   Some twenty years were past; 'twas market-day :
Country and town were met in concourse gay
Within Iölcos' many-circling tow'rs,
All purpos'd to enjoy the fleeting hours.
Bold yeomen from their farms on business bent,
Fair maidens, gallant youths, on mirth intent,
Throng'd the long market-place.   Among them, slow,
The elders mov'd, patriarchs with locks of snow,   190
And comely matrons, keeping each an eye
On her sweet daughter—not distrustfully,
For these were early days, when simple truth
And purity inspir'd the thoughts of youth.
A plashing fountain in the midst was seen,
Twin'd o'er with creeping plants of emerald green.
At one end Pallas' modest temple rose,
Benches in front and shady porticoes,
Reserv'd for the old folk.   Above the pile
Pelion tower'd craggy, and yet seem'd to smile.   200
Meanwhile, like gnats that round the traveller swarm
At sun-down, when the air is soft and warm,
Or motes in noontide's drier sunbeam tost,
Fix'd by the eye one moment, the next lost,

So swarm'd the mingling multitude that day,
So glanc'd their sparkling manifold array;
While questions, answers, quick responsive given,
The buzz of myriad voices rose to heaven.
Thus, e'en as now, life's motley mask went on
In fair Iölcos, 'neath the summer sun.   210

But who is this? Why parts the crowd asunder?
Why do they gaze, why whisper with such wonder?
From the Hill-Gate a single-sandall'd man,
Clad in the garb of the Magnesian clan,
Comes boldly forward through the scatt'ring throng;
A panther's hide upon his shoulders hung,
Two jav'lins in his hand; his locks unshorn
Down his back floating, golden as the morn.
" 'Tis not Apollo, surely! nor the boy
" Of Syrian Byblos, Aphrodite's joy?   220
" And Naxos holds rash Ephialtes' dust.
" Offspring of Gods, if not a God, he must
" Visit these spheres!"—So doubted they; but, lo!
Fierce from the Sea-ward street, as bursts the foe
On herdsmen all unarm'd, came hurrying on,
Drawn by two mules his wicker car upon,
Th' usurping son of Cretheus, Pelias stern.
What caus'd the haughty monarch's cheek to turn
Pale, as he paus'd? He saw and recognis'd
The token, the one sandal; and, surpris'd   230
From dread to fury, thus address'd the youth:—
" Tell me, young Sir! and answer me with truth—
" No subterfuge! what is thy land, thy race?
" And whence, thus single-sandall'd, in this place?"
To whom the youth,—"Old man! thou do'st me wrong;
" No word of falsehood ever sear'd my tongue;

" My heart is true as thine.   No act of shame
" Hath soil'd my conscience or disgrac'd my name.
" From Chiron's cave, his cherish'd ward, I come
" Not to a foreign, but my native home ;   240
" Come to assert my right to Cretheus' throne,
" My father's ravish'd birthright and mine own,
" Which Pelias holds.   He, cruel, set aside
" His weaker brother, and his rights denied,
" And would have slain myself ; but under night
" My friends remov'd me from the tyrant's sight,
" And sent to the wise Centaur.   Chariclo,
" His wife, receiv'd and rear'd me.   Would'st thou know
" How with one sandal only I stand here ?
" This morn, departed from my master dear,   250
" Reaching Anaurus' stream that, swift and deep,
" Bursts from the heart of Pelion's woody steep,
" An agéd woman sought my help to cross ;
" I bore her over in my arms, with loss
" Of that my sandal.   Scarcely cross'd, no more
" A hag's, but heav'n's own lineaments she wore ;
" Her brow, her arms, her deeply-bosom'd breast
" Proclaim'd the Goddess—Hera stood confess'd !
" She smil'd and said, ' Thou hast begun life well :
" ' Go on, and prosper.'—Now, O kinsmen ! tell—   260
" Tell me, no stranger among alien men,
" But your own blood, your kindly citizen—
" Where live my gentle parents ?   Be my guide,
" Some one, in charity, to where abide
" Æson and fair Alcimedé !   My name,
" Once Diomed, is, by the Gods' acclaim,
" Chiron their witness, Jason."—As he spoke,
Tears from the eyes of many around outbroke ;

And an old man, advancing 'fore the rest,
Took by the hand and thus the youth address'd :—   270
" The Gods are righteous.   All things wait their hour.
" Man hath from God but delegated power.
" Long have the sons of Cretheus look'd for thee.
" I am thine uncle Pheres ; come with me."

    Needs not to say how Æson and the mild
Alcimedé receiv'd their long-lost child ;
For one whole day did Æson lay aside
His pen, while she alternate laugh'd and cried ;
They wearied not, beholding him ; nor would
Old scores have rak'd up, but the Fates withstood.   280
    A meeting now was summon'd of the kin
Of Cretheus, - from all quarters they came in.
The feast was spread on Æson's threshing-floor.
Alcimedé brought out her ample store
Of food, and Æson broach'd his choicest wine ;
For men hold freest converse when they dine.
The family council due appointed sat ;
One recommended this, another that,
As suited each his several temperament.
The elder most were on strong measures bent,—   290
" What ! truckle to the tyrant—who was not,
" Moreover, by Æolid loins begot ? "
Resentful less, the young, in many of whom
Their blood ran filter'd through a Minyan womb,
In various risks of commerce too engag'd,
Urg'd patience,—Pelias was infirm and ag'd,
And could not long survive.   Time would redress
All things, and war was bad for business.
Besides, though Jason rightfully complain'd,
Pelias had not tyrannically reign'd ;   300

And young Acastus could be set aside
And Jason put in when the old man died.
Certés the son oft lags behind the sire,
And piping times of peace let down the fire!
Pheres and Amythaon, junior born
Of Cretheus, such cold counsel held in scorn.
Alcestis cried, fire flashing from her eyes,
" Who palter with plain duty I despise!
" The right is Jason's—let him the throne take :—
" But," added, " Spare my father, for my sake!"   310
A few whose ventures had not thriv'n a cloak
Put on of zeal disinterested, spoke
Vaguely of kindred claims and natural laws,
And vow'd they'd peril all in such a cause,—
Hoping, athwart an old world's wreck, to feel
Their way to a new turn of fortune's wheel.
Melampus, son of Amythaon, said
A little bird had whisper'd as he stray'd
Near Pylos, " To Iölcos go ; for thence
" Shall honour spring and modest competence   320
" For those who hazard "—what, the bird said not ;
But nothing hazard, nothing can be got.
Admetus, Pheres' son, had fain shunn'd strife ;
He lov'd not aught might peril his sweet life :
But when Alcestis spoke, his purpose fail'd,
And nobler instincts for the time prevail'd.
Thus they held counsel; and 'twas hard to find
Which way the balance of their will inclin'd.
Meanwhile their hosts kind car'd for every one ;
But heartily they wish'd the talk was done.   330
    Five days they feasted and deliberated
On Æson's threshing-floor, till all were sated

With viands and discourse. The number Five
Is sacred to the Gods that counsel give.
Jason kept silence, cautious 'yond his years,
Though bold; he lent to all attentive ears;
Then, rising last, propos'd, in modest guise,
A thing as yet unknown, a compromise.
" Let Pelias yield up to my sire and me
" The throne and Cretheus' sceptre peaceably,   340
" Then he may keep—for that will we engage—
" The private lands, our righteous heritage,
" Assign'd by Zeus of old to Æolus,
" But wrongfully by him withheld from us,—
" Free, as his own. So shall he end his days,
" Honour'd by Zeus, and with all good men's praise."
—They were all weary, Æson most of all ;
Bandied from one to other round, the ball
Of hot dispute had dropp'd. Th' idea was new ;
Its various merits crowded on their view,—   350
'Twixt right and wrong, 'twixt black and white, till then
No neutral tint, no mean, was known to men ;
Policy had no place,—'twas yea or nay ;
The strong hand of the boldest rul'd the day.
Admetus in a whisper had suggested
Th' idea which Jason thus with form invested :—
He for the moment opportune had tarried ;
They all approv'd it, and the vote was carried.
    Then all, consentient, left the threshing-floor,
And to Iölcos went, to Pelias' door,   360
Enter'd and took their places in the hall,
And bade the trembling slaves their master call.
Pelias, due warn'd, came forth in feign'd surprise,
Gracious his words, but with suspicious eyes.

Whom Jason thus address'd :—" O thou whose birth
" Springs from Poseidon, Shaker of the earth ;
" He who in Petra fill'd the womb of night,
" Whence, son o' the morning, Skyphius sprang to light !
" 'Tis not for us, near kinsmen as we are
" Through Tyro, daughter of Salmoneus, war   370
" To wage together ; for the Gods not love
" Blood-feud betwixt relations, nor approve
" Too rigid construing ev'n of right, if so
" It work our past'ral charge, the people, woe.
" For nations are God's sheepfolds ; their increase
" Is His ; and in their welfare He wills peace.
" Yield then, we pray thee, to my sire and me
" The throne and Cretheus' sceptre peacefully ;
" So shalt thou keep—for that will we engage—
" The private lands, our righteous heritage,   380
" Assign'd by Zeus of old to Æolus,
" But wrongfully withheld by thee from us,—
" Free, as thine own ; so shalt thou end thy days
" Honour'd by Zeus, and with all good men's praise."
    He ceas'd, and Pelias spoke :—" As thou hast said,
" So let it be.   My days are well nigh sped ;
" The hand of age is heavy on my brow,—
" Would it were with me still as thou art now !
" For thou art young ; Hope lightens in thine eyes ;
" Thy bosom pants for gen'rous enterprise ;   390
" Not Orcus can appal nor heav'n elate
" One whom a God stamps master of his fate !
" Come then, be this our compact.   Phrixus' ghost,
" Disquieted, on Ach'ron's whirlwinds tost,
" Came to me in a dream, and crav'd my care
" That some one to bright Æa should repair,

" Thence back to fair Orchomenos and Greece
" To bring the precious spoil, the Golden Fleece,
" Spoil of the Ram that bore through middle sky
" Hellé and him from Ino's envious eye.   400
" This, stern, withholds Æëtes.   And the lip
" Of the true Pythia saith 'tis by a ship
" The conquest shall be won.   Be this thy toil!
" Reclaim, bring home, brave boy! the precious spoil;
" And by great Zeus I swear, a sacred oath,
" Zeus our ancestral God, that, nothing loath,
" That toil accomplish'd, all shall be restor'd,
" Sceptre and crown; and I will own thee lord."
    Thus was the compact set betwixt them twain,
And all departed to their homes again.   410
    Now sacred heralds speed to every land,
By Æson's and by Pelias' joint command,
T' invite the hero demigods of Greece
To the high conquest of the glorious Fleece.
Throughout broad Thessaly, through vocal Thrace,
Through Pelops' isle that the twin seas embrace,
Where Zeus's fane Arcadian tow'rs on high,
And sacred Styx falls mist-like from the sky;
Where'er the scatter'd sons of Hellen reign
O'er subject tribes, on mountain or on plain,   420
They go,—and Hera with them, to inspire
Each hero's youthful heart with sweet desire
Of glory, the acclaim that stamps the brave,
Rings on men's tongues, and shall outlive the grave.
It lighted up each breast, th' immortal flame
Of aspiration high and generous shame;
No more would they with their gray sires abide,
Or loiter, sucklings, at their mothers' side.

Jason the while, not ign'rant of the aid
Of wise Athena, the Tritonian maid,   430
Of every art mother and mistress skill'd,
Address'd himself the fated ship to build.
Through Pelion's forest zone he takes his way,
Like a young panther seeking for his prey ;
Where'er the deeper delf, the richer soil,
There is his morning's task, his evening's toil.
For ev'ry part the fitting wood he chose ;
The far peaks echo to his axe's blows ;
Each river-God sits trembling by his urn ;
The Oreads shriek, the Hamadryads mourn.   440
    For the strong keel a stately oak he slew,
Shap'd it in curving length with much ado ;
Then, for the timbers, lofty firs and spruce,
Straight, ag'd, and dry, time-season'd to his use.
Ribs, planks, and ties, disruption to restrain,
Shap'd he with adze and smoothen'd with the plane,
Limb unto limb adjusting,—each assur'd
Its proper place, by nails of brass secur'd.
Like a vast flower, expanding as the dew
Of morning quickens it, the fabric grew.   450
For the slim mast a lissom pine he sought,
Tall, verdant, seemly, like a maid unthought
Yet of in marriage. " Spare me, spare ! " she cried ;
" I am but young !"—" Sweet sister ! " he replied ;
" It is God's will.   He takes that gave thy breath."
She bow'd her head, and meekly welcom'd death.
Benches athwart the ribs he nail'd, whereon
The rowers should sit ; but parted one by one,
For space in rowing.   Fifty seats—for so
Tritonis bade him, neither fewer nor mo—.   460

He fix'd, a score and five on either side :—
One hundred arms should thus at once be plied ;
The sacred number that infers the dower
Of love consummate and supernal power.
Thus arm'd, bright Briareus his succour gave
To quell Typhœus and Olympus save.
The sailyard of close ilex fashion'd he,
The oars of poplar, great Alcides' tree.
Through rowlock thongs, to tholepins strong fast-made,
The fifty oars in equal cadence play'd. 470
A rudder then he shap'd, that should avail
To guide the vessel's course; a fish's tail
Supplied the model,—then, with prescient hand,
Provided ballast, wood, and stones, and sand.
A wicker bulwark next he fram'd, to hide
The oarsmen and protect on every side,
Well twisted; over which skins should be hung,
Proof against spears and arrows, foes among.
In front he rais'd aloft th' indignant prow,
With ram's-head beak projecting from below. 480
Foremost, deft carv'd, as ruling o'er the tide,
Poseidon's sacred swan appear'd to glide.
Behind he rear'd the stern, strong as was meet,
Embattled, lofty ; with commodious seat,
Whence should the steersman's view at once command
Rowers and ship, the broad sky, sea, and land.
Above it rose a canopy ; behind
The flag-staff, whence the ensign woo'd the wind.
Lockers below, within, for meat and drink,
And stores of all kinds, fill'd up every chink. 490
Beneath the benches was the cordage stow'd ;
A long chest 'midships was the sail's abode.

The sail, a wondrous work, Athena wove,
The cordage skill'd Arachné, for her love;
Not yet had rivalry betwixt them grown;
Each lov'd the art for its sweet sake alone.
With purple dye Arachné's sire the sail
Tinctur'd, the gayer thus to court the gale.
Last, Jason pitch'd the whole, and, joyous, spread
With radiant colours, yellow, black, and red.   500
Thus, like a glancing opal, Argo lay
On the broad beach of Pagasæ's still Bay.

   'Twas eve, and on a rock beside the strand
Apart sat Jason, weary foot and hand,
But happy, and his conscious heart elate
Argo, his finish'd work, to contemplate.
'Twas eve; and a sweet Zephyr softly stole
Down from the uplands, and refresh'd his soul.
Dreams of a prosp'rous voyage, and conquest sure,
And swift return—all things that youth allure   510
To deeds of daring—cours'd his fancy through;
Was it not his a fated work to do,
The Gods subserving him? Had he not sway'd
Men's counsels?   Had not Pelias tribute paid
Prospective to his rights?   He felt a power,
Inborn, yet unsuspected to that hour;
And pride, the failing of his race, had nigh
Surpris'd his heart, lapp'd in complacency,
And would have master'd; but, as thus he mus'd,
Beside him sudden, 'tween the light suffus'd   520
Of evening and the ship, stately and fair,
A woman stood, in the soft twilight air,—
Theano 'twas, or seem'd to be, the child
Of Æolus, austere in brow, yet mild;

C

The married priestess of Athena's fane,—
Her gait, her gesture, all bespoke her plain.
The vestments of her office high she wore,
And heav'n's commission on her brow she bore.
    " Jason!" she said, " thy soaring thought aspires
" To deeds of daring worthy of thy sires ;   530
" But err not in that soar ; for thoughts of pride
" Betray'd Typhœus, who the Gods defied.
" What hadst thou done without Athena's aid ?
" Forget it not. To Heav'n thy thanks be paid,
" Selected to work out the ends of Fate.
" The wise are pious, modest, temperate.
" This thy fair Argo, destin'd to convey
" The sons of heroes on their ocean way,
" How will she stem, frail cockle-shell, the wrath
" Of waves and storm-winds menacing her path ?   540
" How 'scape Symplegades and Scylla's fangs
" When midway tost 'twixt heav'n and earth she hangs ?
" Will Boreas' icy lips her prow caress,
" Or Notus spare her stern's gay comeliness ?
" Fated indeed to immortality,
" But such proud guerdon cometh not from thee.
" Man's weakness felt heralds God's hour,—till then
" He intervenes not for the sons of men.
" What bids the hot blood through thy veins to roll ?
" What would thy dry bones be without a soul ?   550
" Thine Argo is but naught till she receive
" The breath of God inspir'd, to bid her live.
" Speak not! Thy cheeks that thus ingenuous burn
" Answer me. List ; for thou hast much to learn.
    " Beyond Mount Pindus lies a sacred land,
" Chaonia, whence thy sires by heav'n's command

" Came into Thessaly.   Sparse fields of corn,
" Fair pastures, grazing flocks, its slopes adorn.
" A river waters it, without a break
" Descending from the broad and sedgy lake   560
" Pambotis.   Higher still, the vale contracts;
" The stream pours down in foaming cataracts
" From a cleft gorge and single waterfall,
" Which the Perrhæbian hinds the ' Cow's Mouth' call.
" Beyond, once more, the vale expands, and forms
" A sweeping circuit, shelter'd from the storms,
" Still sloping upwards, fertile, tow'rds the sun,
" But virgin as when time his course begun.
" This is Dodona !   From on high looks down
" Tomarus, mount of God, with awful frown   570
" Reproving crime ; but from its base distils
" The river of mercy in one hundred rills
" Sparkling like diamonds, fresh that glide between
" Dark forest, interspers'd with alps of green ;
" Then join and flow in one.   The forest trees
" Now cluster, now stand singly.   All degrees
" Of age are theirs, but all spontaneous grow ;
" No axe presumes to lay their honours low ;
" But, life in each accomplish'd, from the sky
" Lightnings fall, cloudless, on them, and they die.   580
" Oaks are they all, the holy oaks of God.
" Inmost, a spacious circle, never trod
" By mortal foot, was at creation's birth
" By mighty Hermes' wand mark'd out from earth.
" There, in the midst, one Tree stands hoar, sublime,
" Whose date, coëval, knows no peer but Time.
" No sire it owns, no children—there is none
" Like it on earth—it lives to God, alone.

" Through the three worlds its roots extend, profound ;
" Its boughs expand an emerald gloom around ;   590
" Its leaves are written o'er with mystic spells ;
" Beneath each several leaf a spirit dwells,
" Vocal with love and praise, consentient song,
" As of bees murm'ring Hybla's meads among.
" At the Tree's foot the fount of Wisdom springs,
" Limpid ; in oracles of truth it sings.
" Three Virgins stand beside it, rev'rend dames ;
" The Present, Past, and Future are their names.
" Around the precinct, on the circling oaks
" Are tripods hung, that the rous'd wind provokes,   600
" Clashing and echoing round, in fitful breaks,
" As the prophetic breath sleeps or awakes.
" And by them watch, sole guardians of the place,
" The bare-foot Selli, much-enduring race,
" Unwash'd, ascetic, sleeping on the ground,
" None ever to his trust unfaithful found.
" Thus day to day succeeds, and year to year ;
" But, when a hero of thy race draws near,
" Seeking for counsel, from that mighty Tree,
" Echoing from time through vast eternity,   610
" A voice speaks out, the very voice of God ;
" For this his temple is, his dread abode,
" The house, th' inviolate home, where dwelleth He
" Who was, and is, and shall for ever be,—
" Dwelleth on earth thus near, yet far apart ;
" In heav'n thus dwells, and in the humble heart.
    " Thither, my son !—Speak not !—'tis thine to go.
" I will go with thee. Ere the sun be low
" To-morrow thou shalt greet the guardian band,
" The Selli, and before the Presence stand.   620

" First, make thy gift, a tripod, to be hung
" The gifts of patriarchs of thy race among.
" Then ask the triple Virgins for the draught
" Of Wisdom—not mere knowledge, mark ! nor craft,
" Nor for the future's insight, ill or well,—
" Who seek that lore abuse God's oracle ;
" He gives ambiguous answers in such case,
" Which lead, misconstrued, to deserv'd disgrace.
" But ask for knowledge of thyself, for skill
" To probe thy weakness, to discern heav'n's will   630
" In present circumstance from day to day ;
" For heart to do it, and for strength to pray.
" Then turn to Him who dwelleth in the Tree,
" Thy fathers' God, whose shroud is mystery,
" One and alone—for, shadows faint and dim,
" All others are but ministers of Him,—
" Ask him for Power—not to enslave mankind,
" But to endure—to rule thy proper mind,
" Withstand temptation, and fulfil with might
" What conscience' inner voice approves as right ;   640
" For honesty of purpose, singleness
" Of eye and tongue ; and, finally, to bless
" Thyself, thy comrades, and the Ship.   But few,
" Few be thy words—thou hast with God to do.
    " I will be with thee, to sustain thy prayer,
" Thee praying, veil'd thy face and prostrate there ;
" A conscious limb will sever from the Tree,
" That none may near, that none may touch but me,
" Of life and truth ; this within Argo's keel
" Will I imbed, that, long as nightly wheel   650
" The Dancers round the polestar, shall impart
" A life immortal to her, and the art

" Prophetic.   When thou hesitatest, vex'd
" 'Tween lawful courses, which to choose perplex'd,
" To wits' end driv'n the Gods' high will to tell,
" Argo herself shall be thine oracle,
" Shall speak heav'n's message with a living voice,
" Which when thou hear'st, ensue it and rejoice ;
" But, silent, fear, and search thine heart lest guile
" Lurk in thy thought or falsehood in thy smile.   660
" Thus, as a child clings to his mother's breast,
" Obedient to her lightest word's behest ;
" Or, erring, weeps in penitence sincere,
" Marking th' averted gaze, the silent tear ;
" So look to Argo thou, in doubt, distress,
" Thy mother, and thy kindly monitress ;
" Nor, if through guilt thy purpose end in shame,
" Forewarn'd, fore-armour'd, tax the Gods with blame.
" —Prophetic and immortal!   When thy day,
" Thy quest, its joys, its griefs have pass'd away,   670
" Argo shall be translated to the skies,
" Reserv'd for a still loftier enterprise.
" Then, when the year of years shall come again,
" And crush'd Typhœus breaks his Scythian chain,
" And Briareus ends the work he once began
" Ere the fair earth was purified for man ;
" When he who is to come, and watcheth now,
" Fire on his sword and Sirius on his brow,
" Peace to his friends but to his foes a rod,
" In three steps conquers the three worlds to God ;   680
" And earth and heav'n dissolve, and the great Tree,
" The presence gone, sinks in eternity,—
" Then—even as Chrysomallus Phrixus bore
" Through the blue skies to Æa's shelt'ring shore ;

" Or as this Argo bears the flower of Greece
" E'en now, in venture for the Golden Fleece—
" So shall she then, transfigured yet the same,
" Come from her Southern skies, through seas of flame
" Bending her course, God-guided, to convey
" The sons of God on a predestined way,   690
" Sons of his love, escaping from the strife
" Of heav'n's last conflict to a purer life,
" To where the fathers have already come,
" By brighter paths, and to a happier home !

    " Go then !"—and as she spoke, her stature grew
Dilated, and the dark gray eyes he knew,—
No more Theano, gracious, pure from stain,
The married priestess of Athena's fane ;
The robe, the helm, the gleaming crest betray'd,
And the vast ægis, the Tritonian maid.   700
A cloud of glory shone about her form,
Then darken'd as a sea beneath the storm ;
Though still, like distant thunder, the far roll
Of the deep voice resounded through his soul :—

    " Now go," she said, " but not in princely guise,
" For pomp and pride are hateful in God's eyes.
" Go, as thou cam'st, a single-sandall'd man,
" Clad in the garb of the Magnesian clan,
" Two jav'lins in thine hand, thy locks unshorn,—
" For dust thou art, and shalt to dust return ;   710
" And who would at God's gate a suppliant be
" Must go, a pilgrim, in humility."

    The vision pass'd, and Jason was alone,
The voice departed, and the glory gone.

    He rose ; 'twas night. The Zephyr's breath had died,
Or stirr'd but 'mong the pines on Pelion's side.

Heav'n's immemorial watchfires gleam'd on high,
And not a cloud was seen in all the sky.
The little waves came dancing to his feet,
As fain their lord, Poseidon's friend, to greet.   720
The world around him, shelter'd, hush'd from harms,
Lay like an infant in its mother's arms.
One light, most look'd for, steadier than a star,
Shone from his mother's upland home afar.
A prayer to heav'n, one fervent prayer, he pray'd ;
Then on the sand his weary limbs he laid.
A pleasing languor o'er his senses crept ;
Night spread her mantle o'er him, and he slept.

    Morn broke ; but, ere the sun was ris'n, his rest
Ended, his steps were bent unto the West,   730
Dodona-bound ; where all things in accord
Were done, obedient to Athena's word.

BOOK II. ORPHEUS.

Now had the last words of farewell been spoken,
The last bread in his father's house been broken,
The last sage counsel of the Centaur heard ;
All by Athena's care had been prepar'd,—
Farewell to each save one, the saddest, last
Heart-break of all.   His mother round him cast
Her loving arms, and cried, " O Jason, stay !
" Thou know'st not what thou rushest on to-day !
" Last night I dream'd a dream.   I could not close
" Mine eyes for weeping, and the vision rose   10
" Presagic.   News had come that thou wert lost,
" Wreck'd with thine Argo on some foreign coast.
" Pelias straight slew thy sire, and sought for me.
" I fled to his own hearth for sanctuary,—

" Sat down there ; but the cruel king pursued
" With naked sword, insatiate for my blood.
" I saw me plunge a dagger in my breast,
" And curse the impious murd'rer of a guest,
" Sink at his feet, and stain them with my gore.
" O Jason, Jason ! what can I say more ?   20
" Go, and thou seal'st thy gentle father's fate ;
" Go, and thou leav'st thy mother desolate !
" Would I had died before this evil day !
" I am no heroine—O my Jason, stay ! "
     " Mother ! " he said, and sooth'd her with his hand,
" Dreams are delusive when they countermand
" Heav'n's mandates clear express'd.   Rather rejoice,
" Thy son elect by true Athena's voice
" Argo to build, her sons perchance to lead—
" But that as God wills, so we but succeed !   30
" Hera hath bid me prosper ; Delphi's shrine
" Blesses and owns the enterprise divine.
" Then weep not.   Tears are idle,—only this,
" Trust and be doing, Fate's best omen is.
" The heroes wait me.   Farewell, dear one !   Trust
" In them, in me, in Argo !   Heav'n is just ;
" I shall return—and if not, if the sun
" Bring thee such sorrow, still, God's will be done !
" Farewell !   But look not out on them, on me,
" Or Argo—this behest I lay on thee ;   40
" Lest, inadvertent, thy reluctant eyes
" Blight with their glance our brighter auspices."
     He spoke, and broke away, signing adieu.
Obediently Alcimedé withdrew
Into an inner chamber, screen'd from sight,
With her handmaidens, shutting out the light ;

And, kneeling, pour'd her heart out, sobbing, there,—
But Fate, though pitying, granted not her prayer.
  Meanwhile the heroes stood expectant all
In groups, conversing gay, in Æson's hall;   50
When Jason, issuing from his mother's room,
Cried, "Now, O friends! the wish'd-for hour is come.
" Down to the shore with me, brave sons of Greece!
" Descend, where Argo pants for her release.
" There will we choose our chief, and homage pay
" To the kind Gods that bless our work to-day."
The chiefs assembled, joyous, shout applause,
Grasp Æson's hand, and pledge them to his cause.
Æson, as host, their order'd march array'd,
Honour to each by due precedence paid.   60
Foremost of right heav'n's mission'd envoys pass'd,
The young men next, the ripe in years came last;
The envoys singly, for God's work they do;
The rest associate following, two and two;
For friendship stamps the brotherhood of worth,
And the Gods Saviours all are twins on earth.
  First went Æthalides; his lineage springs
From Hermes,—herald he to sceptred kings;
Sacred the office; round his head he wore
The milk-white fillet; and his right hand bore   70
His sire's caduceus, mindful of the hour
When Argeiphontes tam'd the Dragon's power,
And great Athena flung the spiry roll
Of his huge length to coil around the pole.
Him Hermes sends, to herald Argo's path.
Undying mem'ry of all things he hath;
Alternate life in heav'n and earth he leads;
Prompt unto war, but more to peaceful deeds.

Next Orpheus, the sweet singer, came,—from Thrace,
Of pure Calliopé, his spotless race;   80
His lyre Apollo, but the Muses gave
Skill for its use in sweet Pimplæa's cave.
Benthesicymé, nurse of pure desire
For all things lovely—Amphitrité's choir
Own'd her their leader—taught him how the seas
Burst into music, ruffled by the breeze,
When spirit first effus'd itself on ocean,
And the waves danc'd in regulated motion,
Poseidon's ritual service, round the queen—
Recurrent dash, with many a pause between.   90
Thence modell'd, henceforth, to man's use transferr'd,
Are hymns of praise on Thrace's mountains heard;
And the recurrent stamp, the triple round,
Have through the world man's perfect worship crown'd.
Him sends Apollo.   As he walk'd, the lyre
Sang low, untouch'd, stirring with living fire.
Ever, alone or his brave peers among,
He murmur'd verse, or broke forth into song.
     Third, with delib'rate step and look intent,
As always on some distant object bent,   100
Went Tiphys, pilot skill'd to read the sea's
Secrets, and scan the wild skies' auguries.
He knew the rising of each helpful star;
He heard the winds when must'ring from afar,
Within their cave; firm as a grounded rock,
But firmest in the fiercest tempest's shock.
The heroes pray'd, Athena sent him, guide
For Argo, heav'n-taught, o'er th' uncertain tide.
     Fourth walk'd gray Mopsus, true Apollo's seer.
He knew the flight of birds, and to his ear   110

Their songs were as man's speech.   He drew his birth
From Ampyx, nam'd the ' Voice' of heav'n on earth.

Fifth, Idmon, of the same Œchalian race,
Haruspex sage and reverend, had place.
Attendant on each kingly sacrifice,
Learn'd in old rites, and prudent in advice,
He scann'd the steaming entrails with his rod,
And, thus discern'd, proclaim'd the will of God.

Each went content, foreknowing he must die
Far from Tithæron's vale and Thessaly.   120

These five went first, to herald, cheer, protect
From peril, and counsel what the Gods direct.
In Delphi's shrine, inscrib'd, the number Five
Sets forth th' informing power by which we live.

These singly march'd ; then the remaining crew
Of Argo came, as said is, two and two.

With Jason walk'd Acastus, Pelias' son,—
Not yet had thought of rivalry begun
'Tween him and Jason ; much his sire withstood,
But unavailingly, for go he would.   130
Admetus and Melampus follow'd next,
Neither much liking, but found no pretext
T' evade the quest,—then others of the kin
Of Æolus, on fire high fame to win.
They march'd with springy step and heads elate,
Proud of their glorious blood, defying fate.

Next Polyphemus, broad-brow'd, haughty, strode,—
Of great Poseidon son, th' Earth-shaking God ;
And of like birth Euphemus, slight and tall,
Mere youth, the youngest of the heroes all.   140
Him had his mother trusted to the ward
Of Heracles,—his ardent spirit soar'd,

Hating restraint, impatient of the yoke,
Like a young bull, or charger yet unbroke.
Self-will'd, presumptuous, needing discipline,
But born to rule, are all that race divine.

Next them, Oïleus, dull of intellect,
And Butes, given to act and not reflect;
Brave both, and honest, but the one too quick,
T'other too slow; this slim in form, that thick ; 150
Each saw and mourn'd the failing of his friend,
But neither his own fault could comprehend.

Then, scarcely touching earth, their azure hair
Loose on their shoulders, flutt'ring in the air
Ev'n when no breeze was stirring, and with wings
Of every tint bedropt that Eös brings
Ambrosial from her chambers of the East,
Come Zetes, Calaïs,—they the Harpies' feast
Shall end for ever ; sons of Aquilo,
Whose piercing shafts from icy Scythia blow. 160
While Orytheia by Ilissus stray'd,
Boreas beheld and lov'd the Attic maid,
Wrapt her in clouds and ravish'd her to Thrace ;
And thence do Zetes, Calaïs, claim their race.
Ev'n yet in Tenos ye may see their tomb,—
Four pillars rough-shap'd point towards heav'n's dome ;
Three stand deep-bas'd in undisturb'd repose ;
The fourth rocks softly when the North-wind blows.

Idas and Lynceus follow'd.   Long before
Had Periëres, from Pelasgia's shore, 170
The son of Æolus, Messenia won
From the old Leleges.   His elder son
Was Aphareus, the younger Œbalus,
The latter fam'd as sire of Tyndareus ;

Whence, or from Zeus, the twins of high degree,
The Dioscuri, regents of the sea.
But Aphareus, surnam'd the Black, begot
Idas and Lynceus.   Love between was not
These and their kinsmen twins; but each the peace
Held sacred, fellow-champions of the Fleece.   180
Strange was the contrast 'twixt the brother pair;
Lynceus was dark-complexion'd, Idas fair;
Idas full-flesh'd, Lynceus attenuate, dry;
Clear, cold was Lynceus', moist was Idas' eye.
Lynceus' quick glance, like to the lynx's spring,
Flew right and left,—he saw through everything;
Nothing escap'd his ear that pass'd around,—
Idas paid little heed to sight or sound;
But, if contention rose his peers among,
His was the fiercest gesture, loudest tongue.   190
A sneer perpetual dwelt on Lynceus' lip;
Soft-ton'd his voice; his words would smoothly slip
His teeth betwixt, then leaping reach the quick
Of his friend's marrow, like a gnat-sting's prick.
Idas was gloomy, Lynceus full of glee;
That dealt in banter, this in repartee.
By Hermes, the light-finger'd, Lynceus swore;
Idas by Thracian Ares, God of war,—
But what he sought by force, in crafty guise
Lynceus would win, and mock at his surprise;   200
And oft his brother's duller eyes would show,
His hand directing, how to deal the blow.
Idas, in pride, th' immortal Gods resisted;
Lynceus suggested doubts that they existed.
Idas affirm'd that men from mud were born,
Lynceus from air; and each held each in scorn.

On pleasure one, on thought the other bent;
Idas voracious, Lynceus abstinent.
One seldom slept, the other frequent dozed.
Matter and mind in them were still opposed.   210
But when their wrath awoke, one common flame
Inspir'd their weapons and assur'd their aim.
As, when a sheet of lightning fills the sky,
A white spot forms and grows upon the eye,
Right in the midst—then, bursting, flings abroad
Its arrowy terrors, delegate from God,
Not without thunder, roaring through heav'n's halls,
And, death-struck, prone some bull majestic falls—
So blaz'd their ire, so roar'd ; but Idas' part
Was still to thunder, Lynceus wing'd the dart ;   220
And, link'd together, 'twas their portion still,
Idas to stupify, but Lynceus kill.
A sharpen'd pillar of stone, by way of spear,
Torn from his father's grave, did Idas bear ;
Lynceus, slight subtle needles, by his breath
Shot through a tube, and poison-tipp'd with death,—
Brought with him, should be said ; his peers objected :
He laugh'd, and said their scruples he respected ;
And henceforth carried a stout Parthian bow
And shafts, to wound, retreating from the foe.   230
   How different these who next appear !   Zeus sheds,
Their father, light celestial on their heads ;
Light, not as of the sun's but Mené's ray,
Robing them all in brightness, night and day.
This Castor, that strong Polydeuces is,—
Their mother Leda, heav'n-named Nemesis.
How light their step, though strong in manhood's prime !
Castor, the one, is bound to death and time ;

But Polydeuces knows not time or death ;
He draws from his great sire immortal breath.   240
A double nature marks their mingled line,
Bifold but one, both human and divine.
No discord ever mars their perfect love ;
They will no purpose save the Gods approve.
Holy in heart and living, virgins pure,
They shun the gilded baits that youth allure,
And, ever prescient of their destin'd skies,
Chasten their thoughts that they the higher may rise.
Not on their wonted chargers pace they on,
As late they match'd the boar in Calydon,—   250
Foot-soldiers now, and subject to the oar ;
Hence each a slender Thracian buckler bore,
Each with his symbol blazon'd on the field ;
Twin-branches, cross-wise, upon Castor's shield
In token of their mutual love combine ;
The watchful dog is Polydeuces' sign.
Two spears, brass-tipp'd and long, they high uprais'd, —
The stars not yet on their broad foreheads blaz'd,
Which now, twin fires, through tempests streaming bright,
Cheer mariners, and glorify the night.   260
   Thus march'd the Dioscuri, such their name.
Then, with step slower and graver, others came,
Heroes for wisdom and great deeds approv'd ;
All of them fear'd 'mong mortals, many lov'd ;
But conscious all of guilt and penance due
To stern Oceanus, though lenient too ;
Who bears the rod, the stubborn heart to break,
But hides from vengeance those his mercy seek,—
Hence Uranus in later ages known ;
Who dwells in darkness, unapproach'd, alone :—   270

                                                    D

These senior most, but less by years than grief
Subdued, grief constant, hopeless of relief;
Yet still intent to suffer and atone
For crimes, ancestral some, and some their own.

    First pass'd, their drooping heads bestrewn with dust,
The unjust sons of Æacus the Just,
Friend of Olympus,—jealous, they had slain
Their worthier brother; purified, again
They dar'd the sun; but evermore remorse
Clung to them, like corruption to a corse;   280
A tombstone rested on their hearts; and they,
While gay mirth peal'd around, were never gay.
Telamon, Peleus these; in Phthia one,
In Salamis the other fix'd his throne.

    Then Theseus, sorrowing for his father, dead
Through his default, returning, safely sped
His errand by Crete's daughter, scorn'd—disgrace
To manhood, and opprobrium to his race :—
And Meleager, in whose aching heart—
The hot tears ever welling, prone to start—   290
Smoulder'd the fire-brand half consum'd, and worse,
Unjustly though pronounc'd, his mother's curse.
Foredoom'd at birth, though guiltless of offence,
For others suff'ring, mute in innocence,
Like corn, hail-crush'd, but struggling still to rise,
Yet fac'd he firm his adverse destinies.
Like a tall column, shatter'd, the rude jar
Of earthquakes lone surviving, seen from far,
In ruin beautiful, ev'n thus his head
Held he erect, nor conscious shame betray'd.   300

    Last, mated, came Ancæus, Heracles,—
Ancæus, King erst of the Leleges,

Who rul'd from Samos ere th' Olympian Queen,
Born 'neath the willow, earthly light had seen ;
An ancient people, that Demeter's breast
Gender'd, and the seas nurs'd,—now dispossess'd,
And dwindling under Hellen's stronger sway.
For nations have their birth, prime, and decay,—
Like trees, they spring, they flourish fair, and rot,
By Gods forsaken and by men forgot.   310
Priest of his race, and King, he knew each rite
Of other days, before th' ascendant might
Of Zeus had hurl'd the happy Titan Gods,
The Fates decreeing, from their blest abodes.
An axe of stone he bore,—the stone was pass'd,
Cross-wise, athwart a beam of ilex, vast,
Rough-clipp'd, a leathern thong the hand pass'd through ;
With this the sacrificial ox he slew,
Not severing the throat, but with a dull
Contusive rupture breaking in the skull.   320
Such was the weapon, such the rite, and had
Mysterious import, but the Fates forbad
Divulgence.   Him Athena sent to take
Part in each sacrifice and duly make
Atonement, Heracles alone his peer ;
For to the Gods time-honour'd rites are dear.
Him in Arcadia Heracles had found
Exil'd, and with him strictest friendship bound.
Autochthon he, not of Deucalion's blood ;
He speaks an ancient tongue, scarce understood.   330
Tall towers he, like a branching oak that fills
Heav'n with its glories on the Carian hills ;
Past middle age, far-seeing, and sedate,
But mournful, musing on his people's fate.

                                          D 2

Him Tiphys only in the skill excels
Of stars, and storms, and ocean's miracles.
   Less tall, less grand, thus mated, meek content
Triumphant on his brow, his step intent
Forwards—the longer mark'd, observ'd the more—
Pass'd Heracles, the last, from Æson's door.   340
His step not light, nor heavy, but assur'd,
As of a man to daily toils enur'd.
Perfect the symmetry in every limb,
Strength in repose ; but they who gaz'd on him
Saw in his eyes at times a dubious light,
Now inwithdrawn, now ominously bright,
As searching some far future to descry,
Or conscious of a home-felt agony,
Which answer'd not, his quiv'ring lips would frame
Unspoken words, or syllable a name :—   350
Marks of the frenzy all divine that clings
To those whose birth through lunar effluence springs,
When, Gods with men engendering, the root
Of bitterness pursues the mortal fruit,—
Such Hera persecutes, nor without cause ;
But these are myst'ries passing nature's laws.
Born thus from pure Alcmena, married maid,
Herself immaculate, by Zeus betray'd,
Such doom bore Heracles, the suff'ring man,
His heart a wilderness, his life a span ;   360
For whom the Gods most love die ever young, —
Such doom he bore his mortal kind among,
Bore willing, from the cradle to the grave,
Toiling the world to lustrate and to save.
So pass'd he on. Few words of wont he spoke,
But weighty ; and the smile not frequent broke,

Less on his lip than in his eye ; but when
It lighten'd thus, creation laugh'd again.
His soul was full of pity for distress,
Tender to every thing of feebleness ; 370
The very worm that crawl'd beneath his feet,
He turn'd aside, he would not tread on it ;
Children he lov'd, and they lov'd him ; the youth
Ingenuous lov'd, whose thought and speech were truth ;
To women courteous, rev'rent ; for his heart
Own'd one soft mem'ry, cherish'd and apart ;
Gen'rous in friendship, prov'd in match with hell,
As Theseus and Alcestis found full well.
Humble, unselfish, grieving but submiss,
He work'd out, trustful, heav'n's great Nemesis, 380
Unask'd (the Pythia bade) the how, the why ;
But to be crown'd with immortality.
Ten works had he perform'd, the number due
To justice' full accomplishment ; but two
Remain'd, to perfect mercy. He was found
Now on the venture to the furthest bound
Of earth, where guarded by fell Ladon grow
The apples that eternal life bestow,—
The place Eurystheus told not ; and he plann'd
To sail with Argo to the Colchian land, 390
And, pending the great quest he had in view,
Achieve, his toils exceeding, this one too.
He ever went on foot, as fits the slave
Self-sold to life-long servitude,—the brave
Love horses, and he lov'd ; but ask'd no more
Than, willing Fate, to labour at the oar.
The heroes welcom'd him, but Fate's decrees
Sent him ere long on other destinies.

His armour glitter'd as he walk'd along;
The lion's skin, girt with a leathern thong,   400
Fell o'er his shoulders; and the head, with teeth
Clench'd, o'er his brow, and fearful, threaten'd death.
Lightly he walk'd beneath the pond'rous load;
His mail Hephæstus, but the sword bestow'd
Hermes; Apollo gave th' unerring bow
And swift-wing'd arrows, messengers of woe;
These carried Hylas, his Dryopian page;
He spar'd him when, his father's heritage,
Theiodamas', by treach'ry forfeited,
Th' unhappy king in retribution bled.   410
He lov'd the gen'rous youth, and sought to fire
His soul with noble impulse and desire
Of virtue; but untimely Clotho's hour
Cut short the promise ere he rear'd the flower.
The club he carried that none else could wield,—
He ever scorn'd the shelter of a shield.
One scar, alone, his heel confess'd, the bite
Of the foul crab, receiv'd in Lerné's fight.

   These were the chosen fifty, from their birth
Predestin'd by their valour and their worth,   420
The flower and hope combin'd of early Greece,
T' achieve th' adventure of the Golden Fleece,—
Not altogether worthily or well,
But still achieve, as old traditions tell;
Yet not achieve without th' attendant aid
Of Heracles, present or absent, paid.
In him, 'bove all, was found the perfect law
Of God fulfill'd, the stone without a flaw.

   Thus marshall'd, Æson watch'd them pass adown
The path that leads to fair Iölcos' town,   430

Enter the Hill-ward gate, and disappear.
Then, fearful lest the hotly rising tear,
None of them looking back, should overflow,
Offend the Gods, or thus work Argo woe,
He sought Alcimedé's dark chamber, where
She wept, and wept with her, and join'd her prayer.
    They meanwhile march'd on thro' the gath'ring crowds
Of citizens, like stars among the clouds.
The matrons wept, the old men bless'd, and told
How this or that one's sire they'd known of old,   440
Nor seem'd the son degen'rate,—maidens strew'd
Flowers on their path, with morning's drops bedew'd.
The young men, jealous somewhat, still admir'd
Their noble port, the blood of Gods that fir'd
Their cheeks with ardour of high enterprise,
And shot in lightnings from their flashing eyes;
But hush'd their shouts in rev'rence and in awe
When, coming last, the sons of grief they saw.
Onward they swept, with long and stately stride,
As in a ritual dance on Hæmus' side.   450
The envoys and the seniors never spoke;
But from among the younger laughter broke
Incessant, blythe, that could not be repress'd;
For joy and hope were buoyant in each breast,
Up-bubbling like the breath of life that springs
From some fresh fount to its own self that sings,—
Mirth 'mong each other, and in exchange with those
That held unequal step and follow'd close,
Maidens and younger matrons, pressing near,—
Yet jesting none but Artemis might hear.   460
And who shall blame youth's heart-felt merriment,
Starting at morn on life's adventure bent,

The world before them, strength in every limb,
Their God their guardian, and their trust in him?
Little guess these what suns will scorch their noon,
Or how the evening shades come all too soon;
Little their mothers guess'd, when on their knees
They cradled them, their mingled destinies,
What lands they were to see, what stranger sky,
What toils endure, perchance what deaths to die!   470
Now through the Sea-ward gate, and down they pass
The steep descent, rock-hewn, to where the grass
Is green 'round Cretheus' hospitable wells;
The pipe of goat-herd and the tinkling bells
Of goats make music there on summer eves,—
The sea's deep breast the fountains' waste receives.
They reach'd the strand broad-stretching of the Bay,
And halted where expectant Argo lay.

    Then Jason spoke :—" All things are ready now,
" If but the Gods propitious start allow.   480
" But, first, choose we our captain o'er the seas."
The heroes pointed all to Heracles;
But he, advancing, stretch'd his hand, and said,
" Not to me, friends! be such high honour paid;
" To Jason is it due, at whose behest
" Each one of us is here, his father's guest."
Consentient all what Heracles had voic'd
Acclaim'd, and Jason's secret heart rejoic'd.
"If so," he said, " let there be no delay,
" Lest storms should rise and our set purpose stay;   490
" First, let us Argo from her bondage free,
" And drag her to her moorings by the sea;
" And meanwhile shall my father's slaves with care
" For a high sacrifice and feast prepare

" To King Apollo, that he may befriend
" The voyage, and bring it to a prosp'rous end."
  No sooner said, than each his arms, his clothes,
Took off, and laid upon a rock that rose
Shelf-like, dry, flat, long-stretching, and smooth-wash'd
By wintry brine of ages o'er it dash'd,   500
To children dear, within the water-mark,—
Dear, for there yawn'd beneath it caverns, dark
Like Acheron, and many a little pool
Where they would hunt for crabs, escap'd from school.
The urchins, dispossess'd, look'd on, or went
On errands, here or there by Jason sent.
  First pass they ropes round Argo, to debar
Rude shocks, and that she should not rush too far,
Taking the water. Then they clear a space
In front of her, broad as her breadth, and trace   510
A furrow in the midst, and dig it deep,—
This to receive the keel, inclining, steep,
Towards the sea; the furrow next they line
With smooth-plan'd boards along the slope's incline—
A cradle, to transmit the precious life
As from the womb to this our world of strife.
Then Argo's prow towards its mouth they bend,
That smooth, impell'd, she may with ease descend,
Drawn by the heroes,—then fix, each, a thong
Of undress'd leather to the tholepins strong;   520
And take their place, alternate, on each side,
With equal force the impulse to divide.
Tiphys the while his lofty seat ascends,
High on the stern, directs and superintends;
And, all things ready, " Now!" he gives the word,
" Pull, brothers, long and steady!" and, in accord,

The heroes pull and each swell'd muscle strain,—
But Argo moves not; all their force is vain!
As, when Hephæstus, Hera, Pallas strove
To drag down Zeus from his high throne above,   530
Resistent, passive, no success they found,
So strove they vainly—Argo held her ground.
No let or hindrance seemingly was there;
And, baffled, they desisted in despair.

Then Mopsus spoke :—" Man's strength is feebleness,—
" It rests with heav'n his compass'd ends to bless.
" Man sows the grain, and folds his hands in peace;
" 'Tis God alone who giveth the increase.
" Only the weak are strong in God,—with such,
" His humble suppliants, prayer availeth much.   540
" But suppliance needs ere Argo can depart
" Not from each single, but our common heart;
" And Argo too must pray with us before
" Zeus grants departure from Pelasgia's shore.
" Single, ye pray to God, and right ye do;
" But God hath other sons, your brethren, too;
" And highest life not single, corp'rate is,—
" Not isolation, unity is bliss;
" And, individual still, to Argo sworn,
" Of her as of a tender mother born,   550
" Ye bear a life conjunct, the whole in each,
" Each in the whole, by which alone ye reach
" Heav'n's ear in prayer, and may obtain the power
" Argo to loose in this her natal hour.
" I speak strange things.   In earth, in heav'n, in hell,
" All spirits have each their proper vehicle,
" Each man, each God, each dæmon—not of clay—
" Transcendant, supersensual; these obey

" Each spirit's motions, and thus cloth'd alone
" Access we find to the Eternal throne.   560
" Now Argo is your vehicle. So long
" As ye conserve clean hearts and purpose strong
" To work heav'n's will in this great enterprise,
" Your prayers through her to Zeus shall grateful rise,
" Hers rising with them ; for Dodona's tree
" Is life within her, and will pray with ye.
" But who such prayer shall offer, and how pray
" Acceptably ? Things ancient pass away ;
" New take their place. No more as Priest and King
" Let monarchs doubly rule ; but offering   570
" Be made by one, of God elect, and wise,
" They to present, he crown the sacrifice :—
" The prayer a Hymn—all in accordant voice,
" Blended in love ; in such the Gods rejoice.
" Such prayers have life, have wings, ascend to heaven,
" And bring back messages of sin forgiven.
" Your priest be Orpheus,—he is good and wise,
" The Muse-taught master of sweet harmonies.
" Argo shall pray,—ev'n now she 'gins to feel
" The life within her, stirring from her keel."   580
    Then spoke Ancæus,—" Ere Deucalion's flood
" Thoth thus ordain'd ; for so we understood
" The written stones to later days that told,
" Bridging th' abyss, the wisdom of the old.
" And Onka, from whose staff I hold my name,
" Whom ye Athena call, attests the same.
" So taught my sires, in hidden lore conceal'd,
" But now in these last days to men reveal'd.
" Orpheus I own elect of God and wise.
" I but serve henceforth in the sacrifice."   590

Then, Orpheus leading, rose the hymnal strain,
Sublime, which never earth shall hear again ;
Rose prayerful—that Apollo's light should shine
Propitious, and Athena's voice combine
With Hera's and Poseidon's to educe
Assent approving from the brows of Zeus ;
That Argo might from Atè's bonds be freed,
And that the great adventure should succeed.
It rose, that mighty Hymn ; each hero sung
In unison ; the swelling torrent hung   600
Suspended o'er them like a toppling wave
Evok'd by earthquake from dark ocean's cave,—
In unison ; but deep below them all
The voice of Argo, like a waterfall,
Thunder'd a diapason low, which fill'd
The ear, too deep for hearing, and upthrill'd
In permeating streams, detachedly,
Through each voice and through all, in harmony.
It rose, a thing of life, that voice combin'd
Of prayer and homage, in sweet concert join'd ;   610
The rivers join'd in, and the babbling rills,
The forest-voices, and th' eternal hills ;
The Nymphs, the Naiads, Dryads, Oreads, sung
With them, but low subdued ; and the harsh clang
Of war and rapine, rending nature's breast,
Wherefore thus lull'd unconscious, sank to rest.
The sun shone brighter, mists dissolv'd in showers,
And earth, exub'rant, rob'd herself with flowers.
It surg'd, that anthem, o'er th' Æmonian plain,
Up Pindus rush'd, reverb'rate back again ;   620
Thence round Tymphrestis and dark Othrys roll'd,
Woke Œta and Parnassus' peaks of gold.

Faint heard on Helicon ; then, sweeping round,
Notus and Zephyr fav'ring, echo found
In wintry Hæmus, ling'ring meanwhile long
On the Cambunian Mountains and among
The woods Perrhæbian ; then, in tow'ring close,
To high Olympus' sacred summit rose,
Press'd, like a daughter dear, to Zeus's seat,
And sank in suppliant murmurs at his feet.   630
Zeus rais'd the Hymn, and kiss'd, and bent his head,
Assenting.   Heav'n forthwith was carpeted
With amaranth flowers ; and by the Sire's command
Iris shone forth, to tell to every land
That man had learn'd in ritual song to pray ;
And earth and heaven kept all one holiday.
    Then—at that nod ambrosial—as, amaz'd,
The heroes on divinest Argo gaz'd,
They saw a tremor pass throughout her form,
Her cheeks of crimson flush, as it seem'd, warm ;   640
They saw her move spontaneous, touch the line
Of smooth-plan'd boards along the slope's incline—
Which enter'd, sparks on every side out-broke
From the close friction, mix'd with ruddy smoke—
Saw her descend, still without impulse, slow,
Into the watery bason clear below ;
Push forwards, slacken speed, and float at ease,
Her moorings scorning, mistress of the seas :—
Ev'n as a stately swan is seen to glide
Down the slop'd bank of dull Cephissus' tide,   650
Near Lake Copaïs, push forth on the stream,
In easy motion, like an airy dream ;
Then pause and turn, its plumes of snow to dress,
Serene, quiescent, in its loveliness.

Then Jason,—" Eagles soar to heav'n, but food
" Must seek on earth for their dependent brood ;
" Nor, though the Gods thus give our Argo wings,
" Must we neglect the care of common things.
" Quick, then ! the oars, the mast, the sail replace ;
" Stow in the stores, the hauling-ropes unbrace,   660
" Put in the sail-yard, fix each hero's seat ;
" And thus make Argo's panoply complete."
 All, as commanded, straight was done.   Then rose
Mopsus, and a broad-bellied hydria chose ;
The heroes' names on wooden tablets wrote
With iron style, and through the narrow throat
The speaking symbols duly dropp'd ; and shook
The urn ; and then, inverting, his rapt look
Searching the skies and Hermes' aid to show
To which seats, several, should the heroes go,   670
Dropp'd one by one, till all but two were shown,
The midmost seats, of highest honour known.
Ancæus' lot the hydria next out-cast,
And that of Heracles leap'd forth the last.
 Meanwhile, obedient to their lord's command,
Had Æson's slaves an altar on the sand
Built of small shingle-stones compact, and strew'd
With branches, dry and apt, of olive-wood.
Thither the heroes promptly thence repair.
Two noble bulls they find already there,   680
Integral, virgin, white as snow, unbroke
By discipline, unconscious of the yoke,
For King Apollo meet.   Each took his place
Around the altar, suppliants for his grace.
The bulls came forward willingly, unbound,
The cords that tied them trailing on the ground.

Then Orpheus, priest of God, his right hand laid,
Devoting, on each sacred head, and pray'd :—
" O Leto's son, hereditary friend !
" Who, from thy Sire disparted, didst descend   690
" To Delos, earth-born, and shalt yet become
" Slave to a mortal by thy Father's doom,
" And build up Ilion, holy citadel,
" Where men, till wreck'd thro' guilt, shall safely dwell,—
" Hear me !   On these thy types, O Man ! O God !
" I lay our guilt ; in pity spare the rod !
" As thus I cut these hairs and fling, to stray
" On the four winds, so cast our sins away !
" Types of thyself, if these may not suffice,
" Beggar'd in gifts, be thou our sacrifice !   700
" Plead with Oceanus to loose our chains,—
" Send comfort from the sphere where mercy reigns ;
" And bless our Argo, speed to Æa's shore,
" And home to Greece ; so henceforth evermore
" Shall each seventh day be hallow'd to thy praise :—
" And if, returning, ours be length of days,
" Many a rich gift shall decorate thy shrine
" At Delphi and Ortygia divine.
" Lo ! as I speak, I sprinkle now—and now—
" The salted barley on each victim brow,   710
" And thus devote them.   Son of Leto, hear ! "
—Then did, incontinent, Ancæus rear
His vast stone-axe, and, crashing in the skull,
Fell'd the broad front of each expectant bull.
Then Heracles, assum'd the sacred knife,
Cutting the throat of each, let loose the life.
No groans they gave, but voluntary gaz'd
Upwards, the eyes of each submissive rais'd,

Welcoming death, as conscious that thereby
Sin was assur'd forgiv'n, and victory.   720
Then Orpheus with a branch of olive shed
The blood of cleansing on each hero's head.
Others, the limbs dismemb'ring, plac'd the thighs
Upon the wood, reserv'd for sacrifice,
Fat doubling round them, and the raw flesh laid
Above—in all things right observance paid.
Then with a torch he woke the slumb'ring fire,
And pour'd rich wine upon the kindling pyre.
Wise Idmon search'd the entrails with his wand;
Each hero tasted, at the seer's command.   730
The thighs consum'd, the rest in morsell'd bits
The younger roasted, skewer'd on five-prong'd spits,
Five still the sacred number,—thus was all
Done as from old on each high festival.
The flames, the while, to the dry boughs applied,
Rose and shot out, tongue-fork'd, on every side;
While, like a cloud by frequent lightnings riven,
The smoke in purple volumes soar'd to heaven.
    Idmon the heroes then with joy address'd:—
" The omens sanction, Zeus approves, the quest.   740
" Ye shall succeed, return ; but many a scene
" Of pain and peril, dark'ning, lies between,
" Yourselves in fault,—not all return; for I
" And others must, pending the issue, die.
" I mourn not—'tis God's will; but time shall trace
" My name in story, honour to my race."
    He ceas'd.   They drew reliev'd and grateful breath;
But griev'd for Idmon, thus foredoom'd to death.
    Now had the heroes toil'd since rise of sun,
And glad they were that their day's work was done.   750

They dash'd into the waters, sporting free,
Like schoolboys fresh let loose to liberty,
Splashing each other—for lustration part,
Before the feast, partly for joy of heart.
Thus play'd Apollo's dolphins, sent to meet
His priests, the Hosii, Delphi-bound from Crete.

It was the hour when the soft clash of bells,
From all sides nearing, of sweet evening tells;
The lazy kine down from their pastures come,
And every herdsman thinks of wife and home.   760
The slopes that eastward to the bay dip low,
By the hills shaded, lay in darkness now;
But still from Pindus, crimsoning the West,
The ling'ring rays shone full on Pelion's crest;
While, creeping higher and higher, the night upspread,
And each tall pine-tree glow'd a deeper red.
The moon's white crescent, bright'ning, clear and cold,
The wavelets tipp'd with silver and with gold,
Rippling; for, though the breeze had died away,
They would not yet, spoilt children, cease from play.   770
The lamp gleam'd steady 'neath Iölcos' gate,
Few from the farms, for these were lighted late;
From Æson's one, by fair Alcimedé
Kindled betimes, hoping her son might see.
Fireflies were out, and brown bats flitted round;
Owls whoop'd, but kind Athena will'd the sound
Dexter, that no ill omen should be heard,—
All else were nested, save sad Procné's bird,
Night's songstress.   A tall column still of smoke,
Thinning each hour, its skyward journey took   780
Propitious, by no wind disturbing tost,
Above the altar hov'ring, like a ghost.

E

Night's dove-like wings, annulling grief and pain,
Clos'd o'er Iölcos and th' Æmonian plain.
But no soft thought of slumber dream'd the band
Of heroes. Seats of leaves on the dry sand,
Obedient, had the slaves of Æson strew'd.
They sat in order, longing for their food,
Half ripe for mirth, half reverential, all;
For this was King Apollo's festival.   790
In a wide circle, horse-shoe-like, they sat,
Low tables before each; a copper vat
For wine well-mix'd was in the centre plac'd,
The gift of Æson, hospitable, vast.
Beside it planted two tall torches shine,
From time to time renew'd, of blazing pine.
The slaves around it serv'd.   Jason sat first,
I' th' midmost, as their captain.   Frequent burst
Of laughter, quick-suppress'd, and merry joke,
Nearer the entrance, from the juniors broke;   800
The elders, next to Jason, were more grave.
All ready, Jason bade a blessing crave,
Which Orpheus ask'd; and quick the slaves bring in,
On platters heap'd of wood, and bronze, and tin,
Figs, cheese, and cakes—the broadly flapping cake,
Of furmity; these for their plates they take;
Then the bulls' flesh, well roasted at the fire,
And sodden herbs,—they feast to their desire.
One piece each, cutting, to the God devotes,
The rest, no morsel spar'd, goes down their throats.   810
Large appetites they had, as we are told,
Men, demi-gods, and Gods, in days of old.
When all were satisfied, his dexter hand
Each wash'd in the near sea; then, at command

Of Jason, the young men brought in a cup
Of unmix'd wine, that two could scarce hold up,
With words inscrib'd, in old time-honour'd phrase;
" Health to the guests, and to Iacchus praise!"
Of silver, gift of Pheres,—this they pass'd
Around the circle, from the first to last;   820
Each drank a little, and libation made
To the Good Spirit, praying for the aid
Of King Apollo; then the pæan sang,
While flutes and trumpets, blown in concert, rang.

  Then, the high feast concluded, Jason bade
Æthalides, who place near to him had,
His own to take, as ruler of the feast
Symposial; and the hero guests address'd
Themselves to drinking—not to drunkenness,
But cheerful cups—Apollo hates excess.   830
The slaves serv'd out the wine with water mix'd,
Drawn from the vat, a cup each twain betwixt.
The health to Zeus the Saviour first went round;
Then each the other pledg'd; and the gay sound
Of mingling voices, laughter, full content,
Up ev'n to Chiron's cave on Pelion went.
Chiron look'd down and Chariclo, and sigh'd
That their lov'd boy should sail next morningtide.
They meanwhile quaff'd and jested, save the few,
Seniors; but they made mirth, indulgent, too.   840

  But Jason silent sat through anxious thought,
Forecasting much, nor with his neighbours sought
Due fellowship; when, rudely, naming him,
With voice obstrep'rous, sneer malign and grim,
Idas thus spoke:—" O son of Æson! why
" Doth thy pale face damp our festivity?

E 2

" Of thy sweet home and mother thinkest thou ?
" Or, like a maiden, tim'rous ?   Nay, I vow
" By this strong spear, which helps me in the van
" Of battle more than Zeus his own self can,   850
" No evil shall befal thee, nor our quest
" Be fruitless, ev'n if God himself, confess'd,
" Withstand us—Idas fighting by thy side !"
Then, rising, seiz'd the cup unmix'd, applied
His lips, profane, and drank a mighty draught,
And, his cheeks streaming, laid it down, and laugh'd.
Fierce, inarticulate, confus'd, a roar
Of angry voices burst the circle o'er ;
But Idmon rose :—" Art thou inebriate,
" Madman ! t' insult the Gods and provoke Fate,   860
" Thus boasting ?   To exhort to warrior deeds
" Is well ; but this thine insolence exceeds.
" Think of Alöeus' sons, who sought to heap
" Pelion on Ossa, and Olympus deep
" Whelm beneath both,—they by Apollo's bow
" Fell, better far than thou.   Of such a foe
" Beware, nor in thy puny strength rejoice !"
But Idas, glancing round, and with a voice
Derisive, answ'ring,—" Sayest thou, old man,
" That such the fate shall end my earthly span ?   870
" Does true Apollo—some believe, thy sire—
" Not I, forsooth ! thy warning words inspire ?
" See if thou 'scape mine arm if so betide,
" Returning safe, I prove that thou hast lied !"
And higher the strife had rag'd, and Jason made
Motion to speak, but instantly obey'd
Æthalides' loud mandate, " Let this cease !"
And, festive law prevailing, there was peace.

But still, as when the bellows cease to blow,
The smith's strong hand relaxing, the red glow   880
Continues, though subsiding, slow to cool ;
Or, as a generous courser, to the rule
Of voice and rein subject in mid career,
Halts, panting, duteous to his master dear ;
But still his will, impatient, forward flies,
And the red light still flashes from his eyes ;
So they, arrested, curb'd themselves, nor soon
Their heat had cool'd ; when, like a breeze in June
Waking the leaves, or note of earliest bird,
Trilling, the voice of Orpheus' lyre was heard,   890
Spontaneous, ere his hand had touch'd the strings ;
And, like the ointment that soft solace brings
To fev'ring wound, the sound their wrath allay'd.
He join'd his voice, and all attention paid.
An ancient lay he sung, of love and strife,
Of harmony, the sweet accord of life,
Of men of elder days and Gods above,
In a new rhythm which after times should love ;
But ' Iö Pæan ' still recurrent rang
At every pause, all joining, as he sang.   900

I.

" First over all Oceanus reign'd, the Father, the Hidden,
" Reign'd over worlds not ours, through space extending, eternal,
" Infinite.   In the midst subsisted the darkness of Chaos,
" Earth, and sea, and sky in a dead-lock mix'd of confusion.
" Man was not, nor sentient life, nor power to evolve it.
" Then, from Oceanus' breath, proceeded the mighty Ophion,
" Intervening, each realm from each disparted, dividing
" Earth from the sea, and the skies from both, their province assigning
" Each to each, and propell'd them to go in the way he ordain'd them.
" Thus he started the sun, the moon, and the stars in their courses,   910
" Regents of heaven ; Arcturus shone, and Boötes the Warden,

" All the Pleiads, the Dog, and Arctos, watching Orion.
" Slowly, murm'ring, the seas retir'd; and the earth rose above them,
" Teeming, travailing; mountains tower'd, and the valleys descended;
" Green life spread o'er the hills and plains: the musical rivers
" Pour'd from the icy peaks, and the glad earth broke into harvest.
" Fishes, first, in the cold sea gender'd—all but the dolphin,
" Hyperborean, lover of music, the friend of the minstrel;
" Long thereafter, his envoy, sent by lustral Apollo.
" Born from the mud sprang the reptile kind; the Nymphs and the Naiads
" Burst in pellucid fountains forth; the pure Hamadryads   921
" Grew with the trees, and the Oreads roam'd on the slopes of the mountain.
" Then the bees first swarm'd, the holy ones; then did the eagle
" Upwards soar and face the sun, and the song of the skylark
" Herald creation's birth to the Gods: the lion and panther
" Leap'd into life; and man's kindly nurse and strong fellow-worker,
" Lordly bull and bountiful cow, came forth with the morning.
" All in degree was beautiful then, fresh-born and abundant;
" Each their own law kept, the law impos'd by Ophion.
" Long did Ophion reign, and his spouse, on snowy Olympus,   930
" Eurynomé, wide-ruling Queen, the mother of Order;
" Till the new world was ripe for the birth of articulate mortals.
" Then, foreseeing evil, their work fulfill'd, they departed,
" Passing from earth to dwell evermore with the unseen Father.
" —Iö Pæan, vaxat, Iëp.eveon' Apollon!

II.

" Now came the rule of the happy Titans, of Cronos and Rhea,
" Long-enduring, while Zeus was nurs'd by the gentle Melissæ
" In the Dictæan cave, nor the Cyclops yet had the lightnings
" Forg'd, whereby, defied, he visits the wicked with vengeance.
" All was Order still; but who may count on the morning?   940
" Clouds may gather and winds may rise ere the dew hath evanish'd.
" Now from the East came, led by the cow, to fam'd Samothracé
" Cadmus, the breathing man, our sire, to conquer the dragon,
" Build proud Thebes, and people the earth with wide-spreading nations.
" Him the Great Gods their worship taught; and Tritonis Athena
" Met him, leading Harmonia fair, the daughter of Ares,
" Daughter of chaste Urania, whom men call Aphrodité,
" All the Gods in presence, rejoicing, and gave her in marriage.
" Naked was she, nor blush'd, a Goddess born, and a virgin.
" White as snow were her limbs and neck; she stood like a statue,   950

" Calm-possess'd, austere, nor cunning ornament needed.
" Cadmus over her threw a robe, the work of Athena,
" Richly woven; it fell in white folds down from her shoulders,
" Half concealing and half betraying her maidenly beauty,—
" Then, at the touch, flush'd womanly shame in quick-coming blushes
" Over her bosom and cheek suffus'd; and she drew it around her
" Close, and press'd to Athena's side; but she brought her to Cadmus,
" Join'd their hands, and he vow'd to cherish and love her for ever.
" Thus is modesty ever the veil and the honour of woman;
" Thus was marriage ordain'd of old by the counsel of heaven.   960
" Then he clasp'd round her neck the necklace wrought by Hephæstus,
" Fatal, wonderful, parent of joy or grief to the wearer,
" All things good and evil within its circle including,
" Pure desire, and unholy lust, love, hatred, and madness;
" Life to the pure in heart, but to those impure desolation.
" As is the heart, so is the life of man, and its issues.
" Theirs was the Golden Age of mortals; holy and happy,
" Void of care, men work'd with their hands, and the seasons repaid them,
" Fruitful, care of the Gods; and when their days were accomplish'd,
" Gently, not into death they sank, but peacefullest slumber,   970
" Thence to awaken as haunters of earth, the beneficent dæmons.
" They twain meanwhile liv'd in love, till, transform'd into dragons,
" Watchers, trusted of God, they flew to the Isles of the Blessèd
" Far in the West, where the sun never sets, and life is unending—
" Far in the West, and far in the East, near the sources of Ocean.
" This was the Golden Age,—an age of Silver succeeded.
" —Ἰὼ Πᾶαν, ναξατ, Ἰέπεveon' Apollon!

III.

" Needs not to tell how Pandora frail was brought to Prometheus,
" Cloth'd but conscious, blushing, adorn'd, a beautiful evil,
" By the wise Titan shunn'd, but his less wise brother embrac'd her,—
" How, when the deep broad cask, woe's me! she curious open'd,   981
" Forth of it, from the abyss, in swarms multitudinous, issued
" Rapine, and lust, and disease, and war, and famine, and slaughter,
" Light esteem for the Gods, trust-forfeit, and strife between brothers,
" Son 'gainst father and man 'gainst God insanely contending,—
" Concord fled to heav'n, with Peace, and starry Astræa.
" Then the necklace, Harmonia's dower, was hung up at Delphi,
" Once a blessing, but now a curse to all who possess'd it.
" Sweet herbs turn to poisonous weeds when faith has departed.

" Even in heaven came evil days; and the once happy Titans   990
" Rose 'gainst Cronos, and him dethron'd, and drove into exile,
" Zeus still dwelling, a youth, in Crete, with the gentle Melissæ.
" Then in the cave of Nysa was born the redeemer Iacchus,
" Born from pure Melibœdes, by mortals call'd Amalthcia,
" Born from Ammon of ancient days. The nymphs of Ceramnus
" Nurs'd him there, and Athena taught and the wise Aristæus.
" Broad was the cave and lofty, with crystal pillars, transparent,
" Glitt'ring, and through it a fountain ran ; a shadowy ilex
" Over it hung ; and odorous plants and each flower of the mountain,
" Pendent or tufted, grew on the rocks in perennial fragrance,   1000
" Daphné, clematis, thyme ; and the bees murmur'd ever among them.
" There he grew till the time was ripe ; and he fought with the Titans,
" Crush'd their power, and captur'd nor slew, but offer'd forgiveness,
" Either his friends to be, or to go in peace, at their pleasure.
" Gratefully they accepted ; and then a cup in the midmost,
" Fill'd with juice of the grape, his gift, he plac'd, and invited
" All to drink, and pledge him their faith and peace with each other.
" Happy had they but kept that pledge ! But Fate was against them.
" Then the oracle spake :—' In peace is life everlasting.
" ' Do thou good unto all, and become, like me, an immortal.'   1010
" So through the world he travell'd, by all the Graces attended,
" Wars composing and love instilling ; and ever the wine-cup
" Proffer'd, and bound the nations to serve by oath sacramental,
" Zeus to serve, their King acclaim'd, and to love one another—
" Greek or barbarian all as one, to love one another.
" Hence libations we pour to the Gods, and love one another.
" All fulfill'd, descending, he brought his mother, Thyoné
" Henceforth nam'd, from Hades, and rose up with her to heaven
" Thence will he come once more, to save, in the day of Typhœus.
" This was the Silver Age, and the Age of Bronze has succeeded.   1020
" —Iö Pæan, vaxat, Iεπεγεον' Apollon !

IV.

" What remaineth ? O sweet Harmonia, return from thine islands !
" Lovely Peace, return, return ! And starry Astræa !
" Last to leave us, the lov'd and lost, pure daughter of Themis,
" Home, come home ! And thou that sleepest, Creator Ophion !
" —Send him, O Father ! binder of sin, but fountain of mercy,
" Ever from thy vast caldron-cup descending to mortals !
" Where the Twelve Gods repair each year to feast with the blameless

" Æthiop race, and East and West are lost in each other—
" Wake once more, and intervene for a second creation,   1030
" Ours, thy children, of Argo born, of the wood of Dodona!
" Teach us that Order is heaven's first law; that Love begets Order,
" Order Strength ; and Strength consisteth in Unity.   Bind us
" Closer and closer, brethren sworn to the cup of Iacchus,
" Peace to ensue and love upon earth ; by self-abnegation,
" Each for each content to suffer ; by kindly forgiveness,
" Griefs endur'd ; by righting wrong, protecting the widow,
" Orphans fost'ring and all things weak ; each loving a maiden,
" One, unselfishly ; living in chastity, temp'rate in all things.
" Bind us, as here we sit, in the sacred circle of friendship,   1040
" As by Harmonia's ring of old, the symbol of order,
" All unto one work vow'd as sons and servants of Argo,
" Self-devoted to open the path to the land of Æëtes.
" Ours be, in fine, the honest heart, the strong resolution
" Not to seek good by crookéd means, but ever straightforward
" Walk in the eye of day, low cunning fearlessly scorning,
" Ev'n if a God appear to prompt it,—'tis but a trial,
" Fatal yielded to, and the result will bring us disaster.
" Better to fail through good than succeed by evil,— the issue
" Lies with God ; 'tis for us to act, for Him to determine.   1050
" This is noble indeed, to suffer for righteous doing.
" First and last is Iacchus' law, to love one another.
" Phrixus thus, our brother, desir'd to die for his people,
" Fate not willing it,—thus hath our Heracles here accepted
" Bondage lifelong to free mankind ; and thus did Iacchus
" Win an immortal crown by love, and to dwell in Olympus.
" So, when the Iron Age shall come—when again in Olympus
" Strife shall reign, already in germ, and the Gods who assist us
" Now shall arm in mutual hate, and Ilion the Holy,
" City of God, shall fall, ah me ! and the wall that Apollo   1060
" Soon shall build, with the Just Man's aid and the strength of Poseidon,
" Down shall crash, and the dragon enter, and all be ruin—
" Ruin, ruin ! desolate homes, and her children in exile—
" Still, even then, shall our fame endure, ever green in remembrance
" Ev'n till the end of time, when, the age of ages completed,
" Argo shall come from the Southern skies, by the hand of Iacchus
" Steer'd, to rescue the sons of men in the day of Typhœus.
" Night comes fast.   O happier we, the sons of the morning !
" —Ἰὼ Παιάν, vaxat. Ἰήπεύεον' Ἀπόλλων !"

The master ceas'd, the ling'ring notes expire,   1070
But still, low murm'ring, sings the conscious lyre;
The strain no more is heard in Chiron's cave,
The list'ning Nereids sink beneath the wave.
The fervour spent, he droop'd his head, depress'd,
And deep sobs shook the mighty minstrel's breast.
The heroes sat in thought, and silence kept;
Some mourn'd life's wasted prime; the younger wept,
Thinking of sisters lov'd and parents dear;
Ev'n mighty Heracles wip'd off a tear,
For thought of Iölé, his lost one, stole,   1080
The master singing, and subdued his soul.
Some dream'd of doing great things, thinking not
How soon their high resolves would be forgot.
All soften'd were ; and they arose and clasp'd
Each other's hands,—ev'n Idas Jason's grasp'd,
With look of deprecation ; then a prayer
Each mutter'd, and lay down.   The midnight air
Refresh'd their heated brows.   'Neath Argo's shade,
Mother and comforter, themselves they laid.
Now clear, now veil'd, the stars shot fitful gleams ;   1090
And, as they slept, thus chequer'd were their dreams.
Tiphys, alone, sat watching through the night
Apart, expectant of the morning light.

BUT when the dawn appearing shew'd the trees
Distinct on Pelion; and the fresh'ning breeze
Woke the tired wavelets that had slept all night,
And they danc'd merrily in the growing light;
Then Tiphys, rising, cried, "Awake, awake!
" Time 'tis that Argo her departure take."
They rous'd themselves, and stretch'd, for most were young,
And youthful slumbers should be sound and long;
But instantly, fair Argo full in view,
Remember'd gladly all they had to do.   10
First, they haul'd in and coil'd the mooring-line;
Then, on the stern standing, with unmix'd wine,
Pour'd from a golden goblet, Jason made
Libation; and to all the Gods he pray'd,

But most to Zeus, to bless their forward track,
Reward the quest, and bring them safely back.
Quick, a bright flash responsive cross'd the sky,
And Mopsus spake, " Good is the augury."
Then Tiphys, hoisting, to the breeze outshook
The ensign ; and his seat each hero took   20
Prescrib'd, his weapons placing by his side,
Ready.   Ancæus, Heracles divide
The central bench of honour.   'Neath their feet,
With frequent thud, the gurgling waters beat,
Washing the keel.   The mighty club and axe
Tremble, unhandled, new to such attacks.
Then, at the word, all stretch'd them to the oar,
And, fast receding, left Iölcos' shore.
A slow and solemn old tripudial chime
The lyre gave forth, and their true stroke kept time.   30
They cleave the waves ; the struggling waters break,
And leave a long deep furrow in their wake,
A track of silver, as a path is seen
In autumn, white, crossing a meadow green.
And now they near the spot where Nelia stands, --
A verdant nook the sea-ward view commands,
Mouth of a gorge, from which descends a ledge,
Of shelf and sand, down to the waters' edge.
There see they Chiron standing, from his cave
Come down to bless their progress o'er the wave,   40
Beside him Chariclo.   The breakers play
Over their feet.   The babe Achilles lay
In her kind arms.   She held him up to view
Of his great sire ; and Chiron sign'd adieu.
Peleus his hands uprais'd to bless the child,
Then turn'd and hid his face, to tears beguil'd.

Now stretch they forth, quitting the bay, and seek
To cross Pelasgia's gulf tow'rds Tisa's peak,—
Thence, shunning Cicynethus, round the bold
Æantian promontory, in to hold   50
Their course to Aphetæ.   The path was clear
For many an hour, nor shoals nor rocks to fear.
The sons of Boreas pray'd, and there arose
The wind that southward from bleak Hæmus blows.
They fix the mast in its appointed place,
And firm by double ropes on each side brace ;
Then rear the sail-yard and display the sail,
And Argo bounds forth joyous to the gale.
The sun, topping the heights, now crown'd the day,
And Argo, swan-like, glitter'd in the ray.   60
As when the sheep, caring no more to feed,
Follow the shepherd, playing on his reed,
Homeward at folding-time ; so Nereus' brood,
The fishes small and great, her course pursued,
Wond'ring and distanc'd.   From Olympus' height
The Gods look'd down and watch'd her with delight.
The heroes, day advancing, 'gan to feel
Hunger, and each partook a well-earn'd meal ;
Then, resting 'gainst the tholepins, idly sat,
In thought subdued, dreaming of this or that,   70
Some of the past, of the dim future more,
For griefs as well as joys might be in store ;
And after high excitement the bright hue
Of life is soberer in reaction's view.
Not sad they were but pensive, and suppress'd
The gloomier thoughts that waken'd in their breast.
Soft plash'd the waters as they onward sped ;
The wind play'd whistling in the sail o'er-head ;

The younger fell asleep.   Anœreus sung
A low sad chant in his ancestral tongue;   80
How once, beyond Hesperia's furthest bound,
A nation dwelt, for worth and might renown'd,
His kinsmen, in an island Aztlan nam'd,
Their king Evenor, far for justice fam'd;
But, mightier, came Poseidon's sons, and won
The empire, sitting on Evenor's throne,
Himself thenceforth their vassal,—either race,
Submissive one, consenting in embrace.
Hence a mix'd kind, pow'rful, but wise and just
For ages, till corroding wealth and lust   90
Of conquest brought their galleys to the gate
Of Athens—foolish! thus to tempt their fate;
For the Tyrrhenians fierce and the strong spear
Of Pallas crush'd them ere they enter'd there;
And Zeus, by counsel of the Gods, decreed—
Ah! retribution harsh for such a deed—
That Aztlan's sea-laid pillars undermin'd
Should crumble away, nor leave a trace behind
Of the fair island, once the world's delight,—
Her sons, her weak, escaping as they might,   100
Perchance yet further in the West to find
A refuge, altars, fortunes, less unkind.
Still you may see her cities 'neath the waves
Gleaming, and Nereids passing from their caves
To dwell alternate in her palaces,
No mortals near, disporting as they please.
   So sang he on, they slumb'ring; and the day,
The wind still holding steady, wore away.
The hot noon pass'd, and they woke one by one,
Each thinking sleep had come on him alone,   110

But each affirming he had waking kept,
And watch'd with Tiphys while the others slept.
Iölcos, long descried, had long been lost
In distance.   To their right lay Phthia's coast,
The pleasant land that Peleus' sceptre owns,
Land of th' Achæans and the Myrmidons.
The shrine of Artemis on Tisa's brow,
Where watchfires mark the reefs that lurk below,
They fearful see; but, touch'd by Tiphys' hand,
The rudder speeds them tow'rds the adverse land   120
Of Ptelcon.   Orpheus meanwhile seiz'd the lyre,
And sang of Artemis in words of fire,
Arcadian Artemis, who loves to dwell
On mountain top, or by wood-shaded well,
And roam the wilds with bow and arrows, sure
To strike, a huntress and a virgin pure.
But now they lower the mast, and tack,—they see
The bay that leads to shelt'ring Aphetæ,
'Neath Tisa's slopes deep-nestled.   They the oars
Resume once more, and 'tween the narrowing shores   130
Row lustily, till, as the evening sank,
Guided by many a house-light on the bank,
Beneath the city's modest walls they find
Safe harbourage and moorings to their mind.

So pass'd their first, and many a day succeeds;
But such, unless proclaim'd by special deeds,
The Muse will not record.   Well-pleas'd she sings
Of deeds sublime, but scorns indiff'rent things;
Yet still allows the poet's tongue to name
Argo's chief landmarks, thus consign'd to fame.   140

Loos'd from screen'd Aphetæ, a Zephyr, sent
By Zeus, arose.   Again the sail they bent;

And through th' Euboean strait sped swift between
Oreus and Tisa, till, approaching, seen
Gray Sciathus, they furl the sail, the oar
Assume, and Northward skirt Magnesia's shore.
The tomb of Dolops, Hermes' son, afar
A signal rises, like a guiding star
By night to seamen doubtful of their way,—
They land, observance to his shade to pay;   150
Then 'yond Peiresia, Meliboea, pass on,
Still rowing, till, rejoic'd, they gaze upon
Tempé, and hoar Olympus, tow'ring high,
Home of the Gods, commercing with the sky,
And, mindful still, set by Poseidon free,
Peneius, rolling turbid to the sea,—
Thence, Eastward, sailing, tow'rds Pallené cross,
Erst Phlegra, where the Giants suffer'd loss,
Blood-born of Uranus by Gé; when Zeus
Porphyrion slew, and huge Alcyoneus:—   160
Now cornfields wave and the red cattle graze
Where Zeus's lightnings rag'd in ancient days.
Next, distant, they descry dark Athos' cone,
The Holy Mount, high-tow'ring, all alone,
Out-post of Thrace, with Zeus's hallow'd fane
Above Nymphæum, glitt'ring o'er the main.
There, of Zeus shelter'd, shall a remnant long,
In accents soft, speak the Pelasgian tongue.
They breath'd a prayer; but, Zephyr fav'ring still,
Pursued their course, running to Eastward, till   170
The wind, as wont, fell with the setting sun;
But they row'd on till midnight, and then run
Beneath the hills of Lemnos, low and bare,
Enter'd the little port, and moor'd them there.

The morning broke ; the sky was dull and gray,
Wind from the East,—they scarce could start that day.
A town they saw, high on the neighb'ring rocks,
Farmsteads around, scatter'd, and herds and flocks
Going to pasture.   Women to the plough
The oxen harness'd, clumsily enow,   180
And awkward started.   Presently, thrown wide,
The city-gates were open'd ; but they 'spied
No men, but women passing in and out ;
Nor in the fields were lab'ring men about.
'Twas very strange,—and, as the light, more clear,
Shew'd Argo in the port, as if with fear
Seiz'd, like a flock of sheep discomfited
By sight of unknown dog, the women fled
Into the city.   Thence came forth ere long,
Upon the half-moon platform, a fierce throng—   190
Or seem'd such—of arm'd warriors ; but they pac'd
Heavily, with their breastplates but half-lac'd,
Their gait undisciplin'd, greaves fitting ill,—
Nor shew'd they purpose to descend the hill,
Argo to question, whence she daring came,
Her route, her nation, and her captain's name ;
But gaz'd abroad with glance incurious, slow
Dragging their long swords after, to and fro ;
Till, as if weary, they inactive stood,
Propp'd on their spears, like statues carv'd in wood.   200
Strange sight !   Like phantoms all unreal, such
The vision seem'd.   The heroes marvell'd much.
The city, Myrina, they knew,—of old
Had Thoas been 'mong Æson's guests enroll'd,
And those of Œneus, when he urg'd the war
'Gainst Pleuron, after they had slain the boar ;

F

And Thoas' name had to his grandson been
By Œneus given, at instance of his queen—
That Thoas, wise in speech, in years a boy,
Who led th' Ætolians at the siege of Troy:— 210
—A shameful thing, that strangers should await
Unwelcom'd, nay, unnoticed at the gate !

They waited long,—no message came ; and then
Æthalides, herald of peace to men,
At Jason's hest, up tow'rds the city went
Thoas to see, state whither they were bent,
And, if rememb'rance fail'd of days gone by,
Crave as mere strangers hospitality.

Now must the Muse unheard of things record !
The Sintian dames had made themselves abhorr'd 220
Of Aphrodité—Aphrodité bright,
Of wise Hephæstus spouse and sole delight.
Him, when cast out by Zeus, his power defied,
From heav'n for taking his dear mother's side,
The Sintians kind receiv'd ; he lov'd their race,
And will'd with them his chosen home to place.
He in Mosyclos dwells,—thence smoke and fire
Darken the skies ; and strokes that never tire,
The hammer thund'ring constant night and day,
The earth astonish and the seas dismay. 230
She dwells in near Eubœa, save when gone
To Paphos, or some Syrian voyage upon.
Her had the women anger'd, and she wrought
Unnumber'd evils, that fair Lemnos brought
To desolation—sons and husbands dead,
By women, only, now inhabited.

But what th' offence ?   Like to a noxious flower,
It grew not up nor blossom'd in an hour ;

And the foul wrong that blighted Lemnos' fame
Was sown in error ere 'twas reap'd in shame.   240
As from earth's entrails, grounded, wild-vines climb,
So wicked actions have their roots in time ;
Each new event, with all its issues, springs,
As from its fount, from old forgotten things.
As one poor thistle, in a garden sown,
Flow'ring, its seed to every quarter blown,
Corrupts a hundred fields once cultur'd fair,
And the vex'd farmer struggles in despair ;
So one crude speculation, loosely cast,
Hath power a thousand hearts and lives to blast.   250
As when, beneath the Typhaonian rock,
Typhœus stirs in agony, the shock,
Through earth and sea propell'd, uplifts a wave.
Vast, tow'ring, rushing on, a living grave,
Which unexpected bursts on some far shore,
And ruin brings where all was joy before ;
So from a distant land, upheav'd, a throe
Of thought occult, but big with future woe,
Destruction roll'd on Lemnos, wing'd by Fate,
And left her fields and homesteads desolate.   260

    Fount of such error, author, scourge of wrong,
Liv'd gray Polyxo, native not, among
The Sintians, Greek by birth. Of fever'd brain,
A Mœnad once in Dionysus' train,
Daughter of Macris, of Peneius' race,
She to Apollo's sacred loins could trace
Though bold Cyrené's womb her parentage —
Cyrené, who with lions war would wage,
Well-match'd, on Pelion ; hence her heart was stern,
Nor easily from purpose fix'd would turn.   270

F 2

She came with Thoas when he won the heir
Of Lemnos, Myrina, the young and fair,
Child of the Sintian king. She rear'd their child,
Hypsipylé. Strange fancies, dark and wild,
Perverse, distorted mockeries of truth,
Her thought had nourish'd from her early youth,
Mingling with strangers from the Scythian waste,
Where Ares black and Artemis the chaste
Are worshipp'd by the Amazons,—from them
She learn'd the rite of marriage to contemn,   280
And men to hate as tyrants. Upis taught,
Misunderstood, misgloss'd, the tale how brought
Harmonia was to Cadmus—higher than
Her mate in race, a dæmon, he mere man ;
She to such spouse, a minister of heaven,
A loving consort, mistress, mother given ;
One of the class divine, immortal fam'd,
Griffins and dogs of Zeus, or watchers, nam'd,—
Man vassal thus, sub-order'd, woman queen :—
Well, had relation such perpetuate been ;   290
But since those good old times all was revers'd,—
And in her teeming visions she rehears'd
The wrongs of women, brooding over schemes
Such to redress, distemper'd noxious dreams,
Shaping them by her Greek brain's subtilty's
Reas'ning, concluding from false premises,—
Deadliest deceiver, who in honest sooth
Propounds such specious fallacies as truth !
Her sex exalting, mirror'd in herself,
Of influence fond, but caring not for pelf,   300
Sincere in purpose, confident of right,
But seeing all things in an oblique light,

Her ends to compass fear nor shame she had,
And means, successful, reck'd not good or bad.
A dang'rous couns'llor, an Alecto dire,
Should Fate that smould'ring furnace wake to fire!
Experience had she great in little things,
In wise men's folly and the craft of kings;
But, less than woman, would without remorse
In every question take th' extremest course;   310
Nor ever lack'd example pat whereby
To recommend her views, or justify.
Long these her dogmas had she freely flung
To germinate the Sintian dames among;
And 'mong barbarians, knowing Greece, a Greek
Great influence carries when he deigns to speak.
    The Sintians were an old barbarian clan,
Whose race from Scythes, Phrygian sire, began;
Hard workers—for their soil was thin and poor;
But rich—for skill in smelting iron ore   320
Hephæstus grateful gave to them, and taught
The armourer's craft; and swords and shields they wrought
For men, as he for heroes and for Gods.
No thought had they of changing their abodes
For kindlier settlements, but held their own,
And dwelt in their free island, all alone,—
Great smiths, a noble brood! like Dædalus,
Or him of Ares, wise Mamurius.
Swart and broad-built their type,—short, curly hair;
Teeth iv'ry-white; good-humour'd, frank their air;   330
Kind to their wives, but masters in the house;
The wives meet rev'rence paid, each to her spouse,—
Both walking clean, without a thought to hide,
In the pure steps of Cadmus and his bride.

Hard work both sexes did ; and, sooth to say,
The women got through more in one short day
Than all Mæonia's daughters in a week ;
But, work achiev'd, their blythe hearts would outbreak,
Both sexes mingling free, in mirth and joke,
Nor fear'd men's blame, unconscious of a yoke.   340

    Such audience hers, Polyxo dropp'd the seed
Her sex amongst, prompt discontent to breed.
Credulous, open-mouth'd, they learn'd how great
Their birth, how unendurable their fate,
Women so far superior to the men,
But to their tyrant rule subjected,—then
They heard rejoic'd that argument would give
Back their supremacy, their rank retrieve :—
" If man's but earth-born, womanhood divine.
" Man is as water, womanhood as wine.   350
" Woman should at the least man's equal be,
" Nay, owns by right superiority.
" But if superior, then the female sex
" Should rule the male, should ride upon their necks,
" And guide like horses. But alas ! the scales
" Unequal pois'd, the due adjustment fails.
" Men are the stronger, and can tyrannise.
" This to compensate, women should be wise.
" Superior minds superior power imply.
" Women must win o'er men the mastery.   360
" In argument is woman's strength, the tongue
" Thus panoplied to prove a husband wrong ;
" And, such man's simple nature, though the bit
" He champ awhile, yet, silenc'd, he'll submit.
" Lastly, should women train themselves as men
" Athletically,—not indeed to strain

"Strength against strength, but by the fencer's skill
"Make themselves fear'd if wrong'd or cross'd in will ;
" Thus both by tongue and sword against the dense
" Brute force of man accomplish'd in defence.   370
     " But more," she argued ; " if the case stands thus,
" If men, as sex, inferior are to us,
" Then marriage is unequal ; we are slaves
" That should be masters,—this amendment craves.
" 'Tis not so difficult.   The remedy
" Must, as in all things, with your own selves lie.
" Either be celibates—by far the best ;
" Or married, or if love subdue the breast,
" Ye younger ! be your partnership at will,
" Free to consort or sep'rate—better still ;   380
" Free love, on equal terms, and not by law
" Of God or man constrain'd, nor under awe
" Of penalty ; but each to other hold
" No longer than by mutual wish controll'd.
" Thus mated, thus alone can marriage be
" Ought but subjection to man's tyranny,—
" Each woman, doubtless, faithful to her spouse
" Pledg'd for the time—but no religious vows :—
" If Hera sanction, Aphrodité claim
"Such by their priests, those priests are much to blame.
" But in my country we not much appraise   391
" These Goddesses' worn credit now-a-days."
     Such things she secret preach'd, and they drank in,
Mothers and daughters, close, the doors within.
Some hints of what she taught the wiser ones
Their husbands told, or, widows, to their sons,—
These merely laugh'd, nor guess'd what mischief dire
A spark might raise when folly fann'd the fire.

So things went on; and gradually the seed
Thus scatter'd grew into a baleful weed   400
Unseen beneath the waters, poison-rife,
The stream upclogging of domestic life.
Wives, daughters, all endeavour'd, old and young,
Husbands to prove or brothers in the wrong
By argument; nor counted they the cost :—
Vict'ries thus won are worse than battles lost.
Still more provoking 'twas when they withdrew
Defeated, with superior smile, anew
To recommence strife on another tack,
Still to the vain contention coming back.   410
No word men utter'd but occasion gave
Woman to prove man's equal, not his slave.
Soft wheedlings, coaxings, love's caressing mood,
Were now disus'd, badges of servitude.
With men in public, not their husbands, they
Discuss'd whose province 'twas to rule, t' obey,
Woman's or man's, abstractly ; and each spoke
Her own an ox submissive to the yoke.
While thus the wives, the daughters, not to be
Behind-hand, now affected manners free ;   420
Cropp'd their hair close, their robes succinct uptied,
Adopted swinging gait and manhood's stride ;
Pass'd passengers i' th' street with careless brush,—
Swore roundly by men's oaths, and ceas'd to blush ;
Bold, not immodest-meaning, though their tongue
Would haunt delighted on the verge of wrong ;
Yet still, by natural reticence restrain'd,
Stopp'd short, and licence on that verge refrain'd,—
One thought infirmer, one step further on,
And virgin chastity itself were gone.   430

Rev'rence for elders, ancient usages,
Fear of the Gods, they mock'd as prejudice.
Maidens and wives one common impress bore,
Their ign'rance, folly, much, presumption more.
  At last, the husbands, fathers, constant found
Tongue-match'd and conquer'd as each eve came round,
When, labour-weary, they'd been wont to find
Sweet harmony, home-love, and welcome kind,
Prov'd wrong by reas'ning they could not confute,
And taught that woman's heav'n-born, man a brute,   440
Grew wearied, pain'd, disgusted, sour'd at heart,
Abjur'd their firesides, lived a life apart,
Long'd, but too manly were, their wives to strike,
And view'd thier daughters with confirm'd dislike.
These last the young men took without debate
As fellows at their own self-estimate;
Ceas'd to defer in courtesies where none
Bas'd expectation feebler strength upon;
But, equals, follow'd out their natural bent,
And to the wall of course the weaker went.   450
No thought of marriage rose in either case.
Antipathy between them grew apace.
  Meanwhile nor wives nor daughters now would join
In grateful prayer at Aphrodité's shrine.
Some grudging cult they to Athena paid,
And some to Artemis, the Taurian maid;
The other deities neglected quite,
And lame Hephæstus ridicul'd outright.
His spouse, resenting, shed th' indignant tear,
And meditated chastisement severe.   460
  So matters stood. A few short years before
Had those of Singus, on the Thracian shore,

Invaded Lemnos; and the Sintians now
Return'd the visit, rend'ring blow for blow,
Surpris'd the town, spoil'd it of treasures rare,
And brought back captive maidens, many and fair.
These made they concubines; and sweet and kind
They found them,—far more grateful to their mind
Than their polemic spouses or the youth
Of female Lemnos, masculine, uncouth.   470
The men their bastard to their legal brood
Preferr'd, and thus fresh bitterness ensued.
　　Now Aphrodité's time was come. She cast
Madness among the women, and a blast
Of fire on Lemnos, deadlier than the eye
Of basilisk, which seeing man must die;
But most she frenzied ag'd Polyxo's brain,
Till, like a courser fierce, unloos'd the rein,
Trampling at once on God's and mortals' laws—
Or as a fire the forest-bush or straw's   480
Dry stubble kindles in the summer drought—
She spoke th' accursèd counsel of her thought :—
　　" Daughters!" she cried, " is nothing to be done ?
" Shall insult, shall endurance still go on ?
" Ye murmur, No! Then hearken! Long years since,
" Ye sent me to bright Delos, from your prince
" And you to carry gifts to Phœbus' shrine.
" There met I Upis, Argé, nymphs divine,
" Sent by the Hyperboreans to convey
" Tribute to Eileithuia, whom to-day   490
" We honour less than formerly. They told
" Of a great nation, near their dwellings, bold,
" Fear'd far by land and sea, in everything
" Law to themselves, slaves nor to priest nor king,

" All women, worshipping cold Artemis,
" Abhorring Aphrodité.   Mark ye this!
" Be these your model.   Fathers, brothers, sons,
" They own none—own none ye—be Amazons!
" Let every male thing in all Lemnos die!
" So shall ye win, so keep your liberty.   500
" Even boy infants spare not—seed of men
" That, spar'd, will tyrants propagate again.
" I have spoken—and I think the dæmon true
" That prompts my thought.   To act it rests with you."

    Unsex'd already, with applauding throat
All clamour'd ' Aye!' nor put it to the vote.
They thought no more of mercy in their wrath
Than crushing worms or insects in their path.
Short of a God's no power could have prevail'd
O'er woman's natural instincts, thus assail'd.   510

    'Twas done.   That night, when Erebus his pall
Spread o'er black Lemnos, they were murder'd all,
Fathers, husbands, and sons ; some by the knife,
Most by the drugg'd cup, numbing out the life.
Only each dam chang'd sucklings with her friend,
By alien hands their short sweet lives to end.
Each sister, daughter, wife resum'd that eve
Old coaxing ways, the better to deceive.
Since then we speak in Greece of ' Lemnian deeds '
When treach'rous, shameless cruelty exceeds.   520

    One only 'scap'd, the King.   A daughter's love
Prevail'd a heart harder than stone to move.

    When Thoas' bride, sweet Myrina, had pass'd
Her nine months of probation, and at last
Her child was born, the tenth's accomplishment,
Her strength, not great, though weary travail spent,

Fail'd her; and, dying, to Polyxo's care
She gave the babe, Hypsipylé the fair,
With commendation that she should be true
To her, and kind a guardian's duty do.   530
Polyxo swore, and thenceforth dwelt with her,
Her nurse, and Thoas' trusted housekeeper.
She rear'd her loving to the Gods and kind
To all men, taught her truth, and train'd her mind
To maiden modesty, nor conscious sought
To stain her spotless soul with one bad thought.
True to her oath, and guarding undefil'd,
Such single merit hers, her mistress' child,—
But only, abstractly, bade her take to heart
That women were a race, a caste, apart,   540
Holy, divine, but sold to slavery,
By men wrong'd, tyrannis'd, and should be free;
That marriage seal'd their bonds, but freely given,
Freely withdrawn, love, virtuous, was from heaven.
This she took in on trust, nor knew it wrong,
And no God's voice reprov'd the teacher's tongue.
She in the palace lived retir'd; nor car'd
Polyxo her seclusion should be shar'd
By such, the maids of Lemnos, as had grown
To woman's prime since the new doctrine known.   550
Sixteen sweet springs Hypsipylé had seen,
A child in thought, in maiden grace a queen,
But such as Artemis—not loveliness,
But beauty grave; frank kindness in address,
Controll'd by modesty. Her olive cheek
Spoke of her mother, but all else was Greek,
Of purest type. The darling of her sire,
She lov'd him dearly, but she fear'd his ire,

Too hasty; and this fear, alas! repress'd
Her confidence, and lock'd it in her breast;   560
Else had she learn'd the doctrines false to hate
Which, acted on, made Lemnos desolate.

   Needs not to say how, when Polyxo told
The women's counsel, passion, uncontroll'd,
Broke down all barriers; and she strove to reach
Her father's presence; how, repell'd at each
Exit by watchers, she her nurse implor'd
To spare her sceptred king, her trusted lord :—
She drew a dagger from her belt, and swore
By Hecaté to shed her proper gore,   570
Polyxo's guilt, and track her steps, a ghost
Execrate, on the blasts of Acheron tost,
Unless she sav'd her sire :—Polyxo quail'd ;
Her nurseling's threat her one weak point assail'd ;
Fearless of God, to thought of mercy dead,
Thessalian born, spectres she held in dread.
And well she knew the maiden's will. A thought
Of the dead mother cross'd her too, and brought
Remorse,—then shame that a barbarian brood
Should, she their agent, spill the pure Greek blood :—   580
And then she saw her kneeling, late so proud,
Clasping her knees ; and her fell purpose bow'd,
Subdued by the child's touch —and she gave way.
Brief, secretly that night, when the scar'd day
Had fled from guilty Lemnos, all being laid
In sleep's exhaustion, she the King convey'd
Through the chill chambers to the shore. He found
A little boat there moor'd, the rope unbound,
Rais'd the black sail ; and a fresh Eastern breeze
Wing'd the frail vessel to the Sporades ;   590

And Pythian Phœbus in Sicynos' isle
Receiv'd the royal suppliant with a smile.
Henceforward, their child-queen, Hypsipylé
Rul'd these mock Amazons in sovereignty.

All this had chanc'd a twelvemonth ere the oars
Of Argo brought her to the Lemnian shores.

Meanwhile the Sintian women found the life
Of independence hard, the seasons' strife
Worse than their old contentions. The harsh plough
They plied, sow'd, hop'd for harvest. On their brow   600
Toil set her mark. The bees forsook the hive ;
The cattle mutinied. The dust would drive,
Hephæstus' impulse, from Mosyclos' height,
And cover the sad fields with drought and blight.
Small thought of argument was now—such art
Were none to practise on. Worse, qualms of heart,
Late waken'd, made themselves at times be felt.
Fearful, they labour'd, sword in hand, and belt
Chafing their loins, each martial exercise,
Watching by night and day against surprise,   610
Cruel, retributive, from those of Thrace,
Venging their daughters, torn from their embrace.
Only Polyxo falter'd not,—she saw
But one thing at a time ; her will was law ;
And no one dar'd to whisper a weak doubt
That they had acted wisely, but a stout
Bearing maintain'd, vaunted their liberty,
While each in secret mourn'd that she was free.
Not that their hearts were chang'd, their folly seen ;
Dews fall no longer where such waste hath been.   620
But in her heart Hypsipylé each thing
Ponder'd, and nothing said. Bewildering,

Polyxo's teachings dwelt with her ; but still
True instinct, loving right, abhorring ill,
Grew in her day by day ; and the mists clear'd
Partial, though slowly.   Constant she rever'd
Her Gods ancestral, and in secret pray'd
For, 'gainst th' avenging ones, their gracious aid ;
Certain, her people parricides in crime,
Alecto's scourge would find them out in time.   630

   Thus when the women, issuing from the farms,
Saw Argo in the port, wild with alarms,
Like flock of tim'rous sheep discomfited
At sight of an unwonted dog, they fled
Within the gates just open'd of the town,
Fair Myrina, that on the port looks down ;
Thence issuing, in their husbands' breastplates, lac'd
Perforce but loosely, the front platform pac'd ;
Then wearied paus'd, each resting on her spear.
They took the Minyan heroes, in their fear,   640
For Thracians.   Now Æthalides was seen
Mounting the hill ; and presently the Queen
Join'd them.   They crowded round her, like a brood
Of chickens round their dam, in troubled mood,
A hawk seen over-head, unwelcome guest.
But she mov'd calm, anxious though self-possess'd ;
Nor armour wore ; but bade them back, and let
Her meet him as such envoys should be met ;
Then stood, slightly advanc'd, before the gate.
He, wond'ring much, and holding forth elate   650
The wand of peace, drew near with gentle word :—
" Fair Queen !—if Lemnos own no other lord—
" But Thoas certés rul'd this land, of yore
" The guest of Æson on Æmonia's shore,—

" Jason, the son of Æson, with the band
" Of heroes, vow'd to seek the Colchian strand,
" And bring back Chrysomallus' golden Fleece,
" Which stern Æëtes yet withholds from Greece,
" Waits in the port ; and, if thou daughter art
" Of Thoas, claims hereditary part   660
" As guest in thy fair grace, as from thy sire,
" Short shelter in thy port, with food and fire,—
" Or, if remembrance fail of days gone by,
" Craves, as mere stranger, hospitality."

   To whom the Queen :—" Doubt not our friendly will,
" O sacred herald ! nor fear welcome chill
" From Thoas' daughter.   Æson's son I know
" No stranger, nor inhospitable foe.
" But grief o'erwhelms this isle ; and I, alone,
" New, inexperienc'd, fill my father's throne.   670
" I welcome all.   Return,—short while attend ;
" And, counsel ta'en, fit answer I will send."

   Then to the palace went she, at her side
Polyxo ; and the women, in a tide,
Pour'd after, as where seas contending meet,
Confus'd, one babble all.   She took her seat
On Thoas' great stone chair, and still'd the crowd,
And thus address'd, in accents clear, not loud :—
" My words are, Welcome, and supply the wants
" Of these our guests, great Zeus's suppliants ;   680
" Send to them food and gifts, that they remain
" Quietly at the ship, nor knowledge gain
" Of how we stand, of what hath been our crime,
" Or how th' Erinnys still awaits her time."

   Then, skinny, her elf-locks 'scaping from the comb,
Now by a twelvemonth nearer to the tomb,

Leaning upon her staff, and with a croak
As of the Phocian bird, Polyxo spoke,—
Still resolute her heart; her eyes gleam'd fire,
As doth the Mænad or th' insane inspire :—   690
" I say not ' Send not '—Send them food and gifts;
" But our emergency needs special shifts.
" List to me! No one can a summer's day,
" 'Cross country, tow'rds a landmark work his way
" Direct, uncheck'd, on the horizon seen ;
" But if a hostile river roll between,
" Must build a raft, or ford it.   Kept in sight,
" Thus he may reach the landmark before night.
" Free from men are ye and their tyranny,—
" But what your chance, what your security,   700
" Should the fierce Thracians, as these guests have come,
" Swoop down like eagles on your franchis'd home ?
" And when we elders die, how will you live,
" Ye younger, growing old ? Will the fields give
" Their fruit spontaneous, ye too weak to plough ?
" Be this averted ! Do ye ask me how ?
" The way now opens.   Men, our natural foes,
" To circumvent, craft must brute strength oppose.
" Use them as instruments our ends to gain.
" Ev'n the great Amazons make tools of men,   710
" Else would their race expire.   From Upis I
" Learn'd what may serve in this emergency.
" Once yearly to the Mount Riphæan, where
" Dwell the Sauromatæ, their foes, repair
" The Amazons, a band select, on truce,
" Each for one night a warrior mate to choose,
" And each bring home a daughter.   Bearing sons,
" They slay them.   Thus the race of Amazons

G

" Recruited lives. Ask from these strangers each
" A child, daughter or son, to heal the breach   720
" In our estate. But, granted, then dismiss
" The strangers instant; or, refusing, this
" Be signal of their death, as well ye know
" To deal it. These sparse sons will be enow
" To till the fields, strong-handed, bred in due
" Subservience, and, as needs, our race renew,—
" Greeks too their sires, and of the hero race,
" Their dread shall guard you 'gainst attacks from Thrace.
" This then do ye of these our brave guests crave ;
" But keep past counsels secret as the grave."   730
        Thus spoke the hag,—adding instruction wise
How in report they should their state disguise,
Bereft of men. The women, much commov'd,
Debated long, but at the last approv'd.
Hypsipylé, but partially content,
Said, " I will pray, if such be your consent,
" Jason to come up here, unarm'd, alone,
" To hear your common counsel and my own."
        So saying, she the multitude dismiss'd,
And young Iphinöe call'd unto her :—" Hist,   740
" Maiden !" and her a special message gave ;
And she went down, and near'd the ship; and, grave,
With courteous gest, Æthalides her led
To Jason's presence, and she boldly said,—
" Hypsipylé hath sent me here to tell
" Thee, Argo's captain, that she greets thee well,
" And prays thee to come up, unarm'd, alone,
" To hear the city's counsel and her own,—
" The rest to keep the port, nor make debate ;
" For we are women, and unfortunate."   750

Jason much wonder'd, but prepar'd t' obey;
Over his shoulders threw a mantle, gay
With purple and with gold, that skilful wove
Arachné, and her father dyed,—above
His head and o'er him Aphrodité pour'd
Beauty and grace, as of th' Assyrian lord
Of Byblos.   Thus, unarm'd, alone, he went,
Iphinöe with him, up the steep ascent
To Myrina.   The damsels straight unbar
The gate, and curious gaze; but, like a star,   760
Unheeding, cold, though glitt'ring, on the ground
He bent his eyes, advancing.   Up the mound
Where stood the palace they proceed, and thro'
The sculptur'd door beneath the portico,
Into the hall.   She on the great stone chair
Of Thoas sat, Hypsipylé the fair.
Alone she sat, and at a sign the maid
Iphinöe left them.   One quick blush betray'd
Slight tremor, and her heart more hurried beat,
Youthful, unwonted such a peer to meet;   770
But she compos'd herself; and her eye, clear
And pure, met Jason's as the chief drew near;
Then rising, with sweet dignity, address'd,
Call'd him by name, and hail'd as friend and guest:—

" Son of my father's friend, I greet thee well!
" Now list to me; and to thy comrades tell
" This city's counsel and my own,—thereon
" Delib'rate, and resolve what shall be done.
" Then come up here and be our guests awhile,
" A day, or longer, welcome.   Fear no guile,   780
" Ent'ring our walls.   No men inhabit here,—
" Fathers, sons, husbands, all we once held dear,

" For Thrace have left us, to return no more,
" Reaping the harvests of a kindlier shore,
" Forsaking, reckless of our helpless state—
" Left us, our homes and Lemnos, desolate.
" Thus stands our grief.   Thoas, mine honour'd sire,
" Invaded Thrace, whose sons with sword and fire
" Had ravag'd Lemnos.   He, alas! was slain,—
" But home the Sintians captive o'er the main   790
" Brought Thracian damsels; and a madness seiz'd,
" By Aphrodité sent, at what displeas'd
" I know not, the proud victors; and they lay
" With these strange concubines; and day by day
" Their wedded wives despis'd.   We bore this curse
" Patient awhile, hoping a change; but worse
" And worse it grew; for now they held in scorn
" Their children erst in lawful wedlock born,
" The bastards tend'ring; and their daughters lived,
" Legitimate, uncar'd for and unwived.   800
" At last some God inspir'd us; and, when last
" They home return'd, we courage took, and cast
" All love and duty from us, and refus'd
" Access, our trust and weakness thus abus'd.
" They, the male children of the Sintian race
" Collecting, with their captives, sail'd for Thrace,
" There with those fierce barbarians cast their lot,
" Ourselves, their country, and their hearths forgot.
" These things being so, to you, as friends, not foes,
" List what my people by my mouth propose.   810
" We cannot plough, nor sow, nor reap, nor fight,
" Being women, in protection of our right.
" Do ye then, as the proud Sauromatæ
" To the great Amazons, the chaste, the free,

" Give each of us a son, the work to do
" That is beyond our strength ; and then pursue—
" If such your pleasure—your sea-path in peace.
" Or, if content to wed this isle with Greece,
" The fields are fertile and the women fair ;
" Our homes are yours, and I, my father's heir,   820
" Will share with thee the throne, and with firm will
" Thee and thy brave companions guard from ill.
" Do you, in turn, us cherish and defend,
" And we will love ye, faithful, to the end.
" But deem not we would burden your free lives
" With Hymen's shackles, matrimonial gyves ;
" Nor would we suffer vows, that make a slave
" To man of woman, kind soe'er or brave.
" We are well taught, franchis'd from slavery—
" We who are born, should live, and will die free—   830
" That marriage seals such bonds ; while, freely given,
" Freely withdrawn, love, virtuous, is from heaven.
" We women, heirs of pure Harmonia's line,
" Were else degraded from our rank divine.
" Such then our proffer.   Should you wish, in time,
" To quit this Lemnos for another clime,
" At your own option be it,—not a day
" Would sorrow urge us to prolong your stay.
" Thus we propose, in self-respect, not pride.
" Consult your comrades, ponder, and decide.   840
" If you prefer to start this day, this hour,
" All Lemnos owns, all I, is at your power,—
" Needful supplies my servants now prepare.
" Only, in pity, Jason ! grant this prayer,—
" Tell not the Thracians we in Lemnos, few,
" Helpless, survive, abandon'd—e'en by you !'

So speaking, paus'd Hypsipylé; but mute
Stood Jason; nor his soul could ill impute
To her thus urging, little more than child,
By some strange madness seemingly beguil'd.   850
At length, recov'ring, her address'd,—" Fair dame!
" I thank thee for thy kindness, but, for shame,
" May not accept this island and thy throne;
" For a fair land i' th' West I call my own,
" Nor may forswear; and the Great Gods have will'd
" Not without me the Fleece's quest fulfill'd.
" But I will back to Argo, and apprise
" My comrades of thy kindly courtesies."
    So saying, he kiss'd her fair hand and withdrew;
And she gaz'd after as he pass'd from view.   860
    When he came forth, the women throng'd around,
Eager and joyous. Pass'd the gates, he found
Carts waiting of supplies, of wine and bread,
And fruits, with vine-leaves 'gainst the flies o'erspread,
And gifts, rich, various, tokens of good will.
These follow'd his slow footsteps down the hill.
    Jason reported all; and, with one tongue,
The youths acclaim'd consent, nor ask'd if wrong
Such dallying, nor of Mopsus' voice requir'd
The counsel of the Gods. Their hearts were fir'd   870
By Aphrodité, anxious that again
Lemnos should peopled be by living men.
Only the Dioscuri dar'd to say
'Twas sin and shame; they would not go that day.
Euphemus too, revering Heracles,
Obey'd, though never eagle for the breeze
Of freedom panted more, prison'd in a cage,
Than he, in the young fervour of his age.

With Jason, all the rest went up ; but none,
The elders, follow'd their rash steps upon.   880
Anceus with his axe, in thought apart,
Peleus and Telamon, the sad at heart,
Theseus, and Meleager, fire-chastis'd,
Mopsus, and Idmon, stern, the Gods despis'd,
Orpheus, and Tiphys, and Æthalides,
And, youngest 'mong the seniors, Heracles,
Like noble steeds of their dead lord bereav'd,
Sat by deserted Argo, watch'd, and griev'd.

Then, as those truants climb'd the hill, befel
A strange and unexpected miracle.   890
The colours, glorious, Argo that array'd
Like a bright bird, slowly began to fade ;
Till, the gates enter'd, all was neutral gray,
And so continued many a future day.

That night in Myrina this came to pass :—
Hephæstus sent an earthquake, and a mass
Of ruin toppled on Polyxo's head.
Forth from her evil heart the spirit fled.
But Hypnos and his brother Thanatos,
By Hypnos summon'd from dark Tenedos,   900
Lapp'd the foul corpse in lead, and to the gorge
Of red Mosyclos, mouth of the God's forge,
Bore her and dropp'd her in,—that, as a ghost
Unburied, on the blasts of Acheron tost,
She should alternate ride, and in the brains
Of sophists, godless men, that vicious pains
Take to confuse the bounds of right and wrong,
And gloze false morals with their serpent tongue.
Her still our kinsmen the Tyrrhenians call
Mania, whose visions men by night appal ;   910

She poppy-heads in sacrifice requires,
Once children's, - her eyes gleam with dusky fires;
But we fell Lamia give th' accursèd name,
Mem'ry of Lemnos' and Polyxo's shame.

Meanwhile all Myrina rejoic'd, well pleas'd,
And Aphroditè and her spouse appeas'd
With sacrifices.   Nor less constant blew
From Zeus a fav'ring Zephyr, to the crew
Younger reproachful, dallying day by day,
Of duty careless, wasting time away :—   920
Argo, sad, longing to resume her track—
Zeus, patient, urging—they alone hung back.

BOOK IV. HERACLES.

Now days, and weeks, and months pass on ; and still
The truant youths return not down the hill.
The Zephyr constant of their duty warns,
And Argo for her absent children mourns.
 There is a pleasing languor in the air
Of Lemnos. Those who to her shores repair,
Strangers, perceive it. Drowsy, it inspires
Day-dreams and sloth, and high resolve expires.
There, but no eye can see them, are the doors
Of horn and iv'ry, whence the effluence pours   10
Of nightly visions brooding o'er the head
Of sleeping man, with poppy-leaves o'erspread.
Through a vast lab'rinth, deep beneath the ground,
Of many chambers, where nor light nor sound
Terrestrial penetrates, they wand'ring stray
Till summon'd by their God to upper day.
This is the house of Hypnos, God of Sleep.
His brother, Death, in Tenedos doth keep

Watch, with his hammer-axe uprais'd to strike,
As Ker commands him, rich and poor alike.   20
Watchers of Zeus they are; like dogs, they wait
On human life; and most at childhood's gate.
Their keeper Chimareus, Prometheus' son,
On Imbros rude rears his Cimmerian throne.
Not ev'n Hephæstus, touching Lemnos' shore,
The king of toil, by night and day at war
With sloth and folly, could escape defeat
Where Sleep is sov'reign, lam'd in both his feet.
Then well may Zeus in pity spare the rod,
Nor, fearing Night, reprove the sluggard God.   30
The heroes, conscience-lull'd, make still delay;
And swift the hour of duty slips away.

    Their days are spent in mirth and making love;
Now in the swimming circling dance they move,
Or sing in Lydian mode to the soft lyre,
Or looser Lesbian, nurse of sweet desire;
Sometimes in manlier exercise combine,
Ball-play or quoits, in which the damsels join,—
Complaisant they advantage due to give
To each dear partner, nor for vict'ry strive.   40
Then, such their folly, would they tasks perform
At which their cheeks erewhile had redden'd warm,
Unworthy of their noble blood, their name
Of freemen, and to warrior hands a shame;
Would plough, sow, cattle tend,—nor had refus'd
Perchance to milk the cows, if thus abus'd
To degradation.   Ofttimes might be seen
A hero guide the plough, a damsel 'tween
The shafts i' th' furrow treading—she the scourge
Applying frequent the dull steer to urge;   50

Boasting to guide, but guided—fond pretence !
Arcadia's sport without its innocence.
Or, single task'd, a youth would stop the team,
Dart off, and join a group beside some stream,
Cool-shadow'd, dancing—dance a round—and then
To his plebeian task return again.
But, though invok'd, the Graces absent grieve,
Nor will Orchomenos for Lemnos leave.
And all this while the mount of fire shoots high
Its lightnings, and the thunders shake the sky   60
Of the great hammer which Hephæstus wields ;
While, thoughtless they of swords, and spears, and shields,
Inglorious, shun the duty of stern toil,
From which not Gods themselves, exempt, recoil.
    Meanwhile, as from beneath Night's sable wings
Day leaps to life, so good from evil springs.
Plants struggle tow'rds the light.   The female youth
Of Lemnos, from right purity and truth
Perverted, not their seeking, led astray,
Find, one by one, false theories melt away,   70
Love guiding back to truth.   The youths are kind,
Courteous, submiss, to their shortcomings blind,
Constant each to his mate, she constant too :—
They learn to love the strangers, keep in view
Their fancies, curb their own— follow their lead,
Nor feel the yoke—cease to command, but plead,
Sure of obedience ; hasty-speaking, oft
Recall sharp words.   Their manners become soft ;
They learn to know that influence more avails
Than strength, and that, in true affection's scales,   80
Love will outbalance pride ; that liberty
Less sweet is than dependence ; that, being free,

They would be bondsmen ; fearing now to part,
They own, nor scorn, the shackles of the heart.
They would give worlds to know their tie of love
Were such as pure Harmonia would approve.
No fear of Thracians while the heroes stand
Beside them, potent to protect the land ;
But great their dread lest they should quit their shore,
Pursue the quest, nor think of Lemnos more.   90
Then—let the Thracians, all their myriads, come,
'Twould matter nought—a short step to the tomb !
Thus these recover'd their lost sex, became
Women once more ; while those, to manhood shame,
Dallied effeminate, how lost, how chang'd !
Nor beyond Lemnos their weak wishes rang'd.

    But now no longer Heracles, enur'd
To life's hard toil, this living death endur'd.
A feast was set at Aphrodite's shrine ;
The women absent at the rites divine,   100
He sent to call the truants, nor could they
For very shame the summons disobey.
" Kinsmen," he said, " Are we of the high blood
" Of Gods and women whom th' immortals woo'd ?
" Is it your will, ploughmen, to drive the steer
" Through these fat fields of Lemnos, dwelling here ?
" Or, concubines in quest of, did we come,
" And stranger wives, despising those at home ?
" Small credit ours, nay infamous disgrace,
" Chamb'ring with wantons of barbaric race ;   110
" Nor, our swords rusting, will the Gods of Greece
" Grant to our empty pray'rs the glorious Fleece.
" See ye how Argo, once so gay and bright,
" Mourns our suspended march, our waning might ?

" The breeze from Zeus blows steady day by day,
" Tow'rds Colchis urging, and we still delay !
" Rather let each of us go home at once—
" What better counsel offers for the nonce ?
" But this our captain, let him here remain,
" An' so he please, in Aphrodité's chain,   120
" Till he fill Lemnos with male progeny ;
" And mighty honour will he reap thereby ! "

So spoke he, frowning 'neath his beetling brows :
Hoping their manhood's nobler springs to rouse.
All hung their heads abash'd, nor rais'd their eyes ;
Each felt, ingenuous, that the words were wise.
But Jason spoke, incens'd :—" Alcmena's son !
" Thou hast no right to speak as thou hast done.
" If thine arm stronger, thine the weightier voice,
" Still thou art here by thine own act and choice ;   130
" The quest is mine and, leader, mine the rule,—
" No tutor thou, nor I a child at school.
" Natheless thy words are true, though bitter.   I
" Approve them, and will guide myself thereby,—
" But at my own good time, for mine the power ;
" Wait thou in patience till I fix the hour."

Great Heracles kept silence.   But a day,
And five, and ten pass'd, nothing done, away ;
Nor more was said of quitting Lemnos' isle.
Jason, 'twixt pride and love, put off the while   140
Announcement of his purpose form'd to leave
The Sintian land ; for much he fear'd to grieve
Hypsipylé.   He lov'd her ; but his love,
Compar'd with hers, was coldness.   Hers, above
All thought of self, burn'd with a purer flame,
Less dear to her himself than his good name.

The youths said nought, their minds made up to go ;
Hard duty bade it, and it must be so.
But Jason's was the voice to say ' Depart ! '
Till that was utter'd, haste were none to start.   150

    'Twas night,—the elders all slept sound within
The ship ; and, stretch'd upon his lion's skin,
Leaning against a rock round which were cast
The mooring-ropes that held the vessel fast,
Lay Heracles, sole watcher, much perplex'd,
The heroes loit'ring, what he should do next ;
And had resolv'd, in sorrow and in scorn,
Argo to quit with the approaching morn,
His search of the fam'd apples to pursue ;
When 'tween himself and the dim star-lit view   160
Of Argo, 'neath no mortal mask conceal'd,
Her glory veil'd, her eyes, her brow reveal'd,
Stood Hera, Queen of heav'n ; whom to behold
A tide of bitter mem'ries o'er him roll'd,
Griefs that, unjust, the soul corroding burn ;
He gaz'd upon her, unabash'd and stern.

    " I pray thee, Heracles ! by thy great heart,
" Not yet from Argo or her quest depart.
" The Fleece cannot be won, nor the dues paid
" That Fate beyond it claims, without thine aid.   170
" It rests with thee whether thy comrades waste
" Their life and manhood here in beds unchaste,
" Or, thou their rescuer, the great toil resume
" That shall bear fruit, like thine, beyond the tomb.
" Not long unequal match'd shall be thy lot
" With men thy lesser though they know it not.
" Pity their human frailty, thou, the pure !
" And still, as hitherto, great heart ! endure."

" And why endure ? Why should I slave beyond
" My toils' excess, my voluntary bond ?   180
" And at thy bidding ? Thee I venerate,
" Queen of Olympus, ruler of my fate ;
" But thou hast scanty claim to love from me,
" Thou who, remorseless, heap'st with injury
" Me, above all men, singled from my birth,
" Suff'ring, accurs'd, a wand'rer upon earth ;
" Bow'd, with Prometheus parallel'd alone,
" With weight of others' guilt, beside my own.
" Think, Goddess ! canst thou ask it ? A great thing
" Truly, when seeking the last term to bring   190
" To my long toils—two more, unjust, impos'd
" By thy harsh minion, the full reck'ning clos'd—
" That I, so late with these soft Minyans found
" Associate, nor by love nor cov'nant bound,
" Backsliders, should my onward course delay,
" Like Sisyphus, to push them on their way—
" Now, when through parting clouds, the skies more clear,
" I see my promis'd home, Olympus, near ! "
    To whom the Queen :—" Deem not so light of these
" Twin labours, crown of thy high destinies.   200
" Man's ransom paid by thee, these last, in place
" First, if thou knew'st it, shall the ten efface.
" Mission'd by heav'n, with triumph on their wing,
" Immortal life, conquest o'er death, they bring.
" Ten is the law complete of life—the debt
" Cancell'd, the forfeit by acquittance met,
" Due justice satisfied ; but cancell'd sins
" Leave room for a new reck'ning, which begins
" And ends in love, life's object and intent ;
" And Twelve is Delphi's full accomplishment.   210

" Thus much I speak constrain'd ; and do thou well
" Credit me, thine unwilling oracle.
" But when thou speak'st of suff'ring—suff'rings—thine !
" What are thy suff'rings, man ! compar'd to mine ?
" A slave, thou say'st ? But what am I ? Thy heart
" Grasp'd at the bondage proffer'd thee ; thou art
" No slave, but self-devote, a victim free ;
" But I—blest-ruling once, Eurynomé,
" Honour'd before time was—then Cronos' bride,
" Loathing—now doom'd to sleep thy sire beside,   220
" Who heav'n and earth doth and the seas command,
" Crushing us seniors with his iron hand—
" In me alone this horror Fate allows,
" Wife of my brother, mother of my spouse—
" Unknowing why, if just, this awful doom—
" Through generations, more perhaps to come,
" Of my own bowels, pass'd from bed to bed,
" No chance of dying or of beauty fled,
" One after one as each usurper falls,
" Transmitted as a chattel in their halls—   230
" Great, but how humbled !—Man ! thy littleness—
' How can it fathom this divine distress ?
" Thou talk of suff'ring, serfdom ! By this line
" Gauge thine own agony, and think of mine ! "
     " I am not yet a god, but simple man,"
Rejoin'd the hero, " nor presume to scan
" The depth sublime of thine immortal woe.
" I know not, ask not, why these things are so,—
" Why we must struggle in the web of Fate,
" Like flies, to grief and toil subordinate.   240
" Yet know I well—the future is all dim,
" But God is God, my heart is fix'd in Him ;

"He will not fail me,—when this arm is dust,
"My home shall be with Æacus the Just.
"—Then thou too suff"rest! Deem not I compare
"My griefs with thine, I of man's crimes the heir;
"But thou art goddess, I but human be;
"Thou hast a strength and will denied to me."
  "Weak will, scant strength!" the Goddess sad replied;
"But these are counsels the Trimorphi hide   250
"From men and Gods; all that Gods know is this,
"That suff'ring works out a great Nemesis,
"Rightly endur'd, till opposition cease,
"And, love o'er hate prevailing, all be peace—
"Peace save to him, fruit of my pride alone,
"Who writhes beneath the Typhaonian stone.
"By this faith we too live, work, and endure,
"Our expectation, comfort, dim but sure;
"The Shrouded, the Unseen One, dwells afar,
"Lord over Fate, and we his servants are.   260
"Yes! thou say'st rightly, I too suffer,—thou
"And I are fellow-victims, hostile now
"Oppos'd for working out God's purposes,
"But to be friends hereafter. Think then these
"Thy suff'rings at my hand as not from me;
"Grant me my boon!"—"Mother, I pity thee!"
"—A pretty mother have I been, forsooth!
"But I can bear thy pity,—and, in truth,
"Would I could love thee! For thou noble art,
"And brave should brother be to brave man's heart.   270
"Nor hast thou, by thy light, me harshly judg'd,
"Nor, sacrifice withheld, my altars grudg'd.
"As yet I cannot! Thy sire did me wrong,
"And Fate hath steel'd me. Therefore am I strong

" In purpose 'gainst thee—therefore heap I toil
" Upon thee suff'ring, nor in will recoil—
" Of griefs inflicted shall increase the score,
" And, till thy count exhausted, heap on more—
" But, thyself willing!   Recollect the choice,
" Twice proffer'd, ratified by thine own voice!   280
" Yes! thou endurest nobly—I admire,
" If love I cannot, bastard of thy sire!
" Thus valuing thee, not loving, I have spoke
" Words to thee such as never yet outbroke
" The prison of my lips, as to a son,—
" Thou call'st me mother!   Well, the hours run on,
" And I shall be thy mother, in the day
" When all these tears of time are wip'd away.
" Enough! thou understandest me.   And now,
" Once more, be gen'rous, and thy proud heart bow   290
" To mercy.   Intervene, that the great quest
" Of Argo may go on, nor find arrest
" Midway, and shame me.   Jason's heart is weak,
" Willing, but feebled from his bonds to break.
" Thou hast known love thyself, though purer plac'd,
" Have pity on him, me nor him disgrac'd!
" Froward, I grant, but young, thou elder much,—
" Be as his elder brother; act as such;
" Go to Hypsipylé thyself,—her soul
" Is gen'rous as thine own; a dark cloud stole   300
" Between her and the sun, and she has err'd
" Through ignorance, the voice of truth unheard;
" But the cloud lifts apace; her heart is pure,
" And she, as thou, is learning to endure.
" Speak to her kindly, that she may indeed
" Jason dismiss, and Argo may be freed."

" Mother !" he said, " thy bidding I will do.
" I understand thee, and could love thee too,
" As a brave warrior loves an enemy
" By whom, his friend, it is his fate to die.   310
" There is a high-born people in the North,
" The Celtæ, fam'd for valour and for worth,
" Nigh Thulé, where the earth of mortals ends.
" Two men I knew there; they were ancient friends—
" Of kindred nations, but requir'd to fight
" As champions in a cause which each deem'd right,
" Three days' debate within strict barriers clos'd,
" Each as the noblest of his tribe oppos'd.
" They fought with swords, alternate wounding each;
" Each in the intervals the deadly breach   320
" Of his foe tended, pierc'd by his own sword;
" And, constant, interchang'd endearing word,
" Spoke of their happy childhood, blameless youth,
" Walking th' associate path of joy and truth;
" Warn'd each the other of his own weak points,
" Brac'd up each other's slacken'd armour-joints;
" While the two nations, wond'ring, watch'd and wept,
" And wish'd it ended.   Weakness gradual crept
" On one, my dearer friend; and then his foe
" Withheld his own, tempted the other's blow,—   330
" But vain! he totter'd, sank on his friend's breast,
" Thence to the ground.   Cyculnus closely press'd
" His heart to his, receiv'd his dying breath,
" And clos'd his eyes, wishing his own the death,—
" Victor; but lifelong sorrow, not remorse,
" Darken'd his days.—Mother! I think not worse
" Of thee than Pherdias of Cyculnus did—
" I who, by counsel of the Veil'd Ones, hid

" From mortal scrutiny, accept the doom
" Thou urgest unrelenting to the tomb.   340
" Farewell, till that hour come! Meanwhile, with morn
" I seek the Queen, and urge the youths' return.
" I crave thy pardon for my words, with shame ;
" In that I suffer thou art not to blame."

    Great Hera answer'd not, but on his brow
Her hand laid softly, and her lips spoke low
As blessing, but the words he heard not well.
The sense of love and peace ineffable
Stole o'er him, as he watch'd the Goddess rise,
Like to a luminous cloud, and seek the skies,   350
Tending towards the East, less'ning afar
Till seen but faintly as a distant star,
Then lost to view. But still his eyes remain'd
Fix'd, by the constellations' maze enchain'd,
Dazzling but comforting, obedient all,
Like dancers in some heav'nly festival,
Circling around the everlasting pole ;
And deep content possess'd the suff'rer's soul.

    But, when the watches of the night were past,
When the air grew more chill, and the dew fast   360
Dropp'd on the earth—but nothing yet was heard
Save earliest twitter of the wak'ning bird ;
And the stars pal'd, save sweetest Hesperus ;
And from the brink of dark Oceanus
Rose-finger'd Eös urg'd her steeds, the Hours
With equal pace strewing her path with flowers ;
And Zephyr, twin with Hesper, came to meet
His mother from the West, with airy feet
Brushing the clouds aside,—and, broader now,
Redden'd the Orient with the coming glow ;   370

And, last, arose great Helios, glory-clad,
And earth and skies and the dark seas were glad,—
Then—but allowance made by some delay
For night's soft slaves, unworthy of the day,
Who, pillowing on dull ease their drowsy heads,
Forfeit morn's wholesome freshness, lie-a-beds—
Guests such at Lemnos; nor exempt might be,
Perchance, where Hypnos rul'd, Hypsipylé—
Then Heracles his lion-mantle threw
Over his shoulders, and went up unto   380
The gates of Myrina, but without sword,
Or mighty club, or rattling quiver, stor'd
With shafts, or bow—these latter Hylas' charge;
The hero chose not he should roam, at large
From Argo, where such looser rule was kept;
And, wearying of his cage, the poor boy wept.

  The gates he found unguarded—little dread
Now of the Thracians; up the street he sped,
Well-built, devoid of men,—the women gaz'd
At him as at some portent strange, amaz'd,   390
Back-shrinking. He ascended thence the mound
Where rose the palace, on the highest ground,
Closing the street's long vista; then pass'd thro'
The sculptur'd door, beneath the portico,
Into the hall, where stood the great stone chair
Of Thoas,—but all now was vacant there;
And so proceeded forward through a court
With buildings round it, and—the sounds of sport
Hearing beyond it, and faint music—pass'd
Still further, till his steps emerg'd at last   400
Beneath a spacious pillar'd loggia, whence
The startled eyes a vast magnificence

Of sea and land, most sea, expanding hail'd :—
Eastward, Mosyclos the clos'd view curtail'd ;
But to the North high Samothrace's peak
Pierc'd the clear sky ; and, like a misty streak,
Thasos, pine-crested, on th' horizon low
Lay, dim descried.   Westward, stern Athos' brow
Rose cone-like, crown'd by Zeus's guardian fane,
An island seeming, monarch of the main.   410
At summer solstice Athos' shadow falls
With eve on Myrina's fair streets and walls.
Azure, unruffled, like a landlock'd bay,
Mirror for Artemis, the broad sea lay.
   Below him slop'd a garden, lovely, not
Spacious ; four-square, divided into plot
And walk, bisected twice ; one plot for flowers,
Roses and creepers, forming shadowy bowers,
With beds of violet ; two more for trees
Fruit-bearing, apples, pears, and figs, the breeze   420
Stirring their branches ; and a fourth for sport
Gymnastic—most the Minyan youths' resort.
This guarded was by lions, wolves, and bears,
Chimæras dire, and dragons langu'd with spears,
Of box-trees clipp'd, pride of the gard'ner's art,
Cypresses 'tween them, beast from beast to part ;
With a thick 'spalier hedge of ivy green,
Sweet bay, and od'rous myrtles, as a screen.
Central to all, high tower'd a stately plane ;
Six fountains in a row toss'd dewy rain   430
To right and left below the steps that led
Down from the loggia, and a coolness spread
Through the soft air.   A broader walk ran round
The garden, and a low wall was its bound.

At its East end a gentle hillock rose,
The wall the square exceeding, to enclose;
Upon its summit stood a pillar-stone,
A rustic seat beside—sequester'd, lone,
To Consus sacred, who inspires the will
Of secret counsel when the heart is still.   440

   He paus'd. 'Twas a fair scene, and such he lov'd;
But much he saw to scorn and ire that mov'd.
On either hand, beneath the loggia, sat
Groups of the youths at tables, playing at
The golden dice, and draughts, and at the game
Of Cephallenia; but they paus'd for shame,
Seen Heracles, nor spoke, but gaz'd with awe
On his dark-frowning brow. Others he saw
Below, playing at quoits. or ball, or hide
And seek with their fair mates,—or, one espied,   450
The others ran, and oft was pris'ner caught
A hero willing, home in triumph brought.
Others were dancing mingled—*sans* excuse,
The eye too wanton, and the zone too loose.
Apart, upon the mount, beside the stone,
Farthest, he saw Hypsipylé, alone,
Seated and musing; on her hand she leant
Her head, and her eye fix'd on ocean bent.
Slow he the steps descended, and his way
Took through the garden; and sport, dance, and play 460
Ceas'd at his presence, as when, hush'd, at noon
A cloud with thunder charg'd obscures the sun.
She heard his foot's approach, firm, strong, unlike
Other men's tread, and felt its echo strike
Through heart and soul, as of a prophet's doom,—
She knew at once the dreaded end was come.

She glanc'd around, as frighten'd, to escape;
She strove to speak, but words she could not shape;
She rose, sank back; her cheek flush'd crimson-red,
Then pal'd, as to her heart the tumult fled;   470
But clasp'd her hands nor dar'd to scan his face,
And would have caught his knees in her embrace,
Suing for mercy; but he hasten'd and
Prevented, raising her with gentle hand;
And, looking in his eyes, she saw that there,
Which seem'd to give her strength to match despair;
And, gath'ring her scar'd life convulsive in,
Master'd herself, and sign'd him to begin.

    " Lady!" he said; " I come to crave a grace
" At thy fair hands, that years shall not efface   480
" From mem'ry, granted,—not as judge severe,
" But as a suppliant to a sister dear.
" I come to bid thy great soul gen'rous be,
" For great I know it, sweet Hypsipylé!
" To release Jason, let the youths depart;
" That Argo, care of Gods, once more may start
" On the great enterprise for which design'd
" She quests a prize and blessing for mankind.
" I know thou lovest Jason, and would'st fain
" Detain him, hoping he may with thee reign,   490
" Thy husband, o'er the Sintians; that the isle,
" Happy, well-peopled, rich, again may smile
" As in old times, thy father living—now
" Curs'd by the Gods, thee loving. I know how
" To save thy father thou didst intervene,
" Pious, when, like a pois'nous fog between
" Earth and the sun, foul teaching wrought a deed
" Of blood that Pelops' horror did exceed;

" And this the Gods remember to thy praise.

" It may be, Jason will in future days   500

" Return triumphant, thy sweet hope to wed,

" With Hera's sanction to thy marriage bed ;

" But, meanwhile, Argo's is a plighted toil

" From which no forfeit may his debt assoil ;

" To him alone reserv'd, by Fate's decree,

" The task, the travail, and the victory."

—He paus'd, but she replied not,—like a bird

Held in strange hand though kind, her pulses, stirr'd

By terror, flutter'd still ; but words could none

Frame yet, though gaining calm ; and he went on :— 510

—" Brave art thou, pure in heart, and of the line

" Of Zeus not distant, thus of race divine.

" 'Tis not to-day thou hast begun to learn

" Pleasure should yield to duty, mistress stern

" Indeed, but kindly.   Be not further woe

" Heap'd upon Lemnos—bid the heroes go !

" Jason will Lemnos quit but at thy word,

" If thou such grace wilt to my pray'r accord."

    To whom the Queen :—" I know thou dost not ask

" This willingly, nor would'st this heavy task   520

" Impose on my weak shoulders without sure

" Warrant from heav'n.   Grief henceforth to endure,

" Hopeless, must be my portion.   My life's dream

" Is over, a night-taper's transient gleam ;

" My youth's few flow'rs of freshness wither'd all,

" Like wreaths at dawn after a festival !

" But thou art right—thou say'st indeed no more

" Than what my doubts and fears have urg'd before.

" But 'tis more bitter than thou canst conceive ;

" For I have giv'n him all, all I could give,   530

" Heart, person, life, with slight return, nor grudg'd,
" Fearless of wrong, in ign'rance if wrong-judg'd.
" And I had hop'd that here he might remain
" With me, long years, and o'er the Sintians reign,
" As thou hast said, and that we might grow old
" Together, shedding blessings manifold
" On all around us. But, alas! no tie
" Binds us inviolate; for that did I,
" Unknown its sanction, disavow; and free
" He is to cherish or to part with me;   540
" And well I wot, if now the link I sever,
" And thus I lose him, it will be for ever.
" O friend! I am but young; I well may say
" I never had a mother. Day by day,
" Since childhood, has my life been woven in
" With webs of sophistry, that virtue sin,
" Sin virtue gloss'd, till, hopelessly enchain'd,
" My reason deaden'd, heart (it may be) stain'd,
" I scarce know what is right or what is wrong;
" Yet something in me leads me still along,   55)
" I trust, towards the light. It must be so·!
" I feel, I know it—I will let him go;
" But not this instant! Grant me but a few
" Last days of respite ere I say adieu ! "
    But Heracles,—" Alas ! what can I say ?
" Bethink thee, Lady! every hour's delay
" Rivets thy chain.—No! I dare not disguise
" Truth's face, nor screen it from thine aching eyes.
" ' At once!' is duty's word; the present hour
" Is thine; the future lies beyond thy power.   560
" I would not wound thee, sweet one! save to bless;
" Resolve and act twin-born, the pain is less.

" And bless'd thou wilt be by the Gods, who prove
" Virtue by suff'ring, and the suff'rer love.
" Thou art not of those light ones yonder ; thou
" Hast childhood left behind, art woman now "—
—" Alas, too true !" she murmur'd—" and when man
" Is weak, woman is strong, to think, to plan,
" To execute, all in a moment's space,
" Instinctive grasping truth in her embrace.   570
" O Lady ! be thus prompt, thus wise, thus strong !
" And thy resolve shall be the minstrel's song
" For many an age,—but such thy looks disdain :—
" Then ev'n for Jason's sake divorce the chain
" That binds him here, inglorious, at thy side ;
" Point him to Argo's goal, his honour's guide,
" In person absent, but by influence still
" Swaying his steps, his heart, to good from ill.
" —Nay, check these tears !   Two paths there are, of right
" And wrong diverse, that open on our sight   580
" When childhood ends,—thou hast walk'd hitherto
" On lines mark'd out by circumstance, thy view
" Perverted,—his indeed a cruel heart,
" Not mine, that could condemn thee, nor the smart
" Feel as his own that heals thee ; but the hour
" To each one comes, and with the call the power,
" To choose between the guidance of his good
" And evil dæmon.—Hast thou understood
" My purpose, Lady ?   For I would not urge
" My plea, successful own'd, beyond the verge   590
" Of courteous instance, but would pardon crave."
    " Go on, go on !" she answer'd ; " Let me have
" Strength at thy hands, thou strong one, and yet kind !
" Open my eyes, for mine, alas ! are blind,—

" And weak, how weak ! mine heart with grief distraught ;
" Help me to know my duty as I ought !"
   " Then list ! and I will tell thee what befel
" Myself, and it may point this purpose well.
" Not older much than thou, I wander'd out
" From Thebes, my home, pond'ring, perplex'd with doubt,
" The life that lay before me, fresh in youth,   601
" Error intent to shun, to follow truth,—
" But, passion that way prompting, reason this,
" Distracted sore, I fear'd the way to miss ;
" When, lo ! thought-weary, I beheld a hill,
" Spur of Teumissus, on its pinnacle
" An ancient obelisk, the sacred sign
" Of the Gods Saviours and of strength divine.
" Methought I would ascend.   Its lower zone
" Was verdant, trees and flow'rs ; but craggy, lone,   610
" Precipitous, by torrents split, the mid
" And summit tower'd.   The mists alternate hid
" That obelisk, and then, the shroud unroll'd,
" It gleam'd forth in the sun-light as of gold.
" Two paths I saw,—this went straight up the mount,
" Through rocks and tufted thorn, with small account
" Of ledge or torrent, difficult and rude :—
" That, starting from the spot whereon I stood,
" Broad, mossy, green, with flow'rs besprinkled gay,
" Led by a devious but an easier way,   620
" Circling the hill, so seem'd, with scarce-mark'd rise,
" Appearing, disappearing,—but the eyes
" Lost it, still in the wood ; while this, uncheck'd,
" Seen plain throughout, the ob'lisk reach'd direct.
   " As thus I doubted which to choose, in fear
" That might not reach the goal, while this was near,

" Though rugged,—coming from the mount I saw
" Two women tow'rds me near in silence draw,
" Taller than woman's stature, and their mien
" Importing as of men and Gods between.   630
" One down the rugged path majestic strode ;
" The other from the smooth and easy road
" Glided,—this last, by sudden impulse press'd,
" Quicken'd her step, and in soft voice address'd :—
" Her zone relax'd, her eye assur'd and bold,—
" Bright colours, tawdry, deck'd each flutt'ring fold
" Of her loose garments. On her feet she wore
" Rich sandals, and intemp'rance' stamp she bore.
   " ' My Heracles ! thou doubtest which to choose,
" ' The path of roses, that the breath bedews   640
" ' Of softest Zephyr, or the path of thorns,
" ' That Boreas courts and youth's enjoyment scorns.
" ' Follow me ! I will lead thee by a path
" ' Where all is sunshine, and the tempest's wrath
" ' Sweeps past unfelt ; where stone thy tender feet
" ' Shall not offend ; where resting-places sweet
" ' The way-side offers,—by a path which leads
" ' To pastures where each sense insatiate feeds,
" ' Full gratified ; where pleasure rules alone,—
" ' All won by toil of others, not thine own.   650
" ' Such bliss I yield my vot'ries. Come with me !'
" —I ask'd her name. She answer'd hurriedly,
" Her voice a whisper, ' Happiness my name ;
" ' But Vice they call me who would do me shame.'
   " For now beside me stood who from the hill
" Of life had come direct,—sedate and still
" Her aspect ; her long robe of purest white,
" With azure zon'd, studded with starlets bright,

" Flow'd to the ground.   Her naked feet were torn,
" Bleeding by many a rock, bramble, and thorn ;   660
" Her form austere, but beautiful ; her eye
" The throne of light and holy purity.
   " ' I, too,' she said, ' O Heracles ! my hand
" ' In friendship offer ; for by sea and land
" ' Thy race is fam'd, and mortals count on worth
" ' As due of right from those of noble birth.
" ' And I have watch'd thee from thy childhood, pure,
" ' Gen'rous in impulse, and of purpose sure.
" ' Such thou then, come with me ; and we will seek
" ' Together yon lone land-mark on the peak   670
" ' Of life before thee,—not by the soft road
" ' Of moss and roses, treacherous though broad,
" ' That leads bewild'ring but to Lerné's marsh ;
" ' But by the path of thorns, repulsive, harsh,
" ' Direct that mounts there—if thou heark my voice,—
" ' Thy years are ripe ; free, thou must make thy choice.
" ' Not pleasure I offer, women not, nor wine,
" ' Nor idlesse weak ; but happiness divine,
" ' That happiness which Vice can never bring,   679
" ' The heart's pure joys from conscious worth that spring.
   " ' Know then, the Gods ordain that nothing great,
" ' Nor good, shall be achiev'd without debate
" ' 'Twixt toil and ease encount'ring, conqu'ror toil.
" ' Would'st thou earth's harvests ? Cultivate her soil.
" ' Would'st cattle ? Tend them. Fame in arms ? Their use
" ' Learn and employ defenceful, not abuse
" ' Lustful to conquest.   Honour from thy king ?
" ' Win such by faithful service rendering.
" ' Love from thy friends ? Work for them night and day.
" ' The Gods' high favour ? Worship and obey.   690

" ' A body match'd such mast'ry to attain ?
" ' Keep it thy subject ; passion's fires restrain ;
" ' Hard exercise, rough sports, the victor's goal,
" ' Pursue ; be reason sov'reign of thy soul !
" ' My name is Virtue—great is my reward.'
  " ' Thou seest,' Vice broke in, ' the service hard,
" ' The toilsome path to which her counsels tend ;
" ' Mine is the easier path, the happier end.'
  " ' And what that thou call'st happiness hast thou
" ' Worthy the name ?' return'd, with frowning brow, 700
" That one austere—' that wilt not take the pains
" ' To toil for an' it were but sensual gains ?
" ' When felt thou hunger, urging thee to eat ?
" ' When thirst, to drink ? When, worn by toil and heat,
" ' Sleep-weariness ? Satiety's dull'd fire
" ' Ever in thee anticipates desire.
" ' Thou boast of happiness ! Canst thou bestow
" ' That bliss supremest known to man below,
" ' That life's song sweeter than Apollo's lays,
" ' The heart's low music heard of just self-praise ? . 710
" ' When did thy vot'ries show one worthy deed,
" ' One word, one thought, born native to thy creed ?
" ' Ease-lapp'd as youths, as men with luxury
" ' Worn out, untimely, in contempt they die,
" ' Infamous thou, their pandress—scorn'd that art
" ' By the wise Gods and by the pure of heart !
" ' For me, my dwelling is with God alone,
" ' And with good men ; nor ever is aught done
" ' Of excellent and great, in earth or heaven,
" ' But to my impulse first the praise is given.   720
" ' All praise who know me. I make labour sweet,
" ' And relish add to the strong workman's meat ;

" ' Joy and security for kings prepare,

" ' Nor less the slave, poor bondsman, is my care.

" ' Mine are wise counsels in the hour of peace ;

" ' In war my arm brings honour's sure increase,

" ' None such ally ; nor can man friendship find

" ' Associate firm save when the knot I bind.

" ' My feast is sweet, though frugal ; my repose

" ' Sound, though the ground my pillow,—for it flows   730

" ' From toil, well-earn'd ; and yet, though soft it falls,

" ' Cheerful my children rise when duty calls.

" ' Lov'd by the Gods, to friends and country dear,

" ' Their life pure-guided and their hearts sincere,

" ' Youth prais'd by age, age reverenc'd still by youth,

" ' Peace in their soul, ungnaw'd by envy's tooth,

" ' Such live they ; nor, in death, inglorious shame

" ' Find, but an immortality of fame.

" ' And now, O Heracles!' she ended, ' Choose

" ' Betwixt my path and hers—'tween Virtue's use   740

" ' And Vice's waste of being—worthiest mine ;

" ' And happiness, true happiness, is thine !

" ' Yet sterner trials are reserv'd for some

" ' Right-choosing, and perchance to thee may come.'

" So spoke she; and I lowly bent my knee,

" And ' Goddess!' cried ; ' I cast my lot with thee.'

" Thus then my choice was made; and I have found,

" What true she pledg'd, peace, happy and profound,

" Under a grievous burden ; but I took

" The burden willingly, and steadfast look   750

" To hopes that fail not with this earthly breath,

" And Rhadamanthus' judgment after death.

" Now unto thee, Hypsipylé! this choice

" By me is offer'd—Oh! attend my voice!

" Not without counsel of the Gods.   The Queen
" Of Heav'n came to me, night and day between,
" On yester-eve, and bade me seek thee here,
" Act as thy Jason's elder brother dear,
" And, much reluctant I, these hard things say ;
" Praising thee one would listen and obey :—   760
" ' Go to Hypsipylé thyself ; her soul
" ' Is gen'rous as thine own.   A dark cloud stole
" ' Between her and the sun, and she has err'd
" ' Through ignorance, the voice of truth unheard ;
" ' But the cloud lifts apace ; her heart is pure,
" ' And she, as thou, is learning to endure.
" ' Speak to her kindly, that she may indeed
" ' Jason dismiss, and Argo may be freed.' "
 " Alas ! " the Queen replied, " the path is steep,
" The choice is hard, and a sad crop to reap   770
" Of sorrow in the choosing ! Easy 'twere
" Vice to repel ; but up that perilous stair
" Of life, through rocks and thorns that dares the clouds,
" Climbing, to cling as sailor 'mong the shrouds
" Of tempest-struggling bark, to where it ends
" At Virtue's goal, my trembling heart transcends—
" Weak, weak as young ! How can I meet this woe ?
" O Heracles ! how can I bid him go ? "
 " Lady ! thou call'st me strong ; but I reply,
" The weakest maiden is more strong than I !   780
" Strong in her weakness, virtuous tending ; for
" The Gods are tender tow'rds such weakness, nor
" Know'st thou how strong thou art till, virtuous tried,
" Thou hast, thy trust in them, thy fate defied.
" Not thou or I alone, but every one
" Must make this choice that weeps beneath the sun,—

I

" Less difficult than seeming; 'tis the first
" Step in the climbing thou wilt find the worst.
" Only, the obstacles thy path beset
" With woman's, not man's weapons, must be met.　　790
" In gentleness, persuasion's melting tongue,
" Love and endurance, are such weak ones strong.
" The bramble man would force through in his pride,
" Baffled, the woman softly puts aside.
" The rock man fights with that his path would stop,
" She wears down, pouring water, drop by drop.
" The stream man leaps, or finds the effort vain,
" She wades, and the kind Gods her steps sustain.
" The doom proud man resents, untaught to bend,
" She bows to, meek enduring to the end.　　800
" Thus man and woman both climb duty's hill,
" How diff'rent! yet alike in purpose still—
" Happier who climb together, each his mate
" Strength'ning where weak—united, conqu'ring fate.
" But, unto this, they must be bound in love,
" For life and death, such as the Gods approve,
" The path that Cadmus and Harmonia trod,
" By holy marriage, ordinance of God.
" This thou hast not been taught.　To those not bound
" Thus, yon steep path more difficult is found.　　810
" Now Fate hath laid this load on thee and me—
" A solitary path through life; to be
" Cheer'd by no loving voice, no closest tie,
" Husband's or wife's, when darkest glooms the sky ;
" Or if, in waning years, such bonds be worn,
" Not those we sigh'd for in our early morn.
" Poor victim !　Thou must climb the hill alone,
" Victim of others' errors, not thine own,

" With bleeding feet and hands, and many a tear;
" But thou wilt reach the obelisk, and there,   820
" Th' Eternal Gates in view, life's trials past,
" Safe, the Gods Saviours' care, find peace at last.
" But now hath Jason Fate's great work to do,
" And thine must be the voice to bid him go.
" I know I wound thee, sweetest! but, again,
" Do it at once, I say, and less the pain.
" —Nay! do not wring thy hands and look on me—
" I cannot bear it—thus, so piteously!
" My voice and hands are rugged, not my heart;
" And, thus debating, not less mine the smart.   830
" Would I could, bearing, give thy heart relief!
" It may not be—I can but share thy grief.
" Thou fav'rest Iölé, my long-lost love,
" Shy as the violet, timid as the dove;
" But she was strong when by Athena told
" Zeus will'd our mutual passion to withhold,
" Part of my life-long penance,—we shall meet
" Once more in face of death, but as friends greet
" Who part for ever.   Sweet! I not repine;
" I weep thy sorrow—comfort take from mine!"   840
    Thus speaking Heracles, she bow'd her head
On her small hands, and, like thick rainfall shed
By summer show'r, wept, shiv'ring as the storm
Swept like an earthquake through her tender form;
Then, by an effort as for life, subdued
Her agony, repress'd the swelling flood,
By the seat's arm holding convulsive, took
Assur'd resolve, look'd up to him, and spoke :—
" O noble fruit of pure Alcmena's womb,
" My comfort, and of ages yet to come!   850

                        I 2

" I too have heard thy tale—my childhood's eyes
" Wept for thy wrongs, thine untold agonies,
" Lifelong endurance, slaving to make free,
" Thy patience, and thy love for Iölé.
" Yes! I will do thy bidding, though it break
" My heart to do so, and at once will speak
" To Jason.　Should long years bring home his heart,
" True to me, to assume a husband's part—
" But no! he will not come—no vision fond
" Will I indulge, nor claim beyond the bond;　　　　860
" Bond, say I?—claim?—mine is the child's alone
" Who gives a jewel, thinking it a stone!
" Hath the sun mem'ry of the clouds that roll
" Across his orb?　But such is Jason's soul.
" Yes, better done at once!　And I will leave
" This isle, and seek Ætolia's shore, and grieve
" Weeping with Iölé; and she shall be
" My comforter, and we will talk of thee,
" And she shall give me strength.　And now, farewell!
" I thank thee for the drops thine eyelids swell　　　870
" In pity for me.　One last boon—but this;
" Give me before we part a brother's kiss!"
　　Great Heracles bent downward, kiss'd her cheek,
And those brimm'd drops they could not but outbreak.
She took his strong rough hand between her own,
And press'd it to her lips,—one little moan
Escap'd, but wept no more.　So he the mount
Descended, through the garden, little count
Taking of those there; but pursued his way,
The road he'd come by, to where Argo lay.　　　　880
And Hera spread a cloud round him, intent
Men should not see him weeping as he went.

But she, drawing her veil around, to shade
Her face and eyes, pass'd to the loggia, bade
Iphinöe the heroes call, and stood
Expectant in the midst ; and, like a flood
Of sunlight rich outpouring after storm,
Beauty as of a Goddess o'er her form
Shed Aphrodité.   Grace was in her mien,
And dignity as of Olympus' Queen.   890
    " O friends !" she said, " Like swallows ye have come,
" Spring-birds, to make this isle your summer home,
" Nestling beneath our eaves ; but autumn's fall
" Warns ye to fly where sterner duties call ;
" And slight our hope, thus winging o'er the main,
" New springs shall bring our cherish'd guests again !
" Yes ! duty calls ye hence ; the glorious Fleece,
" Still unrecover'd, is your debt to Greece ;
" Argo lies mourning ; Fate will have it so,
" And 'tis my voice that now must bid ye go.   900
" —Jason ! if, homeward bound, your love endures,
" This sceptre, isle, and my poor hand, are yours,—
" But only by the path Harmonia trod,
" In sacred marriage, ordinance of God.
" You found me ign'rant,—guiltless but for you,
" You leave me wiser, ah ! but sadder too !"
    She bent her look upon him searchingly,
But he, embarrass'd, would not meet her eye ;
Resentment, thus dismiss'd, o'ermaster'd love,
While shame 'gainst better impulse, stronger, strove ;   910
Like conscious hound, that half for pardon begs,
Half snarling growls, his tail between his legs.
    " Lady !" he answer'd ; " be all this as God
" Determines.   For myself, no other abode

" To me is pleasant like the slopes that lie
" Below Mount Pelion, tow'rds the evening sky.
" My country claims me. For thy gen'rous part
" To us thy guests I thank thee from my heart."

    She paus'd awhile ; but Jason spoke no more ;
Then, driving back a tear that would run o'er,   920
Said, " One thing more remains.—Friends, give us space,
" But for a moment—nay, not leave this place ;
" One instant only.—Jason ! 'neath my zone
" I bear, thou know'st, a son, thy gift, alone
" Henceforth to mind me of thee. What thy will
" Tell me, that I its purpose may fulfil."

    " I know not," he replied, " whether return
" Be fated me, or that my friends must mourn
" My death, far absent. But if so, command
" My son, when grown to man, to seek the land   930
" Of Thessaly, and with my father live,
" And with my mother, if they still survive,
" Them both protecting, duteous, till they die,
" Their son's bequest, from Pelias' treachery."

    Again she paus'd :—" And nothing more to tell ?
" Not one word more ? Then be it so—farewell !
" —For you, my friends ! may the Gods Saviours keep,
" And guide your flight across yon distant deep,
" And, swift returning, crown'd with conquest, bear
" To happier homes than those ye leave us here !"   940

    So saying, with her hand she sign'd adieu ;
And, turning, from the loggia quick withdrew,
And sought her chamber, lonely, screen'd from sight,
From the court op'ning, and shut out the light ;
And, kneeling, pour'd her heart out sobbing there ;
Nor Hera, pitying, disallow'd her prayer.

Then broke from those poor women the wild cry
Of ill-prepar'd for, homestruck, agony ;
The old sad scene of multiplied farewells
When war's harsh signal of departure knells,—   950
But sadder this, for few their hopes, their fears
Many of no return in future years,—
Parting for ever, in the bloom of youth,
Widow'd of love, of innocence, of truth,
Unwed, without protectors, mark'd for scorn,
Thrace at their gates, forsaken and forlorn—
Blood-guilty too—most through their elders' wrong :—
Thus, like frail barks the breaker-reefs among,
They toss'd and surg'd in mingling passions' roll,
The quick bewild'ring tempest of the soul ;   960
And you might see and hear—but close the eyes
And stop the ears—their confus'd agonies ;
The tears o'erflowing, the beseeching face,
The passionate last clinging long embrace,
Pledges of love undying, tender vows
Of sure return to seek out and espouse,
Vows soon forgotten—but to be the stay
Of each fond heart for many an after day.
Then all was over.   With instinctive shame
At once all parted—for the impulse came   970
From kindly Hera.   Jason took the lead ;
And through the streets the hero band proceed,
With drooping heads, their eyes on the ground bent,
And many among them sobbing as they went.
They walk'd as men going to death, but not
For their dear country—that a happier lot !
The women follow'd wailing in the rear,
And from the platform watch'd them disappear

Down the steep path that, winding, hid from view
Their parting steps.   Then, silent, these withdrew,   980
Each with her heart to commune, and to make
Pray'r to great Hera for her lov'd one's sake.

But soon as Argo saw the heroes come
Back, thus repentant, to their ocean home,
Like mother welcoming her truant boy,
She flush'd all over, bright, with conscious joy,
Then pal'd again.   All sat down to the oar,
Eager the port to leave and Lemnos' shore.
They loos'd the ropes from the great mooring-stone.
The Zephyr blew no longer; wind was none.   990
But soon as clear'd the harbour—like a bird
Swift to her nest, her nestlings' clamour heard;
Or holy bee, with honey satiate found,
Straight to the hive, from Hybla's pasture-ground;
Or stallion's flight 'cross country, ardour-fir'd,
Sudden, by scent of distant mates inspir'd—
More swift, more straight, more sudden, more intent,
Argo sprang forward with a bound, and bent,
The lightning rivalling, spontaneous, forth,
Her course across the water-path, due North,   1000
Where Samothrace's peak they could descry,
Seat of Poseidon, piercing the blue sky.
The ocean seeth'd, the white waves swell'd like clouds.
The tortur'd air sang whistling in the shrouds,
Sky, sea, else tranquil.   Mute they sat in fear—
Need none to row, nor Tiphys' hand to steer.
Then Mopsus spoke ;—" This marvel is from God !
" He wills our footsteps to the dread abode
" Of bright Electra, pure, of Atlas born,
" Whom, wed to earth, her starry sisters mourn.   1010

" She dwells in Samothracé, with her son,
" Wise Dardanus, belov'd of Zeus, who won
" Her virgin love.   There Dardanus awaits
" Your advent, suppliants, at the Great Gods' gates—
" For ye have sinn'd—by penance proof to give
" Of heart-contrition, and new birth receive."
And, nearing fast, they see aloft, afar,
On the high mountain, glitt'ring like a star,
The suppliants' refuge sure, within its shrine,
The great Palladium, tutelar, divine,   1020
Landmark of life, but not reveal'd to sight
Save of the longing eye and heart contrite.
No port yields harbour on that rigid coast;
Ships that approach, not guided thus, are lost.
But Argo drives right on, nor slacks her speed,
Till close below the rocks; then, like a steed
In mid career check'd, halts; then, sweeping round,
Lies motionless upon the calm profound;
And, winding down, they steps saw, and a ledge,
Rock-hewn, forth-jutting to the waters' edge;   1030
And an old man majestic, who appear'd
Expectant standing, as the vessel near'd.

   Thus landed they on pure Electra's isle;
And Dardanus receiv'd them with a smile.

BOOK V. PHINEUS.

ALAS! how hard is it, with falt'ring pace,
False steps of vice or folly to retrace!
The landmarks lost, the sense of right destroy'd,
The heart's pure fountain left an empty void,
The spirit crush'd—although we struggle on,
The spring of youth and happiness is gone;
And, though we reach the spot diverging whence
Our steps to riot turn'd from innocence,
And start afresh, from manhood on to age
Life henceforth is a weary pilgrimage;   10
While, never slumb'ring, following at our back,
Th' Erinnys, scourge of wrong, pursues our track.
Thus men, so nations!   Eager though to leave
Error behind, and their life's loss retrieve,

That life disorder'd, prone to each extreme
As one scale or the other kicks the beam—
'Tween law and licence oscillating still,
Slaves to each impulse, impotent of will—
In spite of effort individual, such
Their weighting load, too little or too much—   20
They, like a ship, her oars, her rudder lost,
Her sail a rag, on ocean's billows tost,
Roll on awhile careering, tempest-driven,
Then founder, while wild shrieks ascend to heaven,—
Honour they may, but more they cannot save ;
And sink exhausted to a nameless grave.
Such fate befel the Lemnians, such dispraise,
Fruit of their early crime, in after days.

     But happier fortunes follow'd Argo's crew.
" Welcome !" the old man cried, inform'd who knew   30
Their story by Athena :—" What ye seek
" Of shrift and blessing the kind Gods bespeak,
" For Argo's sake, your mother,—yet not all
" Who stand before me.   In the gloomy hall
" At Saïs, where the shrouded image stands,
" The key of life was plac'd in thy pure hands,
" O tried Ancæus !   And thou, Heracles !
" Must not the nine days' myst'ry tempt with these
" Thy present friends ; for thee Eumolpus waits,
" Adopt of Athens, at Eleusis' gates,   40
" The apples vanquish'd, to inform thy faith
" For thy last conquest o'er the powers of death.
" Ye twain must watch with Argo.   Prayer from thee,
" Autochthon ! avails much,—then pray with me.
" Ye others, follow !"—And, he leading, they
Mounted the rock-hewn steps to where, half-way

Up the steep cliff, they found a cavern's mouth
Which through the mountain by a path uncouth,
Dark, broken, led them, stumbling much I ween,
But when they slipp'd hands held them up unseen,   50
Till they emerg'd upon a hidden vale
Deep-bosom'd in the circling hills, where sail
Eagles o'erhead screaming in upper air;
But other sound is never echoed there
Save the hoarse voice of many waterfalls
That streak with white the dusky mountain-walls,
Then down the slopes short course impetuous take,
And flow in tribute tow'rds a limpid lake;
Therein twin central pyramids arise
Sheer from the water, pointing to the skies;   60
Round this a belt of gardens,—a thick copse
And pines above it reach to the hill-tops;
And over all, with darkly glooming frown,
High, Samothracé's cone-like peak looks down,
Veil'd by a thin cloud, bright and glittering,
Where sits Poseidon, Samothracé's King.
No access but the cave for mortal men,
Nor, faithless found, can such return again;
But, life forsworn and blessings misenjoy'd,
Pass, exiles spectral, to the further void.   70
    Beyond the lake a narrow avenue
Leads to a temple vast, where, two and two,
Stand unhewn stones, each by a third stone crown'd,
Into a circled space of open ground
Gates two and forty forming; there the shrine
Of the Great Gods,—beyond, yet more divine,
A place by none approach'd, and hid from day,
Where the Great Gods themselves worship and pray.

Close to the circle stands the modest home
Of Dardanus, with cells for those that come,   80
Vot'ries ; the three Cabiri near abide,
And Corybantes nine ; on t'other side
The circle dwells Electra, with the three
Cabirian nymphs, her saintly company.

    Here Dardanus receiv'd them, gave them food
And sympathy, their sorrows understood,
Their sense of penitence, their hope of grace ;
And pledg'd them comfort from that holy place,—
Then pallets 'sign'd to each ; and sweet repose
Refresh'd them wearied, till the morning rose.   90
    Then, with the dawn, the wondrous rites began
By which the life of heav'n is given to man—
Man into union with the Gods receiv'd ;
A triple process, by three Gods achiev'd.
Examin'd, first, they own'd their guilt-link'd bond
To just Oceanus, nor hope beyond—
Save that from man, as sinners, debtors, all,
He looses his own chains at mercy's call.
Next they, as penitents, lustration sought
From the Gods Saviours, most from him who brought 100
Styx and her sons to guard the threaten'd power
Of Zeus, when once Typhœus rul'd the hour ;
Whom stern he crush'd, Ægæon then, but now
Known as Apollo, of the silver bow.
By blood and water purified, they thus
Stood guilt-absolv'd before Oceanus,—
Not all of equal guilt, but all confess'd
A debt incurr'd, a burden on the breast.
Last, they receiv'd new being, born anew
Of the Great Mother of the Gods, and drew   110

Celestial life from the pure seed of heaven
Through wise Poseidon's spirit-effluence given—
To each a second self, a vehicle
Wherein reborn and yet the same to dwell,
Working the will of God—but how conferr'd
May not unblam'd by ears profane be heard.
These are deep myst'ries, only to be learn'd
By those whose chasten'd hearts have heav'nward yearn'd
At Imbros, Lemnos, or Eleusis' fount,
Or Thracian Samos, or the Phrygian Mount.   120
Meanwhile to each of the Twelve Gods they pray'd,
To each devout the due oblations paid—
Cabiri, Corybantes, each his day
Attendant serving; nor forgot to pray
To the Great Mother—at whose hallow'd feet
Electra laid, her priestess, off'rings meet.
Thus for nine days, a triad for each stage,
They meted out their life's new pilgrimage;
Each day one Corybant, each triad one
Cabirus rul'd; and when the nine were run,   130
The sum was found complete of perfect law,
And their new birth's accomplishment they saw.
   But when the tenth sun rose, and, like a ghost,
The shadow touch'd Phœnician Thasos' coast
Of Samothracé's peak, though from the vale
Unseen—then Dardanus, attenuate, pale
With fasting, call'd and bless'd them; and, with hand
Trembling, each cinctur'd with a purple band,
Sign of adoption through the mysteries,
And potent 'gainst the dangers of the seas.   140
   So they took leave, and sought the cave again,
The Corybantes mingling in their train;

While laughter interchang'd and bant'ring joke
Quick 'tween the heroes and their convoy broke,—
Strange merriment, such raptures following !
But bows relax'd eager to freedom spring.
Through the cave pass'd they—rock nor let was there—
Wafted along like light birds through the air ;
Then the long steps descended to the ledge
Where Argo waited by the water's edge ;   150
And Argo, seeing them, flush'd out once more
In the gay colours that at first she wore,
Greeting them purified ; and, glad at heart,
Gave vocal signal they should instant start.
   They seat themselves and stretch them to the oars,
And fast receded Samothracé's shores.
The sun shone brightly ; breeze was none ; but joy
Lighten'd their toil, and flash'd from every eye,
Fresh, laughing, shouting, eager to decrease
Their goal's long distance and redeem the Fleece.   160
Like clouds o' the night driv'n off by morning's wind,
They left their past life and its cares behind.
The younger shunn'd to look tow'rds Lemnos, name
To them associate both with sin and shame ;
But Heracles thought oft, amid their glee,
Of his sweet sister, lone Hypsipylé.
They bend to th' oar, and their sea-pathway trace
'Tween barren Imbros and the shores of Thrace,
Where the long Chersonese projecting lay
Beyond the azure depth of Melas' bay ;   170
And, night approaching, moor them at the mouth
Of the strict Hellespont.   But from the South
A breeze upsprang at dawn,—they spread the sail,
And up the wid'ning channel 'fore the gale

Sped swiftly, between banks with dark wood cloth'd.
Around the prow the troubled waters froth'd,
And the keel left its furrow in their track.
Here Hellé fell from Chrysomallus' back,
Whence Hellé's bridge, ill-omen'd, is it nam'd.
Ida they saw, the village yet unfam'd   180
Of Ilion, old Dardania, and where near
Abydos looks on Sestos.   Past they steer
Percoté and the Pityeian pines,
And the dry strand that Lampsacus conjoins,
Abarnis surnam'd, where the Paphian queen
Dropp'd, but disown'd with shame, her birth obscene.
And now the shores receded, and the broad
Propontis open'd ; but their onward road
Was check'd abruptly ; for, with icy wing,
A blast from Hæmus swept, discomfiting,   190
Down on the ship, and drove them from their course
To where deep grief and impotent remorse
Awaited them—no crime of theirs that brought,
But, Fate so will'd it, came to them unsought.
    There is an island on the Mysian coast—
Isle now indeed no more, for sandstorms toss'd
By ages have fill'd up the space betwixt
Its shore and Mysia.   On the mainland fix'd
Their seat the brave Doliones ; but plac'd
Their city, guarded by the watery waste,   200
On the near isle, where, Northward-looking, rears
Its front the hill surnam'd the stellar Bear's.
This giants tenanted, a race abhorr'd ;
But never with their peaceful neighbours warr'd,
For these were of Poseidon's blood.   The isle
Rose central to a lofty mount, erewhile

By oakwoods cover'd, now a sacred shrine
To the Great Mother, Dindymon divine.
Two ports the city had ; one outer, fam'd
Less shelter'd, Chytus ; one Panormus nam'd,   210
Inner and safer. By the tempest driven,
Chytus her moorings had to Argo given.

   King Cyzicus was in the bloom of youth,
Just Jason's age, for loyalty and truth
Flower of his race ; and on the morn should wed
Fair Clyté, whom King Merops to his bed
Consign'd with a rich dowry. They had felt
Each dear to each from childhood. Now she dwelt
Secluded in the palace, till the rite
Of holy marriage should their hands unite.   220
The night preceding, as the young King slept,
Dreaming of Clyté, Death and Sleep watch kept
Beside him, pitying. They had made debate
Which should possess him, but the will of Fate
Gave Death the early conquest. "He is young!"
Sleep murmur'd. " Aye, but," answer'd Death, " 'twere
" Brother, to stay him whom lewd vice's touch   [wrong,
" Hath never sullied ; and the Gods love such."
Then Sleep, " O Cyzicus ! to-morrow's eve
" Will bring thee guests whom thou must glad receive, 230
" The sons of Argo, questing Æa's strand
" On high adventure. 'Tis the Gods' command
" Thou treat them kindly." Joyful he awoke,
Thinking Apollo or some God had spoke
In pledge of a fair future ; but the dream
Had other import than it did beseem.

   Thus, when the ship arriv'd, at fall of dark,
The chiefs he welcom'd, press'd to disembark,

K

And share his hearth, and sleep beneath his roof;
Nor should, he urg'd them, Argo keep aloof   240
I' th' outer port, but to Panormus come
With morning's dawn, as to her kindly home.
Thus feasted they—due service on the shore
First to Apollo paid.   An ample store
Of gifts gave Cyzicus.   And, when the thirst
Of food and drink was sated, they rehears'd
Thus far their venture, told him everything,
And what they sought for from the Colchian King.
They ask'd him of their onward route, but he
Knew little; for adventure on the sea   250
His people car'd not; within walls they stay'd,
And the Tyrrhenian pirates held in dread.

  Next morn the elder heroes climb'd the Mount
Of Dindymon, from thence to take account
Of the sea-prospect, how the landmarks lay.
They saw the twin shores narrowing melt away
Eastward, till lost in mists that veil'd the strait
Where Io cross'd, sad wanderer, the hate
Of Hera driving on her pilgrimage;
Hence 'Cow's Ford' known in this our later age.   260
Northward, 'yond Proconnesus, arching wide
Like a vast bow new-strung, they Thrace espied;
While from their feet forth stretch'd Mygdonia's strand,
Their destin'd course; and, jutting from the land,
Poseidon's Promontory.   Nearer seen
Ran Rhyndacus, sluggish, through banks of green,
But strong to push his waters' yellow stain,
The blue o'erpow'ring, far into the main.
  Meanwhile the younger, led by Heracles,
Sought to the inner hav'n, for greater ease,   270

Argo to lead from Chytus; but they found
Unlook'd for let, preoccupied the ground.
The giants, fierce, that dwelt on Arctos' hill,
Descending, had, all night, with evil will
Lab'ring, in part the inner passage block'd,
Hoping to trap and stay her, thus landlock'd ;
Forgetting, foolish, as all giants are,
They could not outward her free passage bar.
Surpris'd but unappall'd the giants stood,
And fiercely gaz'd, a grim and grisly brood.   280
Six hairy arms, two from the shoulders, four
Springing from each thick flank, the monsters bore,—
Tall like the Alöcidæ ; twenty-two
Their number, twin elevens ; and each could do
Six heroes' work and more within the space
Of the sun's circle.   Hera had their race
Nurtur'd, as foes for Heracles.   But now
Their hour was come.   The hero bent his bow,
Restrain'd his friends, his quiver emptying shook,
From Hylas arrow after arrow took,   290
And shot, each time one striking.   They vast rocks
Flung blund'ring, wide ; earth reel'd beneath the shocks.
Eleven had fallen when, with shout and cheer,
From Dindymon returning, in their rear
The elder heroes took them, and astound,
Bewilder'd, stupified, cut to the ground.
They lay upon the strand like fallen trees,
Half on the earth's breast cradled, half the sea's,
Half in, half out the water.   Birds, I wis,
And fish devour'd them—fitting Nemesis!   300
Breed vile and hateful,—some survive, 'tis said ;
But most by Theseus were extirpated.

K 2

Such things thus passing, had the marriage-rite
Between those two been ended, and t' invite
The heroes to the nuptial feast, the King
Came courteous, the morn's greeting proffering.
But Mopsus now announc'd a fav'ring gale,
And bade departure. They uprais'd the sail,
And started, bidding their kind host adieu,
Who watch'd them till they disappear'd from view;   310
Then to his young wife's timid arms return'd,
Who still her father's home, her mother, mourn'd,
Cheer'd her and comforted. Meanwhile they steer'd
North-Eastward, dashing on ; but, ere they near'd
Poseidon's Promont'ry, with nightfall came
From Hæmus a rude tempest, sheets of flame
Rending the heav'ns, and driving hail, and blast
Of Boreas which back drove them, scar'd, aghast,
Whither they knew not, but to reach, alas!
The self-same spot their last night's shelter was,   320
Ev'n Cyzicus! They touch'd the friendly shore ;
The night was dark, the lightnings blaz'd no more ;
News quickly spread that a Tyrrhenian host
Unfriendly-will'd had landed on the coast ;
The young King, waken'd by the prompt alarm,
Leap'd from his bed, and call'd on all to arm,—
Himself was foremost. Fierce they rush'd to quell
The so-thought pirates, question'd not, but fell
Sudden upon them—time none to inquire,
One side or t'other. Like a raging fire   330
Dry autumn's grass devouring, the war rag'd.
Neither thus witting, Jason fierce engag'd
With Cyzicus, and through the breast his spear
Drove, the bone breaking. Senseless he fell there,

Like a fair hyacinth, the flower of woe,
By unintending hand in death laid low.
The best men fallen, the remainder fled
Back to the city-gates discomfited,
Bleeding and mourning.   Dawn awoke, and then,
O grief! all knew their error, ne'er again   340
To joy together, but to weep.   Hot tears
Pour'd from the heroes' eyes, as on the biers
They bore their victims and the youthful might
Of Cyzicus, quench'd like a star in night.
Three days they mourn'd for him ; and on the third
Under a stately mound his corpse interr'd,
Thrice circling it in arms, in double rank,
Tripudial marching, to the measur'd clank
Of sword and shield.   But Clité to the hill
Adjacent fled, and slew herself; and still,   350
Herself transmuted, so old men aver,
A fountain springs up there, nam'd after her.
   Now for twelve days, twelve nights, a furious gale
Incessant blew, forbidding them to sail ;
But the night following, while the others slept,
And Mopsus watch with young Acastus kept,
O'er Jason's slumb'ring head a halcyon flew,
Shrill prophesying calm ; and Mopsus knew
The friendly message.   Jason he awoke,
Stretch'd on his sheepskin, and quick urging spoke :— 360
" Ye must ascend the mountain and appease
" The Mighty Mother, so the storm shall cease.
" For Cyzicus' youth blighted she is wrath,
" Though not your crime, and binds your forward path.
" Thus saith a certain envoy.   See'st thou yon
" Bright sea-bird there, the flagstaff sitting on ?

" She was thy grandsire's sister, Ceyx' bride.

" Too happy pair! they call'd themselves in pride

" Hera and Zeus, exulting in a love

" Blissful, they thought, as that of Gods above ;   370

" Hence chang'd to wand'rers o'er the ocean-wave,

" But, kindly warning, potent still to save.

" Thus warns she now.   Great Rhea rules as queen

" Over the regions, life and death between,

" Which now we draw near, ent'ring day by day

" Within their influence, by an untried way,

" The Gods our guides.   But theirs is lesser power,

" Ruling our life, than in the coming hour

" Of deathly conflict.   If they aid us still,

" 'Tis by allowance of her sovereign will.   380

" Great God, kind mother!—hers beneath these skies,

" Barbarian, strange, our trembling destinies."

Then Jason leap'd up, and his comrades all.

Oxen some drove, that from the young King's stall

Had, gifts, been sent them, up the mountain-side,

The easiest path ; others the quick oars plied

Of Argo to a nearer creek, and bent

Their knees and hands to conquer the ascent

Steep to the summit.   There a wild-vine, gray

With age, thick, rugged, half in the ground lay,   390

Half root-expos'd, expecting death, nor sought

For respite, knowing death but honour brought.

This, slaying, Jason fashion'd in the form

Of the Great Goddess, sender of the storm,

And rais'd it on a pedestal where high

Vast oaks o'ershadowing screen'd it from the sky ;

Then built an altar of small stones, with sod

And oakleaves strewing, sacred to the God ;

The oxen offer'd, all observance paid ;
And thus as King, and Priest, and Saviour pray'd :— 400
  "O Goddess ! by whatever title known,
" Rhea or Cybelé—that dwell'st alone,
" The Mighty Mother—Berecynthia ! Queen
" Of heav'n, and earth, and sea, and what between
" Lies interlunar ; or, more dear to thee,
" Antæa prais'd and kindly Hecaté !
" —Henceforth, it may be, not of us asham'd
" Nor of our homage, Dindymené named !
" Thou whom the winds, the storms, the waves obey !
" Thou, of Olympus' floor the prop and stay ;   410
" Which when thou visitest, each God his face
" In rev'rence veils, and Zeus himself gives place !
" All earth thy dwelling, but thy loving eyes
" Most seek the Asian land that fairest lies
" 'Tween the East sea and Cyprian, and afar
" To the world's end, where Ocean's sources are :—
" Dread Titan ! present help to those that school
" Their hearts to truth and live by wisdom's rule,
" Seeking thy smile by prayer and hallow'd rites
" Time-honour'd, such in which thy heart delights : 420
" But dark as Erebus thy frown to those
" Who, conscious, sin, and hate to love oppose :—
" Thine is the power when wildest billows rage,
" The good man praying, promptly to assuage ;
" Earth's harvests reap'd, the teeming ewes, are thine,
" The garden's produce, and the clust'ring vine ;
" Vict'ry in war, and honour, match'd in skill
" When heroes combat, flow but from thy will ;
" Thou standest by kings' thrones, assessor true,
" Dispensing justice, yes ! and mercy too,—   430

" Or, justice hoodwink'd, temperest the scale,
" And biddest truth be mighty and prevail.
" Nor less to generous youth thy cares extend,
" Their kindly nurse, protector, guide, and friend,
" Ev'n as to him we mourn for—by a blow
" Unwitting, else we were not here, laid low !
" Him have we laid in earth, and honour done
" Befitting, as our brother and thy son ;
" Our hearts are sore, with tears our eyes are dim—
" Not one of us but would have died for him !   440
" —Then hear us, Mother ! us thy children hear,
" Adjur'd, propitious, by that title dear,—
" Hear me, thy son, young too, who speak for these
" My betters else, and clasp thy pitying knees !
" Not now through Orpheus, priest of Saviour Gods
" That own in distant Hellas their abodes,
" But in my own right, Argo's chosen chief,
" I, Jason nam'd, demand of thee relief,
" Thus privileg'd beneath a stranger sky,
" Now nearing this our earth's extremity :—   450
" To thee, then, thus I dedicate this shrine,
" Plant thus this image of thyself divine ;
" And in requital pray :—As thou art strong,
" So calm this tempest, speed our course along !
" As thou art just, so bend Æëtes' heart
" Our suit to rev'rence and the Fleece impart !
" As thou art nurse and mother, be to us
" Tender and mild as erst to Cyzicus !
" Guide us throughout the peril and the strife
" That waits on this our path 'tween death and life ;   460
" And bring us home, protecting, safe to Greece,
" Thy boon the treasure of the Golden Fleece !

" Be our sure comfort still in hour of need,—
" So sable lambs shall on thine altars bleed ;
" And triple dogs and honey of the bee,
" Where highways cross, be consecrate to Thee !"
    So Jason pleaded—not without the aid,
Inspiring known, of the Tritonian maid ;
Then due libations pour'd.   Thereafter round
The altar march'd the heroes, with the sound   470
Of shields and swords clashing, the wail to drown
Uprising from those mourners in the town,
Unpleasing to the Goddess.   She the prayer
Accepted.   Music came, sweet, on the air.
Before their eyes, astonish'd, trees took root,
Bourgeon'd, put leaves forth, flourish'd, and bare fruit.
Flow'rs sprang up round their feet.   The lion came
Forth from his cave, and fawn'd upon them tame.
And, lasting portent, a clear spring, hard by
The new-built shrine, where all before was dry,   480
Gush'd forth, bright, joyous singing, down the mount
Flowing perennial, since nam'd Jason's Fount.
    Thus the storms ceas'd ; and, when the earliest ray
Of Eös warn'd them of approaching day,
They left the shore, less sorrowing now, behind.
The sea was calm, no breath was there of wind.
They, bending to the oars, drove Argo on
With sweeping strokes the tranquil sea upon,
That not the horses wing'd who urge the car
Of dark Poseidon, and immortal are,   490
Could match their speed.   But when the west'ring sun
Gave token that his course was nearly run,
And the wind, rising counter, cropp'd the crest
White of each billow, they relax'd, distrest,

Their effects, save the mighty Heracles :—
He, his whole strength exerting, forc'd with ease
The good ship on, while, as each wave she broke,
The timbers groan'd as by an earthquake shook.
Ancæus and a few on t'other side,
The rowlocks urging, match'd his oar's long stride.   500
So toil'd the seniors, the youths resting, till
They saw now near the Arganthonian hill,
Beech-wooded, their night's landmark. Sudden then,
With crash like thunder bursting before rain,
The oar of Heracles snapp'd right across,
O'erstrain'd, thus useless. Half-vex'd at the loss,
Half-smiling, he sat silent, looking round,
His hands first then in life inactive found.
Then all the youths, refresh'd, resum'd the oar,
Their bourne at hand, and soon attain'd the shore   510
Of the great promontory. Weary, worn,
Like ploughmen that at evening hour return
With sweat bedrench'd, and glad their homes to reach,
They landed, and moor'd Argo on the beach.
Whom, kind, the natives, pious peaceful brood,
Welcom'd, and gave them comfort, fire, and food.
    They rais'd an altar, sacred to the Lord
Of Delphi, and with grateful rites ador'd.
Then, the due feast preparing, Heracles
Went to the forest from among the trees   520
One for an oar to choose. He chose a pine,
Well suited, tall, nigh branchless, like the line
To the dropp'd plummet straight—his legs apart,
With both hands grasp'd, he tore it from the heart
Of mother earth—and on his shoulders threw.
Meanwhile his page, young Hylas, by the crew

Deputed, sought for water in the wood,
Where they were told a rustic altar stood,
Not distant; but he miss'd it, further went,
Still on the quest for the cool draught intent,   530
Till, the trees op'ning as he walk'd, he found
A circled space of green and mossy ground,—
I' th' midst a broad clear fount, that sprang with glee
To life, and thence ran murm'ring to the sea,
In devious course. This was the lov'd resort
Of Nymphs and Dryads for their midnight sport,
And prayer to Artemis. 'Twas early still,
And their songs wak'd not forest yet, nor hill.
The full moon shone on Hylas as he near'd
The fountain's brink,—he like a God appear'd;   540
And, when the brazen vase he stooping sank,
And the wave gurgled round it as it drank,
Eudatia, virgin Naiad of the stream,
Saw his bright face refulgent in the beam,
Lov'd him, and o'er his neck her white arm threw,
Seeking to kiss his mouth, and gently drew
Him down to join her. One sharp cry he gave;
Then all was silent o'er him as the grave.

   That cry heard Polyphemus, son of dread
Poseidon, watching friendly for the tread   550
Of Heracles returning. To the fount
He ran; but sign was none to give account
Of the lost Hylas. Heracles too caught
That cry despairing, and his quick stride brought
Those twain together. Terror's clammy sweat
Broke o'er his brow; and anger, as they met,
Scarce gave him utt'rance. Rapid words exchang'd,
Each counter quarters of the forest rang'd,

Seeking the youth, lest by some wild beast slain
He suffer'd, or by robbers captive ta'en.   560
Like bulls by gadflies goaded in the hour
Of Sirius, they the sylvan coverts scour;
Their shouts the Arganthonian echoes wake;
Beasts to their caverns, scar'd, for refuge take;
The Nymphs and Oreads tremble and lie still,
Nymph in her fount and Oread on her hill.
Only Eudatia, conscious, quiet lies,
And gazes on the youth with raptur'd eyes.
He, life-transform'd, to a new nature born,
Earth's ties forgetting, loves her in return.   570
Hour after hour those seek, but not to save,—
He hears nor heeds them 'neath that siren wave.
    Meanwhile the moon calm travell'd on her track,
But neither hero to the ship came back.
They miss'd them not.   The moon went down—the star
Of Hesper rose—and Zephyr from afar
Came, fresh, to greet the morning.   Quick, to start
Tiphys commanded, and they straight depart,
Loosing the ropes, raising the sail, and round
The promontory rapid passage found,   580
Poseidon's swan, carv'd, skimming on before,
So seem'd it,—the wind fresh'ning more and more.
But when the sun was up, dismay'd they find
The twain were left—worst, Heracles—behind;
How chanc'd so, none could guess; and rose debate
Whether to turn or leave them to their fate.
But Jason sat uncertain, griev'd, nor spoke,
Dubious,—then Telamon's quick ire outbroke,
And "Well may'st thou sit silent," fierce he said,
"Thou to whom Heracles were, absent, dead,   590

" More grateful far than living, lest alone
" His glory, present, should eclipse thine own.
" But words avail not—I myself return ! "
—With that, while like twin watch-fires his eyes burn,
He springs on Tiphys—nor the rest say nay—
Seizing the helm ; and had retrac'd their way,
But the two sons of Boreas rais'd their voice
Return forbidding—wretched ones !   That choice
'Tween gen'rous and cold counsel cost them dear !
Them by the hero's arrows death austere   600
O'ertook in Tenos ; but he pitying gave
Due rites, and rais'd a mound above their grave.
Then to them, doubting, Glaucus o'er the brine,
The ancient fisherman, prophet divine
Of Nereus, rais'd his head, with sea-weed crown'd,
And seiz'd the keel and righted, half swung round,
Veering from Æa ; and in stern arrest
Reprov'd the purpose, and the youths addrest :—
" Why seek to bear the hero to the strand
" Of Æa 'gainst th' o'erruling Fates' command ?   610
" His doom ye know, ten labours to fulfil,
" Obedient slave to a proud tyrant's will.
" These toils well ended now, two more achiev'd
" See him a God in yon blue skies receiv'd.
" Fate too hath Polyphemus mark'd, to build
" On Cius' banks a city, and to yield
" Life in the vast land of the Chalybes.
" Hylas sleeps with the water-nymph."   With these
Brief words he sank, submerging, to the grot
Of truthful Nereus ; and they doubted not   620
The word, but as at first held on their course.
But gen'rous Telamon felt swift remorse

For his harsh words to Jason; and he left
His place, and seeking Jason's, " Ire bereft
" My tongue of wisdom, brother! and to live,
" Wrong unredress'd, I cannot brook.   Forgive!"
To whom the chief:—" Certés, thou didst offend;
" But harsh words weigh not, spoken for a friend,
" Flocks, plunder, not in question.   But do thou
" Take my strong part, as I forgive thee now,   630
" Should future cause arise to me of war."
So they sat down in friendship as before.

    Thus they sail'd on, the elders anxious, less
The younger—soon forgotten their distress.
Lightly they parted with the hero—fond
As is youth's heart to leap nor look beyond
The gulf before it!   Thoughtless, their excuse.
Men never value blessings till they lose.
Little thought they, scarce missing him, that he
Must, soon or later, still their saviour be.   640

    Now right across the Astacenian bay
Bounds Argo forth before the breeze all day,
All night, till daybreak; they the oars resume,
The wind abating, and by sunrise come
To the Bebrycian land of Amycus,
Close to th' emerging rush of Bosporus.
Amycus, known most arrogant of men,
Guests on his coast thrown would not suffer again
Departing till they match'd themselves in might,
The cestus wielding, with himself to fight.   650
Thus he to Argo's heroes.   But to catch
And keep are diverse; and he met his match.
Strong Polydeuces slew him with one blow.
Like two fierce bulls debating for a cow,

Like two smiths hamm'ring on an anvil, they
Doubled and tripled strokes for half the day,
Till, planting that strong blow behind the ear,
He fell'd him lifeless like a butcher'd steer.
Madman! Upon his tomb a laurel grows,
Which whoso, plucking, weareth comes to blows   660
With his best friend.   A ship's crew have been known,
Madden'd, to fight till forth the branch was thrown.
There feasted they all night on the sea-shore ;
And Orpheus sang, amid the billows' roar,
That hush'd to listen, of the glorious deeds
Of him who with the cestus most exceeds,
Twin-leader, one with Castor—while the heart
Of Idas envious swell'd, sitting apart—
The son of Zeus, Therapnæ's Spartan King ;
And the long shores rejoic'd to hear him sing.   670

   But when the sun aris'n dispell'd the night,
And clad the dewy hills with roseate light,
Such spoil embark'd as needed, they set sail,
And, driv'n swift onward by the fav'ring gale,
Enter'd the dreaded jaws that pour the tide
Of waters press'd, which North and South divide,
Scythia and Asia, from the further sea.
There Io cross'd, from Hera's cruelty
Seeking a home, hence Bosporus its fame ;
But Thracian Path, the Strait, its ancient name.   680
Approaching, a vast billow, mountain-high,
Roll'd up against them, blotting out the sky,
Like a huge rain-cloud toppling o'er the mast ;
But Tiphys pierc'd it, and unhurt they pass'd,
Though not unterrified.   The mouth pass'd through,
On the right shore a forest came in view,

An ancient world of hoary cypresses,
Ill-omen'd presence, black, funereal trees;
A white rock gleams there, rooted in the deep,—
The scar'd fish eye it, and at distance keep.   690
On their left hand, deep-op'ning, a calm bay,
Untroubled, shining like a mirror lay,
By a curv'd land-spit guarded, like the horn
Of Chrysomallus.   Smiling as the morn,
Untravell'd, crime-unstain'd, nor by the plough
Nor lab'ring oxen till'd, it seem'd, till now.
Lawns slop'd down, verdant,—none that drew life's breath
Harbour'd in those days near that path of death.
Seven hills, thick-wooded, each 'yond each arose
Along the bay, the prospect fair to close.   700
Here a great portent show'd, a sign from heaven.
By a quick flash of light the North was riven;
A mass of fire blaz'd forth, that scatter'd rays
Fiercely around; but, when the eye could gaze
Steadier, it seem'd to take a dragon's form,
Watcher of God; then, sovereign of the storm,
Zeus's great eagle; then, Athena's bird;
Shape changing constant—but, as dying heard
The home-bound peasant's song, with soft'ning light,
The blaze abating, lovelier though less bright:—   710
Next like the dogstar, last like Mené's beam,
Pale and yet beauteous, crescent, it did seem;
And so abided, hovering o'er the hill
That topp'd the bay—a lovely miracle.
And Mopsus spoke:—" Not only from the East
" Good omens spring, but from the North, confess'd
" Home of the Gods.   Yon is the kindly star
" Of Hecaté; of her once more ye are

" Children accepted by her sign, your stay
" And Argo's through this dark and perilous way."   720
    So on they far'd; the wind the ropes among
And in the sail made music, and with long
Strokes too they row'd, and Argo eager press'd,
Swan-like, against the swelling tide her breast.
For now the stream came swifter.   From the world
Of upper waters, through the channel hurl'd
Contracted, struggling with the rival shores,
The stream of Io cat'ract-like down-pours;
From Asia's shore to Scythia's, like a ball,
Bandied; and thence recoiling, from the wall   730
Of Asia back rebounds.   Seven counterthrows,
Suchlike, their slow progressive course oppose,
Lab'ring; while lat'ral currents, swinging round,
Rough, retrogressive, Tiphys' hand confound.
The vex'd waves dash despairing on the shore,—
Like Bacchanals' in Thrace the mingling roar.
It is a perilous road forsooth to tread,
That transit 'tween the living world and dead!
As a man fever'd tosses to and fro
On his rack'd couch—the spirit seeks to go   740
Forth to the void, but nature holds her own,
Not yet to part—so, while her timbers groan,
By the wild fever of the currents toss'd,
The vantage gain'd one instant the next lost,
Argo in agony convulsive toils,
Fights with the surging hell that round her boils,
Flung thither, hither back; yet, constant still,
Her helm obedient owns the steersman's skill,
Defies despair and death, and points the prow
Triumphant tow'rds the goal she nears e'en now.   750

L

Such grief surmounting, joyful they perceive
The calmer wave, the close-press'd strait they leave;
And sudden, inhospitable, black in hue,
Broad the vast Euxine bursts upon their view,
A sight of terror; prayer broke forth from each
Senior, the young gaz'd impotent of speech;
The oars in their slack'd hands suspended hung;
Ev'n Tiphys' arm relax'd, the rudder swung
Loose at that prospect; and the sight seem'd worse
Promise to pledge than all their previous course.   760
Still danger past is pleasant though we see
Threats in the future,—they, content to be
Friends with the present, singing, the long oar
Urg'd strongly onwards, till the Thracian shore
Shew'd them a port and town, the first they'd seen
Since ent'ring those strict perilous jaws between.
They joy'd to mark such tokens of their kind,
Earth's joys and sorrows not yet left behind.
     This was the home of Phineus, ancient seer.
On the last stage of human life, and near   770
Its exit, dwelt he, but constrain'd to wait—
Not calm reposing, after life's debate,
On verge of the great void, escap'd the blast;
One only storm to weather still, the last—
But grief-bow'd down, in penitence and shame,
Waiting a morn's relief that never came.
Him did Apollo, God of light, impart,
Brother of Cadmus, the diviner's art,
Skill'd as Tiresias; but he too betray'd
The counsels of the Gods, and Zeus the shade   780
Of night perpetual cast upon his eyes;
Old age undying, famine's agonies,

He added; and his dogs, the Harpies, sent
Him to deprive of needful nutriment,—
This doom to last till, woe's deep measure full,
The sons of Argo should his grief annul.
For of all crimes trust-forfeit is the worst,
And who betrays heav'n's counsels most accurst.
For crime 'gainst man man may atone and live;
'Gainst God, not man, God only can forgive;   790
But still the penalty remains to pay,
And claims the debtor's forfeit day by day.
Long had he borne such penance, nor repin'd,
Patient and prayerful, seeking not t' unbind
The chain that bound him, waiting for the power
Of Fate to loose it at the fitting hour,—
Hence Phineus, 'Holy,' nam'd of Zeus, who more
Of prescience gave him than he own'd before;
While wise Apollo taught the healing art,
Knowledge of simples—these did he impart   800
To all around, who came for remedies
Through counsel, and for check against disease.
These brought him casual food wherefrom to snatch
A meagre meal, 'scaping the Harpies' watch.

But now his hope drew nigh. 'Twas midnight deep;
Phineus lay stretch'd apart, in broken sleep,
When Hypnos, Lemnian God, above his bed,
His brother Death not distant, stood and said,—
" Phineus! thy penance nears its close. The morn
" Argo ascends the Strait, and ere return   810
" Of sacred night her sons thy guests shall be.
" The sons of Boreas shall deliver thee
" From thy chief plague, the Harpies. For the rest,
" Endure as hitherto, patient and blest.

L 2

" Teach Argo's sons the myst'ry of the path
" That yet awaits them ; but, for fear of wrath
" Thou know'st of, pause within the warrant—not
" A word beyond.　Be not this hest forgot.
" Death will not tarry long.　Zeus sends me here."
Phineus awoke, shedding the grateful tear ;　　　820
And, "Righteous," said, " Thou that impos'd the rod ;
" But, merciful, I thank thee, O my God !"

　　Thus, when the ship approach'd, Phineus who knew
Her advent rose, and his thick mantle drew
Close round his wither'd form, to guard from cold ;
And, groping, felt his way, with staff and hold
Taken of wall and pillar, to his seat
Beneath the portico, prepar'd to greet
The coming heroes,—famish'd, he did seem
Th' incarnate image of a lifeless dream,—　　　830
Giddy sank down ; the earth appear'd to swim
Round him ; and, weak, relax'd each wasted limb,
Dropp'd into slumber.　His long beard hung down,
White, rev'rend, like the snow on Hæmus' crown.
But when he heard their feet draw near, he woke,
And rais'd his sightless eyes, and feebly spoke,
Suppliant ; while they, pausing, upon him gaz'd,
With looks inquiring, silent and amaz'd :—

　　" Hear me, best of the Greeks ! for ye I know
" By a sure witness Argo's sons, who go　　　840
" Glorious to win the Golden Fleece—O ye !
" Care of Athena, kindly Hecaté,
" But most of gracious Hera !　By the power
" Of Zeus, the friend of suppliants, in this hour
" Of my extremest ill, I ye adjure,—
" Pity, relieve the suff'rings I endure !

" I Phineus am—what Greek but knows my tale ?
" The Harpies' victim ; may my prayer prevail !
" By a true dream last night forewarn'd, I claim
" Your friendly aid to end my grief and shame—   850
" Yours chief, ye sons of Boreas !   Present now,
" I feel the breeze that flutters from your brow
" Ambrosial—I your father's daughter wed ;
" But she, alas ! and all I lov'd are dead.
" Ye are my destin'd saviours."—As he spoke,
Soft pity in the heroes' hearts awoke ;
And those twin brethren wept, and Zetes press'd
The old man's hand, and tenderly address'd :—

    " Such be our care ; nor dearer charge we ask,
" If but the powers divine approve the task ;   860
" Else may we not, though eager, intervene
" Thee and the righteous doom of Fate between."
    To whom the seer, raising again his eyes,—
" Apollo's word, the Shrouded Destinies,
" The Gods of Orcus, this dark cloud that dims
" My sight, this palsy of my agéd limbs,
" The Harpies' rapine, my presumption's meed,
" Witness the task as lawful, nay, decreed."
    Then instantly the youths a meal prepare
For Phineus—last those monsters dire should share.   870
Zetes and Calaïs, with their drawn swords, stood
Guarding ; but when the old man touch'd the food,
Like fire from heav'n, that menace heeding not,
Unseen till then, sudden the Harpies shot
Down from a cloud—like women, fair to see ;
Aëllo one, her mate Ocypeté,
Else nam'd Podargé—fair, but with the cheek
Emaciate, hunger-pale, and eyes with streak

Bloody suffus'd, and gleaming with the fire
Of appetite's unsatisfied desire.   880
Their sinewy hands were arm'd with brazen claws ;
Strength absolute dwelt in their close-knit jaws.
Wings, one as of the vulture, one the bird
Of Zeus, had they.   The heroes gaz'd, nor stirr'd,
Stupified, while the fearful monsters fed ;
Then, sudden ending, spread their wings and fled
Over the seas.   The Boreads straight pursued,
Urging their wings and thirsting for their blood.
Zeus gave them force untiring, and with need—
For those e'en Eurus' blast excell'd in speed.   890
As dogs pursue the fleet stag o'er the plain,
Gnashing their teeth, seeking to bite, in vain,
So these two brothers, pressing on the rear
Of the foul maidens, strove in vain to near,
And strike, and kill them with their outstretch'd hands ;
Nor had desisted,—but by Zeus' commands
Iris from heav'n descended to arrest
The well-match'd race, and utter his behest :—
All paus'd, her seeing.   "Those, O youths !" she said,
" Are dogs of Zeus, with honour credited,   900
" God's instruments to punish human crime ;
" Ye may not injure them.   But, Phineus' time
" Of penance ended, ye, dread Harpies ! both
" Must swear by Styx, the Gods' most solemn oath,
" Henceforth to leave the blind old man in peace."
Then, instantly, in the great isle of Greece,
Arcadia's central realm, where falls the river
Of Styx from heav'n, through mists that hovering ever
Veil the cliff's brow from mortal eye, they stood ;
And, the cup dipping in the sacred flood,   910

And placing in the hands of those twin maids
The axe flint-headed that controls the shades,
She pledg'd them on that quest to go no more ;
And Earth, which heard it, trembled as they swore.

   Thus, happy 'scap'd, the Harpies flew to Crete ;
Iris Olympus sought again ; and, fleet,
Zetes and Calaïs glad retrac'd their way,
And reach'd their starting-point near break of day.

MEANWHILE the heroes, those twin brethren gone,
Waited with care the agéd seer upon,
Like duteous sons that a lost father find ;
Wash'd him, and fitter cloth'd, and spoke him kind.
Of the fat sheep they sacrific'd the best,
The spoil of Amycus; and spread the feast
In Phineus' hall, on platters, boil'd and roast;
And he sat with them, rather guest than host.
Eager he eat, nigh famish'd ; and it seem'd,
Friendless, uncar'd for long, as if he dream'd.   10

Wine still he had in store, and the rich draught
Warm'd him and them; and soon they talk'd and laugh'd
Cheerily, like old friends that after years
Of absence meet—but mirth that into tears
Is apt to melt, not bitter, when the thought
Dwells on the changes fleeting time has wrought.
He had their sires, grandsons, and elders known,
Had mem'ries old to tell of every one;
And in the sons' their voices hearing plain,
He almost thought he heard them speak again.   20

  The tables drawn, they watch'd the livelong night,
Conversing round the fire that crackled bright
In mid the hall, expecting the return
Of the twin Boreads, the event to learn
Of their strange chace. I' th' midst the old man bent
Over the blaze, warming his hands, content;
And much he spoke, as by the dream's command,
Of what awaited them by sea and land.

  " I know," he said, " your Argo's birth, the Tree
" That gives her virtue, and her destiny;   30
" Your quest too, and your fortunes hitherto,
" And the events that wait ye where ye go.
" Ye sinn'd in Lemnos, but were wash'd from sin,
" Reborn, and seal'd, the Hall of Truth within;
" Ye pass'd o'er Helle's bridge, the entrance-gate
" Of the long path that through this Thracian Strait
" Leads life's sad pilgrims to the shores of death:—
" There Helle fell, weak soul, through lack of faith
" In Chrysomallus, strong albeit to save.
" Midway that trembling narrow path ye have   40
" The Mighty Mother made your friend—thus far
" Happy; but, losing Heracles, a star

" Of guidance sure have quench'd—your negligence—
" To him a gain, but to yourselves offence.
" Fate will'd it.   Honours higher on him attend ;
" But ye unconscious will he still befriend.
" Now, through the jaws of Bosporus safe-pass'd,
" Ye stand with me, ag'd ling'rer, on the last
" Verge of this world's horizon—in brief space
" On Argo's wings accomplishing life's race ;   50
" But not, like me, dying, to hail the bourne,
" But pass beyond it living, and return.
    " I speak strange things, but by Apollo's word.
" Beyond this shore th' articulate voice is heard
" No more of kindly men—if claim'd as guest,
" Beware your host—strange races, unconfess'd
" Of like conditions with our own, adore
" Gods we scarce know in Hellas, that have o'er
" Those regions power,   Ours thither rarely come,
" Save when as sons to their ancestral home   60
" Near Ocean's sources they each year repair ;
" Or 'light on journeys, crossing through the air.
    " First, when ye leave me, ye the living gates
" Of Death must enter, if the Triform Fates
" Allow the passage.   Twin, huge, floating rocks
" Are they, that constant with alternate shocks
" Together clash, alternate back recoil,
" Eager, like panthers leaping on their spoil.
" No man, no vessel ever pass'd between
" Those awful gates and lived.   They are the keen   70
" Watchdogs of Zeus, 'gainst mortal flesh employ'd
" To guard the passage to the further void.
" These the Symplegades—in times long gone
" Planctæ, Cyanean Rocks, to mortals known.

" They are alive, the ministers of wrath,—
" This the great peril that obstructs your path.
" Ye must make trial first.   Let loose a dove ;
" If she pass through unhurt, then bend above
" The oars, strong-urging—force your onward way —
" Pray'rs less than effort will avail ; but pray.   80
" But if she perish, fly back ere too late ;
" It is not wisdom to contend with Fate.
" Once pass'd, their life expires ; and, by Death's chain
" Themselves arrested, fix'd they shall remain
" Through endless ages, op'ning up the road
" For mercy's freedmen to the throne of God.
  " Escap'd the rocks, a world before you lies
" Strange and untried—new earth, new sea, new skies ;
" Yet neither earth, nor sea, nor sky as we
" Esteem such, but partaking of all three,   90
" Not yet distinguish'd, in crude nature blent.
" Upstretching Eastward, all is thence ascent
" Through th' interlunar space, the second sphere,
" And the third heav'n, till the Bright Hills appear—
" Yet, rising, not perceiv'd.   A vast abyss
" Yawns first before you like an ocean ; this
" Is what, seen yonder, men shall henceforth call
" —Not Axine—Euxine, friendly path for all.
" 'Tis bounded by the pillars which sustain
" The vault of heav'n, rising like steps, twin chain   100
" Of mighty mountains, to the further height
" Of Caucasus.   There ent'ring, day nor night,
" But twilight reigns.   The void is filled with what
" Seems water, realm of Nereus, but is not
" Water or cloud,—to its own denizens
" Substantial, but illusive, vain, to men's

" Perception, and to breathe, mortal, were death,—

" But ye, in Argo, draw immortal breath.

" No vessels traverse that mysterious void,

" Save those by Æa's king or Dis employ'd,   110

" Like those of King Nausithous in the West,

" That move spontaneous at their lord's behest.

" This is the home of genii—not the kind

" Dæmons of earth, but fierce, difform, and blind,

" Warring in conflict rude, confusion wild,

" Matter and spirit not yet reconcil'd :—

" They the mid channel haunt,—destruction 'twere

" Were ye to tempt the powers that harbour there.

" Beyond the gates Northward and Southward trend

" Twin shores that, wid'ning, arching, narrowing, end 120

" Whither ye tend to.   To your left, but lost

" Distant to sight, the land of Ice, a coast

" Barb'rous and rough, where streams congeal'd of snow

" Into th' abyss beneath perpetual flow.

" There giants live and frost-born tribes, the seed

" Of loftier growths that shall yourselves succeed,

" Rulers of men.   Thence Boreas from the pole

" Sends blasts on eagles' wings to chill the soul.

" Beyond him all is temperate, a zone

" Where speak a speech rich, subtle as your own,   130

" And worship your own Gods, the sacred race

" Of Hyperboreans.   Human griefs no place

" Have in that happy sphere,—they dwell in love,

" Nor think a thought that not the Gods approve.

" Them favours great Apollo—all their care

" Him to observe with sacrifice and prayer.

    " But dexter, Southward, stretches forth the land

" Of Clouds, where awful Hades hath command,

" Land of the dead.   There Acheron pours down
" His turbid waves, and mist-clad mountains frown   140
" Over the mouth of hell.   Yet such there are
" That harbour near, nor dread th' infernal war :
" Tribes of strange character, abnormal birth,
" Uncertain own'd whether of hell or earth.
" Be-South that region lies a burnt up world,
" With ashes foul and black rocks over-hurl'd,
" Cones burning, lakes of salt, deep sunken pits,
" Which, ghastly, each a sulph'rous stream emits,—
" For Tart'rus' caverns lie deep under there,
" And their pent vapours thus seek upper air.   150
    " Ye tremble, yet take courage !   Not by path
" Straight 'cross the void to Æa,—for the wrath
" Of the mid genii were too terrible ;
" Nor Northward, where the frost-born giants dwell—
" But by the dexter shores your pathway lies.
" Nor fear the nearer dead.   Their destinies
" And yours are kindred.   Hug that friendlier strand,
" But land not save where the Great Gods command.
" First, pausing, touch at Thynias' desert isle ;
" There heav'n will stoop your terrors to beguile.   160
" Ere passing Acherusia's Mount beyond,
" Quittance of guests' hereditary bond
" Lycus the king will claim,—there, old in years,
" Two friends departing shall ye mourn with tears.
" Thence sailing, touch—not linger—on the shore
" Of the fell Amazons—the God of War,
" Ares, their parent—female born, but male
" By arms, by purpose—lest their might prevail.
" These masculine though women ; further found,
" The joyous Tibareni till the ground,   170

" Born males ; but, sex in those as these revers'd,
" The rites of childbirth are by men rehears'd :—
" An infant born, the father binds his head,
" Limps with feign'd weakness, and retires to bed ;
" The while the mother, rising, serves the house,
" And bathes and feeds with pap her curtain'd spouse.
" Beyond these dwell the Mosynœci rude,
" In childhood ev'n obese, their skins tattoo'd ;
" Like apes they live in trees, like swine they do
" In public all that men conceal from view.   180
" These dwell along the coasts, but in their rear
" The Chalybes, race to Hephæstus dear,
" Dig from the soil, and charcoal burn, to melt
" Ore into metal, for his forge to smelt.
" These tenant, brave, the Amazonian Mount,
" Holding those unsex'd tribes in small account.
" Age after age, changeless, content, by sweat
" Of their knit brows they their scant living get.
  " These all pass'd by, next on the dry isle touch
" Of Ares, so shall ye gain vantage much   190
" Through knowledge from the quarter whence ye least
" Expect it, but with error's risk increas'd.
" Beware soft counsels ; take not dross for gold.
" By-paths are dogg'd by dangers manifold.
" Thence, Philyra pass'd, strike out with sail and oar,
" Like eagles' flight, across to Æa's shore.
  " Warmer, more genial breezes, brighter glow
" Of day, will greet you as ye forward go ;
" For there is Colchis, there the upper land
" Of light and ether. On that Eastern strand,   200
" Enthron'd supreme ere mortal time begun,
" Æëtes rules the children of the sun,

" Rules with his son Absyrtus,—kind and true
" The son, the sire severe and treach'rous too.
" There lies your goal. Thither through middle air
" Did Phrixus fly. The Golden Fleece is there,
" Upon an oak within the sacred grove
" Of Ares hung, the dragon's head above.
" All these, and Hecaté's dark temple, ye
" Approaching, and bright Æa's walls, will see.   210
" Past Æa rolls the Phasis, river of light;
" And beyond Æa tow'rs the sov'reign height
" Of th' Amaranthine Mount, that nears the sky,
" Wearing the crown of immortality,—
" Men call it Caucasus. On either side
" Two peaks soar upward, and the Mount divide
" By a deep cleft, through which from Ocean pours
" The stream of Phasis down to Æa's shores.
" High on the Northern peak, a prey to pangs
" Immortal as himself, Prometheus hangs,   220
" Suff'ring for man, but hid by a thick cloud,
" That summit and his agony to shroud.
" But on the Southern peak perpetual rays
" Of sunshine rest, so that no eye can gaze
" On it unquench'd,—who dwells there is unknown;
" On it the Gods alight, as on a throne,
" Footstool of heav'n, when journeying to the East,
" With their great sire Oceanus to feast.
" These are th' Eternal Gates, of Life, sublime,
" As the Symplegades of Death and Time.   230
    " Beyond all this rolls Ocean's boundless tide.
" Oceanus there dwells. With him abide
" Ophion and Eurynomé. That river
" Ten sources hath,—holiest the tenth, that ever

" Distils to mother earth, and guards the oath
" Compact 'twixt men and Gods, rever'd by both.
" Along that river's bank, of Gods lov'd well,
" Pious, the blameless Ethiopians dwell,
" And share the feast when from his caldron vast
" Oceanus serves out the Gods' repast.   240
 " Now a great myst'ry learn. The living seed
" Whence trees, and brutes, and humankind proceed,
" All spiritual effluence that with matter blends,
" Dwells in the Ocean-stream, and thence descends
" Through Phasis, through mid Euxine, through the twin
" Symplegades, where lives end and begin,
" Thence through this Thracian Strait and Hellespont—
" Where Sleep with milder, Death with sterner front
" Nigh Imbros watch, threat'ning our morning's birth—
" Thence through unnumber'd springs diffus'd o'er earth,—
" Reserv'd in Samothracé, and reveal'd   251
" In those by the Great Mother's myst'ries seal'd;
" Who, like yourselves, their Eös overcast
" By youthful sin and retribution's blast,
" Those sins confess'd, by water wash'd and blood,
" Receive a second life, their first renew'd.
 " Up this same river of light ye now ascend;
" All spirits do— where they began they end.
" But life embodied cannot tread the way
" 'Yond the Symplegades save, when men pray,   260
" Their prayers, daughters of Zeus, have power to rise
" And seek their native home beyond the skies.
" And, as the serpent shelters her young brood
" Living within her, so within the wood
" Of Argo born and shelter'd, and with fresh
" Life from Electris, ye, though in the flesh,

" Shall op'n a path where none is, but shall be,—
" For, by your act, yon sea, which is not sea,
" Shall by a victim, yours, ordain'd by Fate,
" But willing, render'd be consolidate,—   270
" Pathway for ships and men return to find
" To Ocean's sources, long since left behind.
" Then shall the genii, that their drear abode
" Have in the void, be reconcil'd to God ;
" Then on its shores shall men, our kinsmen, dwell,
" And tales of distant Greece their children tell.
" I may not say who that great victim is,
" Nor how accomplish'd such our Nemesis.
" Hidden as yet the Gods these secrets keep ;
" But ye will know hereafter, and will weep."   280
      He ceas'd.   The heroes sat in silence round,
Their hearts with doubt oppress'd and grief profound,
Hearing such things, contemplating a doom
Worse than of passage speedy to the tomb.
      Then Jason spoke.   " We have had much to learn !
" But say yet further,—should the Fates return
" Grant us, the Fleece attain'd, how lies our way
" Homeward—new paths, or those we tread to-day ?
" For Æa lies beyond the furthest ken
" Of mortal eye, and we are ign'rant men."   290
      " My son," the sage replied, " if ye pass through
" The rocks, and trustful win—as he would do,
" Your comrade late—fear not what may betide ;
" For God himself shall be your strength and guide.
" But if less worthily attain'd your end,
" Much on Ancæus' knowledge will depend."
      " Alas ! " said Jason ; " we are weak, and hard
" The task !   What kindest God shall be our guard,

M

" Our guide athwart such perils?   Whom address,
" Propitiate whom, in that our worst distress?"   300
    To whom the seer,—" Athena hitherto
" Hath been your guardian, and will still be so ;
" And mighty Hera,—but beyond this shore
" Of mortal life, re-ent'ring by the door
" Of worlds supernal, other Gods have power
" More than co-equal, of superior dower,—
" Ares ; Laphæstius, who requir'd the blood
" Of Phrixus, self-devote, but Fate withstood
" And Chrysomallus ; Hecaté, severe,
" But kindly ; and the dame to Paphos dear,   310
" White Goddess, Black, alternate yet the same,
" Whom ye adore by Aphrodité's name.
" She, born from Ocean, whom the Zephyrs bore,
" On the crisp billow wafting, to the shore,
" In heav'n Urania, Queen of love below,
" Most will your venture further ; this I know,
" But how know not.   Yet know I, she is light
" To the clean heart, but to the unclean, night.
" Seek good by worthy means—she grants and crowns
" With honour ; by unworthy compass'd, frowns,   320
" Dishonouring while she grants—your penance great
" Ev'n though your weakness work the ends of Fate.
" She tempts for trial,—yours the choice to test,
" Proffer'd ambiguous, and embrace the best.
" Credit me, 'tis not favour, not applause
" Of Gods or men, that wins in virtue's cause ;
" Gods ye may change, this for another sky,
" But your own selves control your destiny.
" Yet deem not your belovéd Gods and kind
" Of Hellas ye forsake, leaving behind ;   330

" Rather ye bear them with ye. They shall own
" Part in your struggle ; lands till now unknown
" Shall learn to love them ; altars ye shall raise,
" Their advent echoing to far distant days :
" And, long as hero worth or fame endures,
" Their praise shall live throughout the world, and yours."
    Then broke in Idas,—" I approve thy word,
" Thou worthy prophet !   'Tis in the good sword
" Heroes should trust, not Zeus, not Hecaté ;
" I ask no other guide or guarantee."   340
—Therewith around a pillar outside the hall,
Within the heroes' sight, a lizard small
Darted, by a black serpent swift pursued,
Intent to seize it for its young ones' food ;
Whom a thin, arrowy, lightning-flash struck dead,
From the unclouded sky ; the lizard fled,
And under Phineus' mantle shelter sought.
Then Mopsus spoke,—" Scoffer ! thy words have brought
" This instant omen.   Fear the Gods and live.
" Not to man's strength or craft the Shrouded give   350
" Ungrudging conquest.   Won in faith's defect,
" The Fleece may 'scape us when we least expect."
To whom the sage,—" Blame not o'er much.   The youth
" Sees half, but half is not the sum, of truth.
" Fight as thine arm were all in all ; but pray
" As prayer were all,—such concert wins the day."
    So speaking, Eös woke, and a fresh breeze
Rush'd through the hall ; and the Boreades,
Borne on its blast, descended, glitt'ring bright,
Their long hair streaming with their rapid flight,   360
Panting but joyous.   Up the heroes sprang ;
And they, folding their wings, amid the clang

M 2

Of eager questions, through the midway pass'd,
Saluted Phineus, and his knees embrac'd :—
" Father !" said Zetes, " Hail ! The Harpies both,
" Sworn upon Styx, the Gods' most solemn oath,
" By Zeus' command have sought the Cretan shore,
" Thine age and frailty to molest no more.
" Give us thy blessing !" And the blind seer laid
His hands upon them, bless'd, and grateful pray'd.   370
      Thus all rejoic'd ; and Jason,—" Good old man,
" Would Zeus but grant thine eyesight too, thy span
" Of life to comfort !" But he bent his head,
Humble. " My son, such may not be," he said.
" God's mercies measur'd are. We may not seek
" Beyond allowance, nor excess bespeak
" Save in the prayer for death,—when that he grant,
" I of all bliss shall be participant."
      And now the sun was ris'n, and from around
The country-folk came in, and Phineus found   380
Cloth'd and rejoicing, from the Harpies freed.
They food had brought, and he supplied their need
Of counsel, wise divining. On that day
Had Jason plann'd to prosecute their way ;
But with the Dog-star, strong opposing, rose
The blast for forty days from Thrace that blows,
Earth to refresh and the Ægean main.
Thus, like keen horses whom their bits refrain,
Eager but curb'd, impatient, they sat still.
But, forty days accomplish'd, on a hill   390
Across the Strait, they rear'd an altar high
To the Twelve Gods, perpetual memory
Of that their venture, and red Thracian bulls
Slew to Poseidon, who the wild wave lulls

And rouses at his pleasure; and to all
The Gods of Greece made solemn festival,
Praying clear passage 'tween the rocks, their bourne
To reach unharm'd, and victors to return.
Nor were the elder Gods less nam'd,—but here,
On this side still of the dread rocks, were fear   400
Lest the Olympian Gods, of impotence
Suspect beyond, might slighted take offence.
    Then, all being ready, with an anxious heart
They enter Argo, loose the ropes, and start.
The dove was not forgotten,—in his breast
Euphemus held it, flutt'ring, ill at rest.
Nor less Athena knew the desp'rate strife
The heroes rush'd upon, for death or life.
On Thynias' desert isle descending, she
Stood watching, aid to give if need should be.   410
They through the narrows of the tortuous track,
Where the swift central current show'd most black,
'Tween labyrinths of rocks, sharp, net-like, close,
Whence thousand eddying whirls their path oppose,
Urge with the oar; while Tiphys guides the helm,
The floods evading that would else o'erwhelm,
With steady eye.   They hear the nearer roar,
The clashing rocks, and the resounding shore;
Till, sudden emerging, burst upon their sight,
While each bronz'd cheek grows pallid with affright,   420
Those living gates that guard that unknown sea,
Op'ning and shutting in their agony,
Like the twin jaws of some tremendous birth
Foul gender'd from the womb of nether earth—
The very mouth, it seem'd to them, of Hell,
Yawning t' engulf, dread, unavoidable.

Their oars suspended, eyes and heart uprais'd
To heav'n appealing, stupified they gaz'd.

　As in the morning, ere the sun is high,
Two bearded goats contend for mastery,—　　　　430
The conscious fair one, prize of their debate,
Rear'd 'gainst the rock the while, her head elate,
Crops the spring-shoots,—they simultaneous rise,
Dash brow 'gainst brow; the dull thud shakes the skies,—
Recoil; then, back returning, blow with blow
Persistent meet, nor pause for rest allow :—
The lazy goat-herd watches, slumbers,—noon
Creeps on, he wakes; nor yet the fight is done;
The ev'ning shadows lengthen—still the same
Recurrent blows—neither will yield the game :—　　　　440
So the Symplegades, the living rocks,
Propell'd, persistent, with alternate shocks
Together clash, alternate back recoil ;
While sea, earth, sky, echo the wild turmoil.

　Suspended thus the oars, they gaze, until
Mopsus commands to test the oracle
Prescrib'd by Phineus.　Young Euphemus stands
On Argo's prow, the white dove in his hands,
Th' Idalian bird to Aphrodité dear.
He waits the moment due with hope, yet fear :—　　　　450
Now the rocks part, but space too brief will bring
Their forward rush,—may Fate inspire her wing!
He looses tow'rds the op'ning,—they their heads
Stretch, their eyes strain, to witness how she speeds.
Straight, steady, tow'rds the gap she takes her way,
Contemptuous seeming of the rude affray,
Poising when half-way through,—why not more swift,
Foolish! distrustful of that jealous shrift ?

Back come the monsters; the rebounding waves
Rush to the shore, and in the hollow caves   460
Fight, gurgling, chuckling, as in fiendish sport;
The white foam blinds the sight—and ill report
Seems of th' event,—but no! kind Gods prevail—
She passes safe—bereft but of her tail,
The last soft feathers, tribute paid to death!
Reliev'd, the heroes draw exultant breath;
And shout their thanks to Aphrodité, warm,
Heartfelt in transport, louder than the storm.

    Then Tiphys cries each muscle's strength to strain
The rocks to pass through ere they close again;   470
And from the shore the surf's returning race
Drives the good ship into the middle space
Betwixt those watch-dogs.   Shudderingly they see
Reach'd their full tether's far extremity,
Return commenc'd.   In front the main lay clear;
But in their teeth an adverse wave rose near,
Like a huge mountain; and with heads oblique
They cow'ring sat, expecting it to strike;
But Tiphys eas'd the helm—the timbers reel,
But harmless rolls the death 'neath Argo's keel.   480
They row—the strong oars bend like archers' bows—
But small way gain compar'd with what they lose;
Rather suspended, like a cork, she hangs,
Motionless.   Nearer now the monsters' fangs
Press forward,—they in fancy felt their breath,
Their teeth sharp clenching in the gripe of death;
When, by a rearward surge propell'd, she rush'd
Down like an arrow,—yet the rocks had crush'd,
Had not Athena, as the ruin clos'd,
To the near rock her strong right arm oppos'd,   490

Checking; but, with the right the stern above,
The panting ship beyond their clasp she drove,
Shot forward like an eagle on the wind;
Nor lost they save the ensign, crush'd behind.
All drew deep breath, achiev'd the victory,
The rocks behind, in front the open sea.
She heav'nward rose, mutt'ring in under tone,
" Less Aphrodité's succour than mine own !"
They meanwhile whence the succour came guess'd not.
Old friends for newer are too oft forgot.   500
But Mopsus taught to give the Goddess praise :—
" Brothers," he said, " behoves our hearts to raise
" In grateful thanks most for Athena's aid;
" For she hath sav'd us, the Tritonian maid.
" I saw her arm outstretch'd, the rocks withheld,
" And our safe exit, by her thrust impell'd.
" Now we may hope what else we have to do
" Well to achieve, this first worst grief pass'd through."
    The rocks the while, astonied, in their course
Arrested, trembling—like the Isthmian horse   510
That Taraxippus sees, or 'neath the glare
Of the fix'd eyes of Gorgo's dead despair,
Fast'ning upon their victim—back recoil'd,
Then rooted stood, of life and dread despoil'd,—
No more the living gates of Death, but given
Of God a door of Life from earth to heaven.
    But sad the hearts now of the heroes grew,
Their old familiar world shut out from view;
Retreat cut off, the step decisive ta'en,
Before them the vast Euxine's dreary plain.   520
The waters darker gloom'd, and overhead
A twilight dim the sunless sky o'erspread;

Their faces each to other stranger seem'd ;
All things unreal look'd, as if they dream'd.
They row'd on, silent, aw'd ; but noble race
Is never slack chang'd circumstance to face ;
And soon, as the black waste they travell'd o'er,
They laugh'd and jested as they did before.

   So on they row'd, following the Southern coast,
Past Rheba's stream and Phylla's, where as host   530
Dipsacus welcom'd Phrixus when he fled
On the wing'd ram—past thirsty Psilis sped,
And Calpé's rocks.   As oxen toil all day,
Their hoofs firm planting in the deep strong clay ;
The sweat pours from their brows ; their eyes askance
Up from the yoke look with beseeching glance,
Panting, longing for rest, nor rest to find,
For the keen goad still urges them behind ;
So toil'd the heroes, nor in sleep repos'd
When, the day ended, darkness o'er them clos'd ;   540
But urg'd on Argo, till at morning-tide
The desert isle of Thynias they espied.
There saw they joyful a propitious sight.
Apollo, God of Delos, on his flight
From Lycia to the Hyperborean land,
Stoop'd from his course to greet the hero band,
To cheer with memory of their Grecian home,
To strengthen them for trials soon to come.
The golden locks, unshorn, at once they know ;
In his left hand he held the silver bow,—   550
The island trembled as it felt his feet.
They gaz'd mute on the ground, fearing to meet
Those eyes of glory that like Helios glow'd.
But he went on, rejoicing, on his road,

Northwards, across the sea.   Landing, they built
An altar of small stones, and the blood spilt
Of the wild he-goats ; and they danc'd around,
Singing the Pæan—how, arriv'd, he found
At Delphi the great serpent, how assail'd
And slew—nor Gæa's mother-love avail'd—   560
As th' old song tells, all in the early morn,—
" Hail Pæan, Hail Eöns ! pure, unshorn ;
" Only thy mother's loving hands may dare
" To part the tresses of thy golden hair !"
  Then Orpheus took, ended the festival,
A cup of wine unmix'd in name of all ;
Each, his arm piercing, a red drop of blood
Commingled with the consecrated flood ;
Each touch'd, and drank, and pour'd on earth ; and swore
True friends to be and brethren ever-more.   570
  Two days then pass'd, the wind adverse ; the third,
It dropp'd ; and Zephyr came at Zeus's word,
Helpful ; and they the sail rear'd, and, their heart
Of love and grateful rev'rence full, depart.
They pass Sangarius, River of Hunger nam'd,
As Psilis, late, of Thirst,—the marsh ill-fam'd
Anthemois, and Elæus.   Rivers nine
Flow Northward, sons of Acheron divine,
On dark Celæno gender'd.   Zephyr blew
Fresher and fresher, driving them unto   580
The Acherusian Promont'ry, but short
To halt of it, at rapid Lycus' port,
Where dwelt the Mariandyni and their King,
Lycus.   They land.   The natives quickly bring
News of their advent, and the King came down
At once, t' invite them courteous to the town,

As guests ancestral —none could reckon how ;
But sought not the fair claim to disallow.

'Twas a strange land, strange race that there they found,
A land of visions, race of phantasms, bound   590
To life, yet not of life, to death, but free
Of death's dominion—being, that not be.
All contradictions odd were gather'd here ;
For this th' ambiguous interlunar sphere,
The middle term 'tween light and dark, the home
Where Larvæ, Lemures, and spectres roam,
That visit earth and converse in the brains
Of men where folly, vice, or madness reigns.
The land Bithynia, but the people hight
The Dead-Alive, in twilight that delight.   600
These stand half-way between the tribes whose birth
The great void owns and us of nether earth.
A white pall o'er the land, as of the moon,
Hung constant,—hard and chilly ev'n at noon
The sharp-cut outlines ; but, the clouds between
That flitted past, the moon was never seen.
Strange aspect wore the natives, pallid, thin,
Like corpses beautiful in death ; within
The sockets their dull eyes seem'd plates of horn,
Thro' which light as of lamps glow'd pulsing, born   610
Of flick'ring thoughts that now arose, now fell,
Fitful, like music's varying fall or swell.
They bore no weapons ; wild and fast they talk'd ;
Laugh'd much ; and rather glided they than walk'd.
But warm they greeted their new friends ; and these,
Expecting such, return'd their courtesies.

    The feast preparing, Lycus a torch-race
Proclaim'd, in Greece once known, the starting-place

Prometheus' altar. Each youth, running, sought
His rival's torch t' extinguish ; and who brought   620
His own in first, still burning, won the prize,—
Mem'ry of him who stole fire from the skies.

      And now, the feast set, meats were serv'd like those
Of earth, but tasteless, scanty-fed where flows
Sangarius ; much they eat, unsatisfied,
Much drank, from Psilis' grudging stream supplied ;
But drink nor meat their thirst nor hunger tam'd,
And they desisted, being Greeks, asham'd.

      Meanwhile their hosts' shrill laughter shook the hall,
Measureless, senseless, but with grave face all ;   630
Uprising oft, oft they sat down again ;
Now rock'd themselves, now groan'd as if in pain ;
Now arms and legs, here, there, at random sent,
Toss'd as if jointless, in their merriment ;
Like Tyrrhene jesters, or Manducus' jaws
Chatt'ring, or puppets dancing, without pause.
Nor, though the guests could no connection find
'Twixt act and thought, could they refrain ; but join'd.
These were the younger guests ; the elder near
Lycus sat graver ; but sensation queer   640
Of unreality each to his seat
Glued acquiescent, as if fascinate.

      Lycus alone sat cold and uncompell'd
By such vagaries, and low converse held
With Jason. Much he ask'd of Argo's tale,
How 'gainst the living rocks did she prevail,
What ventures gone through, whither they were bound,
And what their object, in these strange seas found ?
Much he bemoan'd their loss in Heracles ;
Much joy'd that Amycus, the Bebryces'   650

Fell tyrant, Polydeuces' hand had slain ;
And full cups call'd for, to his health to drain.
" Heracles," said he, " help'd me when on foot
" He with the Amazon's girdle came, and put
" Bithynia's breadth beneath me.   Amycus
" All 'yond the Rheba since reft back from us,—
" Faith-breakers, liars, the Bebrycian race !
" I joy thy brave friend brought on them disgrace."
   But Jason, " Whence thine own high blood, and how
" Ancestral host ?   Why do these mop and mow,   660
" Gibbering, around us ?   Thy own face appears
" Now as my equal, now as old in years ;
" Now as a man's, now as a wolf's thine eye,
" Now a cold serpent's—whence thy mystery ?
" Mine eye is steady—do I see or dream ? "
   To whom the King,—" Things are not as they seem,
" O sage young Sir !—and few, I think, have eyes
" Keener than thine to see through fallacies.
" Thou ask'st my race ?   I am, like thee, a Greek ;
" These shapes confess'd their barb'rous kind bespeak. 670
" Ancestral host ?   I am that Lycus, son
" Of wise Prometheus who Deucalion
" Begat, and through him thine Æolid strain.
" I and Deucalion thus were brothers twain,
" And all Deucalion's race is kin to me—
" And tied besides by hospitality.
" Each generation have I visited
" Once in their lives at least, and compacts made
" Solemn for sport—nor found we pastime dull,
" 'Specially when the moon was at the full.   680
" From my advances none can stand aloof,—
" Is not this wild chase of thine own a proof ?

" Third query, whence my myst'ry ? Hearken then.

" Thou know'st how he, the craftiest born of men,

" Prometheus, at Meconé slew the ox,

" And parting, in observance orthodox,

" Hid the white bones beneath the fat, the thighs

" Beneath the belly, which the Gods despise,

" And bade Zeus choose. Deceiv'd, the bones he chose.

" Laughter from Gods and men immortal rose.   690

" But man comes ill off playing tricks with Zeus.

" Myself and my twin-brother Chimareus

" Slaughter'd were found, by some strange issue chang'd,

" In place o' the ox—thus was the God aveng'd.

" My sire the worst, Zeus had the best of it ;

" And hence your proverb stands, ' the biter bit.'

" Prometheus tore his beard, in turn deceiv'd,

" Of both his sons by his own act bereav'd.

" But Chimareus and I had been reborn,

" Like you, in Samos. I, indeed, in scorn   700

" Such mumm'ries held, for from my childhood I

" With Hermes had convers'd, the sleek, the sly—

" He with Apollo—he believ'd them all ;

" Therefore I hated him. I still recall

" How standing, like two fools, of flesh bereft

" Both of us, but our reborn being left,

" He, disconcerted, wine'd beneath my scoff,

" Eyeing his fleshly garment thus cast off.

" For, after all, old Dardanus spoke truth,

" And each of us had blossom'd into youth.   710

" Our destiny henceforward diff'rent, him

" The Gods in Imbros plac'd, to guard the dim

" Entrance of life ; but me they station'd here,

" King of these interlunar regions drear,

" Ruling o'er phantoms, immaterial things,
" Substantial less than the winds' whisperings,
" Real to minds, like these thy friends', of clay—
" A joke to you and me, who watch the play.
" More wouldest know ?   Thine eye prevents thy speech.
" Thine ear—while I a deeper myst'ry teach.   720
" Think not true life consists, reborn, in this
" Thy fleshly tissue—independent 'tis
" Of finite being, no confinement owns—
" Can pass at will—feel me ! I have no bones—
" What once were mine, aha ! are relics, stor'd
" A famine-fuge in Sparta, and ador'd
" Throughout all Greece—can pass at will, no bar
" Impeding, matter through, and from afar
" Control, and over animals hath power,
" Least then resistent, at the midnight hour—   730
" Possess'd can enter, fashion to its use
" Each kind, and be wolf, serpent—what we choose ;
" Condition'd merely that we free elect
" With Zeus the dry bones and the thighs reject.
" Thus am I what thou too, reborn, may'st be,
" Native to two worlds, death and life, like me.
" Thus am I old at once and young—and thou
" Both young and old appearest to me now.
" Thus can I roam a wolf the forest wide,
" Thus as a serpent through the coverts glide,   740
" Tasting, else bodiless, of sense denude,
" Crafty or fierce alternate, mortal food ;
" But otherwise enfranchis'd, free to roam,
" And through creation make myself at home.
"Why should'st not thou too thus true life enjoy,
" Freed, disconnected from the dull alloy

" Of human flesh ? Ev'n now I could by art
" Thy newer being from the old dispart,—
" Say but the word, and we as wolves will go,
" Or serpents, as thou wilt, my kingdom through,   750
" And make a night on't ?   Or if better please,
" Hell's mouth is near, and I have sure pass-keys ;
" I, as a wolf, am friends with Cerberus,
" And Orthrus too will welcome both of us.
" Rare sport to see the waters flee the touch
" Of Tantalus, the fruit evade his clutch !
" What say'st thou? Come ! " And now the laughter yell'd
Wild and more wild ; and Jason him beheld
Glorious, dilated, like a demi-God,—
Fierce, with red flames, the horny eyeballs glow'd.   760
His senses reel'd, while through his veins desire
Ran riot for the venture ; but the fire
He by one gripe of desp'rate will repress'd,
And thus, recovering, cool, his host address'd :—
" Lycus !   I thank thee ; let me but achieve
" The task before me, and I will not grieve
" Myself or thee, returning here, unshar'd
" The merry sport of which I now have heard.
" Till then, excuse me."—" Be it so," replied
The King.   But Jason, loudly, " Time we hied   770
" Home to our ship for slumber.   Ho ! my friends ! "
And each, rous'd as from sleep, the word attends.
       Then Lycus, " Of our damsels, young and bright,
" Take each one a companion for the night."
But Jason cried, " Remember Lemnos ! " and
All answer'd " Nay "—save, youngest of the band,
Euphemus, amorous and elate of heart,
The dove's purveyor, Aphrodité's part ;

He would not be gainsaid by fear or shame ;
The rest departed ; and a mate, by name,   780
Lycus bestow'd, Celæno.   " She," he said,
" Of Thirst and Hunger, twins, was brought to bed,
" Her name is Sin—some as my mother give her—
" What matter ?   Sin is young and fresh for ever."
They at the ship continuous vigil keep,
In such strange neighbourhood distrusting sleep ;
But young Euphemus woke, half through the night,
Bristling his hair, and panting with affright ;
And found—for the new life subserv'd him still—
A lean hag on his breast, sucking her fill   790
Of his heart's blood—'twas red upon her lip.
He fled, pursued by phantoms, to the ship,
Chasing and mocking,—eyes bloodshot and dim,
He swoon'd as, dragging in, they rescued him.
Then Orpheus pray'r to the Gods Saviours rais'd,
And Hecaté, weak children's patron, prais'd ;
And Mopsus spoke :—" These things have been decreed
" To test your truth in thought, in word, in deed ;
" 'Gainst life's illusions ye have held it fast ;
" Faith in God's power remains for proof, the last.   800
" For thee, boy ! fear not, truant 'scap'd from school ;
" Pardon'd though guilty, vow'd to sterner rule.
" But think not light, convict of such offence,
" Nor shun th' Erinnys of lost innocence.
" That scar upon thy breast is hight Remorse ;
" Sleeping or waking thou wilt feel its force ;
" Its smart will haunt thee to thy dying day,—
" Meanwhile, thy lapse repenting, fast and pray ! "
    Morn rose.   Lycus supplies of meat and wine
Had sent o'ernight, with grapes too of the vine ;   810

N

But wolf's flesh their eyes saw, unseal'd, the food;
The grapes were nightshade and the wine was blood.
And Mopsus, " Five goats, spoil of Amycus,
" Two skins of Phineus' wine, remain to us;
" These shall our needs suffice till we return;
" Night after night consum'd, renew'd at morn,—
" The gift of Zeus and of Iacchus this,
" While wand'ring, pilgrims, through the dread abyss.
" Meanwhile these spectres' close approach repel;
" For they too surely are the spawn of hell."   820
So, the shapes friendly nearing, Lynceus shot
Arrows, which pass'd them through, but harm'd them not;
And Lycus cried, " If these be hypocrites,
" Zeus made them so, mere masks; but thou, thy wits
" Keen-edg'd about thee, wolf in a sheep's hide,
" Slaying them, an' thou could'st, 'twere fratricide!"
   All hurrying now to start, they heard the cry
Of Idmon, bathing in the marsh hard by;
Idas and Peleus rush'd there—'twas too late!
From a vast boar the sage had met his fate.   830
Lurking, disturb'd, it from the bank above
Attack'd, and through his thigh the keen tusks drove.
His life-blood drain'd, relax'd each quiv'ring limb,
He died as to the ship they carried him.
Some say a grisly wolf the monster seem'd,
Escaping through the reeds,—perchance they dream'd.
   Three days they mourn'd; but on the fourth befel
Like fate to Tiphys,—who the truth can tell?
Most say, a fever, some a serpent, stirr'd
By his foot, smote him,—but perchance these err'd.   840
What can I say?   God gives, God takes our breath;
God's time, God's will, is best, in life and death.

Idmon his own and Phineus' words had not—
But Tiphys and the others had—forgot.
Two lofty mounds record their memory there.
 Now on the heroes settled chill despair.
But more for Tiphys than the sage they griev'd.
Of their sure pilot and the helm bereav'd ;
And would have linger'd hopeless on that strand,
Had not Ancæus urg'd them,—"Thus unmann'd, 850
" Thus faithless, how shall we achieve the Fleece ?
" Bethink ye ! no return remains to Greece : —
" Forward our course ; no other choice is given—
" If worsted, why ! we can retreat on heaven !
" Tiphys is lost,—granted !—no surer guide
" Could e'er have led us o'er this treach'rous tide ;
" But pilots still, inferior scarce, are left,
" Worthy of Argo's helm, of him bereft.
" My words are few, I seldom care to speak ;
" Self-praise hath ne'er uncall'd for sham'd my cheek ; 860
" But I, youth-cradled by barbaric seas
" Unknown to Greece, am match'd to cope with these,—
" Mid perils train'd, by wilder tempests tost
" Than those that rage within th' Ægëan coast.
" Such, I my service offer."—Peleus said,
" Th' Autochthon's claim is just, long credited
" For skill ; perchance too more acceptable
" To the strange Gods that in these regions dwell."
But Jason, " Where these pilots ? Who shall steer
" Argo to Æa safe, and back ? I fear 870
" Nothing remains but, mute, our hands to fold,
" And wear out life here, hopeless, growing old."
Then sprung Ancæus to the helm, and seiz'd,
Indignant ; others sprung too ; but it pleas'd

The heroes; and a halcyon from the brine
Flew o'er his head, and Mopsus own'd the sign.
    Thus they took heart, encourag'd; and now more
Griev'd for sage Idmon than they did before.
    Next day, being the twelfth, the Zephyr blew,
And to that sorrowful strand they bade adieu.   880
Rowing, the better the smooth rocks to shun
That, shelving, seaward from its steep base run,
They round the dreaded Acherusian height,
Gazing with wonder mingled with affright.
Its terrors shading, green, above, below,
The birth of ages, hoary plane-trees grow ;
Deep, in a hollow, yawns a cavern vast,
The mouth of Hades, whence an ice-cold blast,
Perpetual, breathing death, a veil of frost
Flings o'er the trees.   The branches, wildly tost,   890
Shriek in their agony ; while from the shore
The surf's swell mingles with the cavern's roar.
Never by night or day doth silence win
One hour of respite from that hideous din.
Rounded, a valley from the Mount descends,
Whence Ach'ron, rushing, with the sea contends.
The current drove them Northwards ; but, the sail
Raising, they thus against its force prevail.
And soon they pass Callichorus, the cave
Of Aulion, that Iacchus shelter gave   900
From the far East returning ; and behold
The tomb of Sthenelus, of Actor bold
The strong-arm'd son.   Him the sweet breath of life
Forsook, returning from Thermodon's strife,
With Heracles ; an Amazon's fierce hand
By a swift arrow slew him on the strand.

He, meanwhile, stood up, weeping, at the knee
Suppliant of Hades' queen, Persephoné;
And pray'd that he might look upon once more
Men of his kindred as they pass'd the shore;   910
And, granted, standing on the tomb, with awe
The hero gazing on the ship they saw,
Arm'd as in life, sword, shield, and spear, and zone,
And glitt'ring helmet with its purple cone,
His sad eyes watching with a stony glare,
But sign nor motion might of life declare,—
Then, slowly sinking, disappear'd from sight
Into the darkness of eternal night.
Furling the sail, and rowing to the beach,
They rites perform'd, appeasing, tribute each   920
Off'ring of wine; and, love's accost repaid,
Within his tomb rejoic'd the mighty shade.

   But they, the Zephyr fresh'ning, reembark,
Hoping to pass Parthenia's stream ere dark.
Zeus fills the sail; and, as an eagle springs
Forth through the ether thin, nor moves his wings,
But like an arrow forward sailing glides
Borne on the blast, so Argo through the tide's
Clear azure shoots.   They pass the Virgin river,
Where Artemis, her bow aside and quiver   920
Laid on the tranquil bank, her zone unlac'd,
Naked as earliest morning and as chaste,
Bathes her lithe limbs at eve, her lov'd resort,
Wearied, among the Amazons, of sport;
Then springs up heav'nward through the pure serene,
Her seat to take near the Olympian queen.

   Thence, without pause, they onward through the night
Along the still shores skim, with, faint in sight,

Cytorus, by perennial box-trees crown'd;
And, as the morn broke, rowing, struggle round   940
Carambis, that the Tauric Chersonese
Haughty confronts,—then once more 'fore the breeze
Pass where the nymph Sinopé, fearing shame,
Stak'd her virginity, and won the game.
Night once more day succeeding, Halys' red
Waters they pass'd, through many mouths disspread;
And Iris, that her tide white-eddying rolls;
And, the sea rough'ning, fearing the sunk shoals
Form'd by Thermodon's river, that distils
Through many founts from th' Amazonian hills,   950
But broad, united, seaward finds her way,
Earth-charg'd,—they anchor'd in the quiet bay
Where Heracles by stratagem betray'd
Fair Melanippé, Amazonian maid,
Questing the girdle, trapp'd her; and the Queen
Ransom'd her sister, rend'ring it, between
Anger and love—grateful, unharm'd that he
Restor'd her, rev'rent of her purity.
A pleasant spot it was around them; grain
Slop'd up the hills, rich orchards cloth'd the plain;   960
Horses and oxen graz'd; 'mong shadowy bowers
Birds nestling sang, bees humm'd among the flowers;
And lighter day, though but scant sun, appear'd,—
Life was more genial as its source they near'd.
Perchance it all seem'd fairer than it was,—
Contrast oft makes things worse for better pass;
But they esteem'd it lovely; and their hearts
Drank the sweet solace welcome rest imparts.
Still it was dang'rous ground,—they joy'd with fear,
For the fierce Amazons rul'd far and near   970

Around the bay.   Three gallant tribes they are,
But scatter'd, not prepar'd for sudden war.
Perchance they knew, perchance had gather'd round
The little band that there had shelter found,—
Attack'd, had these reap'd glory's large increase,
But the Gods watch'd, and the night pass'd in peace.
Kind Zeus ! that present sent the fav'ring gale ;
Kind Hecaté ! whose mercies never fail
Those who her love maternal not distrust—
The triple-fac'd, the pitiful, the just !   980
    Away ! away !   Argo herself gives forth
The word for starting ere the pinions swarth
Of Night are folded.   Hurrying up the mast,
The sail wings Argo faster and more fast.
Swift gliding, they the jagged coast-lines view'd
Where the soft Tibareni dwell, and rude
The Mosynœci.   Evening came, and while
The heroes watch'd, expecting Ares' isle
Soon to descry, a bird of those that haunt
That desolate rock and those approaching daunt   990
By their fierce aspect, soaring over, dropp'd
A feather, sharper than a lance brass-topp'd,
Which struck Oïleus' shoulder ; and the oar
Fell from his hand.   His strokesman Idas tore
The sharp shaft forth.   The wound his wond'ring eyes
Examin'd, less in pain than dull surprise.
Lynceus and Butes, who behind him sat,
Laugh'd softly, this in mirth, sarcastic that.
Then spoke Ancæus,—" When with Heracles,
" Nearing Stymphalia's lake, we birds like these   1000
" Encount'red ; ye must frighten them away,
" Or they will work us mischief while we stay."

Scarcely was said when they were at the shore
Of that rude throne of Ares.   Prompt for war,
The birds rush'd down; but they with sword and spear
Made clangour, hideous clashing; and in fear
Those monsters fled, and from their shouts; nor car'd
Attempt return while there the heroes far'd.

  Landing, there met them straightway, with accost
Humble, as strangers suppliant to a host,   1010
Four naked youths, but of a gentle kind,
With eyes that glow'd as if from fire behind.

  " Brethren ! for such ye seem, of kindred blood,"
Began the foremost; " give us clothes and food !
" Yourselves, as Gods, to us as men extend
" The hand of helpful Zeus, the suppliants' friend !"

  To whom the chief, rememb'ring Phineus' word,—
" This to your prayer we willingly accord ;
" But what your country, what your name, your race ?
" And why, thus wretched, naked, in this place ?"   1020
  Whom Argus answer'd :—" We are born of one
" By two descents of Æolus the son,
" Phrixus, who fled to Æa on the ram
" From Ino's wrath.   Well known the tale.   I am
" His eldest born,—my brothers these.   To fame
" As yet unknown, yet, since ye ask, my name
" Is Argus.   This is Cytisorus, that
" Melas, and Phrontes fourth.   Arriving at
" Colchis, Hermes commanding it, my sire
" Slew that, his kind preserver ; and the fire   1030
" Of dark Laphystius' altar fierce consum'd.
" The fleece hangs in the grove of Ares, doom'd
" To rest there till a destined champion come
" To win the fated spoil and bear it home.

" Æëtes to his daughter Phrixus wed,
" Chalciopé.   But now my sire is dead ;
" And we, the king commanding to repair
" To Greece, to claim the riches—I the heir—
" Of Athamas—our duteous purpose cross'd,
" Storm-driven and shipwreck'd men, to this rude coast
" Escap'd, with life but nothing more, are thus   1041
" Naked and starving.   Kind, then, succour us."
    Whom Jason, marvelling, answer'd ; while, each breast
Swelling with joy, the heroes forward press'd :—
" The storm was sent by Zeus ; the Gods bespeak
" The succour ye of us as suppliants seek.
" No strangers ye, but kinsmen.   Athamas
" Brother of Cretheus, sire of Æson, was,—
" Æson my sire.   We, by the Gods' command,
" Are on our journey to the Colchian land,   1050
" Where dwells Æëtes ; and, our ends to speed,
" Your aid in guidance is by heaven decreed.
" Of this hereafter.   All things that ye crave,
" Clothes, food, and cheerful comfort ye shall have."
So saying, he gave them clothing from his store.
    There is a modest temple on the shore,
Built by Otrera, queen and Amazon,
To Ares.   Hid within is a black stone,
The Amazons' vow'd worship,—horses they,
Morsell'd in pieces, sacrificial, slay ;   1060
In front an altar of small pebbles,—sheep
Jason slew there, peace with the God to keep.
    The feast concluded and the social reign
Of cups beginning, Jason spoke again :—
" Zeus all things sees ; he guards the pure, the just.
" Your sire he rescued, from the tempest's gust

" Yourselves protected, and this ship hath given
" Your refuge, and ourselves as friends from heaven.
" Athena built this Argo by my arm,
" And, shelter'd in her, ye need fear no harm, 1070
" May visit Greece, land of your father's birth,
" Orchomenos, or where ye will on earth.
" Friends we will be, and carry your ends through,—
" Now hearken what in turn we ask of you.
" Æa we seek, to win the Golden Fleece,
" And bring the prize in triumph back to Greece:
" But we the people know not, nor the place :—
" Ye native are, own part in Æa's race ;
" Return then with us, counsel for the best,
" Not fight—our swords shall, needed, do the rest. 1080
" Then home in Argo come with us, and we
" Will claim and yield your heirship loyally."
  " Alas !" said Argus, " desp'rate is your plan.
" Æëtes beard ? Ye little know the man !
" Return we will, and counsel—choice is none—
" But much I doubt. He prides himself upon
" His race from Helios, and the Colchians dwell
" Devoted round him, swarth, innumerable.
" Like Ares' is his voice, his strength ; his eyes
" Strike terror. Nor the risks should you despise 1090
" That guard the Fleece. A dragon 'neath the oak
" Watches, all-seeing, sleepless, that awoke
" To life immortal from the gore distill'd
" From crush'd Typhœus, when his fierce cry fill'd
" Three worlds with terror. Who shall face that eye ?
" Who wrest the treasure from such custody ?"
  He paus'd. The heroes trembled, but replied
Peleus,—" Nay, fear not ! Have we not defied

" Symplegades, Gods aiding us, and death ?
" And who shall daunt us drawing mortal breath ?   1100
" Æëtes ? No ! We of the blood divine
" Of Gods and heroes boast a prouder line.
" Yielding the Fleece, contented home we sail ;
" Refusing, little will his hosts avail,—
" For Fate is with us, and we must succeed
" If but our faith be sure and bold our deed."
    So too Ancæus and the elders all,
But languish'd ne'ertheless the festival.
Ev'n Jason's cheek by Argus' words was blanch'd.
Each felt himself by the grim monster cranch'd.   1110
Their strength so few, Æëtes' countless swarms,
The thousand vague indefinite alarms
Unthought of till we peril face to face
Scant means, hope-gilded, with forecast disgrace—
They, on such doubts and terrors tempest-tost,
Counted their lives, their honour, all but lost.
Each youth, asham'd, his fears kept out of sight ;
But Jason waking lay, long into night.
    Morn rose.   Their prospects brighter seem'd by day,
Lighter the load that on their bosoms lay.   1120
They start, still coasting—pass the island bed
Of Chiron's mother ; but she blushing fled
To Pelion, by the scornful Rhea found
With Cronos—further sail, nor labour round
The Sacred Mount ; for thence the great bay's sweep
Trends off, curv'd like a bow, round-arching, deep,—
But from that landmark stern, with sail and oar,
Dart off, as Phineus bade, for Æa's shore—
Straight as the cord that binds the well-strung bow,
Swift as, well-notch'd and loos'd, its arrows go.   1130

Warmer and warmer now the sun is felt;
Their frosty fears under its influence melt.
But courage on sensation that depends
Can ill supply ambition's nobler ends.
As day wore on, more and more silent grew,
Thoughtful, the younger and more num'rous crew:
The Minyan blood, commingled with the Greek,
Began in secret to their hearts to speak,
Alloying, not less firm, their purpose high,
With thoughts, in God's distrust, of policy.   1140
Jason scarce spoke to any save compell'd,
But frequent converse low with Argus held.

Long had the eye since morn of Lynceus keen
Discern'd the outline, but more plainly seen
The Amaranth Mountains now broad propp'd the skies,
Furrowing th' horizon.   North and South arise
Distinct the parted peaks, the one with cloud,
Pale terror's veil, Prometheus' living shroud;
Footstool of heav'n the other, tow'ring bright,
Clad in eternal robes of liquid light.   1150
The cloud their beacon, evening's sunnier glow
Redden'd it hourly; when, behind them, low,
Far, but like thunder loud'ning, near, more near,
Continuous sound of rushing plumes they hear;
And o'er them passing high, his wings like oars
Sweeping the heav'n, direct tow'rds Æa's shores,
They saw th' immortal vulture bend his course
Straight to that awful height, where nor remorse
Spares one keen pang, nor firm endurance quails,
But love for man sublime o'er hate prevails.   1160
Then, as they trembling sat, they distant heard
The suff'rer's groans, and mingled, softly stirr'd

By pity, the faint accents, sorrow's tide,
Of Ocean's daughter, weeping at his side;
Then, the groans ceasing, saw the monster back
Returning, satiate, by the self-same track;
Heard, shudd'ring, pass the sweep, the rush, the roar,
Till, lost in distance, all was still once more.
No one for many a league the silence broke,
And afterwards they still in whispers spoke.   1170

   Now nearing land, and evening sinking, they
On their still'd oars, Argus advising, lay,—
Not to approach the shore till fall of dark.
The distant city and black grove they mark
Of Ares, the Fleece glitt'ring through the trees.
Their terror quicken'd, lying thus at ease.
The words of Peleus and the seniors all,
Urging a bold advance, unheeded fall
On Jason's ears.   Good Phineus' mandate true
Less weigh'd than the cold caution of his new   1180
Adviser, Argus.   Night come, tow'rds the reeds
That Phasis' soil-beladen torrent feeds
On the North bank, they push their stealthy way,
Like midnight thieves slow creeping on their prey,
Not fearless to attack while watch he keeps,
But circumvent and rob him while he sleeps.
Through the tall reeds they push, putting aside,
The reeds closing behind as on they glide,
Argus directing, to fit lurking-place,—
Approach unworthy, forecast of disgrace!   1190
O Faith, once bright! that at the first assault
Should'st dimm'd, inglorious, make such base default!

   Moor'd to the bank, safe hid, they wade to land;
And Jason, while the Minyæ round him stand,

Of wine unmix'd a golden goblet takes,
And, falt'ring, to the Gods libation makes
Of land and heaven that be prepotent there,
In ancient chant preferring thus his prayer:—
 " O Zeus Laphystius, Shaper, Master, Best!
" O Helios, Lord of Light, man's daily guest! 1200
" Thou, Mother Earth, or best-nam'd Hecaté!
" Thou, Aphrodité, gender'd from the sea!
" Thou, Ares! at whose well the dragon-brood
" Paid each to each, save five, the debt of blood!
" O ye Indigetes, to godhead rais'd,
" Mortal, in this especial land most prais'd!
" Ye Manes of dead heroes!   Ye below,
" Gods of black Hades and the realms of woe!
" All ye who here in earth or water dwell,
" And guard bright Æa's realm and citadel! 1210
" I ven'rate, worship, name ye, and require
" A master's welcome, comfort, food, and fire!
" To city, wall, and country till now powers
" Propitious, be no more their Gods but ours!
" Terror and Blight, Defeat and Death, oppose
" Against your former friends, henceforth your foes,
" Deserting, imprecated.   Aid our quest;
" And be our moorings with good omens blest!"
—Words not unheard, but no response succeeds.
The distant surf o' the beach, the whisp'ring reeds, 1220
Alone break silence, comfort none impart,
Scarce heard for beating of each hero's heart.
 Night deepen'd,—the youths slept on board, dismay'd;
The elders through the long night watch'd and pray'd.

Book VII. Medea.

THE younger, sleep-refresh'd, awoke with dawn,
Their terrors less, the veil of night withdrawn ;
But still the words of Argus, and the sight
Of that dire vulture, and th' approach by night,
Stealthy, the sense of shame, their courage bow'd
To such low ebb, hung o'er them like a cloud.

    Whom, with the seniors, Jason thus address'd :—
" Perils beset us doubtless, but the quest
" Is certain ours, by Phineus' pledge that, pass'd
" Symplegades, we shall succeed at last.   10
" But, at this latest starting-point, how next
" My foot to plant I hesitate, perplex'd.

" Two courses open,—one, to claim the Fleece
" As Hera's envoys and a debt to Greece ;
" T'other to beg it of the King, and seek
" His favour by fair words and bearing meek ;
" Or 'tween these two a mean perchance may be
" Expedient found, through wary policy.
" I fain would hear your counsel."—Mopsus rose :—
" Thus much in warning would I interpose,   20
" Speaking from God.   Unlock'd the gates of Death
" And Lycus quell'd, the trial-proof of faith
" Awaits ye now—faith in the power of God.
" Who walks with Him must the straightforward road
" Of right pursue and devious craft abhor,
" Ev'n if heav'n's hand appear to ope the door,
" Tempting, to sure success—the penance great,
" Ev'n though your weakness work the ends of Fate.
" These too were Phineus' words.   The path of right
" Now lies before you—choose it, God will fight   30
" Along with you ; rejecting, free your choice,
" Forewarn'd, his wrath will follow ye.   My voice
" Must silent be from henceforth.   Light from heaven
" Was at Electra's isle to guide ye given."
    " My voice," cried Idas, " is at once to claim
" The Fleece in Argo's and in Greece's name,
" As debt withheld, in strength of deeds, not words.
" I ask no other help than our good swords."
    " Hear me ! " said Peleus. " 'Tis not yet too late
" To quit this thief's hole, seek Æëtes' gate,   40
" Boldly, as sceptred kings, ambassadors
" Accredited by Gods to these far shores,—
" Rather by Him who, above all Gods God,
" Hath nor in Greece nor Asia his abode,

" Of whom all other powers but vassals are,
" Known at Dodona King, dwelling afar,—
" Strong in His strength, and with all courtesy,
" To claim the Fleece ; and, if he will grant free,
" Proffer such friendship and alliance close,
" As equal may to equal, match'd, propose :—   50
" But—beg as suppliants, flatter, bear us meek !
" Such counsels like I not—they burn my cheek."
　　Thus too the sons of Leda, ever among
The youth found faithful ; but with weightier tongue
Anceus spoke :—" I say too, claim as right,
" Courteous but firm ; refus'd, defy and fight.
" Why seek to covert ere the tempest come ?
" Is God's power here less mighty than at home ?
" Your fears are phantoms that but substance ape,
" Mere masks of Lycus in another shape.   60
" Face such, in God your trust, they disappear.
" Thus Heracles—would that he were but here !
" Thus Hera, thus Athena, strong as wise—
" Thus should your own brave hearts and wills advise ;
" And Argo's voice, if rais'd, would urge the like.
" There is a time to parley, time to strike."
　　While these were speaking, Argo trembled, flush'd,
Like Orpheus' lyre by his light fingers brush'd,
Murm'ring approval ; but at this appeal,
As fire from flint sharp-stricken by the steel,   70
She broke forth into utt'rance, voicing " Claim !"
The elders recognis'd ; the rest, O shame !
Ears seal'd through lack of faith in truth divine,
Said it but thunder'd, and ignor'd the sign.
　　Then Argus spoke, the man of glosing speech,
Tongue-silver'd, fond low ends by guile to reach,—

His brow unwrinkled, but the eye betray'd
Craft that had older men than Jason sway'd:—
"—Young still, nor in such counsels meet my lot,
" Yet have I knowledge here which ye have not—   80
" Perchance not useless—proffer'd as your guest—
" But yours to judge, deciding for the best.
" What ye determine on, e'en through the worst
" Me-seeming, I will speed; but ponder first:—
" No more in Greece, but in a stranger land,
" Where life, race, Gods are diff'rent all, ye stand;
" 'Mid those will hold ye cheap, and of ye deem
" As to yourselves the tribes barbarian seem—
" Untaught! but they are numerous as the sands,
" And proud Æëtes all their hosts commands.   90
" Born of the sun, their veins with subtle fire
" Burn fierce in wrath, or melt in soft desire;
" Cruel if thwarted, kindly if appeas'd
" By deferent speech, nor in accost displeas'd.
" None fiercer than Æëtes. Claim as right
" The Fleece ye quest, not deadlier is the bite
" Of the fell dragon than his wrath will fall
" On me, my brethren, Argo, one and all.
" Ask'd as a boon, it may be he will grant
" As to a kindly Zeus-sent suppliant,   100
" Thus gaining by an easy road your ends,
" Not making foes but, rather, gaining friends.
" Refus'd, ye are not worse off than before;
" And win ye must, so say ye, ev'n by war.
" But no-wise need is, so it doth me seem,
" In this our case to come to such extreme;
" For water dropp'd, we know, will soften rocks
" Proof 'gainst the rudest sea's intemperate shocks.

" Two daughters hath the King, Chalciopé,
" And young Medea, of dread Hecaté   110
" Priestess, accomplish'd in all magic art,
" But pure, and pitiful, and kind of heart.
" Queen o'er the elements, her spells have force
" T'extinguish fire, stop rivers in their course,
" Bridle the hateful moon to impotence,
" Control ev'n Sirius to beneficence ;
" But, pow'rful thus, untouch'd by passion, mild,
" Self-diffident, and humble as a child ;
" Ever for good exerting, not for ill,
" Her tongue's seduction and her magic skill.   120
" Her most Æëtes loves, child of his age,—
" Her voice can soothe him in his wildest rage.
" Chalciopé, my mother, was as hers
" In infancy ; she much to her defers ;
" And I will urge my mother to obtain
" Her int'rest that your suit be not in vain.
" For we too are in danger, as she knows.
" But that strong Hermes did the wish oppose,
" He would have Phrixus slain.   'Twas Hermes led
" My mother, 'gainst his will, to Phrixus' bed.   130
" He loves her not, because she lov'd him well.
" Us too he dreads, warn'd by an oracle
" Our star his adverse ; hence to Greece he sent,
" Hoping that years in the adventure spent
" Might rid him of us, or by tempests' chance,
" Or hate engender'd when we should advance
" Our claim to the rich stores of Athamas.
" Much need then for Medea, in this our pass,
" Returning, unexpected, and with you,
" Strangers, all strangers hateful in his view,   140

" To intervene, if haply she may soothe

" His rising fury, and a pathway smoothe,

" Ours to his pardon, yours to win your quest.

" For all our sakes, this, credit me, is best."

He ended, and the youths murmur'd applause.

But Jason hasty rose, precluding pause

For counter counsel in the claims of truth :—

—" Greeks are we, not barbarians, as in sooth

" These Colchians are.   Heroes and sons of Zeus,

" Who could withstand us, or our rights refuse ?   150

" But force, brute force, befits not, such our race,—

" Not ours the sword of Ares, God of Thrace ;

" Not to such madness should we have recourse.

" Greeks know that wisdom stronger is than force ;

" And wisdom speeds by matching means to ends,

" Nor, reckless, making foes that else were friends.

" 'Twas Metis bore Athena, by the will

" Of Zeus ; we need no surer oracle.

" My sentence is, that we should ask the Fleece

" As a boon first,—so we return to Greece,   160

" Granted, successful ; if the King deny,

" Or make conditions, then 'twere time to try

" 'Tween such, or, threat'ning war, as right demand,—

" Nor mine, thus claim'd, shall be the weakest hand.

" Still, we are few—ill-match'd 'gainst hosts like these ;

" The dragon too—mate but for Heracles.

" Not vain I therefore Argus' word approve,

" That he should aid us through the virgin's love

" Our quest t' achieve,—and Phineus' voice was clear

" That Aphrodité most would aid us here."   170

Ev'n as he spoke, a milkwhite dove, pursued

By a fierce hawk, her pinions ruffled rude,

Rush'd down, and refuge sought in Jason's breast.
The hawk sat on the flag-staff.   Thanks address'd
They to the Goddess, grateful for the sign.
But Idas shouted, " O ye powers divine !
" Is't come to this ? that we, to Argo pledg'd,
" Like sucking babes, like nestlings yet unfledg'd,
" Like tender maidens—poltroons as we are—
" Court Aphrodité's smile, hang back from war,   180
" Take note of doves and hawks, but types that be
" Of woman's trust and manhood's treachery !
" Jason ! thou ne'er wilt win a nobler prize
" Than Aphrodité's by such stratagies ! "
       The youths blush'd scarlet, half with ire, half shame ;
But Jason pass'd it by.   " The Paphian dame,"
He said, " decides it thus.   At once I go
" With Phrixus' sons to greet the King, and know
" The issue.   Either way, I straight return.
" They will remain,—and, if Æëtes burn   190
" With anger, or conditions hard impose,
" Engage Medea's aid.   Ere evening close
" Argus will send us word."   So saying, he sign'd
The council ended.—Heady, self-will'd, blind,
Self-deeming wise, too little self-afraid,
Himself most trusting, by himself betray'd,
Jealous of counsel from his equals, but
All ears to whisper'd hints, adroitly put ;
Intriguer born, but still in craft at school,
Guide, as he thought, of Argus, but his tool,--   200
Brave as the bravest, but delighting more
In subtilty of act and wordy war ;
Proud of his rule o'er heroes and the choice
Of Gods that gave him the potential voice ;

Cold, well nigh passionless, nor wise, nor great—
He work'd out ne'ertheless the ends of Fate.
  Meanwhile, such things resolv'd on, Argo groan'd;
And the bright colours faded she had donn'd
Once more since Samothracé—pale to sight
Thenceforth, till rob'd ere long in deeper night.   210
  But Hera and Athena sat apart
In high Olympus, anxious, sad at heart.
  " Alas!" said Pallas; " bitter is my grief!
" Manhood at fault—in-creeping like a thief—
" Plotting with Argus, all my words forgot—
" How hath this youth made shipwreck! I would not
" Save him, thus dastard. But his elder crew,
" And Argo, mine own ship—I loathe to do
" What still, I fear, must be."—" Thou sayest sooth;"
Hera replied. " 'Tis fated that the youth   220
" Win the bright Fleece by Aphrodité's smile.
" Thereto must we her vanity beguile,
" Already willing, urging by our prayers.
" I know thou lik'st her not, her beauty's airs,
" Her soft seductions, and her fond caprice.
" But we must stoop to this, to win the Fleece.
" Good points she hath, too,—nor did me refuse
" The cestus more than once when cross'd by Zeus."
  " Go then," said Pallas; " better urg'd by thee.
" I love her not, and, virgin, she hates me."   230
  " Nay! thou must come; for not by me alone
" Persuaded will she grant, and send her son
" To fire Medea's soul with Jason's love.
" To this thy presence flatt'ring must her move,
" Woo'd by Athena. Nay! whate'er the cost—
" Curl not thy lip—the Fleece must not be lost!"

" Nothing," said Pallas, yielding, " do I know
" Of such soft wheedlings,—natheless, I will go."
    So saying, they went together to the fair
Palace of Aphrodité, and stood there,   240
In front of her bed-chamber.   She, alone,
Within was sitting on an ivory throne,
Combing the locks that o'er her shoulders flow'd
In rippled waves that all around her glow'd.
These had she plaited next, but sudden seen
That guest unwonted and th' Olympian Queen,
She rose, and eager greeting, welcome made,—
Quick coil'd those radiant masses round her head,
And then, with smile malicious-sweet, address'd :—
—" Hail, reverend matrons,—now, at last, my guest,   250
" I greet thee, Pallas !—Hera, if thou seek
" Aught I can please thee in, I pray thee, speak !"
    To whom great Hera,—" Laugh you may to see
" Such vot'ries here ; but sore calamity
" Impels our suit. The heroes boune from Greece
" T' achieve th' adventure of the Golden Fleece—
" Most Jason dear to me--the will of Fate
" Bent to accomplish, are in evil strait
" On Æa's shore, Æëtes' cruel heart
" Steel'd and the dragon 'gainst them. O ! take part   260
" In my great sorrow, suppliant, and befriend !"
    To whom that fair one, sham'd that thus should bend
Those haughty heads, in rev'rence thus replied :—
" Dear Hera ! great Athena ! 'twere my pride,
" Yea, joy, thus to befriend, so far as may
" These hands unwarlike your behest obey."
    " Nought from these hands, unwarlike, sooth ! we ask,"
Rejoin'd the Queen, " but a more genial task,—

" To send thy son Medea's heart to fire
" With love for Jason; for, if she conspire   270
" With him thereto, the Fleece will soon be won."

    " Promise I might; but easier said than done,"
Replied she, her eyes clouding,—" Rather ye
" Should ask this of him; he cares not for me,
" Ingrate! but grave respect pretends for such
" As light esteem me. T' other day, I, much
" Anger'd, to break his bow and shafts had sworn:
" But the young rebel held the threat in scorn,
" And vow'd to shoot me with the selfsame bow,
" Myself, his mother! if I spoke him so.   280
" Both threats and blandishments he doth despise;
" And I am nothing—nothing—in his eyes!"

    Thereat did those two Goddesses askance
Seek each the other's eye with merry glance;
But, " Nay!" continued she, " my griefs may seem
" Trifles to you, yet not, methinks, a theme
" For mocking mirth. I should have spar'd me this;
" Sufficient to myself my heart-break is.
" But since ye urge it, I will seek my boy,
" Caress and coax,—I know he will be coy—   290
" And, after all, perchance he may refuse.
" We cannot guide such issues as we choose."

    Then Hera took her slender hand, and, soft
Stroking it, smil'd :—" Don't be dishearten'd!   Oft
" Will he refuse perchance, but persevere;
" Thee intervening, I have no more fear.
" And Phineus true hath said that victory,
" In Asia potent, must proceed from thee.
" Do thy best only—do it—and at once."

    Pleas'd Aphrodité smil'd, but no response   300

Made further, and led Hera to the door ;
And Pallas follow'd, friendlier than before.
Some say she kiss'd that siren, as without
Great Hera stately stepp'd—but this I doubt.

　　Then Cythereia, plaiting first her hair,
Sought through th' Olympian valleys, here and there,
Her son to find, and found him, not alone,
But playing for dice with Ganymed, the son
Of Tros.　The youth was losing ; two remain'd,
Golden,—the rest had greedy Eros gain'd ;　　　　310
Who rudely scoff'd as, standing on the grass,
He view'd his rival near the bankrupt's pass.
Once more the youth, kneeling, for conquest toss'd,
But those two last, beggar'd, he likewise lost.
He went his way disconsolate, aggriev'd,
Nor Aphrodité's soft approach perceiv'd.

　　She kiss'd her boy, and clasp'd her arm about
His neck ; but he hung back with frown and pout :—
" Why did'st thou laugh, thou mischief? Cheating? What !
" Hast thou not yet these naughty tricks forgot ?　　320
" But come, I pray thee, do this thing for me ;
" And in requital I will give to thee
" A plaything Cretan Adrasteia gave,
" His nurse, to Zeus in the Idæan cave,—
" A wondrous work, once to Harmonia given,
" When trick'd out by the Gods with gauds from heaven.
" She flouted, scorning—foolish ! without art
" Nature is impotent to bind man's heart.
" 'Tis a fair sphere, a circling wheel, of gold,
" Nave, axle, spokes ; with bright stones manifold　　330
" Studded, and ivy-tendrils twining through,
" Around, within, without.　A bird, of hue

" Bright-brindled, lies transfix'd against the spokes,
" Wings, legs, coherent, that desire provokes,
" By mortals seen. That wheel hath power to draw
" Hearts in obedience, charm'd by magic law ;
" Can make the coldest vestal am'rous burn,
" And truant loves to their first vows return.
" Thrown at your will, a furrowing track, afar
" Shooting, it makes, as of a falling star ;   340
" But quick comes back into your hands again.
" This pretty toy shall yours be, for the pain
" Of one slight service. Send a burning dart
" Of love for Jason through Medea's heart,
" The maid of Æa,—do it *sans* delay,
" If thou would'st win the Wheel of Love to-day."
    Pleas'd Eros listen'd, and her white robe caught
With both his hands, and eagerly besought
To give him instant ; but she pinch'd his cheek,
Smiling, and answer'd,—" Love's own God must seek 350
" Favour by wooing, grace by service done.
" Do this ; and, the maid's heart for Jason won,
" I swear to thee, by this dear hand and mine,
" The bauble and my thanks shall both be thine."
    So said, the dice he gather'd, counting lest
One should be miss'd, and in his mother's breast
Threw them, and seiz'd his bow, that lay among
The flowers, and quiver, on a myrtle hung
Hard by ; and through the vale, the palace, ran,
And Zeus's field, and through the gates that span   360
Olympus' entrance—pausing to survey
Earth's seas, realms, deserts that beneath him lay ;
Paus'd but one instant ; thence a path shoots down
To that twin peak Caucasian, silv'ry, crown

Of earth, heav'n's footstool, which the earliest sun
Illumines,—that path taking, lighted on
Dull earth, which shot forth verdure as he trod;
And to Æetes' palace took his road.

Meanwhile, the council ended at the ship,
Jason, success triumphant on his lip,   370
With Phrixus' sons and Telamon, whom most
He trusted, pardon'd late that rough accost —
But he, the purpose disapproving, went
To guard, if need, his captain's life intent—
Set forth for stately Æa, Hermes' wand
Of peace and friendship taking in his hand.
Hera around them cast a cloud, to hide
Their steps, approaching from the river's side.

They through the plain, of Circé nam'd, proceed
Through broken ground, where every deadly weed   380
Rank flourish'd; hoary alders their arms spread,
Twisted like ghastly skeletons, o'erhead,
Thin-foliag'd, their moss'd roots half hid i' th' mud,—
To right and left dank tombstones thick were strew'd
Of women buried; but suspended hung
Corpses of males, by chains in raw hides slung
From those branch'd arms, expos'd to birds of prey,
Which, scar'd from their feast hideous, fled away—
Such custom 'mong the Colchians.   From the plain
Emerging, to the left they see the fane   390
Of Hecaté, which sable poplars screen.
This passing, and the town at right hand seen,
They mounted tow'rds the palace, that on high
Seem'd, lofty-tow'ring, to approach the sky,—
Paus'd and admir'd.   On a vast platform, square,
The palace stood i' th' midst; a broad steep stair

Led up to it; fair terraces all round
Left space for concourse; on a rising mound
A pyramid at each fourth angle rose.
Two vast bulls, human-headed, watchful, close   400
To the great portal stood.   A central dome
Soar'd high o'er all, glitt'ring, as 'twere the home
Of Gods etherial; ·spiral pinnacles
Rose from its ring-like base, whence merry bells
Kept up continual concert, endless change,—
To their Greek eyes barbarian all, and strange.
Now, Argus leading, enter'd they the hall,
Where all was laid as for high festival,
Beneath that dome.   The arching roof display'd
The stellar vault, in colours bright array'd ;—   410
Orion and Boötes pictur'd were,
And the great Wain, which others call the Bear ;
The Ocean-stream round serpent-like was roll'd,
Half veil'd in darkness, gorgeous half in gold ;
While in his crystal bark through signs eleven
The God of light pursued his path through heaven,—
Through day's bright hours they saw the vessel sail
Exulting, buoyant, bounding 'fore the gale ;
Through night's dark shadows tardier seek her road,
Ascending then the stream, by Hermes tow'd.   420
All was in motion, wondrous; Helios light
Gave from that dome by day, the stars by night.

   Thence, passing through a gate, themselves they found
In a vast atrium, columns ranging round.
Four fountains in the angles music made,
With milk and wine, water and oil that play'd,—
An owl's beak oil, water a lion's maw,
Milk a cow's mouth, wine a fierce tiger's jaw

Forth pouring ; but a central fount on high
Flung up a jet of ocean to the sky.   430
Three flights of stairs, breaking the columns, led
By steps of marble, yellow, blue, and red,
To three fair dwellings, terrac'd high, apart.
The heroes gaz'd around with beating heart,
And Phrontes whisper'd,—"In yon furthest house
" Æëtes lives, Iduia too, his spouse,
" My mother's mother.   Nearer, to the right,
" His son Absyrtus, borne to him by bright
" Asterodæa, Syrian maid,—the youth
" Is loving, generous, and the soul of truth ;   440
" But his sire loves him not.   There, to the left,
" My mother dwells, who mourns, of us bereft,
" Her mansion desolate.   And, chamber'd nigh,
" Medea sleeps when not attendant by
" The shrine of Hecaté."—But then the cloud
Hera withdrew.   They stood reveal'd.   A crowd
Of women pour'd out, like a river-tide.
" Behold herself, Medea !" Argus cried,—
Who, glancing but, to call her sister ran,
Chalciopé.   She rush'd forth, pale and wan   450
With weeping, and her sons in her embrace
Lock'd, and with tears bedew'd each long'd for face ;
And question quick and quick response ensued.
Meanwhile Æëtes, in no placid mood
At the loud tumult, enter'd stern, and saw
Ill-pleas'd his grandsons and their friends ; but, law
Of host constraining, welcomed,—those, austere ;
These, keen regarding, with less stinted cheer ;
Bade the slave-women wash them ; and, with fair
Words, to the hall invited, to feast there.   460

Thus Jason feasted 'neath that wondrous dome,
Guest, least expecting, in Æëtes' home.
Æëtes sat upon his marble throne,
Medea beside, a lower seat upon;
For he would ever have the maiden by,
Pride of his heart and apple of his eye.
Her dusky robe down to her ankles flow'd;
Above her brow a silver crescent glow'd;
Her brow, broad, lofty, seem'd the hallow'd seat
Of knowledge fathomless and purpose great;   470
Her eyes shone with a lustre pure and keen,
Temper'd, howe'er, as night and day between;
But his, the son of Helios, terrible,
Cast shadows from the forms on which they fell.
They feasted on the flesh of beeves that feed
In rich Trinacria, of celestial breed;
They drank the wine from that deep fountain first
Unseal'd by Dionysus, and which burst
In torrents from the tiger's jaw within
The central court, its neighbours with its din   480
Joyous o'erpow'ring—Jason sparingly,
Cautious,—less guarded Telamon than he.
But when desire was sated, then, with voice
Unsteady, while his eyes with no fix'd choice
Rov'd o'er his guests, with jealous ire that burn'd,—
"How," ask'd the King, "my grandsons! how return'd
"So soon, your quest accomplish'd? Well I know
"The distance great, my sister long ago,
"Circé, conveying in my father's car
"To the Tyrrhene Hesperia, yet more far   490
"Remote than Greece:—Link'd too by what new fate
"With these your friends, and where your ship, relate."

Argus replied :—"O gracious King and sire !
" Our ship a storm destroy'd, and we in dire
" Extremity escap'd to Ares' isle.
" There had we perish'd on that desert soil,
" Prey to the birds ; but, thither sent by Zeus,
" These to our prayers, thy guests, did not refuse,
" Thy name with rev'rence heard, comfort and aid.
" Themselves to Æa journeying, as they said,   500
" To crave a boon, thus have they brought us here.
" Their names, their purpose these :—Th' Æolids fear
" Most Pelias, this man's uncle,—he excels
" In arms and wealth, and at Iölcos dwells.
" Warn'd by an oracle, in fear of wrath
" Of Zeus impending, he, constraining, hath
" Sent Jason here, to ask the Golden Fleece
" At thy hands, fav'ring, as a boon to Greece.
" For this hath wise Athena built for him
" A ship that Nereus rough and Boreas grim   510
" Defies invulnerable—that, like the wind,
" Baffles the sight, and leaves mischance behind.
" In this embark'd, the flower of Greece, from each
" Island and realm, lie waiting, off the beach,
" Thy good will seeking—Heracles, of late
" Their partner, absent, but may join them yet—
" So may'st thou grant.   No thought have they of force ;
" They come constrain'd thereto, without resource ;
" Nor ask without fair proffer—to subdue
" The Sauromats ; for they are Greeks, though few.   520
" This know thou Jason, Æson's son, the son
" Of Cretheus, near our kin,—that, Telamon,
" Son of just Æacus.   What further ?   All
" Father or grandsire each a God they call."

Argus thus speaking, lightly, on tiptoe,
Glancing round merrily, with his bended bow
Came Eros ent'ring—a sweet breeze of spring
Wafted, advancing, from each folding wing—
Unmark'd, like ray that woos the morning dew.
From his stor'd quiver forth a shaft he drew,   530
Slight, glossy-feather'd, barb'd, with poison-groove;
'Twas wing'd by pity, sharpen'd 'twas by love,
With juice of fond Narcissus deadly tipp'd,—
Withal had been in Lethé's waters dipp'd,
That strong affection, sleep-bound, former ties
Forgetting, should make perfect sacrifice.
This, by the notch adjusting to the string,
He loos'd at that bright maid who by the King
Sat, doom'd, Medea.   She perceiv'd the smart,
But knew not what the sting, nor whence the dart.   540
Then, softly laughing, turn'd upon his heel,
And sought Olympus.   But the subtle steel
Burnt in her heart, unconscious; her cheek burn'd,
From red to pale, from pale to red return'd;
Her heart beat quicker as she look'd upon
Jason, but save of pity thought was none—
Fear for her father's anger, known so fell;
But pity leads to love, as all know well.
She drew her veil around her face, to hide,
Instinctive, her emotion's swelling tide.   550
Henceforth the light effulgent of her eyes
Was soft-subdued by human sympathies,
Unless when mov'd to scorn, and then her ire
Wak'd in those sunny orbs the slumb'ring fire.

But the King frown'd, hearing what Argus spoke,
Doubting the sons of Phrixus; and he broke

Silence, indignant :—" Wretches, and ingrate !
" How dare ye seek my presence with such prate
" Of storms and strangers, fallen from the sky ?
" Better had been mine eyes and wrath to fly,   560
" Timely, than tempt me thus.   What ! see I not
" Your scheme, your cunning ? with these Greeks in plot,
" Not the Fleece only, but my crown to gain,
" And ye yourselves over the Colchians reign ?
" But that as guests, not grandsons, ye this day
" Have eat my bread, I would your guile repay,
" Your tongues cut out, forth from my presence driven :—
" How have ye lied before the Gods of heaven !"

    Then Telamon, wine-heated, fierce up-sprung ;
But Jason curb'd him, and with gentle tongue   570
Answer'd, his own stirr'd anger strong refrain'd.
And Hera o'er his person beauty rain'd,
And grace, and dignity ; and 'tween her veil
Medea watch'd him, list'ning to his tale.

    " Æetes ! be not angry with the youth,
" Nor these his brethren,—they have spoken truth.
" All is as they have said.   They met with us,
" Suppliants, as we to thee, of sacred Zeus ;
" And we are here with no intent of ill,
" But seeking, as thou hear'st, of thy good will   580
" The fleece of Chrysomallus, kind that bore
" Phrixus, their father, sav'd,.to Æa's shore ;
" Here sacrific'd, and the Fleece hung above
" The dragon's head in Ares' hallow'd grove.
" This would I beg of thee, a friendly boon,
" In name of Greece,—nor, sooth, of Greece alone :—
" Gods have commanded me to seek thy face ;
" Gods claim for Hellas, for themselves, this grace,

                                                        P

" The Fleece kind yielding. Mission'd such, I come
" In all good faith, a guest, unto thy home,—   590
" Else had we not as suppliants sought thy gate.
" Be counsell'd then ; nor, weaker, strive with Fate.
" This grant, and through all Greece thy name shall ring
" In songs sublime, that fame immortal bring.
" This grant, and Sauromat and Celt, compell'd,
" Shall kiss thy footstool, by our valour quell'd."
    Thus ending Jason, his averted eyes,
Blazing, the King turn'd on him, blank surprise
Master'd by fury ; but Medea laid
Her hand on his, and the fierce outburst stay'd,   600
Calming.   He doubting sat, whether at once
To slay them there, or, wiser, for the nonce,
Put their assum'd pretensions to the test
By some stern trial ; and this seem'd the best ;
So answer'd :—" Women, Amazons, enow
" Allies have we the Sauromats to cow ;
" Gramercy for your offer !   But if ye,
" Sons of the Gods, nor of less high degree
" Than we of Æa, come from distant Greece
" On such sole errand, I will yield the Fleece,—   610
" But on such tried conditions as shall prove
" Your worth a warrant for my answering love.
" For, when a bold brave man with iron hand
" Rules, strong in will, supreme, a subject land —
" Thy master Pelias such, as well I judge—
" To such would I, his friend and equal, grudge
" Nothing, not e'en the Fleece.   This then your proof :—
" Two bulls, with iron horn and brazen hoof,
" And breathing fire—Hephæstus' gift to me,
" When in my father's car I bore him free   620

" Escap'd from Phlegra and the Giants' war—
" Range in the field of Ares,—fierce they are,
" Untam'd, save by my hand.   These, day by day,
" Yok'd to an iron plough my goad obey,
" Ploughing four acres of the fallow land.
" Such plough'd, I sow—not with Demeter's hand,
" Seed-scatt'ring—but with dragon's teeth that, spar'd
" By Cadmus, he with me in friendship shar'd.
" These spring up armour'd giants, and attack,
" From all sides rushing, me, my breast, my back,   630
" Senseless! whom mow I down, like flow'rs, for sport.
" What say you now?   The morrow's morn, my court
" And I spectators, you shall yoke these twain,
" Plough the four acres, sow the dragon grain,
" And mow the harvest—boaster! if you can :—
" For strong 'twere shame to yield to weaker man,
" As me to you, not equall'd in such game.
" Ha! doth the pastime like you?—Speak, for shame !"
    For Jason, as he spoke, bent down his e'en,
Speechless, much troubled hope and dread between ;   640
Nor spoke at once ; but then, with words astute,—
" The test, O King ! is hard ; nor I impute
" Injustice, thus imposing.   Be it so.
" I can but die if need be—if the blow
" Fall fatal, debt of dire necessity :—
" But God's hand rules such issues,—we shall see."
    " Then get ye gone," rejoin'd the King, and rose ;
" The prompt event will prove ye friends or foes.
" But, fail to plough the field, the harvest shun—
" By yon bright orb ! your mortal race is run !   650
" Warning to stripling braggarts, over-bold
" That match themselves with men of stronger mould."

So spoke Æëtes, with scant courtesy;
And Jason took curt leave. But, sad, the eye
And heart of that fair virgin, doubting, seem'd
His parting steps to follow, as if she dream'd.

Argus remain'd behind, as was agreed,
To win his mother's voice to intercede—
And Phrontes too, the younger, whom the maid
Lov'd sister-like, and he the love repaid,   660
Warm, trustful—that she should her power exert
To smoothe the trial, in such arts expert;
And Argus, sending, should by Phrontes' lip
Report th' event to Jason at the ship.

But in her chamber sat Medea, pale
And troubled, questioning her heart:—" What gale
" Of unknown passion is't disturbs my soul?
" Why do my pulses beat, my senses roll
" Confus'dly thus?—That youth too, why so bright
" Stands his sole image still before my sight?   670
" Open or shut mine eyes, or here or there,
" Where'er I turn, the form is everywhere!
" Am I bewitch'd? Is there some subtler spell
" Than mine that masters me? Incredible!
" Yet, not so master'd, what avails my skill
" That cannot rule my sight, my thought, my will?
" Present, he fascinates my thought, my sense;
" Absent, the presence is the more intense.
" I've heard of love—creeping weak mortals o'er;
" But this is pity, pity—nothing more.   680
" Love, and for such as him—love! a mere Greek?
" A son of clay? The thought on't shames my cheek.
" 'Tis pity—and well may pity dim my eye,
" So fair, so graceful, and so young to die!

" For die he must—who could those monsters tame,
" Bend their proud necks, endure their throats of flame ?
" Or, bending, 'scape from the fierce giants' death,
" Or draw unscath'd the watchful dragon's breath ?
"—So young ! not much my elder—yet how wise
" His speech, how temp'rate, reverent his replies !   690
" I saw red anger flush his cheek, yet not
" One word resenting, nor respect forgot.
" Hardly entreated, certés !   How harsh my sire !
" Not his the crime if jealousy and ire
" Of his own Gods have driv'n him to this pass :—
" And I must see him die, and he, alas !
" Deem me consenting— see that noble crest
" Abas'd, unduly match'd—and he a guest,
" Stranger, and suppliant—surely true advis'd
" Son of a God, if not a God disguis'd.   700
" Perchance a mother, sister, wife—but no !
" For such too young—to share with me the woe.
" How they will mourn him—how the thick dust spread
" In mortal anguish on each drooping head !
"—'Twere impious !   Will not Zeus, the suppliants' friend,
" Grace to such suppliant, stranger, guest extend ?
" What punishment perchance attends my sire,
" Thus trampling love and justice 'neath his ire ?
" Would I could intervene—but see not how,—
" How gladly, would but maiden shame allow !   710
"—How hot this air ! how my brain burns ! my tongue,
" Parch'd, I scarce recognise ! "—With that she flung
Her sandals off, and robe, and on her bed
Threw herself, fever'd ; Hypnos o'er her head
Soft hover'd ; and she dream'd that he had come
Upon that venture from his distant home—

Not for the Fleece's, but her own sweet sake,
Her to his father's house his wife to take,—
That she had quell'd the bulls for him; and then
He by her help had slain the armour'd men;   720
But, victor thus, her sire the suit refus'd—
Then, soften'd, said, it should be as she choos'd;
And she elected wife to go with him;
And tears fell anguish'd from that visage grim
Of her fond father—and she woke in tears,
All trembling, throbbing with strange virgin fears;
And, on her elbow rising, gaz'd around
The chamber, like a doe unwitting found
Caught in the toils—already one sharp dart,
Scarce felt for terror, drinking at her heart;   730
Then, struggling from her sleep, sat up; but still
The vision vivid glow'd; till, all her will
Summoning, she drove off th' unwonted spell,
And cried, "O Hecaté! if ever well
"I serv'd thine altar, aid me in this strait;
"'Tis nothing vile, O mother! but some fate
"Impels me—help thy child!"—"Nay, 'tis not love,
"But pity's fancies thus my spirit prove;
"For what to me this youth?—Yet what excuse,
"Thus wet my cheek?—Nay! let him fitting choose 740
"From his own race some fair Greek maid his wife—
"Ah me! But be it so,—my virgin life,
"My father's care, priesthood, suffice for me!
"—But Phrontes, and those brethren, will they free
"Escape my father's ire? And if it fall,
"As fall it will, o'erwhelming one and all,
"Save me, most trusted, in one common lot?
" Would but their mother ask me! I could not,

" So sued, refuse—would I could wake her fears !"
—With that she rose, repressing the hot tears, 750
Open'd her own and sought her sister's door,
The vestibule foot-naked crossing o'er ;
But lifted not the latch, for her cheek burn'd
With shame, and back again in haste return'd,—
Then sought again, but fruitless—thrice it sought ;
Then to her bed crept back, wilder'd, distraught ;
Buried her face i' th' clothes, to shut out day,
And moaning, tossing, there convulsive lay.

Whom saw a little maid, and pitying told
Chalciopé. She counsels manifold 760
Was with her sons debating, how to win
Medea's help ; but, hearing this, rush'd in,
And cried, " Alas ! my child, what hidden grief
" Seeks at thy weeping eyes this sad relief ?
" Ill ? or for me and mine dost sorrow ? Speak ! "
—But she, with blushes dyeing her pale cheek,
No words found answ'ring—" Would that I had died
" Long years since, quitting Æa, Phrixus' bride !
" Or that these luckless strangers ne'er had come,
" Bringing my sons back to this hated home ! " 770
Whereat, as touchwood catches prompt the spark
Struck by the flint, light opening through the dark,
Medea, with timid guile, new hope conceiv'd,—
" Ask'st thou my grief ?—late of thy spouse bereav'd,
" Soon of thy sons to be, if true my dream !
" I saw yon pavement with their hearts'-blood stream,
" Slain by our sire, their fancied treason's meed,—
" Canst wonder that my heart should also bleed ?
" My sons, my sons ! " she sobb'd ; " I fear'd the worst,
" And this is worst !—O child ! if e'er I nurs'd 780

" Thee as an infant, shar'd my mother-breast
" 'Tween thee and Phrontes, whom thou lovest best
" Of all thy brethren, help, O! help us now,
" As help thou canst; or—hear, ye Gods! the vow—
" I, thine Erinnys, and my sons, will be,
" Through life and beyond death, a curse to thee!
" But thou wilt help?"—With that she clasp'd her knees
With both her hands; and, as a sudden breeze
Ruffles twin rose-bushes surcharg'd with dew,
They wept a mingling shower, and closer drew,   790
Embracing each the other; but her face,
Close-press'd, Medea hid, fearing the trace
Read by her sister of her new-born joy;
Then answer'd, " Heav'n best knows if, that dear boy
" To save, and others thine, I saw the way,
" I would by slackness thy tried love repay."

    " Then," said Chalciopé, seeking her eyes,
" Canst thou not give some drug, some art devise,
" That stranger aiding, for my children's sake?
" Nay, himself prays thee, Argus sent to take   800
" Counsel with me, and seek thy fav'ring aid."

    Which hearing, joyous, flushing bright, the maid
Had eager spoke, but checking, frown'd, and pause
Short making,—" Hard the task; nor without cause
" Would I our father anger, as I fear.
" But, if I grant, beware lest should appear
" Aught in thine eyes or action to suggest
" Doubts of our purpose. Send word to the guest
" To meet me near the temple when, withdrawn
" The veil of night, the first ray gleams of dawn;   810
" And I will bring him succour. Mine the care
" The drugs, far-sought, at midnight to prepare."

So said, Chalciopé retir'd ; and straight
Phrontes went to the ship, all to relate
To Jason and the rest. The youths took heart,
Gladden'd, reliev'd ; the seniors no such part
Rejoicing shar'd ; and Peleus said, " Where now
" Our nobler thoughts ? 'Twas base to bend the brow,
" Suppliants, I ween,—'tis wicked to conspire
" With child, trust-forfeiting, against her sire—   820
" Crime to the Gods most hateful. Nemesis
" Will sure avenge it, if we win by this."
     Whom Jason answer'd not, but said, " No more
" Bide we among these reeds, but to the shore
" Row Argo, and moor openly ; lest fright
" Appear to daunt us, lurking from the fight."
Which heard, they row'd to land, and the ship moor'd,
The mooring-lines round a huge stone secur'd.
     And now delusive pity's fond disguise
No more the truth hid from Medea's eyes.   830
She lov'd the youth—but now debate ensued ;
Rather, cool judging, in reaction's mood,
Her promise pledg'd, bitter, unloos'd remorse
Rush'd, unexpected, with a torrent's force,
Whelming her soul with thought of what she must
Down-trample, kept such promise,—breach of trust,
Her father's will defeating—he so kind,
Trust but in her reposing. Strong her mind
Strove 'gainst such thoughts' distraction ; and she saw,
Or seem'd to see, prescrib'd a higher law   840
Than blind obedience—that, her sire to save
From crime, she ought his bitt'rest wrath to brave,
Best serving him.—Could she the means conceal ?
Impossible ; such works themselves reveal—

She must accept the cost.   But then, worse fear
Of misconstruction, Jason now so dear,—
How should she such her action justify
To that calm, resolute, clear-judging eye?
What if he should impute to love the thought,
Mere pity's birth, that to his presence brought?   850
Were such vile doubt to touch her virgin fame,
In his soul imag'd, she would die with shame!
—To bid him come himself—to seek his face,
Not send—bold, shameless, was it not disgrace?
But whom with such instructions' service trust?
Ev'n though he misinterpret, go she must!
" O Artemis! " she cried, " why didst thou not
" In guileless infancy, my happier lot,
" With thy pure arrow me, thy vot'ry, slay?
" Is there, kind Hecaté! no other way   860
" Than my poor sacrifice of heart, of home,
" With ills unnumber'd, well I know, to come?"
" —Nay, let him die, if such his fate, and mine;
" If both thus perish, I shall not repine,
" Surviving not."   But then the thought of guest
Misus'd return'd; and bitter, unrepress'd,
Her tears burst forth.   She wrung her hands, and pac'd
With broken steps the room,—misjudg'd, disgrac'd,
Torn by the bulls, or by the giants grim
Butcher'd, her own hand with them arm'd at him,   870
Preventing not—"No, no!" she cried at last;
" Meet him I will, my promise shall stand fast;
" Coldly will give the drug, say nought, and go
" Away, and bear as best I may my woe.
" What matter if in distant Greece he wed
" Another maid, fit partner of his bed?

" What matter if the Colchian dames to shame
" In songs he ne'er will hear consign my name?
" ' There liv'd a maid in Æa,—little thought
" ' Her blind fond father she unsought—unsought—	880
" ' Love lavish'd on a stranger; she defied
" ' All shame, the wanton, and to save him died.
" ' And he'—no more ! no more !—Nay ! welcome death,
" Sooner than tainted live by such foul breath—
" Short pang, quick ending—and I have the means !' "
	With that she sought within a secret screen's
Recess fell drugs that master human life,
Beneficent well us'd, but now the strife
Of her soul's anguish sought to quell. She laid
These on her knees, and the rich store survey'd ;	890
And a strange calm, exhausted, o'er her crept,
Sweet peace in prospect; and she softly wept,
Pitying herself—so young ; such pleasant hours
As she had pass'd among the birds and flowers
With her girl-friends, companions of her youth,
All passing now away. 'Twas sad, in truth ;
But was not all life sadness ? Why, oh ! why
Had this Greek's coming thus disturb'd her sky
So tranquil late, so passionless serene ;
She o'er her heart's unclouded world a queen ?	900
The sweet warm sunshine she should feel no more ;
And brighter seem'd the sun than e'er before,
Like her, now setting—she of kindred birth ;
And her heart clung to the fond breast of earth,
Thus quitting—wept again—then seiz'd the death
Would quickest, surest, easiest seal her breath.
But Hera sudden a great horror flash'd
Of death upon her, and she loathing dash'd

The poison from her, shudd'ring—all the thought
Of such great loss and crime before her brought—   910
Sober'd as in an instant, instant calm ;
And the kind unseen presence fell like balm
On her vex'd heart, resolv'd.   She firmly trod
The floor, replacing, and her fate to God
Commended, doing what she felt was right ;
And watch'd and pray'd till far into the night.

     Thus, as within a laver, brazen, vast,
Disturb'd, the waters varying shadows cast
On wall and roof of some fair loggia, bright
With sunshine, or the full moon's mellow light ;   920
The shadows undefin'd, uncertain, dance,
Tremulous—now retreat they, now advance—
Perpetual change, nor soon subside to rest :—
So stirr'd the tide tumultuous in the breast
Of that sad maid.   But, as those waters, smooth,
Mirror once more th' unruffled sky of truth,
So the wild waves disturb'd of passion's smart
Subsided o'er the deep sea of her heart ;
And heav'n and earth on that chaste empire met
In clear resolve, on generous purpose set.   930
If some slight lurking hope should fond remain,
Scarce conscious, that her love return might gain,
Who shall condemn ?—Thymœtes ?—Nay, the tongue
Of age deals milder judgments than the young.
Nay, not condemn.   Fate that hour's issue wrought ;
Duty was first, love second in her thought.

THE hours roll'd on, and now 'twas midnight deep,
When sailors watch the timid Bear, and steep
Orion climbs, her threat'ning,—travellers rest;
Earth's human cares lie folded to her breast;
And ev'n the mother of dead sons relief,
Fall'n for their country, findeth from her grief.
No bark of dogs was heard, no living sound,
But silence reign'd below, above, around;

And Day's young majesty and late-born Light
Confess'd, obscur'd, the elder rule of Night.   10
    Then rose Medea and rob'd herself, and fleet,
Gliding, with anxious eyes, with noiseless feet,
The steps descended, through the atrium pass'd,
The vaulted hall, where those starr'd monsters cast
Strange looks as fell her shadow, eyeing her,
Through the black poplars, where no bird did stir,
To Hecaté's dark fane—there, to her cell.
Seven times she wash'd her in the sacred well,
And seven times strove articulate to invoke
Dread Brimo, nor her tongue the stillness broke,   20
Awe-stricken but hopeful; yet her heart spoke loud.
Then, donning a black mantle like a shroud,
She three times stamp'd, and call'd her dragon car;
And the bright dragons, wing'd, came from afar;
And she ascended and to swiftness urg'd,
And, laggard-seeming, them impatient scourg'd,
And they flew swiftly; and she press'd their flight
To that lone cliff where, screen'd from mortal sight,
Prometheus hangs, ent'ring the cloud. The moon
Shone bright within, a brightness as of noon   30
Veil'd by eclipse. Snow-deserts, showing green
In that dimm'd glory, sable depths, were seen,
And pinnacles storm-blasted by the shock
Of Zeus's lightnings frequent. 'Gainst a rock
Rising, i' th' midst, a rugged pyramid,
Chain'd, pierc'd, a mighty form lay stretch'd, but hid
The face from view, motionless. In his side
A wound, the vulture's daily feast, gap'd wide;
And from that wound a stream of ichor, slow
Oozing, dropp'd black upon the earth below.   40

Pale, sad, with hollow eyes and wasted limb,
The Oceanid watch'd for love of him ;
As from far distant days so watch'd she now,
Wiping the sweat that gather'd on his brow.
She to Medea in whisper, like the deep's
Low voice, far heard, said, " Lightly tread ! he sleeps."
   Beneath that rock, born of the gory shower,
A plant grows wondrous, saffron-hued its flower ;
Two stalks uprearing ; but the deep-prong'd root
Shews red, up-torn, like raw flesh newly cut.   50
The juice is black, distilling from the core.
Gods call it ' Savan,' mortals ' Mandragore.'
None such grows else on earth. Its power is great,
Gender'd to work th' unerring ends of Fate.
She, mutt'ring thrice the prayer to Brimo pure,
Bade the thick cloud the curious moon obscure ;
And, grasping the two stalks, the root pluck'd up,
The first gush gath'ring in a golden cup ;
While shudd'ring earth through her deep caverns groan'd,
And that sad suff'rer, quiv'ring, mov'd and moan'd,   60
But woke not. And the watcher said at last,
" Maiden, approach ! That wrench's anguish pass'd,
" Now will he sleep more sound." And she replied,
" O Goddess, loving known ! that last defied
" Zeus, watching here thus steadfast, by thy sire's
" Great mercy sanction'd ! tell him when the fires
" With morn rekindle, how I hop'd to hear
" Once more his voice, to feel his presence near—
" Voice long mine oracle 'twixt guile and truth ;
" Presence most priz'd, now parting from my youth,   70
" Now ent'ring a strange road, without a friend—
" I know not whither borne, or for what end,

" Impell'd by some strange fate.   I cannot tell
" Why, but I know this is my last farewell.
" Give me, O faithful one! his blessing,—he,
" Waking, would give it,—it may profit me."
    " I dare not," said that watcher; " but I know
" This, that the path thou ent'rest on is woe ;
" Yet tread thou must, a minister of Fate,
" A dog of Zeus, to such predestinate,   80
" Thyself the forfeit ; but to win at length
" Truth from thy guile, and from thy weakness strength,—
" Each human pang must undergo, and, worse,
" Unjustly though pronounc'd, thy father's curse ;
" For such with irons hot the Gods in-burn.
" Pray thou it do not on his head return.
" All will be clear to thee beyond the tomb."
" —But Jason"—the maid whisper'd ; " What will come
" Of this our concert ? "   " Misery in his love."   89
" But love me ? " " Yes." " And what fate shall he prove
" Returning, the Fleece won ?   And when shall I—"
—" By Argo, whom he lives by, he shall die.
" Ask not thy proper fate, thy Nemesis.
" Now go.   My blessing on thee, if not his ! "
    Then back to Æa and to Brimo's cell
Return'd Medea, and the oracle
Once more sought, weeping.   " O sweet Mother, speak !
" Unknown my purpose bless'd, blind, wav'ring, weak,
" Ev'n at this last hour, bid me aye or no ! "
And the veil'd presence answer'd, sadly, " Go."   100
    Then, home return'd, she in her chamber bray'd
Between twin stones the mandragore, and made,
With the juice thence and in the cup express'd,
Mixing with drugs that in the secret chest

Garner'd she kept, an unguent of a force
Could drag the stars and planets from their course,
And bend to please her, and that should have power
To shield the champion in the coming hour.

   This done, she bath'd her limbs anew, and wove
Her tresses in a knot that wakens love;   110
And chose her robe most Greek-like, to invest,
Else innocent of art, her throbbing breast;
With long white veil o'er head and shoulders drawn:
And waited longing for the ling'ring dawn.

   But when that bright one, coming from the East,
Outlin'd the mountains, and the glow increas'd,
Medea bade her maidens twelve prepare
Her mules and chariot—by a secret stair
Descending to the basement, whence a door
Gave exit. At her girdle hung, she bore   120
The drug in a gold casket. She, the car
Ascending, seiz'd the reins and whip, and, far
Stretching, she lash'd and urg'd the mules to go;
And they ran swiftly,—yet, in sooth, more slow
Than those twelve fair ones, young, that ran beside,
Sportive like fawns, each with her white robe tied
Up to her knees, for freedom. Artemis,
With her chaste bevy, oft, in guise like this,
Is seen to drive her fleet stags through the glades
Of Mount Cyllené and th' Arcadian shades.   130
Nigh to the temple halting, where a mound,
Tree-shaded, secret, yet gave sight around,
And of the path ascending from the strand,
She 'lighted, and to her maidens gave command:—
" Bide here, and take your pastime 'mong the flowers.
" I go, not without warrant from the powers

" In yon dark fane, and pure Chalciopé
" Thus urging, the Greek stranger's life to free
" From the wild bulls, and from Æëtes' wrath
" Her sons, my brethren.   He by yonder path   140
" Coming, withdraw ; but go not out of view.
"—Be trustful in all this ; or ye will rue ! "
    So blythe those sported.   Some glanc'd in and out
The wood's green lab'rinth, chasing chas'd, with shout
And laughter.   Some sang songs of love or mirth.
Some, lazier, gather'd flow'rs ; or, on the earth
Stretch'd, watch'd the insect world ; or, giddier, ran—
Emulous of th' ambitious quests of man—
After bright butterflies,—oft, in disgrace,
Stumbling o'er roots, and worsted in the race.   150
Thus, resting that pure Goddess, her nymphs play,
The long chace ended, at the close of day.
    But she apart sat watching, and it seem'd
As if her soul, time thus suspended, dream'd ;
Yet, wakeful, each leaf's fall, each distant sound
Startled her ear, and made her quick heart bound.
Fresh, though scarce felt, refreshing still, the breeze
Of the cool morning fann'd her through the trees.
There sitting, the bright Phasian bird o'erhead
Thus to a black crow of the temple said :—   160
" Why are these here ?   Why doth Medea muse
" Thus pensive ?   Why the river-path peruse
" Constant ?—Why dost thou laugh so ?   Dost thou ken ?"
—" She the young Greek expects here."—" And what then ?"
—" What then ! are you so blind ?   When two such meet,
" Love, and heav'n knows what worse, will come of it.
" Go to, you silly bird —gorgeous and bright,
" Yet duller than an owlet !—But aright,

" Sorrow, I see, on her, on him, on all,
" Through this ill-omen'd meeting will befall."   170
    Grieving she heard, yet not without a smile.
The black dogs of the temple came the while,
And fawn'd upon her, and she patted them,
Absently ; and bright glist'ring serpents came,
And lick'd her hand ; and, gliding through the grass,
Would first in stately slow procession pass,
As vassals 'fore their queen ; then lightly shoot
Between her arms, now soft caress her foot,
Now like a girdle twine around her waist ;
Or in and out her long robe, chasing chas'd,   180
Innocent as those maidens, dart ; and, known
A fav'rite, one sat climb'd as on a throne
Her brow upon, and rearing seem'd to say,
" A proud precedence here I hold to-day !"
Cresting defiance.   But he came not—till,
Too long expected, rising o'er the hill,
She saw his form ; and, instant starting, all
Those strange guests fled, as from a festival,
Foes at the gate ; and she her long veil drew
Closer, and arm'd her for the interview.   190
    As over ocean Sirius rises, star
Brightest of heav'n, but baleful, from afar
Distress to mortals bringing, thus did rise
Jason, bright, baleful, on Medea's eyes.
Unarm'd he came, but in his hand he bore
The wand of peace, and on his shoulders wore
A glorious mantle, that Polyxo wove,
Gift of Hypsipylé's first dawn of love.
Eager she rose ; but, calm composure fled,
Her heart sank low, a mist her eyes o'erspread,   200

Blushes her cheek ; nor forward nor retreat
Serve would her trembling knees, her rooted feet ;
And all her purpos'd words she straight forgot,
Blank, like a schoolboy's lesson learnt by rote.
    Meanwhile those maids discreetly had retir'd,
Not out of sight but distant, as requir'd.
But these—as, rooted near, two cypresses,
Rock-born, kind-will'd, converse not till the breeze
Rising provokes their love—so these two stood
Motionless, mute ; she with the pent up flood   210
Of thoughts embarrass'd ; he expecting her
First to begin, cool, wary not to err,
Her bent untried. But, silence keeping still,
As from the pressure of some infelt ill—
She young and bashful, never perchance yet
With such as him on such high counsel met—
Time for self-mast'ry willing to afford,
He pitied and first spoke, in courteous word :—
    " Why hast thou sought to speak with me alone,
" Fair princess ? Young, but wise in counsel known, 220
" I am not one by youth's conceits impell'd,
" But, trusted, have with Gods communion held.
" Then blush not, fear not. By thyself I swear,
" And by the Goddess dread who dwelleth there—
' For this place holy is, and word of guile
" Or ill intent may not my lips defile—
" I seek this land and thus embrace thy knee,
" Suppliant, in Fate's enforc'd necessity,
" Save by thine aid unequal to the task.
" Such thou hast promis'd, and I humbly ask,   230
" And will requite by gratitude, receiv'd,
" As suits our diverse spheres—thy meed, achiev'd,

" Glory from Greece. My comrades in their songs
" Shall voice such virtue, and barbaric tongues
" Beyond bright Hellas celebrate thy praise.
" The wives and mothers that wear out their days
" On the drear sea-beach sitting, watching for
" Return of those they fear to greet no more,
" Shall bless thee saving—if, indeed, thy grace
" Give us, with joy return'd, to see their face.   240
" Thus Ariadné, daughter bright of Crete,
" Her father grudging, guided Theseus' feet
" To slay the Minotaur, and with him fled,
" The Gods approving,—such too credited
" Thy guerdon, the world's praise, if thou too lend
" Thy wit to guide, thy favour to befriend."
  She, with droop'd eyelids list'ning, sweetly smil'd,
By the soft subtle flattery beguil'd ;
Then look'd up to his eyes, intent to speak,
Which cold, self-centred, chill'd again her cheek ;   250
Then, child-like, rallying from her hope's eclipse,
Such jealous guard ! essay'd, but from her lips
No words would come ; so, simply, in his hand
Plac'd the rich casket ; and, with that, command
Surrender'd of all terms, all self-reserve,
Save of pure modesty. He, every nerve
Quiv'ring with secret joy, receiv'd. She fix'd
On his her eyes, where speaking love commix'd
With maiden shame entreated, wishing strong
Him hers, her his, to bind, though tied her tongue—   260
Scarce conscious so entreating, wishing ; he
Felt, but resisted, fearing what might be
That occult drawing ; and dishearten'd, pain'd,
She spoke at last, in accents clear, constrain'd :—

" Misconstrue not my presence, son of Greece !

" Fate's warrant mine to win for thee the Fleece ;

" Thus acting, my sire's friend, Zeus fearing, lest

" Unduly match'd, unjustly slain, a guest.

" Return'd, send to the palace to require

" The dragon's teeth, Cadmeian, from my sire.   270

" Receiv'd the teeth, do thou at midnight hour,

" When the Great Gods of nether earth have power,

" In living waters wash'd, in black array'd,

" Dig a deep circling trench, and having pray'd,

" There immolate an ewe, and, on a pyre

" Built in the trench, burn bleeding and entire ;

" And to the Mighty Mother, Brimo, pour

" Honey, appeaseful, the sweet off'ring o'er ;

" Then turn thy back, nor let the sound of feet

" Or barking dogs arrest thy prompt retreat,—   280

" Thy life the forfeit, loit'ring.   In the morn,

" When griefs to man with waking light return,

" Thou with this unguent helmet and spear-point,

" Thy sword, thy shield, and each thy limb anoint,

" Invulnerable dower'd, with strength immense,

" A God's not more, that not the bulls' offence,

" Their flaming breath, dragg'd struggling to the yoke,

" Nor multiplied the teeth-born giants' stroke,

" Shall hurt thee.   But in no wise stint from fight ;

" Its virtue lasts but between dawn and night.   290

" Yet more,—the bulls well yok'd and plough'd the field,

" When the sown teeth the giant harvest yield,

" They rushing on thee, fling unseen a stone

" Among them : they will leave thee unharm'd, alone,

" And slay each other—then press on and slay ;

" And thou shalt carry hence the Fleece that day—

" Go where you will—if you indeed will go ! "
—With that the pent-up tears would overflow,
Grieving that he should sail away, far o'er
The dreary sea, never to see him more.   300
Then, taking his right hand, for shame had left
Her cheek, betray'd thus, nigh of hope bereft,
But wishing strong, she went on,—" Say, at least,
" By me befriended in thy need, distress'd,
" Thy heart shall record keep of me, albeit
" In distant lands, keep in remembrance sweet—
" Slight such the recompense—yet swear to me ;
" As I, O Jason ! will remember thee !
" And tell me, where thy household Gods ? the strand
" Ye tend to ? rich Orchomenos ? the land   310
" Hesperian ?   And of Ariadné, late
" Beprais'd by thee as minister of fate,
" And lov'd in Hellas,—this was not her gift ?
" Thou signest nay—but, to compel thy shrift,
" Tell me, scarce pardon'd, hast thou wife, or spouse
" Virgin-betroth'd, expectant, in thine house ?
" That I may love her sister-like, and send,
" If such there be, the greeting of a friend."
     Falt'ring she spoke ; and, not unmov'd, replied
Jason :—" No wife have I, nor promise-tied   320
" Virgin at home, expectant of my bed.
" My home, Iölcos,—there the reverend head
" Of my sire Æson, and my mother, fair
" Alcimedé, lament me, absent ; there
" Dwell the strong Minyæ, strong in wealth's increase—
" The land Æmonia, fairest land of Greece.
" Deem not I shall forget thee, safely stemm'd
" This adverse tide, nor to worse proof condemn'd.

" The Greeks are grateful, and, thus succour'd here,

" I have most cause to hold thy memory dear,—   330

" Such succour through all coming time a grace

" To me and mine, and all th' Æolid race.

" Of Ariadné—never seen of me—

" I know nought, save that, left in Naxos, she—

" By no pledg'd marriage-bond to Theseus tied—

" Became, there found, great Dionysus' bride.

" Happier, had Minos timely compact made

" With that his guest, nor thus himself betray'd,

" Furth'rer of heav'n's high purpose, 'gainst his will.

" So too thy sire had 'scap'd this present ill,   340

" Example ta'en,—but thus rule Zeus and Fate."

    " Talk not to me of compacts ! "—quick, irate,

Eyes flashing, instant shadow'd ; and, with voice

Broken, continuing, spoke she :—" Not rejoice

" The Fates, such ord'ring ; nor of guest nor host

" Speak me—not such Æëtes—unlike most

" I Ariadné,—loving, lost, betray'd,

" Poor innocent, to give such traitor aid !

" Nor such guest thou ; the parallel holds not,—

" Unjust the thought.   Only, be not forgot   350

" My service done—I will remember thee,

" True, gentle, gracious—O ! remember me !

" —Forgetting—ah ! that some swift bird may bring

" Such word of sorrow on its storm-bound wing ;

" That storm shall bear me back on its cold breath

" To mind thee how by me thou 'scapedst death,

" A living accusation to thine eyes—

" Me, the poor maiden thou wilt then despise ! "

    With that, anguish'd, worn out, heart-dead as stone,

Wishing no longer, for all hope was gone,   360

She clasp'd her hands across her eyes, to hide
The light; but through that floodgate the prison'd tide
Of grief would out, of crush'd hopes, quicken'd fears
Of his soon parting, miserable tears;
And he was human, after all; and took
Her hand, and conquer'd by that passion spoke;
For youth in him and wish in her prevail'd
To prompt the vow, and calmer prudence fail'd :—
" Nay, sweet! thy words are naught.   If e'er thou come
" To fair Iölcos, my Thessalian home,   370
" Honour'd thou shalt be, surely, by all Greece,
" Owning thy gift, attain'd, the glorious Fleece;
" But I, thy debtor most, such purpose sped,
" Will hail thee wife, with thee will share my bed,
" Harmonia's gift, and cherish ever and aye,
" Loving, be Hera witness! till I die."
    Such heard, believing scarce, lifting her eyes,
His seeking with a bright unfledg'd surprise,
And reading there true purpose, her soul rush'd
Home from far distance, and the hot blood flush'd   380
Cheek, brow, neck, bosom; and her eyes suffus'd
With tears, but sweetest drops, thus disabus'd
Of fears and hopes at once in certain bliss,—
Nor, melted all, had scrupled, upon this
Sure cov'nant stricken, to have fled at once,
Had he but ask'd it, with him, in response ;
But that those maidens, fearing for the time
Elapsing, great the risk and known their crime
Thus privy, forward came, though tim'rous, bold ;
And Jason, cautious, his new wish controll'd   390
Of converse, urg'd :—" Such sweetest compact seal'd,
" Part we, lest this our meeting be reveal'd

" To envious eyes, and to thy sire made known."
—So parted they—he to the ship alone—
She with her maids, they prescient sad of ill,
Returning; but her soul went with him still.
He paus'd oft, going, musing, half in scorn
Blaming himself, beyond fix'd purpose borne,
Repentant half of that ill-omen'd plight,
But glad of present comfort 'gainst the fight;   400
Nor, strangely heart-mov'd, wish'd his word effac'd,
Though such step taken could not be retrac'd.
She, reach'd her chamber, greeted anxious, heard
Her sister's words but answer'd not, nor stirr'd,
On the low footstool sitting; for thoughts roll'd
O'er her heart's sea, confus'd and manifold,
Till her brain reel'd—most, what her father stern
Might say or do, should he the secret learn,—
Stirr'd not; and, but for now and then a moan,
Seem'd a pale image, mourning, carv'd in stone.   410
As when the waves, breast-heav'd, not breaking, swell,
And dark th' horizon glooms round, terrible,
One white bird only, floating, dimly seen—
Such Jason's love those dark'ning cares between.
She rose at length, and with one strong embrace
Her wond'ring sister clasp'd, and kiss'd her face;
Then on her bed exhaustion's slumber slept,
Which the kind Hours long, calm, and dreamless kept.
    Reach'd Argo, Jason the rich casket show'd
Exulting, passport for their homeward road,   420
Winning the Fleece; but, sham'd, kept unreveal'd
The compact with the maid of marriage seal'd.
Idas apart sat gloomily, nor voic'd
His discontent; the others, most, rejoic'd.

But Telamon, by Jason's order, and
Sacred Æthalides, with Hermes' wand,
Herald of Kings, up to the palace went
To crave the dragon's teeth; and the King sent
Gladly, as certain they his death ensur'd
Ev'n were the wild bulls' fiery breath endur'd.   430

    Thus pass'd the day's long hours. Oppression reign'd
On all their hearts, and mirth's relief restrain'd.
But, when the night deep darken'd, and the Bear
Declining slop'd in heav'n, and the still'd air
Slept in the vast profound, and in repose
His comrades lay, Jason, long watching, rose;
And, Argus question'd, answer render'd, brief,
Through those dank alders ghastly, like a thief,
Stole; and round-glancing, anxious, climb'd the hill
To a place desert, there, lone, to fulfil   440
The rites to Hecaté. The ewe he found,
Which Argus, leading, to a stump had bound.
All was dead silence. A dull stream flow'd down,
Living, but with black leaves of poplar, brown
With death's decay, thick cover'd. Wash'd therein
Seven times, and rob'd in black, man's shroud of sin,
He, cubit-broad, dug the round trench, and slew
On wood pil'd altar-wise the sable ewe,
And fir'd the pile, and milk and honey pour'd
Grateful, and triform Hecaté ador'd,   450
Praying,—retreated then, nor look'd behind.
And Brimo, hearing, came. With oak-leaves twin'd,
A crown hung o'er her head; but, save her eyes
Dark-glowing, scarce was seen. The blighted skies
Clouded themselves,—darkness fell over all,
Deeper than night, creation's funeral pall;

But torches here and there like lightnings play'd,
And the black dogs incessant bark'd and bay'd ;
While quaking, groaning, heaving, the vex'd earth
Disgorg'd herself of some vast monstrous birth,   460
Which, circling all, rose up in spires convolv'd,
In substance part, in vapour more resolv'd,
And, like the wild-vine rampant, knotting clung,
The trees embrac'd, and hideous overhung,
Emitting sounds so undefin'd, so drear,
The black dogs' howling died away in fear ;
The waves of Phasis shudd'ring fled the shore,
And Ocean's daughter heard th' infernal roar.
Jason, with stagg'ring feet and ashen'd lip,
Fled panting, stumbling, till he reach'd the ship.   470
His comrades comforted.   Thus pass'd the night,
Till hopes more cheerful came with morning light.

How do the soul's dark terrors roll away
With the bright blessing of returning day !
Sweet day, bright sun, that glowing hope impart,
Dispel pale doubt, and fortify the heart !
When Helios shines, our thoughts and spirits rise ;
When clouds obscure, firm purpose droops or dies.
Such tides, being human, even heroes know,
And own, with us, alternate ebb and flow.   480

Thus, when sweet Eös, ris'n from Ocean's fount,
Fresh, dewy, climb'd the Amaranthian Mount,
And Helios following in her track appear'd,
These thought no more of what they late had fear'd,
But from each lip light mirth and laughter broke,
Jubilant, nor of aught but conquest spoke.

Beyond the city, far as is the space
'Tween starting-point and goal i' th' chariot-race,

A dead king honour'd, lies a grassy plain,
Sacred to Ares,—fallow kept from grain,   490
Four acres there the hero's task to plough.
Æëtes rose, dark triumph on his brow,
And arm'd himself.   His breastplate Ares gave
When he slew Mimas in Phlegræa's cave.
His four-con'd helmet lightnings shot; but on
The vast orb'd sevenfold shield a blazing sun
The eye confounded, pictur'd bright,—his spear,
Save Heracles', no mortal arm might rear.
His son Absyrtus held the chariot fair,
Gold-wheel'd, and steeds, that snuff'd the morning air, 500
Tossing their heads; and he, ascending, took
The reins and lash'd them, and their trampling shook
Earth to her centre.   Through the streets he drove,
With " Follow all ! " and urg'd, bending above.
Thus, arm'd, thus strong, from Ægæ's crystal dome,
Mounting his chariot, o'er the ocean foam
Poseidon, giver of life, the fresh, the free,
Drives the sea-horses, Tyrant of the Sea.
Pure Amphitrité sits beside the King,
Tritons and sea-nymphs follow gambolling;   510
While Nereus mourns his superseded reign,
His subjects swelling the Olympian's train.
For Gods to Gods as men to men succeed,
And victors these to-day to-morrow bleed.
   Meanwhile did Jason each his limb anoint,
His sword, his shield, his helmet, and spear-point,
Invulnerable thus; and strength immense
Came to him therewith.   Strong Idas, in offence,
Hew'd at his naked limbs, his armour tried
By blow on blow, which harmless glanc'd aside.   520

And as a high-born charger, haughty, fierce,
Whinnies and paws the ground; his keen eyes pierce
Heav'n, earth, with transport, longing for a foe,
Tossing his mane, his ears erecting; so
Jason exulted, hew'd the air, with shout
Defiant, lofty pacing, as about
To leap to heaven; or watch'd complacently
His image in the river that glided by :—
Foolish! to credit his, in pride's display,
Strength not his own, nor lent but for a day!   530
But who of us in youth's vain prime have not
Split on such rock? So be the prank forgot.

Then, sitting on the benches, swift they row'd
Past Æa, up the river, to the broad
Plain of dark Ares, landing; and the King
Receiv'd them; and to heav'n the clamouring
Of multitudes innumerous rose, like bees
Of Hybla clust'ring, on the rough rocks these
Seated of Caucasus, the plain around.
Close by their landing-place a rocky mound   540
Rose from the river, rifted, rough to climb,
Tufted with shrubs, sweet myrtle, fragrant thyme,
Conspicuous from the plain. That climbing, all
Sat watching, as at some strange festival
Unbidden guests,—whiling by speech or song
Th' expectant hour; and, hearing the soft tongue
Pelasgian, out o' the clefts bright lizards came,
List'ning, heads bent aside, well-pleas'd and tame.
Blue sky o'erhead, warm sun,—a fresh breeze blew;
On one side Amaranthus topp'd the view;   550
On t'other the vast Euxine smooth out-roll'd,
Unbroken by a sail, dreary and cold.

Conspicuous thus, the dusky Colchians gaz'd
At their strong limbs, their careless grace, amaz'd.
  Now Jason, naked, took his spear and shield,
His sword back-slung, and forward on the field
Went, seeking the wild bulls,—he bore the teeth
In a bronze helm, the harvest doom'd of death.
The fallow space he found, lists for the fight;
The teeth laid down; and fix'd his spear upright   560
Beside, that ready lay, the brazen yoke
And iron plough compact; then, to provoke
The bulls, fierce shouted; they from their dark caves
Came rushing, bounding, like the ocean waves,
But fire for foam forth-breathing. Like a rock
Breasting the torrent, he withstood the shock,
His shield opposing, back repuls'd in scorn
Their jaws' red terror and their iron horn.
As when Hephæstus wakes Mosyclos' fires,
And, lab'ring strong, the bellows' life inspires,   570
The dormant embers red rekindle first;
Then, plied more urgent, fierce and fiercer burst
Of flame forth belches, and the furnace roars,
And Athos hears it and the Mysian shores;
So fierce the flames belch'd from those bulls' red maw,
Roaring, that all men held their breath with awe;
Swallowing up Jason seem'd they, every limb,
Like lightnings' blaze, yet could not injure him.
Then by the nearer horn each bull to seize,
Drag to the plough, and force him to his knees,   580
A moment serves—resisting, but compell'd
Breathless, by such assault confounded, quell'd.
Then the Tyndaridæ, come close behind,
Fit the strong yoke and to each strong neck bind,

Attach the iron plough, and thence with fleet
Steps, the flame fearing, to the rock retreat.
O'er his broad shoulders flinging now the shield,
The twin bulls harness'd, Jason plough'd the field,
With his spear goading,—snorting, they puff'd flame,
Indignant, but soon yielded, going tame ;   590
And following, as the furrows clean he cleft,
The dragon seed he threw to right and left ;
And the strong bulls, their brass hoofs planting deep,
Lab'ring, did steady pace and equal keep,
Till, three parts of the day the sun's course run,
The ploughing of the acres four was done.
Then glad he loos'd the bulls, and with a shout
Terrified ; and, like birds escaping out
A shaken bush, they fled, in utter fright,
Home to their caves, and shrouded them in night.   600
    Then Jason, seeing as yet the furrows bare
Of harvest, slow retrac'd his steps to where
His comrades sat, and with his helm cool drew
Water to drink,—then on the green bank threw
His limbs in lazy ease ; but his soul long'd
For battle, as a boar, by hunters throng'd,
Whets his tusks, foams, and glares with blood-red eyes,
Impatient of the covert where he lies.
    But, horrent, soon above the fresh-sown plain
Began to bud and shoot the dragon grain,   610
Shot up in blade and ear, as giants grim,
With helm, greaves, breast-plate armour'd every limb,
And sword and spear ; full-grown they were, and fierce ;
Their bright arms' flashing coruscations pierce
The golden skies. Ev'n as at night, when snow
Has whiten'd the broad waste of earth below,

And winds have clear'd the heav'n, spark after spark,
Star after star bursts brilliant through the dark ;
So these sprang up from earth,—and, minding well
Medea's word, throughout his oracle,   620
A vast round stone Jason upheaving flung
The gath'ring host of grisly monsters 'mong,
Then crouch'd behind his shield ; and they the war,
Blinded, infatuate, as all giants are,
Address'd each 'gainst the other, and sword plied
And spear relentless, each a fratricide.
They fell like oaks by storms uptorn and riv'n.
Then, as a meteor darts athwart the heav'n,
Furrowing th' expanse, a portent dire to men,
So Jason rush'd, like panther from his den,   630
On that vile crew, and slew them as they fought ;
Others by earth as yet but half out-brought,
Or shoulder-high, mow'd he like poppies down ;
Till, like a field of grain, Demeter's crown,
Laid, broken, by fierce hail—peasant and lord,
Beholding, in one common grief accord—
So lay that giant harvest, reap'd in death,
Not one surviving to draw sentient breath,—
So griev'd Æëtes ; but the Greeks with pride
Shouted and joy, till Caucasus replied   640
In echoes, which the winds far-wafting bore
To distant Halys and the Pontic shore.
All home return'd now, with the setting sun,—
The day was ended, and the fight was won.
    But, like a mountain torrent, swoll'n by rains,
That downward rushing scarce its bank contains,
Æëtes' mind roll'd turbid, troubled, bent
To crush the Greeks and frustrate their intent,—

R

Marv'lling by what God's favour, whence the skill
Had quench'd in naught his meditated ill.   650
Not on Medea, the cherish'd of his heart—
Such doubt could never in his breast have part
Nor on Chalciopé, submissive known—
But Phrixus' sons, Greek-born, on them alone
Fasten'd his thought; and with his council late
Held he thereon, and how to act, debate, —
What sterner trial he should next impose,
Price of the Fleece, to rid him of his foes.

    Such council sitting, pale Medea heard,
And all her soul with conscious terror stirr'd ;   660
Whom Hera, Fate's will known and Jason dear,
Fill'd with distrust and sudden blighting fear
That, the late meeting by her maids reveal'd,
Her guilt was blazon'd and her doom was seal'd,—
Doubtless to die in torments on the morn,
Her sire's stern sentence, and her people's scorn.
And, as a spark dropp'd in dry grass will glide
From blade to bush, from bush to tree, till wide
The forest blazes, so conviction stole
On her till mast'ring dread possess'd her soul,   670
No force to reason with her terror left,
Of strength, of calm, almost of sense bereft.
Thus the fawn trembling in the copsewood lies,
And feels ere the dogs' gripe death's agonies.
Her eyes with flashing light were fill'd, her ears
With sounds, the echoed discord of her fears.
Shudd'ring, the locks she open'd where her hoard
Of drugs potent for death and life were stor'd,—
But Hera whisper'd inwardly, " Nay ! fly,
" With Phrontes, Argus, to another sky ;   680

" Argo awaits thee,"—and her vanish'd guest,
Hope, sweet return'd, and she reclos'd the chest,—
Yet sweet with bitter mix'd so in the cup,
Seem'd almost worse than death to drink it up.
Weeping, she kiss'd her bed, the walls, and twain
The door-posts of her chamber, pure domain
Of peace, now lost, where fresh from childhood's hour
Her heart had blossom'd like an unseen flower;
And, loosing the long tresses of her hair,
Cut off one lock, golden, and left it there,   690
For her lone mother's heart, of days gone by
Memorial sad, and her virginity.
" Take this, my mother! this is all," she cried,
" Now lives of me! Would that yon guest had died,
" Prey of the billows, ere this evil day!
" Forget me not when I am far away!"
Then, her long veil around her wrapp'd, affright
Blanching her cheek, she went into the night—
With naked noiseless feet, stole like a ghost
Through the hush'd palace; her long tresses, tost,   700
Stream'd in the night-wind,— gates and bars oppos'd
Spontaneous open'd and behind her clos'd;
And, holding up her robe for speedier pace,
Her veil drawn close to hide her eyes and face,
She sped on, running, through the narrow ways;
And the moon shone on her, and in dispraise
And spite address'd :—" Not only I, it seems,
" Seek love at Latmos, where Endymion dreams!
" How oft, thou vixen! hast thou dimm'd my light,
" Seeking to wake him—banish'd from thy sight   710
" By numbered verses, binding, witching staves,
" Questing thy noxious weeds 'mong dead men's graves!

R 2

" Seek thine Endymion, wanton one, and find —
" 'Tis thy turn now—how callous, cold, unkind !
" Thou, dog of Zeus ? I spit at thee—begone ! "
But, heeding not the scoff, she hurried on,
And, reaching the steep verge of the descent
Down to the river, saw the smoke up-sent
By the wan'd watchfire where the ship was moor'd ;
And three times, in a voice but ill assur'd,   720
Cried, " Phrontes, Phrontes, Phrontes ! " and the youth
Heard, and the Minyans, and they guess'd the truth,
Some evil pending.   Jason from the stern,
Argus and Phrontes, leapt, intent to learn
The tidings; climb'd the hill ; and she, the knees
Of Jason clasping, " Save me ! " cried ; " the breeze
" Of fate blows adverse—all is known—my sire
" Counsels to slay ye, Argo burn with fire—
" The dawn the signal.   Fly then swift to Greece !
" I will myself this instant give the Fleece,   730
" Lulling the dragon.   But, O Jason ! thou
" Make Gods and men first privy to thy vow,
" Nor shame me, kin-bereft, all for thy sake ! "
—With that her right hand he with his did take,
Affiance pledg'd, and tenderly up-rear'd,
Pitying, she crouching at his feet, affear'd
As of some savage beast.   He calm'd her dread,
And swore anew, and sooth'd and comforted,
Hera and Zeus attesting.   They return'd
Swift to the shore, where the faint watch-fire burn'd,   740
And row'd, the maid directing, to the bank
Counter of Phasis.   Through the sedges dank
He and Medea, mounting, took the road
To Ares' grove, the dragon's dark abode ;

And reach'd the open space, flowery and green,
Where the ram lighted,—near was, ruin'd, seen
The stone-built altar where, by Hermes' word,
Meeting him, Phrixus sacrificing pour'd
To Zeus Laphystius the atoning blood :—
Thence, the maid leading, enter'd deep the wood,   750
And saw the Fleece, hung the vast oak upon,
Like a cloud redden'd by the rising sun.
But the huge dragon, sleepless, fierce, gray-ey'd,
Heard their quick steps, the maiden's form espied,
Hiss'd, and uprear'd, coil'd, tow'ring spire o'er spire,
Like smoke that soars up, culming higher and higher,
Wood smould'ring moist, upvortic'd from below,—
His dry scales crackled, dire his eyeballs' glow,
Menacing, fearful.   But Medea a song,
Lulling and sweet, and adjuration strong   760
To Hypnos chanting and to Hecaté,
Went forward to the monster fearlessly,
Whose gyres late tow'ring sank subdued, but roll'd
In orbs like chains still round the guarded gold.
He, struggling, strove to raise his head and cranch
Those twain, his spoilers ; but with new-cut branch
Of juniper she touch'd his head, and cast
Spells slumb'rous on his eyes ; and sleep at last
Conquer'd, and her low chanting, strong to bind ;
And he lay lengthwise stretch'd, those orbs untwin'd,   770
Like some tall pine that late the sceptre held
Of Pontus' sylvan hills, by woodman fell'd.
    Then Jason, by her mandate, straight took down
The Fleece ; and she the dragon's head and crown
Of crested pride steep'd with the drug of power,
Potent to keep him slumb'ring many an hour.

Jason, exultant, warily retir'd;
And light shone round him from the Fleece, that fir'd
The trees and coverts, and the forest path,
Flashing like eye of lion in his wrath.   780
Large as a stag's or yearling bull's the hide.
He silent strode, but sad the maid beside,
Unequal pac'd.   Now from his shoulders hung,
Now 'cross his breast the glitt'ring spoil he flung,
With both hands grasping, lest some envious God
Should seek to rob him of the precious load.
Near'd Argo, joyful those the maiden saw
With Jason swift approaching; and with awe,
Mingled with joy, beheld the glorious Fleece.
But first spoke Jason :—" Brothers, this increase,   790
" Crown of our venture, guerdon of our strife,
" We owe this maiden.   Know her for my wife
" Affianc'd,—henceforth to your trust approv'd,
" All ye her brethren, as a sister lov'd,—
" All Greece her debtor—most her debtors we,
" By her sole aid achiev'd the victory.
" And now behoves, no ling'ring, straight to fly,
" Swift, the wind fav'ring and our oars, this sky
" Hostile and strange ; for soon the King must know
" The quest achiev'd, and who hath dealt the blow.   800
" Then hoist the sail at once, and let us start ;
" The prize is scarcely ours till we depart ;
" And soon will Eös greet us from the East.
" Choice is 'tween flight and loss,—quick, choose the best ;
" One way or other, ours is certain fame —
" Won, lasting glory ; lost, eternal shame."
    He urg'd, but on the Fleece the elders sad
Gaz'd, earn'd unworthy ; while the youths were glad,

And sought to touch, to feel, to wear; but now
Desisted, and address'd themselves to row,   810
And the sail hoisted, and keen Eurus blew,
And swiftly o'er the dusk wave Argo flew,
Fresh'ning and fresh'ning ever more the wind,
And long ere dawn left that strange world behind.
Thus, coming like a thief, like thieves they bore,
Still under night, the Fleece from Æa's shore.

But in the stern that maiden sad they plac'd,
Under Ancæus' care—a flower that grac'd
That high seat well; and a new influence stole
O'er those rough warriors and subdued their soul;   820
Rev'rent they lov'd, nor ever word would speak
To shame the virgin roses of her cheek;
And gentler grew their voices; and their aid
Waited, as brothers, constant on the maid.
But most with sage Ancæus, and with those
The elders, convers'd she at evening's close,—
Most with Ancæus, nearer-kinn'd in thought,
In race, and lore in lands barbarian taught;
And when at times her heart grew lone and chill,
She felt a sire's protection round her still.   830

Meanwhile the sun had ris'n, the day grew bright,
Before the maids perceiv'd their mistress' flight.
The news spread quick, and soon was likewise known
That Argo and the Minyan chiefs were gone;
And worse, no longer through the forest leaves
The Fleece shone glitt'ring— who but they the thieves?
Æëtes heard, but scoffing at the thought
His daughter privy, straight her chamber sought,
And found that tress, with those sad tears bedew'd;
And then the bitter truth he understood.   840

Big sobs broke struggling, but he stern controll'd,
And sought the roof's high vantage, to behold
If still in sight that Argo. With him went
Absyrtus. Scanning the wide waste, intent,
He saw the mast-head, and hope's curtain fell,
And wrath rush'd o'er him, fierce and terrible :—
" Arm all, and man the ships, my thousands ! scour
" The seas," he cried, " pursue, strike down, devour
" Those wolves, those felons, following on their track ;
" And, dead or living, bring my daughter back,   850
" Your lives else forfeit !—Fool'd, betray'd, beguil'd,
" Ye Gods ! ye Gods ! how I have loved that child !
" O Nature, prodigal of miracles !
" Match this—my flesh against my flesh rebels !
" Smooth traitress ! yester-morn she kiss'd my cheek—
" At night, vile harlot of a lying Greek,
" She robs, flies, mocks at me !   Break, break, my heart !
" I never knew till now how tough thou art !
" O thou foul toad ! be this thy guile a womb
" Of frauds and treasons through all days to come;   860
" Thy lust's fond food to poison—dog thy door
" With terrors—alienate thy paramour—
" Steel thine own hand against thy flesh and blood—
" To die an outcast, by their ghosts pursued !
" On all that love or converse with thee blight
" Fall deadly—blasting and eternal night !
" Him most "—But here Absyrtus cried, " Recall
" Thy words, my sire ! thou know'st not where they fall !
" Shake not the urn—let Zeus dispose the lot."
—" My curse on thee too if thou curse her not ! "   870
Rejoin'd the King :—" Thou wilt not ?   Art thou too
" Rebel against me ?   I will not undo

" The web I have woven.   Go, thou badge of woe !
" How have I joy'd to see those tresses flow
" Wantoning round her bright head—wanton prov'd,—
" Oh God ! that such so fondly I have lov'd !
" Fly on the winds, thou golden tress ! each hair
" To bind her heart with anguish and despair
" To an unpitied rock of penitence,
" Prometheus-like, but without hope from thence   880
" Peace to work out by noble suffering !
" Fly hence, and round her with my curses cling !
" O Father Helios ! scorch her head by day !
" O Moon, her counsels to her foes betray !
" O Water, wash not out her sins !   O Wind,
" Blow not away—no scape-goat may she find !
" Shake off, O Earth ! her footsteps, that she have
" No home in life—deny her corpse a grave !
" And thou, Oceanus ! when to thy breast
" She sues in death, receive not to thy rest !   890
" When she returns by the old paths, and seeks
" Th' Eternal Lights, may no breeze fan her cheeks,
" Sweet and refreshing ; when she nears thy throne,
" May no bright form her life's pure image own,
" Waiting as escort, for thy grace to plead,
" Her life's embodied thought, and word, and deed ;
" But a foul beldam, burning with the fire
" Of wasted life's unsatisfied desire,
" Accuse her at thy footstool, bow'd with shame,
" And with her sink whelm'd in that gulf of flame !   900
—" O son, true heart ! those tears that wet my cheek
" Belie my words—'tis Fate, not I that speak."
    He fell convuls'd ; and tenderly the youth
Uprais'd and comforted, though known the truth,

Himself, not cursing, by those words accurs'd ;
And such, thus utter'd, hop'd he not revers'd.
But he accepted duteous ; and the King
Oceanus receiv'd the offering,
Allow'd the curse ; but, secret understood
His own deep counsels, overrul'd to good.   910

MEANWHILE those fugitives their straight course held
Across the gulf, by Eurus' breath impell'd,
And reach'd red Halys' banks on the third day,—
There to dread Hecaté due rites to pay,
Medea's behest, appeaseful.   What those were,
Mysterious, veil'd, the Muse may not declare.

But, gath'ring swift, Æëtes' ships went forth,
Seeking the maid, Absyrtus tow'rds the North,
Others to Ister's mouth ; and some pass'd through
Symplegades, and wander'd far.   But few   10

Returned to Æa, where their master kept
Watch constant on the lofty roof, and wept.
   That East-wind fallen, on th' ensuing morn
The Minyans started, rowing, thus to turn
Sinopé's point and Syrias, and retrace
Their path of venture to its starting-place ;
But, like a hound escaping from the slip,
Or horse, his teeth seizing the bit, the ship
Shot off spontaneous, prescient of Fate's will,
The vex'd air whistling in her cordage shrill,   20
Nor halted till the dreaded Tauric coast
Of Scythian Artemis, unkindly host,
They reach'd, breath-distanc'd, and within a bay
Rocky, secluded, 'neath the temple lay.
   On one side o'er them tower'd a rock, cut smooth
By human art, scor'd o'er with lines, uncouth
Seeming at first, sinuous, irregular :—
A stately king presided, in a car
Fair sculptur'd, rob'd in purple and in gold ;
And soon they knew, below his feet unroll'd,   30
Rivers and spreading gulfs, and hill, and plain,
Long winding shores and towns of living men,
Pictur'd, with rows of sacred signs, like strings ;
While, highest, the rock projecting spread her wings
Roof-like, from rains to guard the subject scene.
All wonder'd, doubting, hope and fear between ;
And sought Ancæus' eye, from him to learn,
So Phineus spoke, the law of their return.
And Argus said :—" Ere yet the signs of heaven
" Were fully known, or heritage was given   40
" Of fair Pelasgia to Deucalion's brood—
" While, elder than the moon, th' Arcadians rude

" Eat acorns on Cyllené—rich and great,
" Egyptian Thebes by Nile's fat waters sat ;
" And sent her kings throughout the world to find
" New realms as vassals to her wheels to bind,—
" Her greatest imag'd there.   Superb he came,
" Lighting his path with ruin and with flame ;
" Crush'd Scythia, Asia ; then, like whirlwind's blast,
" Away for ever into darkness pass'd,--   50
" Left but a handful here, to garrison
" The transient empire that his arms had won,
" Sires of the dusky Colchians, meek that now
" 'Neath stern Æëtes and his sceptre bow.
" Tablets like these he carv'd in many a spot,
" Tarrying,—their import we conjecture not."
—" But that," rejoin'd Ancæus, " I know well,
" Thus taught at Saïs.   They are scripts that tell
" His wand'rings, and the bounds of mother earth.
" See, how vast ocean from his Eastern birth   60
" Rolls round the whole, and how the rivers pour
" Their waves in tribute to his circling shore—
" Hence most where now, most high, we midway stand
" 'Tween the third heav'n and Hellas' sacred land.
" See yonder, how that stream, swift, single, broad,
" Hence starting, through vast Scythia takes his road ;
" And there, how Ister, multiform, divides
" His rock-split bed in three disparting tides,—
" One Boreas distances ; one seeks the Sea
" Midland, beyond Pelasgian Thessaly ;   70
" The third, by-past Tyrrhenia and the plains
" Of Drepané, where wise Nausithous reigns.
" If Fate return by your first path refuse,
" Such choice she gives you.   Ponder then, and choose."

But, gazing thus, lo! Peleus turn'd his head;
And, like a swarm of waterfowl, o'erspread
Beheld the sea with ships, Absyrtus' fleet,
Black, threat'ning.   Pow'rless, trapp'd, was no retreat
By land or sea.   Those shouted while they near'd,
As instant grasping; and the Minyans fear'd.   80

   And now had Argo's children match'd them there
As Gods with Titans, in sublime despair,
Hewing their way to bright Elysium's rest;
But pity spoke in pure Absyrtus' breast,
Lover of peace and justice; and he sent
A herald, craving conf'rence.   Jason went.
And he propos'd that he the Fleece would yield
A gift to Greece, if, certain tasks fulfill'd,
They would commit Medea to the shrine
Of Artemis, till of the kings divine   90
That rule on earth one should her fate decide;
Or to proceed to Greece as Jason's bride,
Or home return to Æa to her sire.
Jason assented, straiten'd in that dire
Extremity; but scarce the youths approv'd;
The seniors loud denounc'd it, anger-mov'd: —
" Abandon her by whom we won the Fleece?
" Sworn to protect her to our homes in Greece?
" Better to lose it, die, than such disgrace!"
—Each thought he saw in hers a daughter's face.   100
But, equal all, where numbers weight the scale,
How can the noble, gen'rous, wise prevail?

   Thus then the day pass'd on, no onset made:
When she to Jason, prescient and afraid,—
" Why do they not attack us?   Hast thou not
" Dealt to abandon me?   O foul, foul blot

"On hero honour! Fool me not,—say, where
"Thy vows, thy pledges? Vanished into air?
"Thine oaths to Hera, Zeus, the suppliants' friend—
"Were all these lavish'd but to gain thine end,   110
"Poor me the dupe, the tool?—My trust forsworn,
"My home forsaken, name bequeath'd to scorn,
"For thy sole sake, worse traitor—O, 'tis shame!
"Slay me at once, in Ariadné's name,
"Thou Theseus, this thy Naxos! Gallant praise
"Thine, certés, this story told in after days!
"How, think'st thou, shall I meet my father's face,
"Vile leman seeming, flung back in disgrace—
"Not worth a blow, a death? And what the price
"To pay—my debt—in torture, sacrifice—   120
"To clear my country's fame, if scarce my own?
"Bethink thee, vile success cannot atone
"For honour's breach, trust-forfeit; and thou art
"Pledg'd mine in honour, compact's better part.
"Nor count success assur'd in breach of right,—
"The Fleece itself may vanish into night,
"Withdrawn by Zeus; for Themis holds accurst
"New compacts seal'd by breaking of the first."
  Blazing her eyes, she spoke in scorn and grief;
Till, chok'd her words, she found in sobs relief.   130
And he in honey'd accents sooth'd and cheer'd,
For, while he lov'd her much, yet more he fear'd :—
"Be calm and listen. Thou art wise, and know'st
"One arm avails not match'd against a host—
"That host with single voice demanding thee;
"Nor way to save thee but through policy.
"Time is our only friend, and such to win
"By stratagem is neither crime nor sin.

" The present peril have I thus stav'd off,
" O'ermatch'd for fight; but this is not enough :—   140
" Deem not we ever dreamt to give thee o'er,
" A treaty's seal, save in the mimic war
" Of craft to craft oppos'd, wherein the stake
" Falls to the hand that best can vantage take.
" Now is thy turn to move—a stroke for power
" Shall turn to vict'ry this suspended hour.
" Do this then,—to the prince a herald send,
" With gifts as from a sister and a friend,
" And bid him seek the temple under night
" To meet thee alone, unarm'd, with assur'd plight   150
" Of personal safety—thou unwilling borne
" By me from Æa—longing to return—
" Thou too the Fleece, by Phrixus' sons betray'd,
" Wishful to render.   I, beneath the shade
" Of the tall columns watching, at his back,
" Conversing ye, the moment of attack
" Will seize, o'erpow'ring,—then, a pris'ner, he
" Shall be our ransom in exchange for thee.
" Thee shall we rescue thus, retain the Fleece,
" Pass free ourselves, and safe return to Greece.   160
" Credit me, this indeed our wisest course.
" What offers else?   Th' alternative is worse."
      " Worse? hardly,—but," she groan'd, " the die is cast.
" I like not double shifts—but that is past.
" Oh! what a web, net within net, we weave
" When once we stoop to practise and deceive!
" Be it so then ; but harm him not!—this swear :—
" Or else —I weigh not his head's singlest hair
" 'Gainst your priz'd Fleece—tender he is and just ;
" Nor save for life would I abuse his trust.   170

" Thou swearest ? well,—and I will likewise throw
" Words on the winds that, willingly or no,
" Will bring him to the temple at the hour
" Of midnight, when such summons most hath power ;
" Words that would draw a wild beast from her den
" To seek her consort 'mong the haunts of men."
    So said, they parted ; and the Minyans joy'd,
The maid safe hop'd through the device employ'd.
    But when black Erebus had couch'd with Night,
The moon dark-hidden, but the stars were bright ;   180
Medea and Jason—Jason with stone-axe
Light held in hand 'gainst savage beasts' attacks—
Ascended to the Virgin Goddess' fane.
She in the portico, conspicuous plain,
Stood looking seaward, anguish in her heart ;
He, 'neath a column ambush'd, stood apart,
Exulting, as the hunter views his prey
Advance unconscious on a pitfall'd way.
He came, predestin'd victim, up the path
Oppos'd, his bosom stirr'd with righteous wrath ;   190
Fearless his tread, unarm'd, and in his hand
Held, ill-discern'd, great Hermes' peaceful wand ;
And, seeing the maid, came forward with a frown
On his broad brow, while she abash'd look'd down :—
    " Medea, thou traitress to thy sire and me ! "
Began the youth ; " Deem not I think of thee
" Unwilling captive, nor had come to plot
" Unworthy treason 'gainst these Greeks, forgot
" The rights of Themis—had not thy strong spells
" Drawn me by cords 'gainst which my will rebels,—   200
" For which now answer :—But receive back first,
" By virtue of this wand, thy charm accurs'd,

S

" As thus I lay it back upon thy brow:"—
Wherewith he touch'd her with an unfelt blow.
She, tearful, stoop'd; but Jason thought her slain;
And leaping, like a panther from his den—
While she her arms around her brother flung,
" He did not strike me!" bursting from her tongue—
Too late the not ungenerous stroke to check—
The fated stone-axe fell upon his neck;   210
And he sank stricken like a lovely flower,
By scythe cut down in summer's opening hour.
And Jason recognis'd the wand, and cried,
" I will'd not this!" but stern the youth replied,
" I doubt thee, Greek."—" But she is innocent,—
" Nor she nor I, O God! this issue meant!"
—Then, as the blood came pouring, gasp'd the youth;
" I knew my life was forfeit.   Thou, that truth
" Work'st out thro' falsehood, love through hate, be thine
" This young pure life that, willing, I resign!   220
" For what full purpose I but dimly know—
" Sufficient that thy wisdom wills it so!
"—Jason! I pardon thee—thine axe hath cut
" Knots that thou know'st not of.   Sweet sister! put
" Thine arm around me—listen—for the choice
" Of life awaits thee by my dying voice.
" Quit this Greek stranger, clasp the pitying knees
" Of Artemis, hers vow'd thy destinies,
" Thus shalt thou sackless be of this sad deed;
" Else shall thy crimes, thy griefs, thy wrongs exceed, 230
" Sharing my blood's Erinnys and the score
" Of heap'd trust-forfeit which the Gods abhor.
" Know'st thou our father curs'd thee?   Not too late,
" Choose! Thou art yet the mistress of thy fate."

—But she faint answer'd, " Nay ! his fate I share."
—" Then thus, poor darling ! I, rude nurse, prepare
" Thy bridal veil ;" and, feebly scoop'd the blood,
He ting'd her white robe with the sacred flood.
She turn'd, crushing her eyes.—" And thou, my foe !
" Friend, rather—hearken !   Bend thine ear more low, 240
" Lest she should hear.   When I am dead, divide
" My members, right and left, on either side,
" And pass between—then fly, and look not back ;
" For the avenger's foot is on thy track.
" Thy stone-axe, friend ! hath done priest's work. Farewell!
" Things dark in life seem clearer now."—Then fell
Night on his eyes, relax'd his limbs, and dank
With death's cold sweat.   But down Medea sank,
Senseless.   Then Jason, first, the warm blood thrice
Tasted, and thrice spat out the sacrifice,   250
The murd'rer's expiation—off then shred
The victim's first-fruits with the axe—and spread
The limbs in twin rows, sev'ring, and pass'd through ;
Then flung them heav'nward the four winds unto ;
And the winds caught and carried them away ;
And lifting up the maiden where she lay—
Her brother's blood yet red upon his lip—
Bore in his arms, still senseless, to the ship.
    But lo ! a mighty marvel now befel.
The winds, as old Dodona's legends tell,   260
Those limbs, receiv'd, laid rev'rent on the breast
Of the vast void ; and they, by Fate's behest,
Became a path, in every future age,
For human souls, in heav'nward pilgrimage,
From death's chain'd rocks to th' Amaranth hills to rise,
And seek their Father's throne beyond the skies—

                                          s 2

Henceforth that void a hospitable home
For ships at will to traverse, go and come,
Rejoicing—Euxine known; a glassy sea,
Mirroring perfect love's infinity.   270
For now through that great sacrifice, the race
Of Atè vanquish'd, hate to love gave place.
Rushing with troubled wings, the genii fled,
Low heard like thunder, disinherited
By that chaste terror, pure Urania's birth—
And sought th' extremest limits of the earth.
She, Aphroditè known, re-born, transform'd,
From that abyss by love creative warm'd,
First-fruits of that perturbid waste's increase,
Those morsell'd members linking all in peace,   280
Rose dewy, shell-thron'd, by soft Zephyrs driven,
Touch'd the still'd shores, and joyous soar'd to heaven.
But of those limbs dissever'd, stor'd apart,
Athena's power reserv'd Absyrtus' heart,
In a clos'd shrine—but for what destinies
Ask not; for these are hidden mysteries.
Thus, by God's counsels, secret understood,
Were fraud, wrath, bloodshed overrul'd to good.
     Black, henceforth, Argo went her sorrowing way;
And so continued many a future day.   290
     Much griev'd the Minyans, by their chief appris'd
Of the sad chance; and Peleus flight advis'd
Instant:—" This fortune is beyond recall.
" The Colchians soon, misjudging, must know all.
" Seek we then Westward, by yon river's gate,
" Electra's shrine, our guilt to expiate."
So said, they started, rowing; and the ship
Pass'd through the Colchians, giving them the slip,

Unwatchful ; and they rowed to Peucé's isle.
But in the morning—'scap'd, by what strange guile   300
They knew not, Argo, and Absyrtus lost—
Baffled, the Colchians sail'd for Æa's coast.
But Zeus irate, and Hera, for the death
Of young Absyrtus, loos'd the lightning's breath,
That once quell'd Titans, 'gainst the Minyans' path ;
And Argo fled, recoiling 'fore the wrath,
Back to the place they started from, in fear,
But soon reliev'd—their foes no longer there.
And at the twilight hour the sacred oak
In Argo's keel Fate's will predestin'd spoke :—   310
" But once in life, re-born, Electra's day.
" That light, guilt-clouded, now hath pass'd away.
" Far must ye rove o'er the vex'd seas, nor rest
" Till reach'd, long sought, the Æa of the West,
" Where Circé dwells ; there shall ye lay aside
" Your guilt's sore burden, and be purified.
" Meanwhile, ye Dioscuri ! pray that God,
" By-paths that hateth, may avert the rod,
" Stay storm and tempest with his pitying hand,
" And bring ye safely to Ausonia's strand."   320
Then those two, praying, hush'd the elements' war :
And on each youthful brow blaz'd forth a star,—
Twin stars that still, through tempests streaming bright,
Cheer mariners, and glorify the night.
      Then Jason said,—" Now see I no resource
" Save that we take that fearful Northern course,
" Our first forbidden, this last disallow'd."
Whereon kind Hera sent a luminous cloud,
That, through the air inclining, streaming low,
Seem'd to point out the way they were to go,   330

So, when the night her mantle had withdrawn
From sleeping eyes, and gloomy gleam'd the dawn,
They loos'd and parted from that doleful strand,
Rowing, cold terror with her iron hand
Their hearts compressing—turn'd their backs on Greece,
Unknowing whence or when their thrall's release,
Nor whither bound—perchance on Ocean's river,
Dark, terrible, unsearch'd, to float for ever,—
Row'd Eastward 'long the coast, the cloud before
Guiding them, till, on either hand the shore   340
Narrowing, a gaping mouth, that seem'd the maw
Of some sea-monster, entering, they saw
Mæotis' dreary waste expanding forth.
Then that bright cloud, out-streaming tow'rds the North,
Shot forward and evanish'd; and despair
Sank on their hearts, abandon'd-seeming there.
    And now, as when a piece of driftwood, flung
Into a mountain brook, its path among
The rough stones feeling, gradual works its way
Into mid-channel, and, escap'd all stay,   350
Swims swiftly onward; so they felt the ship,
Swift hurrying downward, with a constant dip,
Her own sole master and the stream's, glide on
In the mid stream, less ample now—the sun
Appearing not—and right and left a waste
Beyond it, nor by tree nor meadow grac'd—
Gray wilderness of desert; save that hills
Rose distant faint, and on their pinnacles
Black tents seem'd dotted, giving hope that life
Might still exist there, though with death at strife :—   360
For here, in truth, innumerous tribes of men,
Barbarian, strange to Hellas' kindly ken,

Tent-dwellers, shepherds, ever moving West,
Wave after wave, each by the hindmost press'd,
From life's rich sources in the East, are found,
Nor tenure know of stationary ground ;
Iberian urged by Celt, and Celt in turn
By Sauromat, to Atlas' furthest bourne,—
There, check'd, they know not where to plant their feet,
Pent close, nor forward progress, nor retreat.   370
    Nine days, nine nights thus floated they adown.
On the ninth day they saw the distant frown
Of steep Riphæus, 'neath whose shadow dwell
The happy Hyperboreans ; but, when fell
Night once more, scarce discernible from day,
The cloud reappear'd and led them on their way,
Ancæus steering, through vex'd rocks, till dawn ;
When, with the veil of that half-night withdrawn,
And with it that cloud's cheering luminous beam,
The tenth day launch'd them on the Ocean stream,   380
That, from light's orient fount deriv'd his birth,
Rolls Westward round the habitable earth.
    Darker and darker now th' horizon grew ;
And Hermes' city and the gates they knew
Of Northern Hades, and the Land of Dreams,
Where nothing is in nature as it seems ;
Then into utter darkness plung'd, the coast
Cimmerian, where pure consciousness is lost,
Stupor their sense o'erpow'ring ; till, emerg'd,
Through many islands winding, where, upsurg'd,   390
Amber, like pebbles, strew'd the shore, they saw
The cliffs of Thulé tow'ring, by Fate's law
Bound of life's ken ; but on the rock, scarp'd smooth,
Ancæus, passing, read, in scroll uncouth,

Words strange, prophetic, in an ancient tongue
Which he had known th' Iberian tribes among :—
" Thus Hermes saith :—A time will come when, kind,
" Oceanus shall Nature's chains unbind,
" Tiphys disclose new worlds, nor Thulé be
" Earth's utmost bound.   This, late, your sons shall see."
    Still on they floated, boundless all around   401
The waste of waters, many days ; nor found
Prospect of land, but steady kept their course,
Sitting in dreary silence, late remorse
For faithlessness, trust-forfeit, preying keen,—
No songs, no jests ; and each one's face was seen
To others strange—till, with the setting sun,
The islands of the fierce Deucaledon
They sighted, rugged, numerous tow'rds the West.
There, in the Isle of Mists, Cyculnus' guest,   410
Dwelt Heracles in youth.   There, in the isle
' Bless'd' nam'd, or ' of the Waters,' sleeps, the while
This age endureth, on a stately bed
Stretch'd, bound, while years like waves roll o'er his head,
Peaceful, the mighty Cronos,—Briareus
Guarding him, till Typhœus be let loose.
Sacred the spot.   Seven years before that hour,
A deluge shall the sister isles devour,
Loftier, opposing in their pride ; but she
Shall sole survive, in her humility.   420
These pass'd, though distant, Argo, like a swan
Fresh-launch'd, put out her strength, and eager ran
Tow'rds a green island, lustrous, holy fam'd,
By Gods Æthalia, men Iërne nam'd ;
Where, landing, they with living waters sweet
Wash'd their stain'd armour and their swollen feet.

There, as they tarried, resting on the shore,
They saw a boat, impell'd by sail nor oar,
Void of all tenant, come in tow'rds them straight,
And off the beach, as if expectant, wait.   430
All save Ancæus watch'd it wond'ringly,
But he, the sign known, said, " It is for me."
Then, round him press'd, grief's broken accents rung,
And to his neck Medea weeping clung ;
But, as they gaz'd, a glory o'er him fell,
And they drew back in awe ; and kind farewell
He said to each, and to Medea word
Of special comfort, by the rest unheard,
Her arms unloos'd, and gave her to the care
Of Peleus, blessing, as a daughter dear,—   440
Then to the sea-side, follow'd by the rest,
Clasping his mighty stone-axe to his breast
With both arms cross'd, sought to the boat ; and it
Press'd eager forward his approach to meet ;
And, enter'd, swiftly tow'rds the waning light
Of ended day receded from their sight ;
He standing, but the stone axe held on high,
And gazing tow'rds the West with steady eye ;
Till, lost to view, they from the beach return'd,
And him, their friend and father, wept and mourn'd.   450
Peleus, as if of right, the helm assum'd ;
Nor fear'd they as when, Tiphys lost, for doom'd
They reckon'd them ; for hourly brighter day
Cheer'd them, as Southward now they made their way ;
And knew ere long, passing, th' Iberian shores,
Where golden sands redundant Tagus pours ;
And, Eastward urg'd, enter'd the spacious bay
Where, lately built, Phœnician Gadir lay,

Nigh the Red Isle, where Geryon's oxen fed
Till thence by Heracles unwilling led.   460
Welcom'd by those wise merchants, Syrian men,
They well nigh thought themselves at home again.

Next morn, they loos'd and row'd, in hopes to win
Entrance the friendly Midland Sea within,
Between those pillars stern of Heracles;
When sudden rose—not genial Zephyr's breeze—
But Boreas fierce, that drove with mast'ring force
Reluctant Argo from her wish'd for course,
Drifting before it, struggling hopelessly.
Then Peleus shouted with a mighty cry,   470
" Pray, O ye Boreads! pray—pray, one and all ! "
And rowing, praying, panting, 'gainst the wall
Of adverse waves they strove, but all in vain ;
Till kindly Zeus, compassionate their pain,
Bade Boreas fly, and eager Zephyr sent,
Fretting, long-chain'd.   They to the long oars bent,
Rearing the sail, and through the columns pass'd,
Barely.   Escap'd that death, they breath'd at last ;
Else, vortex-drawn, suck'd in, down Ocean's river
They'd floated on, in weary round, for ever.   480
They murmur'd thanks to Zeus, the suppliant's friend,
And almost hop'd their trials at an end.

But no ! their bitt'rest griefs were yet in store.
Th' Erinnys follow'd on their track, yet more
Powerful within the pillars than without.
Thus many a day they drove on, blind, in doubt
Whither their course, along rude Afric's coast,
Far as th' Hermaic Promont'ry, out-post
Of Libya—thence, by Boreas' kindling blast
Flung helpless 'tween the jaws, absorbing, vast,   490

Of Syrtis' bay.   There ships, engulf'd, abide
Sure death, the flux and reflux of the tide
Banding them to and fro, till ag'd they rot,
Or, on the shoals fast-stranded, lie forgot,
Dying by inches, as within the grasp
Of polypus, whose arms the seaman clasp,
Sucking his life.   Boreas, by Zeus' command,
Drove them at length in pity to the land.

But land to them seem'd worse than sea, retrac'd
Their thither path,—a dreary desolate waste,   500
Sand-hillocks endless rolling—not a blade
Of grass, nor muddy pool, nor shelt'ring shade
'Gainst Helios' fires that fiercely o'er them glow'd,—
No path, no hovel, sign of man's abode ;
Deep silence reigned around—no cry of bird ;
No serpent hiss'd, nor rustling lizard stirr'd.
" What may this land be ? " groan'd the youths' despair,—
" Better t' have forc'd Symplegades, and there,
" Zeus, Fate, defying, perish'd—whence, at least,
" Our doom through certain, yet renown increas'd,   510
" Essaying nobly—than die helpless thus,
" Like stranded fish.   God hath abandon'd us ! "
—Fools, and distrustful, so Fate's wrath to brave,
And deem that God is impotent to save !
The elders spoke not save to murmur, " Pray ! "
From them too hope had almost pass'd away.
Like men that flit as ghosts about the streets,
Words utt'ring rare when one the other meets ;
But each in hopelessness his doom awaits,
Famine or fever 'leaguering at the gates,   520
Or storm that blasts the crop, or when with sweat
Of blood the sacred images run wet,

And hollow bellowings through the temples roar,
Or some fierce monster crawls the sun's disk o'er,
And stars appear at noon—the Minyans crept
Along the shore; and, when they would have slept,
Chill words of terror falter'd on their tongue,
Or speechless each the other's hands they wrung;
Then turn'd away and laid them down apart,
Or, wakeful, commun'd each man with his heart.   530

So pass'd the night—of food nor drink they thought;
Nor brighter hope the coming morrow brought;
And certés had perished in that utter grief,
Had not Athena sent to their relief
The Libyan nymphs, familiar, tutelar,
Who erst receiv'd her leaping, arm'd for war,
From Metis' womb, and her in Triton's tide,
Whence nam'd Tritonis, bath'd and purified.

'Twas mid-day, and th' unclouded sun o'er-head
Unpitying down his fiercest arrows shed,   540
When these, the Libyan Heroines, sisters three,
In shaggy goatskins kirtled to the knee,
Stood at the head of Jason, from his eyes
The mantle gently drew, and said, " Arise!
" Why this despair? Sleeps God or wakes? Attend!
" I come from him," the eldest spoke, " a friend."
—He rose and, known the envoys and who sent
The message, low his eyes in rev'rence bent :—
" When next Poseidon's car from Ægæ's caves,
" By Amphitrité loos'd, bounds o'er the waves,   550
" Do ye your mother the long debt repay
" Incurr'd while in her womb conceiv'd ye lay,
" Travailing your birth. Bear her as she bore you."
So said, straightway they vanish'd from his view.

He, his companions call'd, the vision told,
But what it meant they doubted; when, behold,
A giant horse leap'd from the sea to land,
Pie-bald, broad-chested, shaggy, golden-man'd;
And, shaking from his flanks the briny dew,
Swift as the wind across the desert flew.   560
And Peleus cried,—" Ev'n thus Poseidon flies,
" His chariot loos'd—I read their auguries!
" Nor Argo less our dam, that in her womb
" Bore us, and travail'd for the birth to come!
" The mandate is, that, on our shoulders plac'd,
" We bear our Argo 'cross yon sandy waste,
" Tracking the horse—thus love's scor'd debt to pay,
" And find, such duty paid, our homeward way."
    It pleas'd them all; so, bearing her elate,
Twelve days, twelve nights they carried Argo's weight,
Groaning and travailing, over plain and hill,   571
Nor let nor pause, a constant miracle;
On the tenth day their wine and goats'-flesh fail'd,
But struggled on, though hunger, thirst assail'd,—
No mere man's strength that suff'ring had withstood,
But, sons of Gods, theirs was immortal blood;
Till, the twelfth night completed, with the morn
They reach'd that landward travail's furthest bourne,
The land-lock'd marsh that brackish Triton laves,
And laid her gently down upon the waves.   580
    Then, as when dogs rabid with thirst, the tongue
Protruding, search with eager eyes among
Dry rocks for water, voiceless, finding none;
So those went questing, parted, one by one,
The shores such seeking, silent, parch'd, nor found;
Till, crossing some a rugged rising ground,

They reached the sacred field, by Heracles
Despoil'd, laid waste, of the Hesperides;
Where late those watch'd the golden apples, given
To Hera, wed with Zeus, the Queen of heaven,　　　590
Gift of great mother Gaia, healthful food
Of Gods, their waning life by such renew'd.
Ladon, the dragon, sleepless, prompt for war,
Whom fell Echidna to Typhœus bore
In Scythia's cave, by Gods and mortals fear'd,
His hundred heads of terror there had rear'd,
With those maids guarding; prostrate now he lay,
His spires uncoil'd, ebbing his life away,
His gray eyes glaz'd, his spotted coat all pale,
Nor life save in the quiv'ring of his tail.　　　600
Bitterly weeping, sitting sad, apart,
Dust heaping on their heads in sorrow's smart,
Atlas' daughters they saw; but, themselves seen,
Like morning's mist, those vanish'd from their een.
But Orpheus, blameless bard, the purport guess'd
Of what they saw, and rev'rent them address'd :—
" Bright ones and dear ! whether of Mother Earth
" Daughters, or heroines, of celestial birth !
" Speak, we implore ye, who and what your race,
" This dragon whence, and how this sacred place,　　　610
" Late fair and lovely, now thus desolate ?
" And tell, unless thirst deathly be our fate,
" Where water we may find, boon earth's increase :—
" So shall we honour ye, return'd to Greece."
　　He spoke, and the maids pitied them ; and first
Green grass, then stems as of three trees, outburst
That sorrowing soil, and boughs that, leafy, made
From that fierce Libyan sun a grateful shade,

Black poplar, elm, and tearful willow known.
Ægle, the willow, spoke in kindly tone :—   620
" O strangers, pity us !   Would ye had come
" But yesterday, nor suffer'd spoil'd our home !
" Here grew the golden apples—daughters we
" Of ancient Atlas.   If thou Orpheus be,
" As thy lyre speaks thee, needs not voice the rest.
" But yester-eve, ah me !—no friendly guest,
" But vengeful foe, most impious of mankind—
" Came one, dark-brow'd, a lion's skin behind
" His shoulders flung, a knotted club in hand,
" Bow and keen arrows bearing, and a brand   630
" That scatter'd lightnings—came on foot, across
" Yon Eastern desert and achiev'd our loss,
" Mocking with courteous pity, nor refrain'd
" Entreated, but replied 'twas thus ordain'd,
" Bruising the dragon's head, and pierc'd him through
" With his wing'd arrows ; fearless then unto
" The tree he strode, and, rooting from the ground,
" Ravish'd our treasure.   Then he gaz'd around,
" Questing for water, vainly ; but, some God
" Impelling, yonder, searching as he trod   640
" The hill Tritonian, with his foot a rock
" Struck careless, and pure water from the shock
" Gush'd pouring, welcome.   On his knees he sank,
" And thank'd the Gods, and, stooping, largely drank.
" Seek there and ye shall find."   This heard, they rush'd
Impatient to the spot where the fount gush'd
Perennial, fresh.   And, as around a hole
In some grass'd rock, or hoary oak-tree's bole,
Laborious ants swarm busily, or flies
Cluster where some sweet drop of honey lies ;   650

So clust'ring, swarming, eager, closely press'd,
Knees bent, neck-humbled, grovelling on the breast,
They at that fount of largesse largely quaff'd,
And, rising, with relief and pleasure laugh'd;
Nor grateful prais'd, as that bold peer had done,
Him whose prompt gifts man's lagging hope outrun;
And Castor answer'd, "Laugh, as well ye may!
" But who hath timely quench'd our thirst this day,
" Water evoking from the rock, save he,
" Next God, our life in this extremity?   660
" Whom we esteem'd no more than of our kith
" Conversing common—lightly parted with—
" Too long forgot; yet, absent, present still!"
—But now the youth Euphemus, faint and ill
With fasting, reel'd and fell; and, thirst assuag'd,
The pangs of late remember'd hunger rag'd.
And Orpheus cried,—" O maiden, pure and kind!
" Thou see'st our anguish. Tell us where to find
" Sweet water's brother, holy food; take ruth,
" Less on us stronger than this tender youth!"   670
And Æglé said,—" Food have we none to give;
" But pray, if God may grant the dead to live."
Then, praying, lo! that tree which late the fruit
Bore golden, healthful—torn up by the root
That lay before them, spoil'd—flower'd forth once more,
And piteous, dying, one last harvest bore.
And Æglé spoke,—" The Gods have heard your vow.
" Wise Argo's sons! reveal'd I know ye now.
" Your meat and drink, from day to day renew'd,
" Fail'd with the tenth; but heav'n celestial food   680
" Grants to the few who work on without pay
" Beyond the limit of the reck'ning day.

" Such feeds she with the Gods' ambrosia,—take
" And, eating, live, for holy Argo's sake !
" But touch not mortal food, 'tis Fate's command,
" Till purg'd by Circé on Tyrrhenia's strand.
" This shall suffice for many days.   More clear
" Previsions brighten as the end draws near.
" Old worlds give place to new.   Zeus ! I approve
" And own thee just.   Thy chastisements are love."   690
  Then Polydeuces,—" Here but yesterday,
" He cannot yet have pass'd so far away
" But we may find and bless him."   Instant thought
By action follow'd, they dispersing sought
On all sides ; but light sand-drifts, o'er the waste
Night-blown, the hero's foot-steps had effac'd.
Sad they return'd.   Only keen Lynceus' eyes
Seem'd to discern a dark form cresting rise,
Topping the far horizon, shadowy, lone,
Toiling, on foot, inexorably on,   700
Returning Eastward, whence his steps had come,
Seeking victorious his Trœzenian home
And his taskmaster's presence.   Like the ghost
Thin of th' extinguish'd moon, when light hath cross'd
The orient hills, to Lynceus' eyes so seem'd
That dim departing form.   Perchance he dream'd.
  Now to the shore return'd they.   Helios shed
Less fiery shower ; when Mopsus chanc'd to tread
On a fell serpent that beneath his feet
Unseen lurk'd, sand-embedded, from the heat   710
Such refuge seeking— of the race that sprung
From Gorgo's blood by Perseus dropp'd among
The Libyan sands, home-flying.   Deadly rear'd
The asp, and bit ; nor much the hurt appear'd

Harmful at first; but darkness rapid crept
Over his eyes, and death's cold sleep he slept.
Follow'd immediate change to black; and they
Interr'd him hastily ev'n where he lay,
Three times that lone grave circling, weeping sore
That they should see that honour'd head no more;　　720
Flung too on faith's sole guidance, ere the dawn
Of happier days, God's oracle withdrawn.

Then, hurrying, they in terror, and perplex'd
What death that fearful coast might vomit next,
Embark'd on Argo, ev'n as fly distress'd
Children, fear-stricken, to their mother's breast;
And sought that deadly marsh to leave behind;
But, seeking long, no exit could they find.
Ev'n as a serpent, coil'd, his head projects,
Searching for shade, nor finds what he expects,　　730
Tries divers paths, rejecting till he sees
Some hole i' th' rock, through which to creep with ease;
So questing they sought exit, nor despair
Allow'd, now better taught; but, by the prayer
Of Orpheus urg'd, relanded, with the load
Of a vast tripod given by Delphi's God,
Warning that such the powers would not disdain
Indigenous when other help was vain.
This carrying, Triton met them on the shore,
Like a fair youth; a sod of earth he bore,　　740
Off'ring in gift as seizin of the soil
To Greece and young Euphemus, destin'd spoil
Of his late progeny. Then, to their tale
Of baffled quest he answer'd,—" Hoist the sail;
" Notus shall blow,—follow where blackest hue
" The water shews; and soon will be in view

" A narrow strait which leads to the broad sea."
With that, the mighty tripod should'ring, he
Plung'd in the deep; and they the God rever'd.
Libation made; and straight he reappear'd   750
In his own form, to the mid-waist a God,
Below a mighty sea-horse, chested broad,
His tail lashing the brine with double prong.
He seiz'd the keel and drove the ship along
The unseen channel to the open main;
Then, signing kind farewell, plung'd down again.

Book X.　Circé.

HAPPIER that night they laid them down to rest,
For, faint, hope's star was rising in their breast.
Peleus watch'd, careful, lest some pirate fleet,
Tyrrhenian, lurking near, cut off retreat,
Should sudden steal their thoughtless sleep upon.
But with the morning's rise strong Libya's son,
Libs, blew; and they rejoicing rear'd the mast,
And spread the sail, and flew before the blast,
Unknowing whither; but ere long, impell'd,
Trinacria's fertile meadows they beheld,　　　　　10
That endless spring with every flower adorns,
And sheep and oxen, white, with golden horns,

Grazing; and fierce the lust for mortal food
Woke, but Medea their eager eyes withstood,
Terrified, recognizing. "Those," she cried,
" Are Helios' flocks; death watches at their side,
" Unseen,—fatal, assail'd. Beware them. Look!
" Yonder Phaëthusa, with her silver crook,
" My father's youngest sister, and, with goad
" Golden, Lampetïe, marshalling their road,   20
" Sated with herbage, to the crystal springs!"
—So, like the hawk that with suspended wings
Pauses, but, seen the watchful farm-wife nigh,
Resumes his flight, they pass'd that trial by ;
And rowing, by Libs still aided, swept the sea,
Joyous, and reach'd Phæacian Drepané,
And Eryx saw lone tow'ring, 'neath whose root
The sickle lies that reap'd from whence the fruit—
Unutterable deed, that Chaos' strife
Ended—of love and beauty sprang to life,—   30
Hence Drepané that gracious island's name.
Demeter there the Titans taught to tame
The earth by tillage. 'Neath that earthly heaven
Alcinous' sire, from Hypereia driven,
Planted the mild Phæacians. Seen the ship,
They the beach crowded, welcome on each lip,
Strangers approaching ; and Alcinous spoke
Kind words of greeting ; and the shouting woke
Glad Eryx' echoes, as if brethren come,
Or sons, receiv'd, long truant from their home.   40
    But on the heels of joy sure sorrow treads!
Who sleep should lie sword drawn beside their beds,
Foes at the gate. With morning, ere their tale
Had ask'd been told, a strong fleet under sail

Appear'd of Colchians, that, Symplegades
Passing, had travers'd .Egeus,' Pelops' seas,
Questing Medea.   Stern, they claim'd the maid,
And threaten'd vengeance, their demand gainsaid.
Nought knew they of Absyrtus.   Prompt address'd
To fight, the Minyan youth the King repress'd,   50
The Colchians fair entreating, hopeful war
T' avert, which most that gentle race abhor.

    Few months had flown since King Alcinous reign'd.
His worth and love Areté's hand had gain'd,
Kindly and wise.   Generous he was, but just,
And held his sceptre as from Zeus in trust.
Light-hearted, bright, were both, and lov'd to see
All round them happy, 'Now Medea, the knee
Of that sweet queen embracing, urg'd her prayer,
Weeping :—" 'Twas not from love, but in despair   60
" I fled—this stranger sav'd, unjustly doom'd
" To perish, by the bulls' fell breath consum'd—
" My sire the Fleece withholding—his by right—
" My part betray'd, no counsel was but flight—
" And Hecaté, my mistress, bade me go.
" Or deem'st me Jason's leman? Think not so,—
" My flower is fresh, unloos'd my maiden zone,
" As, thy young spouse unknown yet, was thine own;
" But, Greece once reach'd, I am his promis'd wife.
" Give me not up, then! So may Hera life   70
" Long with Alcinous give thee, and increase
" Of children duteous-loving, wealth, and peace!"
    Areté sooth'd and comforted the maid;
And when the night had come, and mortals laid
Their burdens down—only the heroes kept
Close vigil, or by snatches anxious slept—

She, on the genial bed beside her spouse
Lying half-embrac'd, all silent in the house,
Retold Medea's tale, and urg'd, " Be kind
" To her and to these Greeks, that, well inclin'd,   80
" We keep them friends.   Not far from us they dwell,
" Æëtes distant, and his wrath less fell
" Than theirs, ill-willing.   Hers may be just blame ;
" But she is Jason's bride, betroth'd in name
" Of Hera,—make not Jason then forsworn,
" Nor in Æëtes' breast remorse's thorn
" Plant, his child's murd'rer—Spare them all such woe,—
" Protect the maid,—shall it not, love ! be so ?"
    To whom the King : " Small suasion, least from thee,
" Would need to move me, were not God's decree   90
" Stern 'gainst trust-forfeit—tow'rds a father most.
" Nor lightly deem, compar'd with theirs, the host
" Of great Æëtes,—thron'd, he rules afar
" From Asia to Hesperia's setting star.
" Just sentence I must pass, a sceptred king.
" Awards unrighteous retribution bring.
" Yet penal laws for mild construction press,
" And greater obligations rule the less.
" Would she were not a virgin ! Then, forsooth,
" No longer maiden free, but to this youth   100
" Link'd, like us two, by sweet Harmonia's chain,
" I could not yield her to her sire again."
    He smil'd,—her wit would take the hint, he deem'd ;
Then kiss'd her, turn'd, and slept, or sleeping seem'd.
    She rose ere long, quick-witted, glad at heart,
And sent a herald sure the news t' impart
To Jason at the ship—that thus the King
Deem'd of the case impendent ; whispering

Suggestive complot.   He sped through the town.
She, return'd noiseless, by her lord laid down,—   110
Whether her absence noted, or such plot
Suspected, who can tell ? The Muse knows not.
      The herald found them watching by the ship,
Moor'd in the Hyllic port,—with rapid lip
The message gave, and glad the heroes heard.
The genial couch they straightway due prepar'd
In Macris' cave, where she had dwelt of yore
Whom sweet Melissa t' Aristæus bore,
Patron of bees, belov'd.   When Zeus the bed,
Grieving, of Semelé last visited,   120
And Hermes drew forth from the searching flame
Him whom dull mortals Dionysus name,
Macris, that pure one, in her fragrant breast
Pitying receiv'd and sooth'd the babe to rest,
Touch'd his parch'd lip with honey.   Hera knew ;
And, fierce forth-driv'n, the exil'd nymph withdrew
From rude Eubœa to Trinacria's isle,
Where brighter suns and kindlier seasons smile.
There in the cave she dwelt, and agéd died,
Dear to the mild Phæacians.   Deep and wide,   130
The cavern yawn'd.   Its level floor was strown
With snow-white sand ; its crystal pillars shone
Ev'n in the dark by their own loveliness.
There at the end, in a retir'd recess,
They strew'd the bed, and o'er it spread the Fleece,
For such high nuptials honour's large increase ;
And Naiads, Nymphs, Oreads, and Dryades
From all sides came to grace those mysteries,
By Hera sent, decking the grot with flowers.
And o'er the walls the Fleece pour'd dazzling showers, 140

And on those nymphs, of light that wax'd and wan'd.
They long'd to touch, but modesty restrain'd.
   Then, forth the cave, the starry hosts above
Witnessing, first, was mix'd the cup of love,
Harmonia's hallowing wine, which both partook.
Hera's white ewe was slain, its upward look
Propitious tending.   Then, her eyes bent low,
The nymphs that maiden urg'd, reluctant, slow,
Within the cavern, to the genial bed;
And Jason follow'd, by Euphemus led.   150
And all the rest, their brows with myrtle bound—
But spear in hand, and watchful glancing round,
Attack suspecting, ill-assur'd their tongue—
Before the threshold 'Hymenæus' sung.
Sad bridal, certés! Not such had Jason plann'd,
Ill-starr'd, returning to his native land.
   But, when bright Eös from Tithonus' arms,
Yet youthful, broke, and her dishevell'd charms
Betray'd her blushing from th' embrace of night,
And all the shores were bath'd in rosy light,   160
And birds broke into song, and stir of men
Proclaim'd day's busy life begun again;
Alcinous, with Areté by his side,
Mounted his chariot, through the city's wide
Fair streets slow-driving.   Helm nor shield he wore,
But holy justice' kingly sceptre bore.
She, fresh as spring, shed gracious looks on all;
A lurking smile round her lips play'd withal,
Conscious; but he, impassive, forward gaz'd.
The citizens throng'd after them, and prais'd   170
That princely pair, saying, "Sure were never seen
"So fair a monarch or so bright a queen!"

Forth issuing from the gates, a field was seen
Before them, centred by a hillock green,
Of Themis nam'd.   On one side, soft, the wave
Of Nereus plash'd; in front was Macris' cave.
From all the farms around, with shout and din
Joyful, the country folks were pouring in,
Gifts bringing for those princes and their guests.
—But, o'er the sea black hov'ring, like some pest's   180
Dark wings that shadow life with death's eclipse,
They saw near-drawing, stern, the Colchian ships;
Whence their chiefs, landing, came the King to greet.

All paus'd; but at that moment music sweet
Broke from the cave; and Orpheus with his lyre
Came forth, loud singing, with that hero choir
And nymphs attendant, Hymenæus' song,
Exultant, that the echoes round prolong,—
Till, last, Medea and Jason, hand in hand,
The choir bi-parting, 'fore the monarch stand,   190
She lowly-ey'd, but he with triumph fir'd;
While, shouting, all that host the twain admir'd.

Then rising up, and grave, Alcinous spoke :—
" Oft after sunset fair have men awoke
" To sunrise clouded.   Zeus commands the skies,
" Marshals man's path, controls his destinies.
" Just claims, conceiv'd, fall through preferr'd too late.
" Kings cannot traverse ends ordain'd by Fate.
" Part man and wife, bound by Harmonia's vow,
" Nor laws of man nor God's decrees allow.   200
" Content ye then, ye Colchians ! "—Then arose
Triumph and jubilee.   And those dusk foes
Look'd at each other, mutt'ring, well perceiv'd
Out-witted, and therewith of hope bereav'd

To 'scape Æëtes' anger; so they sought
For friendship, tribute to Alcinous brought,
There settling; nor to Æa's towers return'd,
Where lone Æëtes watch'd for them and mourn'd.
    Thus were the Colchians foil'd, the knot was tied,
The Minyans sav'd, the maiden Jason's bride.   210
But fraud's conceptions die ere brought to birth,—
The Golden Fleece was seen no more on earth.
They sought it in the cave,—it was not there;
And ev'ry visage darken'd in despair.
Whether resenting such high trust's misuse,
That sacred thing profan'd to earthly use
In Macris' grot—or that, through guile acquir'd,
Stern Nemesis her righteous dues desir'd—
Or that the Fleece belong'd to Gods by right,
Lent but an hour to man's unworthy sight;   220
Hera withdrew it to the heav'nly spheres,
And that dawn's laughter ended, sad, in tears.
They learnt thus late that the immortals love
Straightforward paths, nor devious craft approve;
And, though success may stamp the issue, blame
The means, and visit all such acts with shame;
And the maid's words now did prophetic seem,
The Fleece itself might vanish like a dream.
Thus they repented, sorrowing,—but their praise
Natheless survives in song from elder days.   230
    Six days they mourn'd, but, when the seventh appear'd,
An altar of small stones compact they rear'd
To bright Apollo, sacrifice and song
And pray'r sad off'ring, intermitted long,—
Perchance, uncleans'd, presumptuous; like a cloud
The smoke hung dense, nor grac'd nor disallow'd.

Then, when the eighth fresh Eös shed her smile
On dewy earth, they left Trinacria's isle.
Gifts many gave Alcinous; and, to grace
Medea, twelve handmaids of Phæacian race   240
Areté. Thus they parted lovingly.
The sun shone golden on the silver sea.
The sail they hoisted. Notus softly blew;
And eager Argo like a sea-bird flew.
The King and Queen stood watching on the shore
Till they could see that less'ning sail no more.

Thus Argo flew, life's halcyon, but obscur'd
Her plumage bright by storms and griefs endur'd,
'Cross the broad sea Tyrrhenian, to fulfil
Eager her mistress Fate's benignant will,—   250
Flew all that day and through the following night;
Till with the morning Æa came in sight
Hesperian, and the mount where Circé dwells,
Æetes' sister, skill'd the oracles
Of God to read, and peace from heav'n impart,
Crime's debt absolving, to the contrite heart.
Swift Argo flew, questing for each her son
Shrift for faith's forfeit, own'd the Fleece ill won,
Repented of, and for Absyrtus' blood
Unsought, but that fraud's issue understood.   260

But not with terror's gloom that mountain frown'd.
Its flanks, its brow, with oaks and bays were crown'd,
And myrtles overshadowing crystal caves,
With sunny slopes th' Ausonian billow laves.

They saw the Goddess, washing on the shore
Her head and hands in the salt sea from gore.
The roof, the walls that night had blood distill'd,
And fire the cave, her drugs devouring, fill'd.

Rav'nous; but with the blood she quench'd the flame.
Hence washing, troubled, to the shore she came.   270
   They, rev'rent, distant moor'd, and landed.   She
Observ'd them.   They drew near, but fearfully;
For creatures coming and going strange they saw,
Their limbs commix'd in kind, 'gainst nature's law
Familiar; such as budded from the breast
Of wat'ry earth, not yet by heat compress'd,
Ere Order's rule had each their limbs assign'd
To bird, beast, fish, or creeping thing, confin'd,—
Monsters abnormal, these, on what intent
They guess'd not, quaint but harmless, came and went.
   Medea and Jason, forth advancing, sought   281
T' address; but, warn'd deterrent, utter'd nought.
She turn'd; they follow'd silent to the grot.
She ey'd them keen, their purpose knowing not.
They, to the hearth approaching, there sat down,
Their eyes abash'd, her hand on her head's crown
Resting, the axe in his tow'rds earth revers'd.
Instant that priestess knew the sign accurs'd
Of holy blood under safe-conduct spilt,
And rites prepar'd to purge them from their guilt.   290
For such Zeus sanctions, hating the offence,
But pard'ning those who seek in penitence.
A sucking pig, atonement's type, she slew,
And with the blood, lustration's healing dew,
Sprinkled, and pray'd, and burnt the cakes, and pour'd
Milk, water, honey on the hearth,—restor'd
That thus their innocence in sight of heaven,
Peace and remission of guilt's debt be given,
The just Erinnys stay'd, her claim withstood,
Whether for kinsman's or a stranger's blood.   300

All due accomplish'd, she arose, and spoke
Kind words, and ask'd—for memory awoke
Of that night's dream—what brought them to that place;
But when Medea look'd up, she knew the race
Of Helios in her eyes, that shone above
Earth's brightest fires, though soften'd now by love.
And then Medea related all—no need
Reciting the sad tale—that she indeed
Had fear'd and fled—but now was Jason's bride—
She had not willingly her sire defied—   310
Some impulse urg'd her she could not restrain—
The Goddess had said "Go!"—her brother slain
By Jason's hand mis-deeming—she the curse
Accepting shar'd, for to break vows were worse,
Such plighted—but her father's heart would break—
Yet all she welcom'd for her husband's sake :—
So spoke she, broken-sobbing; nor that stern
Monitress all condemn'd :—" Poor victim! learn
" That guilt absolv'd 'fore heav'n doth not infer   319
" Cancell'd earth's debts. Who by one hair's breadth err
" From right's straight path are on the road to crime,
" Which, reach'd, bears bitter fruit for after time.
" Sin not again. Keep thy heart soft and pure,
" And, patient, life's out-running dregs endure.
" Now go—I may not tender thee—I would
" 'Twere not so—Go!—Touch not my knees; the blood
" Betwixt us is too near, too far remov'd.
" I knew thy blameless brother, and I lov'd.
" Go with this stranger, whosoe'er he be,
" Not of our race."—Medea bitterly   330
Wept hearing, nor obey'd her,—sorrow's tide
Her hands, the eyes compressing, could not hide;

But Jason led her, trembling, from the cave,
Soothing, nor thanks nor word to Circé gave,
Indignant—impious! for she spoke by Fate.
Return'd, brief did he to his friends relate
All that had pass'd, and they rejoic'd, the load
Of guilt remov'd, and reconcil'd to God.

    Ev'n while he spoke, her mourning veil of black
Argo threw off, reliev'd; but never back   340
Return'd her pristine colours,—pale her hue,
'Tween light and darkness, neutral, to the view.
Electra's life, once sullied, ne'er regains
The rose's spring untouch'd by summer's rains.
Like Psyche's wings rude brush'd, the soul, her bloom
Deflower'd, flits sad, though pardon'd, to the tomb.

    Meanwhile had Iris, watching from the height
Of glittering Anxur, Circé's cave in sight,
Seen those two issue forth, and instant sought
Hera, her mistress.—" For these tidings brought   350
" Thanks," she replied :—" Now, if thou lov'st me, go
" To Nereus' hall, where Ægæ's fountains flow,
" And crave of Thetis, with my greeting dear,
" Her instant presence and her counsel here :—
" Next to th' Æolian Isles—to Hiera first,
" And bid Hephæstus intermit the burst
" Of his red cinders, and his fiery blast,
" Till, with the morning, Argo shall have pass'd :—
" Then pray the lord of blust'ring Strongylé
" His winds to bind, and ruffle not the sea.   360
" For now, with time, that linketh age to age,
" Argo hath rounded her long pilgrimage ;
" And, life revers'd, from Æa of the West
" Tends through the last brief struggle to her rest."

Radiant, that envoy down heav'n's pathway flew,
Eager great Hera's welcome hest to do ;
And Ægæ's depths and each Æolian isle
Laugh'd out and brighten'd, answering to her smile.

From Nereus parting, and her sisters fair,
Thetis sprang up obedient through the air ;   370
And Hera spoke her, seating courteous near :—
" Honour'd and pure ! thou know'st to me how dear
" Jason ; and now must Argo, purified,
" Fight her last battle through the treach'rous tide
" Of Planctæ, past Charybdis, and the rock
" Of envious Scylla.   Through this last death's shock
" Urge her, my sister, saving !   Hear my prayer,
" Entreated—lov'd by me, since thou to share
" My bed with Zeus refusedst, scorn'd his ire,
" Till warn'd an offspring greater than his sire,   380
" So righteous Themis spoke, from thee should spring,—
" Hence, doom'd to mortal wedlock, I a king,
" Noblest of mortals, husband gave to thee,
" Whence thine Achilles, doubly dear to me.
" I, with the Gods, thy nuptial banquet spread,
" And held the torch of Hymen o'er thy head,—
" And this I know, that, when thy son shall come
" To bright Elysium, an immortal home,
" Babe though he be on Pelion now, that hour
" Medea shall meet him as a virgin flower,   390
" His bride predestin'd after death,—for she
" Is but awhile lent to mortality,
" Like yon young Helen, Fate's sad delegate
" Awhile on earth, but to resume her state
" Of youth immortal 'mong the watchers pure,
" Whose lot it is life's contact to endure,

" For great ends suff'ring.   Wise ev'n now she is,
" Only of thy son worthy.   Then in this
" Please me, dear sister ! nor thy daughter less,
" Thus destin'd ; and—nay ! why wilt thou distress   400
" Peleus, obdurate, still ?   If anger'd, say
" Have I not wrongs to grieve for day by day ?
" Pardon him, pitying—to his bed return ! "
—But Thetis that last prayer not answer'd, stern ;
Granting the first, responsive,--" Queen ! I go
" To seek my sisters' help, that Argo so,
" Thy boon, pass safe ; and will the heroes warn
" For prompt departure with the breaking morn."
    Swift plung'd she in the waters, and sent round
Word that those nymphs should with the dawn be found
Betwixt the Planctæ and the Sirens' Isle.   411
Then, swift as lightning, or the ready smile
Of earth, perceiv'd the sun, to Circé's shore
Flew, where the heroes, early banquet o'er,
Play'd with the quoits, while eve's cool Zephyr blew ;
And, beck'ning him, unseen, her husband drew
Aside, and spoke :—" Tarry no longer here ;
" But in the morning, soon as dawn is clear,
" Loose and set sail ; for Hera's dread command
" Urges the Nereids tow'rds Æmonia's strand   420
" To speed your progress,—fated is your path.
" But, seen, remark me not, nor wake my wrath
" Worse than of old."   Scarce list'ning, on her gaz'd
Peleus, and would have spoke to her, amaz'd ;
Unknown her sight since he incurr'd her ire,
Indignant, she bathing his son with fire,
Immortal temp'ring ; but she vanish'd straight,
Nursing, resentful still, immortal hate.

He spoke the heroes,—they rejoic'd, reliev'd,
Such succour known ; but, loving still, he griev'd.   430
    And now sweet day died with the setting sun ;
No moon yet shone, but peeping, one by one,
The timid stars came out ; and night her breast
Unveil'd for men to pillow on and rest.
But watching they, too happy yet to close
Their eyes in weariness' well-earn'd repose,
They saw in heav'n, work'd as by magic spell,
A lovely and henceforth lasting miracle,—
An avenue's long vista stretching, star
Seen beyond star, like lamps, soaring afar   440
Endless, that path seem'd leading to a shrine
At some vast distance, hid from sight, divine ;
And more stars glimps'd and more, till heav'n was bound
As by a luminous girdle all around.
And, as they gaz'd, and doubted if they dream'd,
Argo, or her self's image, parting, seem'd,
Emancipate from earth's control, to rise
And sail along that pathway through the skies,
Themselves within her recognis'd, till lost
In the white sea of that celestial host.   450
Yet was she still beside them.   Then awoke
Dodona's life within her, and she spoke :—
" By you new path, the ancient pass'd away,
" Henceforth shall man ascend to upper day,
" From earth's dim footstool, by that starry road,
" To light eternal, near the throne of God !
" That galaxy of light ye there behold,
" Wedding the spheres as by a ring of gold,
" Is your own Fleece, once more, awhile withdrawn,
" Restor'd, in promise of life's better dawn :—   460

" By it shall I, like Phrixus, soon ascend,
" And ye in me; but when time's measur'd end
" Draws nigh, and dark Typhœus breaks his chain,
" As Orpheus sang, I shall return again
" To bear your children and Ancæus' race,
" Found faithful, to a lasting dwelling-place,
" Where, garner'd in a new Hesperides,
" The fruit awaits ye, won by Heracles.
" Short space now rests, and your day's work is done.
" God's blessing and my own on every one!　　470
" Henceforth my voice is silent.　Friends, farewell!"
—With that the drops of tender sorrow fell
From their dimm'd eyes, sorrowing that thus should end
That commune sweet—their mother and their friend.
　　But when the watches of the night were past,
And, long expected, Eös came at last
Across the hills—the dancing waves grew bright,
And the earth joy'd and every heart was light—
They loos'd, and rais'd the sail; Iäpyx blew,
And, like an eagle skimming, Argo flew.　　480
And soon the sound of liquid singing, clear,
Announc'd the Sirens' fatal islets near,
Accurs'd, that, charming with their bird-like song,
Lure mariners to death their shoals among.
But Orpheus seiz'd the lyre, and with a lay
Answer'd, more bird-like, sweeter-voic'd than they.
Silenc'd, those listen'd,—nor his voice and lyre
Less chain'd the heroes' ill-subdued desire,
Save only Butes; he, in soft despair,
Leap'd in the waters, and had perish'd there,　　490
But Aphrodité, from Idalia's bower
Speeding, shell-borne, t' assume imperial power

O'er Lilybænm's long-projecting shore,
Saw him and sav'd.   She to him secret bore
Eryx, who on the mount that bears his name
Her temple built.   Lapp'd in those bonds of shame,
Butes lived on, his better life forgot,
In dalliance, by his friends remember'd not.

And now th' Æolian Islands came in sight,
Seven number'd; but innumerous islets bright,   500
Sparkling i' th' sun, form labyrinths of rock,
O'er which the wave breaks with incessant shock
Of earth and sea confus'd,—then over shoals,
Shallow but seeming deep, deceptive, rolls;
While prison'd currents or in eddies spin,
Or fume and fret oppos'd the maze within.
Such nam'd the Planctæ—' Wand'rers,'—once, 'tis said,
Floating, now tether'd deep in ocean's bed.
These nearing they, swift sprang up from the caves
Of ancient Ægæ, rising o'er the waves,   510
Wise Nereus' daughters, gracious, young and fair,
Shaking the wet brine from their ebon hair,
With Thetis, matron-veil'd; but they offence
Knew not, all naked in their innocence.
Twin'd in her locks rich chains of pearl she wore,
And a pellucid wand of amber bore;
They strings of coral, armlets, necklaces,
And flowers nurs'd deep i' th' sea's obscurities.
She 'gainst the rudder lean'd—those, as at noon
Bright dolphins sport, rejoicing in the sun,   520
Round some lov'd vessel—now in front they dart,
Now this way, that, on all sides—every heart
Praises Apollo, and keeps holiday;
So sported these round Argo, convoy gay,—

Till, the close lab'rinth ent'ring, Thetis sprung,
With finger sign'd binding her husband's tongue,
And, standing by him, coldly laid her hand,
Steadying, on his, the rudder to command ;
And guided skilful.   They the while, like maids
Who by the seaside, 'neath the evening shades,   530
Close-cinctur'd, men unthought of, play at ball,
Standing apart, nor let the light weight fall,
Flung one to t'other, none unskilful found,—
Shame due to her who lets it reach the ground !
So the bright Nereids, springing rock to rock,
Oft stagg'ring 'neath the blinding waters' shock,
But quick recov'ring, laughter on each lip,
On the waves' crest o'er shoals and reefs the ship
Pass'd, easing, tossing—rocks and waves defied,
Bounding along and battling with the tide.   540
On Hiera's top meanwhile, in sullen mood,
His hammer idle on his shoulder, stood
Hephæstus, watching,—Æolus refrain'd
Scarcely his winds on Strongylé, constrain'd ;
And Hera from Olympus, with her arm
Athena round, breathless, and dreading harm
To Jason from that conflict, forward bent,
Nor ear to Pallas' calm assurance lent
That all the elements might 'gainst Argo chafe,
Immortal, fruitless, but her boy was safe ;   550
While Zeus beside her, pois'd the scales aright,
Glanc'd at Athena, and enjoyed her fright ;
And all the Gods, sitting around, rejoic'd,
Foreknown th' event, and gratulation voic'd,
Argo, the heroes, sav'd, their guilt forgiven ;
And all was jubilee in earth and heaven.

Now had the third part of the day been run ;
The rocks were clear'd ; and, tow'rds the setting sun,
The narrow strait they enter'd, and between
Scylla and fell Charybdis; but the Queen   560
Surnam'd Cratæis, mighty Hecaté,
Her daughter bade the ship should pass through free,
Medea her priestess ; and Charybdis, kind,
From her stern brow the wild-fig's head inclin'd,
Sweet figs them off'ring, to allay their thirst.
Pass'd whom, impell'd, the clear sea opening burst
On their glad eyes ; and, tir'd as when with play
The dolphins end their pleasant holiday,
So the bright Nereids, Rhegion as they near'd,
Love's farewell signing, plung'd and disappear'd.   570
    Little rests now to tell ere Phthia's shore
Hears ag'd Thymœtes' feeble voice no more.
Sweet after toil is eventide's repose,
Slight work remaining ere day's eyelid close ;
The placid hours uncounted lapse, and seem
Past griefs, look'd back on, like a fading dream.
As fishermen, achiev'd their deep-sea's sport,
Watch pleas'd the sail, returning to the port ;
Or, nearer thrown and heavy felt, to land
Draw in their nets, low chanting on the strand ;   580
So these in Argo ran o'er tranquil seas
Day after day before the Western breeze,
Sail set, nor with the oars impatient urg'd ;
All eag'rer thought in calm contentment merg'd,
Their sin forgiv'n, their debt of blood wip'd out,
Th' Erinnys banish'd, hearts at ease, nor doubt
Of port assur'd ; and, lesser cares above,
Trust sweet, confirm'd, in heav'n's presiding love ;

Nor ask'd their several morrows' Nemesis,
Parting—the hour sufficient in its bliss:—   590
While if, the Fleece withdrawn, regret would rise,
Humbled, each night they saw it in the skies,
A sign to mortals, grateful. Thus did day,
And night, and day, succeeding, glide away.
    Now lack'd but one last test ere, faithful found,
Endurance should by perfect peace be crown'd.
Cythera pass'd, and Pelops' distant isle,
And adverse Crete, while sea and heav'n to smile
Seem'd on their homeward progress, sudden broke
The winds from Strongylé, blank Night her cloak   600
Flung o'er the sky, Poseidon striking rais'd
The waves in fury, Zeus's lightnings blaz'd—
Seem'd Chaos once more in confusion hurl'd,
Or loos'd Typhœus coiling round the world.
Yet blench'd they not ; nor, worse, when darkness fell,
Utter, a solid gloom, dense, horrible—
Themselves and day with night commix'd—no spark
Of star or hope to animate the dark :—
Cheering had been Zeus' fiercest lightnings, tost
Trembling 'twixt earth and sky, time's reck'ning lost,
Borne hither and thither, whither they knew not.   611
By God himself, it seem'd to them, forgot,—
Till, death expecting, but to death resign'd,
Orpheus, their bidding, pray'd that they might find
Deliv'rance, or to live, or welcome die.
And him Apollo heard, and from the sky
Down darted, joyous, and alighted on
A rock, in mem'ry thence Ascania known,
The 'Wish'd for'—from that 'Wish'd for' of all time.
He, standing, rais'd his silver bow sublime,   620

Lighting up all that darkness, glorious seen
The purple sky and the dusk wave between,
Pointing to one bright island, from the seas
Rising, the youngest of the Sporades,
Hence Anaphé surnam'd.   The tempest still'd,
Instant, love's last consummate proof fulfill'd ;
And the three worlds rejoic'd.   There landing, they
Built glad an altar to the God of day,
Ægletes hail'd ; and sacrific'd, and pour'd
Libation, and that Saviour's grace implor'd,   630
And knew him gracious, all the past forgiven,
The sweet smoke rising pillar-like to heaven.
Day shone without a cloud ; the storms were past ;
And he most long'd for reconcil'd at last.
Lustrated, happy, children-like, their laugh
Rang to the welkin, and with jeer and chaff
The maids Phæacian mock'd them ; they in turn
Repaid the banter back, in playful scorn.
Thus strong hearts wanton, fierce excitement o'er,—
Thus, life's bridge cross'd, contend in mimic war   640
Eleusis' pilgrims,—thus at Anaphé,
Yearly, the youth, in that day's memory.
    That night Euphemus dream'd a dream, some God
Inspiring ; and, instructed, flung the sod
Giv'n him by Triton seaward, tow'rds the West.
Therefrom, like Mené's crescent, from the breast
Of waters Thera rose, his children's home,
Where they shall dwell till, to Cyrené come
In years long future, they acclaim the soil
Pledg'd to the Delphian tripod, Triton's spoil.   650
    Morning awoke in beauty, heaven and earth
Bright, youthful, fresh, as from creation's birth ;

The breeze propitious; the light cloudlets play'd
With it in sport, its impulse scarce obey'd.
The waves danc'd merrily, sparkling in the sun.
They, their sweet goal approaching, almost won,
Joy'd once more feeling amongst kindly men,
And prais'd the Gods, again and yet again,
Of their own Greece—great Hera—Leto's child,
Lustral Apollo—Aphrodité mild—   660
Poseidon holy—Hermes, gentle, kind,
Leader of souls, eye-wakener of the blind—
And wise Athena—and Dodona's lord,
Pelasgian Zeus, far-ruling, One-ador'd;
Then loos'd and started, skimming 'fore the breeze.
Amorgos pass'd, between the Cyclades
Gliding, would each to each, with eager shout,
This island bright, that well-known crag, point out,—
Save that from Naxos each one turn'd his eye,
Rev'rent, asham'd for Theseus standing by :—   670
" There Myconos frowns bare, the giants' grave !
" Here Delos smiles, late wand'rer o'er the wave !
" This Tenos, where Poseidon's waters flow,
" Scorning to mix with wine,—not Andros so
" Deems of her Dionysus !—to the North
" Euboea's small champion, Myrtos, bold stands forth,
" Threat'ning ; and o'er him mass'd, with wind-swept crown
" Half hid by clouds, black Oché's height looks down ;
" A temple of old days stands on its brow,
" Poseidon's shrine,—perchance he eyes us now !   680
" And see ye, Westward, Ceös, known for laws
" Equal from Themis, and the Gods' applause,
" The Lion's isle !—Beyond it lies the strand
" Harbour'd by sure Panormus, Cecrops' land.

X

" And now we near the Hollows, perilous strait !"
—But grief nor perils from the Gods await
Those pilgrims now ; and through Euripus, near.
'Tween Aulis, Chalcis, safe, the rock they clear ;
Coast rich Bœotia's, rude Eubœa's shores,
Rounding Cenæus, labouring with the oars ;   690
Leave Malia's depth behind and Œta's mount ;
Sweep round Poseidon's Cape ; and, ta'en account
Of those low reefs below th' Æantian height,
Stretch swift across Pelasgia's gulf—to right
And left hand all familiar.   Swifter flew
Argo, and silenter the heroes grew,
Nearing the end.   Now Pelion tower'd on high,
Her tall pines redd'ning with the sunset sky ;
Iölcos' waters ent'ring, show'd the town
Distinct, while Jason's tears fast trickled down,—   700
But one lamp only burning 'neath the gate,
Those on the farms were lighted not till late ;
So, with the last soft beam of parting day,
They moor'd her in the Pagasæan bay.

THE END.

LONDON PRINTED BY WILLIAM CLOWES AND SONS, STAMFORD STREET AND CHARING CROSS.

ALBEMARLE STREET, LONDON,
January, 1875.

MR. MURRAY'S

GENERAL LIST OF WORKS.

ALBERT (THE) MEMORIAL. A Descriptive and Illustrated
Account of the National Monument erected to the PRINCE CONSORT
at Kensington. Illustrated by Engravings of its Architecture, Decora-
tions, Sculptured Groups, Statues, Mosaics, Metalwork, &c. With
Descriptive Text. By DOYNE C. BELL. With 24 Plates. Folio. 12l. 12s.

———— (PRINCE) SPEECHES AND ADDRESSES with an Introduction, giving some outline of his Character. With Portrait. 8vo.
10s. 6d.; or Popular Edition, fcap. 8vo. 1s.

ABBOTT'S (REV. J.) Memoirs of a Church of England Missionary
in the North American Colonies. Post 8vo. 2s.

ABERCROMBIE'S (JOHN) Enquiries concerning the Intellectual
Powers and the Investigation of Truth. 19th Edition. Fcap. 8vo. 3s. 6d.

———————————— Philosophy of the Moral Feelings. 14th
Edition. Fcap. 8vo. 2s. 6d.

ACLAND'S (REV. CHARLES) Popular Account of the Manners and
Customs of India. Post 8vo. 2s.

ÆSOP'S FABLES. A New Version. With Historical Preface.
By Rev. THOMAS JAMES. With 100 Woodcuts, by TENNIEL and WOLF.
64th Thousand. Post 8vo. 2s. 6d.

AGRICULTURAL (ROYAL) JOURNAL. (Published half yearly.)

AIDS TO FAITH: a Series of Theological Essays. 8vo. 9s.

CONTENTS.

Miracles	DEAN MANSEL.
Evidences of Christianity	BISHOP FITZGERALD.
Prophecy & Mosaic Record of Creation	Dr. McCAUL.
Ideology and Subscription	Canon COOK.
The Pentateuch	Canon RAWLINSON.
Inspiration	BISHOP HAROLD BROWNE.
Death of Christ	ARCHBISHOP THOMSON.
Scripture and its Interpretation	BISHOP ELLICOTT.

AMBER-WITCH (THE). A most interesting Trial for Witchcraft. Translated by LADY DUFF GORDON. Post 8vo. 2s.

ARMY LIST (THE). Published Monthly by Authority.

ARTHUR'S (LITTLE) History of England. By LADY CALLCOTT.
New and Cheaper Edition, continued to 1872. With 36 Woodcuts. Fcap.
8vo. 1s. 6d.

AUSTIN'S (JOHN) LECTURES ON GENERAL JURISPRUDENCE; or, the
Philosophy of Positive Law. 5th Edition. Edited by ROBERT CAMP-
BELL. 2 Vols. 8vo. 32s.

———— Student's Edition, compiled from the above work. By
ROBERT CAMPBELL. Post 8vo.

ARNOLD'S (THOS.) Ecclesiastical and Secular Architecture of
Scotland: The Abbeys, Churches, Castles, and Mansions. With Illustrations. Medium 8vo.   [In Preparation.

B

ADMIRALTY PUBLICATIONS; Issued by direction of the Lords
Commissioners of the Admiralty:—

A MANUAL OF SCIENTIFIC ENQUIRY, for the Use of Travellers. Edited by Sir JOHN F. HERSCHEL and ROBERT MAIN, M.A. *Fourth Edition.* Woodcuts. Post 8vo. 3*s.* 6*d.*

GREENWICH ASTRONOMICAL OBSERVATIONS 1841 to 1846, and 1847 to 1871. Royal 4to. 20*s.* each.

MAGNETICAL AND METEOROLOGICAL OBSERVATIONS. 1840 to 1847. Royal 4to. 20*s.* each.

APPENDICES TO OBSERVATIONS.
1837. Logarithms of Sines and Cosines in Time. 3*s.*
1842. Catalogue of 1439 Stars, from Observations made in 1836 to 1841. 4*s.*
1845. Longitude of Valentia (Chronometrical). 3*s.*
1847. Description of Altazimuth. 3*s.*
    Twelve Years' Catalogue of Stars, from Observations made in 1836 to 1847. 4*s.*
    Description of Photographic Apparatus. 2*s.*
1851. Maskelyne's Ledger of Stars. 3*s.*
1852. I. Description of the Transit Circle. 3*s.*
1853. Refraction Tables. 3*s.*
1854. Description of the Zenith Tube. 3*s.*
    Six Years' Catalogue of Stars, from Observations. 1848 to 1853. 4*s.*
1862. Seven Years' Catalogue of Stars, from Observations. 1854 to 1860. 10*s.*
    Plan of Ground Buildings. 3*s.*
    Longitude of Valentia (Galvanic). 2*s.*
1864. Moon's Semid. from Occultations. 2*s.*
    Planetary Observations, 1831 to 1835. 2*s.*
1868. Corrections of Elements of Jupiter and Saturn. 2*s.*
    Second Seven Years' Catalogue of 2760 Stars for 1861 to 1867. 4*s.*
    Description of the Great Equatorial. 3*s.*
1856. Descriptive Chronograph. 3*s.*
1860. Reduction of Deep Thermometer Observations. 2*s.*
1871. History and Description of Water Telescope. 3*s.*

Cape of Good Hope Observations (Star Ledgers). 1856 to 1863. 2*s.*
    —   — — 1856. 5*s.*
——————— Astronomical Results. 1857 to 1858. 5*s.*
Report on Teneriffe Astronomical Experiment. 1856. 5*s.*
Paramatta Catalogue of 7385 Stars. 1822 to 1826. 4*s.*

ASTRONOMICAL RESULTS. 1847 to 1871. 4to. 3*s.* each.

MAGNETICAL AND METEOROLOGICAL RESULTS. 1847 to 1871. 4to. 3*s.* each.

REDUCTION OF THE OBSERVATIONS OF PLANETS. 1750 to 1830. Royal 4to. 20*s.* each.

— ——————————— LUNAR OBSERVATIONS. 1750 to 1830. 2 Vols. Royal 4to. 20*s.* each.
——————— 1831 to 1851. 4to. 10*s.* each.

BERNOULLI'S SEXCENTENARY TABLE. 1779. 4to. 5*s.*

BESSEL'S AUXILIARY TABLES FOR HIS METHOD OF CLEARING LUNAR DISTANCES. 8vo. 2*s.*

ENCKE'S BERLINER JAHRBUCH, for 1830. *Berlin,* 1828. 8vo. 9*s.*

HANSEN'S TABLES DE LA LUNE. 4to. 20*s.*

LAX'S TABLES FOR FINDING THE LATITUDE AND LONGITUDE. 1821. 8vo. 10*s.*

ADMIRALTY PUBLICATIONS—*continued.*

LUNAR OBSERVATIONS at GREENWICH. 1783 to 1819. Compared with the Tables, 1821. 4to. 7s. 6d.

MACLEAR ON LACAILLE'S ARC OF MERIDIAN. 2 Vols. 20s. each.

MAYER'S DISTANCES of the MOON'S CENTRE from the PLANETS. 1822, 3s.; 1823, 4s. 6d. 1824 to 1835. 8vo. 4s. each.

———— TABULÆ MOTUUM SOLIS ET LUNÆ. 1770. 5s.

———— ASTRONOMICAL OBSERVATIONS MADE AT GOTTINGEN, from 1756 to 1761. 1826. Folio. 7s. 6d.

NAUTICAL ALMANACS, from 1767 to 1877. 2s. 6d. each.

———— SELECTIONS FROM, up to 1812. 8vo. 5s. 1834-54. 5s.

———— SUPPLEMENTS, 1828 to 1833, 1837 and 1838. 2s. each.

———— TABLE requisite to be used with the N.A. 1781. 8vo. 5s.

SABINE'S PENDULUM EXPERIMENTS to DETERMINE THE FIGURE OF THE EARTH. 1825. 4to. 40s.

SHEPHERD'S TABLES for CORRECTING LUNAR DISTANCES. 1772. Royal 4to. 21s.

———— TABLES, GENERAL, of the MOON'S DISTANCE from the SUN, and 10 STARS. 1787. Folio. 5s. 6d.

TAYLOR'S SEXAGESIMAL TABLE. 1780. 4to. 15s.

———— TABLES OF LOGARITHMS. 4to. 60s.

TIARK'S ASTRONOMICAL OBSERVATIONS for the LONGITUDE of MADEIRA. 1822. 4to. 5s.

———— CHRONOMETRICAL OBSERVATIONS for DIFFERENCES of LONGITUDE between DOVER, PORTSMOUTH, and FALMOUTH. 1823. 4to. 5s.

VENUS and JUPITER: OBSERVATIONS of, compared with the TABLES. *London*, 1822. 4to. 2s.

WALES' AND BAYLY'S ASTRONOMICAL OBSERVATIONS. 1777. 4to. 21s.

———— REDUCTION OF ASTRONOMICAL OBSERVATIONS MADE IN THE SOUTHERN HEMISPHERE. 1764—1771. 1788. 4to. 10s. 6d.

BARBAULD'S (MRS.) Hymns in Prose for Children. With 112 Illustrations. Crown 8vo. 5s.

BARROW'S (SIR JOHN) Autobiographical Memoir, from Early Life to Advanced Age. Portrait. 8vo. 16s.

———— (JOHN) Life, Exploits, and Voyages of Sir Francis Drake. Post 8vo. 2s.

BARRY'S (SIR CHARLES) Life and Works. By CANON BARRY. *Second Edition.* With Portrait and Illustrations. Medium 8vo. 15s.

BATES' (H. W.) Records of a Naturalist on the River Amazon during eleven years of Adventure and Travel. *Third Edition.* Illustrations. Post 8vo. 7s. 6d.

BEAUCLERK'S (LADY DIANA) Summer and Winter in Norway. *Third Edition.* With Illustrations. Small 8vo. 6s.

BELCHER'S (LADY) Account of the Mutineers of the 'Bounty,' and their Descendants; with their Settlements in Pitcairn and Norfolk Islands. With Illustrations. Post 8vo. 12s.

BELL'S (SIR CHAS.) Familiar Letters. Portrait. Post 8vo. 12s.

BELT'S (Thos.) Naturalist in Nicaragua, including a Residence at the Gold Mines of Chontales; with Journeys in the Savannahs
and Forests; and Observations on Animals and Plants. Illustrations.
Post 8vo. 12s.

BERTRAM'S (Jas. G.) Harvest of the Sea: an Account of British
Food Fishes, including sketches of Fisheries and Fisher Folk. *Third
Edition.* With 50 Illustrations. 8vo. 9s.

BIBLE COMMENTARY. Explanatory and Critical. With
a Revision of the Translation. By BISHOPS and CLERGY of the
ANGLICAN CHURCH. Edited by F. C. Cook, M.A., Canon of Exeter.
Medium 8vo. Vol. I., 30s. Vols. II. and III., 36s. Vol. IV., 24s.

Vol. I.	Genesis	Bishop of Ely.
	Exodus	Canon Cook; Rev. Sam. Clark.
	Leviticus	Rev. Samuel Clark.
	Numbers	Canon Espin; Rev. J. F. Thrupp.
Vols. II. and III.	Deuteronomy .... }Canon Espin.	
	Joshua	
	Judges, Ruth, Samuel.	Bishop of Bath and Wells.
	Kings, Chronicles, Ez-ra, Nehemiah, Esther }	Canon Rawlinson.
Vol. IV.	Job	Canon Cook.
	Psalms	{Dean of Wells, Canon Cook Rev. C. I. Elliott.
	Proverbs	Rev. E. H. Plumptre.
	Ecclesiastes	Rev. W. T. Bullock.
	Song of Solomon	Rev. T. Kingsbury.
Vol. V.	Isaiah................	Rev. W. Kay, D.D.
	Jeremiah	Dean of Canterbury.

BICKMORE'S (A. S.) Travels in the Eastern Archipelago,
1865-6; a Popular Description of the Islands, with their Natural History, Geography, Manners and Customs of the People, &c. With Maps
and Illustrations. 8vo. 21s.

BIRCH'S (Samuel) History of Ancient Pottery and Porcelain:
Egyptian, Assyrian, Greek, Roman, and Etruscan. *Second Edition.*
With Coloured Plates and 200 Illustrations. Medium 8vo. 42s.

BIRD'S (Isabella) Hawaiian Archipelago; or Six Months Among
the Palm Groves, Coral Reefs, and Volcanoes of the Sandwich Islands.
With Illustrations. Crown 8vo.

BISSET'S (Andrew) History of the Commonwealth of England,
from the Death of Charles I. to the Expulsion of the Long Parliament
by Cromwell. Chiefly from the MSS. in the State Paper Office. 2 vols.
8vo. 30s.

BLUNT'S (Rev. J. J.) Undesigned Coincidences in the Writings of
the Old and New Testament, an Argument of their Veracity: containing
the Books of Moses, Historical and Prophetical Scriptures, and the
Gospels and Acts. *Eleventh Edition.* Post 8vo. 6s.
———— History of the Church in the First Three Centuries.
Fifth Edition. Post 8vo. 6s.
—— Parish Priest; His Duties, Acquirements and Obliga-
tions. *Sixth Edition.* Post 8vo. 6s.
———— Lectures on the Right Use of the Early Fathers.
Third Edition. 8vo. 9s.
University Sermons. *Second Edition.* Post 8vo. 6s.
———— Plain Sermons. *Sixth Edition.* 2 vols. Post 8vo. 12s.

BLOMFIELD'S (Bishop) Memoir, with Selections from his Correspondence. By his Son. *Second Edition.* Portrait, post 8vo. 12s.

BOSWELL'S (James) Life of Samuel Johnson, LL.D. Including
the Tour to the Hebrides. By Mr. Croker. *A new and revised Library
Edition.* Portraits. 4 vols. 8vo. [*In Preparation.*

BRACE'S (C. L.) Manual of Ethnology; or the Races of the Old World. Post 8vo. 6s.

BOOK OF COMMON PRAYER. Illustrated with Coloured Borders, Initial Letters, and Woodcuts. 8vo. 18s.

BORROW'S (George) Bible in Spain; or the Journeys, Adventures, and Imprisonments of an Englishman in an Attempt to circulate the Scriptures in the Peninsula. Post 8vo. 5s.

———— Zincali, or the Gypsies of Spain; their Manners, Customs, Religion, and Language. With Portrait. Post 8vo. 5s.

———— Lavengro; The Scholar—The Gypsy—and the Priest. Post 8vo. 5s.

———— Romany Rye—a Sequel to "Lavengro." Post 8vo. 5s.

———— Wild Wales: its People, Language, and Scenery. Post 8vo. 5s.

———— Romano Lavo-Lil; Word-Book of the Romany, or English Gypsy Language; with Specimens of their Poetry, and an account of certain Gypsyries. Post 8vo. 10s. 6d.

BRAY'S (Mrs.) Life of Thomas Stothard, R.A. With Portrait and 60 Woodcuts. 4to. 21s.

———— Revolt of the Protestants in the Cevennes. With some Account of the Huguenots in the Seventeenth Century. Post 8vo. 10s. 6d.

BRITISH ASSOCIATION REPORTS. 8vo.

York and Oxford, 1831-32, 13s. 6d.	Hull, 1853, 10s. 6d.
Cambridge, 1833, 12s.	Liverpool, 1854, 18s.
Edinburgh, 1834, 15s.	Glasgow, 1855, 15s.
Dublin, 1835, 13s. 6d.	Cheltenham, 1856, 18s.
Bristol, 1836, 12s.	Dublin, 1857, 15s.
Liverpool, 1837, 16s. 6d.	Leeds, 1858, 20s.
Newcastle, 1838, 15s.	Aberdeen, 1859, 15s.
Birmingham, 1839, 13s. 6d.	Oxford, 1860, 25s.
Glasgow, 1840, 15s.	Manchester, 1861, 15s.
Plymouth, 1841, 13s. 6d.	Cambridge, 1862, 20s.
Manchester, 1842, 10s. 6d.	Newcastle, 1863, 25s.
Cork, 1843, 12s.	Bath, 1864, 18s.
York, 1844, 20s.	Birmingham, 1865, 25s
Cambridge, 1845, 12s.	Nottingham, 1866, 24s.
Southampton, 1846, 15s.	Dundee, 1867, 26s.
Oxford, 1847, 18s.	Norwich, 1868, 25s.
Swansea, 1848, 9s.	Exeter, 1869, 22s.
Birmingham, 1849, 10s.	Liverpool, 1870, 18s.
Edinburgh, 1850, 15s.	Edinburgh, 1871, 16s.
Ipswich, 1851, 16s. 6d.	Brighton, 1872, 24s.
Belfast, 1852, 15s.	Bradford, 1873, 25s.

BROUGHTON'S (Lord) Journey through Albania, Turkey in Europe and Asia, to Constantinople. Illustrations. 2 Vols. 8vo. 30s.

———— Visits to Italy. 2 Vols. Post 8vo. 18s.

BROWNLOW'S (Lady) Reminiscences of a Septuagenarian. From the year 1802 to 1815 Third Edition. Post 8vo. 7s. 6d.

BRUGSCH'S (Professor) History of Ancient Egypt. Derived from Monuments and Inscriptions. New Edition. Translated by H. Danby Seymour. 8vo. [In Preparation.

BURGON'S (Rev. J. W.) Christian Gentleman; or, Memoir of Patrick Fraser Tytler. Second Edition. Post 8vo. 9s.

———— Letters from Rome. Post 8vo. 12s.

BURN'S (Col.) Dictionary of Naval and Military Technical Terms, English and French—French and English. Fourth Edition. Crown 8vo. 15s.

BURROW'S (Montagu) Constitutional Progress. A Series of Lectures delivered before the University of Oxford. 2nd Edition. Post 8vo. 5s.

BUXTON'S (CHARLES) Memoirs of Sir Thomas Fowell Buxton, Bart. With Selections from his Correspondence. Portrait. 8vo. 16s. *Popular Edition.* Fcap. 8vo. 5s.

———— - Notes of Thought. With Biographical Sketch. By Rev. LLEWELLYN DAVIES. With Portrait. Crown 8vo. 10s. 6d.

BURCKHARDT'S (DR. JACOB) Cicerone; or Art Guide to Painting in Italy. Edited by REV. DR. A. VON ZAHN, and Translated from the German by MRS. A. CLOUGH. Post 8vo. 6s.

BYLES' (SIR JOHN) Foundations of Religion in the Mind and Heart of Man. Post 8vo.   [*Nearly ready.*

BYRON'S (LORD) Life, Letters, and Journals. By THOMAS MOORE. *Cabinet Edition.* Plates. 6 Vols. Fcap. 8vo. 18s.; or One Volume, Portraits. Royal 8vo., 7s. 6d.

———————— - and Poetical Works. *Popular Edition.* Portraits. 2 vols. Royal 8vo. 15s.

———— Poetical Works. *Library Edition.* Portrait. 6 Vols. 8vo. 45s. *Cabinet Edition.* Plates. 10 Vols. 12mo. 30s.

———— - *Pocket Edition.* 8 Vols. 24mo. 21s. *In a case.*

———— *Popular Edition.* Plates. Royal 8vo. 7s. 6d. *Pearl Edition.* Crown 8vo. 2s. 6d.

———————— Childe Harold. With 80 Engravings. Crown 8vo. 12s.

————   ———— . 16mo. 2s. 6d.

————   ———— Vignettes. 16mo. 1s.

. ———————— Portrait. 16mo. 6d.

———————— Tales and Poems. 24mo. 2s. 6d.

———————— Miscellaneous. 2 Vols. 24mo. 5s.

———————— Dramas and Plays. 2 Vols. 24mo. 5s.

———————— Don Juan and Beppo. 2 Vols. 24mo. 5s.

———————— Beauties. Poetry and Prose. Portrait. Fcap. 8vo. 3s. 6d.

BUTTMAN'S LEXILOGUS; a Critical Examination of the Meaning of numerous Greek Words, chiefly in Homer and Hesiod. By Rev. J. R. FISHLAKE. *Fifth Edition.* 8vo. 12s.

———— — IRREGULAR GREEK VERBS. With all the Tenses extant—their Formation, Meaning, and Usage, with Notes, by Rev. J. R. FISHLAKE. *Fifth Edition.* Post 8vo. 6s.

CALLCOTT'S (LADY) Little Arthur's History of England. *New and Cheaper Edition, brought down to* 1872. With Woodcuts. Fcap. 8vo. 1s. 6d.

CARNARVON'S (LORD) Portugal, Gallicia, and the Basque Provinces. *Third Edition.* Post 8vo. 3s. 6d.

———   ————— Reminiscences of Athens and the Morea. With Map. Crown 8vo. 7s. 6d.

———   —— Recollections of the Druses of Lebanon. With Notes on their Religion. *Third Edition.* Post 8vo. 5s. 6d.

CASTLEREAGH (THE) DESPATCHES, from the commencement of the official career of Viscount Castlereagh to the close of his life. 12 Vols. 8vo. 14s. each.

CAMPBELL'S (Lord) Lord Chancellors and Keepers of the Great Seal of England. From the Earliest Times to the Death of Lord Eldon in 1838. *Fifth Edition.* 10 Vols. Crown 8vo. *6s.* each.

———— Chief Justices of England. From the Norman Conquest to the Death of Lord Tenterden. *Third Edition.* 4 Vols. Crown 8vo. *6s.* each.

———— . Lords Lyndhurst and Brougham. 8vo. 16s.

———— Shakspeare's Legal Acquirements. 8vo. 5s. 6d.

— — Lord Bacon. Fcap. 8vo. 2s. 6d.

— ———— (Sir Neil) Account of Napoleon at Fontainebleau and Elba. Being a Journal of Occurrences and Notes of his Conversations, &c. Portrait. 8vo. 15s.

———— (Sir George) India as it may be: an Outline of a proposed Government and Policy. 8vo.

———— (Thos.) Essay on English Poetry. With Short Lives of the British Poets. Post 8vo. 3s. 6d.

CATHCART'S (Sir George) Commentaries on the War in Russia and Germany, 1812-13. Plans. 8vo. 14s.

CAVALCASELLE and CROWE'S History of Painting in Italy, from the 2nd to the 16th Century. With Illustrations. 5 Vols. 8vo. 21s. each.

———— Early Flemish Painters, their Lives and Works. Illustrations. Post 8vo. 10s. 6d.; or Large Paper, 8vo. 15s.

CHILD'S (G. Chaplin, M.D.) Benedicite; or, Song of the Three Children; being Illustrations of the Power, Beneficence, and Design manifested by the Creator in his works. *10th Thousand.* Post 8vo. 6s.

CHISHOLM'S (Mrs.) Perils of the Polar Seas; True Stories of Arctic Discovery and Adventure. Illustrations. Post 8vo. 6s.

CHURTON'S (Archdeacon) Gongora. An Historical Essay on the Age of Philip III. and IV. of Spain. With Translations. Portrait. 2 Vols. Small 8vo. 12s.

———— New Testament. Edited with a Plain Practical Commentary for the use of Families and General Readers. With 100 Panoramic and other Views, from Sketches and Photographs made on the Spot. 2 vols. 8vo. 21s.

CICERO'S LIFE AND TIMES. His Character as a Statesman, Orator, and Friend, with a Selection from his Correspondence and Orations. By William Forsyth, M.P. *Third Edition.* With Illustrations. 8vo. 10s. 6d.

CLARK'S (Sir James) Memoir of Dr. John Conolly. Comprising a Sketch of the Treatment of the Insane in Europe and America. With Portrait. Post 8vo. 10s. 6d.

CLIVE'S (Lord) Life. By Rev. G. R. Gleig. Post 8vo. 3s. 6d.

CLODE'S (C. M.) Military Forces of the Crown; their Administration and Government. 2 Vols. 8vo. 21s. each.

———— Administration of Justice under Military and Martial Law, as applicable to the Army, Navy, Marine, and Auxiliary Forces. 2nd Edition. 8vo. 12s.

COLCHESTER (The) PAPERS. The Diary and Correspondence of Charles Abbott, Lord Colchester, Speaker of the House of Commons 1802-1817. Portrait. 3 Vols. 8vo. 42s.

CHURCH (THE) & THE AGE. Essays on the Principles and Present Position of the Anglican Church. 2 vols. 8vo. 26s. Contents :—

VOL. I.

Anglican Principles.—Dean Hook.
Modern Religious Thought.—Bishop Ellicott.
State, Church, and Synods.—Rev. Dr. Irons.
Religious Use of Taste.—Rev. R. St. John Tyrwhitt.
Place of the Laity.— Professor Burrows
Parish Priest.—Rev. Walsham How.
Divines of 16th and 17th Centuries. —Rev. A. W. Haddan.
Liturgies and Ritual, Rev. M. F. Sadler.
Church & Education.—Canon Barry.
Indian Missions.— Sir Bartle Frere.
Church and the People.—Rev. W. D. Maclagan.
Conciliation and Comprehension.— Rev. Dr. Weir.

VOL. II.

Church and Pauperism.—Earl Nelson.
American Church.—Bishop of Western New York.
Church and Science. — Prebendary Clark.
Ecclesiastical Law.—Isambard Brunel.
Church & National Education.— Canon Norris.
Church and Universities.—John G. Talbot.
Toleration.—Dean Cowie.
Eastern Church and Anglican Communion.—Rev. Geo. Williams.
A Disestablished Church.—Dean of Cashel.
Christian Tradition.—Rev. Dr. Irons.
Dogma.—Rev. Dr. Weir.
Parochial Councils. — Archdeacon Chapman.

COLERIDGE'S (SAMUEL TAYLOR) Table-Talk. Portrait. 12mo. 3s. 6d.

COLLINGWOOD'S (CUTHBERT) Rambles of a Naturalist on the Shores and Waters of the China Sea. Being Observations in Natural History during a Voyage to China, &c. With Illustrations. 8vo. 16s.

COLONIAL LIBRARY. [See Home and Colonial Library.]

COOK'S (Canon) Sermons Preached at Lincoln's Inn. 8vo. 9s.

COOKERY (MODERN DOMESTIC). Founded on Principles of Economy and Practical Knowledge, and adapted for Private Families. By a Lady. Woodcuts. Fcap. 8vo. 5s.

COOPER'S (T. T.) Travels of a Pioneer of Commerce on an Overland Journey from China towards India. Illustrations. 8vo. 16s.

CORNWALLIS (THE) Papers and Correspondence during the American War,—Administrations in India,—Union with Ireland, and Peace of Amiens. *Second Edition.* 3 Vols. 8vo. 63s.

COWPER'S (COUNTESS) Diary while Lady of the Bedchamber to Caroline Princess of Wales, 1714–20. Edited by Hon. SPENCER COWPER. *Second Edition.* Portrait. 8vo. 10s. 6d.

CRABBE'S (REV. GEORGE) Life and Poetical Works. With Illustrations. Royal 8vo. 7s.

CROKER'S (J. W.) Progressive Geography for Children. *Fifth Edition.* 16mo. 1s. 6d.

—————— Stories for Children, Selected from the History of England. *Fifteenth Edition.* Woodcuts. 16mo. 2s. 6d.

—— Boswell's Life of Johnson. Including the Tour to the Hebrides. *New and revised Library Edition.* Portraits. 4 vols. 8vo. [In Preparation.

—————— Essays on the Early Period of the French Revolution. 8vo. 15s.

——— Historical Essay on the Guillotine. Fcap. 8vo. 1s.

CUMMING'S (R. Gordon) Five Years of a Hunter's Life in the Far Interior of South Africa. *Sixth Edition.* Woodcuts. Post 8vo. 6s.

CROWE'S and CAVALCASELLE'S Lives of the Early Flemish Painters. Woodcuts. Post 8vo, 10s. 6d.; or Large Paper, 8vo, 15s.

——— History of Painting in Italy, from 2nd to 16th Century. Derived from Researches into the Works of Art in that Country. With 100 Illustrations. 5 Vols. 8vo. 21s. each.

CUNYNGHAME'S (Sir Arthur) Travels in the Eastern Caucasus, on the Caspian, and Black Seas, in Daghestan and the Frontiers of Persia and Turkey. With Map and Illustrations. 8vo. 18s.

CURTIUS' (Professor) Student's Greek Grammar, for the Upper Forms. Edited by Dr. Wm. Smith. Post 8vo. 6s.

——— Elucidations of the above Grammar. Translated by Evelyn Abbot. Post 8vo. 7s. 6d.

——— Smaller Greek Grammar for the Middle and Lower Forms. Abridged from the larger work. 12mo. 3s. 6d.

——— Accidence of the Greek Language. Extracted from the above work. 12mo. 2s. 6d.

——— Principles of Greek Etymology. Translated by A. S. Wilkins, M.A., and E. B. England, B.A. 8vo. *Nearly Ready.*

CURZON'S (Hon. Robert) Armenia and Erzeroum. A Year on the Frontiers of Russia, Turkey, and Persia. *Third Edition.* Woodcuts. Post 8vo. 7s. 6d.

——— Visits to the Monasteries of the Levant. *Fifth Edition.* Illustrations. Post 8vo. 7s. 6d.

CUST'S (General) Lives of the Warriors of the 17th Century—The Thirty Years' War. 2 Vols. 16s. Civil Wars of France and England. 2 Vols. 16s. Commanders of Fleets and Armies before the Enemy. 2 Vols. 18s.

——— Annals of the Wars—18th & 19th Century, 1700—1815. With Maps. 9 Vols. Post 8vo. 5s. each.

DAVIS'S (Nathan) Ruined Cities of Numidia and Carthaginia. Illustrations. 8vo. 16s.

DAVY'S (Sir Humphry) Consolations in Travel; or, Last Days of a Philosopher. *Seventh Edition.* Woodcuts. Fcap. 8vo. 3s 6d.

——— Salmonia; or, Days of Fly Fishing. *Fifth Edition.* Woodcuts. Fcap. 8vo. 3s. 6d.

DARWIN'S (Charles) Journal of Researches into the Natural History of the Countries visited during a Voyage round the World. *Eleventh Thousand.* Post 8vo. 9s.

——— Origin of Species by Means of Natural Selection : or, the Preservation of Favoured Races in the Struggle for Life. *Sixth Edition.* Post 8vo. 7s. 6d.

——— Variation of Animals and Plants under Domestication. With Illustrations. 2 Vols. 8vo. 28s.

——— Descent of Man, and Selection in Relation to Sex. With Illustrations. Crown 8vo. 9s.

——— Expressions of the Emotions in Man and Animals. With Illustrations. Crown 8vo. 12s.

——— Fertilization of Orchids through Insect Agency, and as to the good of Intercrossing. Woodcuts. Post 8vo. 9s.

——— Fact and Argument for Darwin. By Fritz Muller. With numerous Illustrations and Additions by the Author. Translated from the German by W. S. Dallas. Woodcuts. Post 8vo. 6s.

DELEPIERRE'S (OCTAVE) History of Flemish Literature. 8vo. 9s.

———— —— Historic Difficulties & Contested Events. Post 8vo. 6s.

DENISON'S (E. B.) Life of Bishop Lonsdale. With Selections from his Writings. With Portrait. Crown 8vo. 10s. 6d.

DERBY'S (EARL OF) Iliad of Homer rendered into English Blank Verse. 7th Edition. 2 Vols. Post 8vo. 10s.

DE ROS'S (LORD) Young Officer's Companion; or, Essays on Military Duties and Qualities; with Examples and Illustrations from History. Post 8vo. 9s.

DEUTSCH'S (EMANUEL) Talmud, Islam, The Targums and other Literary Remains. 8vo. 12s.

DOG-BREAKING; the Most Expeditious, Certain, and Easy Method, whether great excellence or only mediocrity be required. With a Few Hints for those who Love the Dog and the Gun. By LIEUT.-GEN. HUTCHINSON. Fifth Edition. With 40 Woodcuts. Crown 8vo. 9s.

DOMESTIC MODERN COOKERY. Founded on Principles of Economy and Practical Knowledge, and adapted for Private Families. Woodcuts. Fcap. 8vo. 5s.

DOUGLAS'S (SIR HOWARD) Life and Adventures. Portrait. 8vo. 15s.

———————— Theory and Practice of Gunnery. Plates. 8vo. 21s.

——————— — Construction of Bridges and the Passage of Rivers, in Military Operations. Plates. 8vo. 21s.

——————— (WM.) Horse-Shoeing; As it Is, and As it Should be. Illustrations. Post 8vo. 7s. 6d.

DRAKE'S (SIR FRANCIS) Life, Voyages, and Exploits, by Sea and Land. By JOHN BARROW. Third Edition. Post 8vo. 2s.

DRINKWATER'S (JOHN) History of the Siege of Gibraltar, 1779-1783. With a Description and Account of that Garrison from the Earliest Periods. Post 8vo. 2s.

DUCANGE'S MEDIÆVAL LATIN-ENGLISH DICTIONARY. Translated by Rev. E. A. DAYMAN, M.A. Small 4to. [In preparation.

DU CHAILLU'S (PAUL B.) EQUATORIAL AFRICA, with Accounts of the Gorilla, the Nest-building Ape, Chimpanzee, Crocodile, &c. Illustrations. 8vo. 21s.

——————————— Journey to Ashango Land; and Further Penetration into Equatorial Africa. Illustrations. 8vo. 21s.

DUFFERIN'S (LORD) Letters from High Latitudes; an Account of a Yacht Voyage to Iceland, Jan Mayen, and Spitzbergen. Fifth Edition. Woodcuts. Post 8vo. 7s. 6d.

DUNCAN'S (MAJOR) History of the Royal Artillery. Compiled from the Original Records. Second Edition. With Portraits. 2 Vols. 8vo. 30s.

DYER'S (THOS. H.) History of Modern Europe, from the taking of Constantinople by the Turks to the close of the War in the Crimea. With Index. 4 Vols. 8vo. 42s.

EASTLAKE'S (SIR CHARLES) Contributions to the Literature of the Fine Arts. With Memoir of the Author, and Selections from his Correspondence. By LADY EASTLAKE. 2 Vols. 8vo. 24s.

EDWARDS' (W. H.) Voyage up the River Amazons, including a Visit to Para. Post 8vo. 2s.

ELDON'S (Lord) Public and Private Life, with Selections from his Correspondence and Diaries. By Horace Twiss. *Third Edition.* Portrait. 2 Vols. Post 8vo. 21s.

ELGIN'S (Lord) Letters and Journals. Edited by Theodore Walrond. With Preface by Dean Stanley. *Second Edition.* 8vo. 14s.

ELLESMERE'S (Lord) Two Sieges of Vienna by the Turks. Translated from the German. Post 8vo. 2s.

ELLIS'S (W.) Madagascar, including a Journey to the Capital, with notices of Natural History and the People. Woodcuts. 8vo. 16s.

———————— Madagascar Revisited. Setting forth the Persecutions and Heroic Sufferings of the Native Christians. Illustrations. 8vo. 16s.

———————— Memoir. By His Son. With his Character and Work. By Rev. Henry Allon, D.D. Portrait. 8vo. 10s. 6d.

— (Robinson) Poems and Fragments of Catullus. 16mo. 5s.

ELPHINSTONE'S (Hon. Mountstuart) History of India—the Hindoo and Mahomedan Periods. *Sixth Edition.* Map. 8vo. 18s.

———————— ———— (H. W.) Patterns for Turning; Comprising Elliptical and other Figures cut on the Lathe without the use of any Ornamental Chuck. With 70 Illustrations. Small 4to. 15s.

ENGEL'S (Carl) Music of the Most Ancient Nations; particularly of the Assyrians, Egyptians, and Hebrews; with Special Reference to the Discoveries in Western Asia and in Egypt. *Second Edition.* With 100 Illustrations. 8vo. 10s. 6d.

ENGLAND. See Callcott, Croker, Hume, Markham, Smith, and Stanhope.

ENGLISHWOMAN IN AMERICA. Post 8vo. 10s. 6d.

ESSAYS ON CATHEDRALS. With an Introduction. By Dean Howson. 8vo. 12s.

CONTENTS.

Recollections of a Dean.—Bishop of Carlisle.	Cathedral Churches of the Old Foundation.—Edward A. Freeman.
Cathedral Canons and their Work.—Canon Norris	Welsh Cathedrals.—Canon Perowne.
Cathedrals in Ireland, Past and Future.—Dean of Cashel.	Education of Choristers.—Sir F. Gore Ouseley.
Cathedrals in their Missionary Aspect.—A. J. B. Beresford Hope.	Cathedral Schools.—Canon Durham.
Cathedral Foundations in Relation to Religious Thought.—Canon Westcott.	Cathedral Reform.—Chancellor Massingberd.
	Relation of the Chapter to the Bishop. Chancellor Benson.
	Architecture of the Cathedral Churches.—Canon Venables.

ETHNOLOGICAL SOCIETY'S TRANSACTIONS. Vols. I. to VI. 8vo.

ELZE'S (Karl) Life of Lord Byron. With a Critical Essay on his Place in Literature. Translated from the German, and Edited with Notes. With Original Portrait and Facsimile. 8vo. 16s.

FAMILY RECEIPT-BOOK. A Collection of a Thousand Valuable and Useful Receipts. Fcap. 8vo. 5s. 6d.

FARRAR'S (A. S.) Critical History of Free Thought in reference to the Christian Religion. 8vo. 16s.

———————— (F. W.) Origin of Language, based on Modern Researches. Fcap. 8vo. 5s.

FERGUSSON'S (JAMES) History of Architecture in all Countries from the Earliest Times. Vols. I. and II. Ancient and Mediæval. With 1,000 Illustrations. Medium 8vo. 63s.

———————— Vol. III. Indian and Eastern. With 300 Illustrations. Medium 8vo. *[In the Press.*

———————— Vol. IV. Modern. With 330 Illustrations. Medium 8vo. 31s. 6d.

———————— Rude Stone Monuments in all Countries; their Age and Uses. With 230 Illustrations. Medium 8vo. 24s.

———————— Holy Sepulchre and the Temple at Jerusalem. Woodcuts. 8vo. 7s. 6d.

FLEMING'S (PROFESSOR) Student's Manual of Moral Philosophy. With Quotations and References. Post 8vo. 7s. 6d.

FLOWER GARDEN. By REV. THOS. JAMES. Fcap. 8vo. 1s.

FORD'S (RICHARD) Gatherings from Spain. Post 8vo. 3s. 6d.

FORSYTH'S (WILLIAM) Life and Times of Cicero. With Selections from his Correspondence and Orations. *Third Edition.* Illustrations. 8vo. 10s. 6d.

———————— Hortensius; an Historical Essay on the Office and Duties of an Advocate. *Second Edition.* Illustrations. 8vo. 12s.

———————— History of Ancient Manuscripts. Post 8vo. 2s. 6d.

———————— Novels and Novelists of the 18th Century, in Illustration of the Manners and Morals of the Age. Post 8vo. 10s. 6d.

FORTUNE'S (ROBERT) Narrative of Two Visits to the Tea Countries of China, 1843-52. *Third Edition.* Woodcuts. 2 Vols. Post 8vo. 18s.

FOSS' (Edward) Biographia Juridica, or Biographical Dictionary of the Judges of England, from the Conquest to the Present Time, 1066-1870. Medium 8vo. 21s.

———————— Tabulæ Curiales; or, Tables of the Superior Courts of Westminster Hall. Showing the Judges who sat in them from 1066 to 1864. 8vo. 10s. 6d.

FRANCE. *⁎* See MARKHAM, SMITH, Student's.

FRENCH (THE) in Algiers; The Soldier of the Foreign Legion— and the Prisoners of Abd-el-Kadir. Translated by LADY DUFF GORDON. Post 8vo. 2s.

FRERE'S (SIR BARTLE) Indian Missions. *Third Edition.* Small 8vo. 2s. 6d.

———————— Eastern Africa as a field for Missionary Labour. With Map. Crown 8vo. 5s.

———————— Bengal Famine. How it will be Met and How to Prevent Future Famines in India. With Maps. Crown 8vo. 5s.

———————— (M.) Old Deccan Days; or Fairy Legends Current in Southern India. With Notes, by SIR BARTLE FRERE. With Illustrations. Fcap. 8vo. 6s.

GALTON'S (FRANCIS) Art of Travel; or, Hints on the Shifts and Contrivances available in Wild Countries. *Fifth Edition.* Woodcuts. Post 8vo. 7s. 6d.

GEOGRAPHICAL SOCIETY'S JOURNAL. (*Published Yearly.*)

GEORGE'S (ERNEST) Mosel; a Series of Twenty Etchings, with Descriptive Letterpress. Imperial 4to. 42s.

———————— Loire and South of France; a Series of Twenty Etchings, with Descriptive Text. Folio. 42s.

GERMANY (HISTORY OF). See MARKHAM.

GIBBON'S (EDWARD) History of the Decline and Fall of the Roman Empire. Edited by MILMAN and GUIZOT. *A New Edition*. Edited, with Notes, by Dr. WM. SMITH. Maps. 8 Vols. 8vo. 60s.

———— (The Student's Gibbon); Being an Epitome of the above work, incorporating the Researches of Recent Commentators. By Dr. WM. SMITH. Woodcuts. Post 8vo. 7s. 6d.

GIFFARD'S (EDWARD) Deeds of Naval Daring; or, Anecdotes of the British Navy. Fcap. 8vo. 3s. 6d.

GLADSTONE'S (W. E.) Financial Statements of 1853, 1860, 63–65. 8vo. 12s.

GLEIG'S (G. R.) Campaigns of the British Army at Washington and New Orleans. Post 8vo. 2s.

———— Story of the Battle of Waterloo. Post 8vo. 3s. 6d.

———— Narrative of Sale's Brigade in Affghanistan. Post 8vo. 2s.

———— Life of Lord Clive. Post 8vo. 3s. 6d.

———————— Sir Thomas Munro. Post 8vo. 3s. 6d.

GOLDSMITH'S (OLIVER) Works. Edited with Notes by PETER CUNNINGHAM. Vignettes. 4 Vols. 8vo. 30s.

GORDON'S (SIR ALEX.) Sketches of German Life, and Scenes from the War of Liberation. Post 8vo. 3s. 6d.

———— (LADY DUFF) Amber-Witch: A Trial for Witchcraft. Post 8vo. 2s.

———— French in Algiers. 1. The Soldier of the Foreign Legion. 2. The Prisoners of Abd-el-Kadir. Post 8vo. 2s.

GRAMMARS. See CURTIUS ; HALL; HUTTON; KING EDWARD ; MATTHIÆ; MAETZNER; SMITH.

GREECE. *See* GROTE—SMITH—Student.

GREY'S (EARL) Correspondence with King William IVth and Sir Herbert Taylor, from 1830 to 1832. 2 Vols. 8vo. 30s.

———————— Parliamentary Government and Reform ; with Suggestions for the Improvement of our Representative System. *Second Edition*. 8vo. 9s.

GRUNER'S (LEWIS) Terra-Cotta Architecture of North Italy, from careful Drawings and Restorations. With Illustrations, engraved and printed in Colours. Small folio. 5l. 5s.

GUIZOT'S (M.) Meditations on Christianity, and on the Religious Questions of the Day. Part I. The Essence. Part II. Present State. Part III. Relation to Society and Opinion. 3 Vols. Post 8vo. 30s.

GROTE'S (GEORGE) History of Greece. From the Earliest Times to the close of the generation contemporary with the death of Alexander the Great. *Library Edition*. Portrait, Maps, and Plans. 10 Vols. 8vo. 120s. *Cabinet Edition*. Portrait and Plans. 12 Vols. Post 8vo. 6s. each.

———— PLATO, and other Companions of Socrates. 3 Vols. 8vo. 45s.

———— ARISTOTLE. Edited by Professors BAIN and ROBERTSON. 2 Vols. 8vo. 32s.

———— Minor Works. With Critical Remarks on his Intellectual Character, Writings, and Speeches. By ALEX.BAIN, LL.D. Portrait. 8vo. 14s.

———— Personal Life. Compiled from Family Documents, Private Memoranda, and Original Letters to and from Various Friends. By Mrs. Grote. Portrait. 8vo. 12s.

———— (MRS.) Memoir of Ary Scheffer. Portrait. 8vo. 8s. 6d.

HALL'S (T. D.) School Manual of English Grammar. With
Copious Exercises. 12mo, 3s. 6d.
——— Primary English Grammar for Elementary Schools.
16mo, 1s.
——— Child's First Latin Book, including a Systematic Treatment of the New Pronunciation, and a full Praxis of Nouns, Adjec-
tives, and Pronouns. 16mo. 1s. 6d.

HALLAM'S (Henry) Constitutional History of England, from the
Accession of Henry the Seventh to the Death of George the Second.
Library Edition. 3 Vols. 8vo. 30s. Cabinet Edition. 3 Vols. Post 8vo. 12s.
——— Student's Edition of the above work. Edited by
Wm. Smith, D.C.L. Post 8vo. 7s. 6d.
——— History of Europe during the Middle Ages. Library
Edition. 3 Vols. 8vo. 30s. Cabinet Edition, 3 Vols. Post 8vo. 12s.
— ... — Student's Edition of the above work. Edited by
Wm. Smith, D.C.L. Post 8vo. 7s. 6d.
——— Literary History of Europe, during the 15th, 16th and
17th Centuries. Library Edition. 3 Vols. 8vo. 36s. Cabinet Edition.
4 Vols. Post 8vo. 16s.
——— (Arthur) Literary Remains; in Verse and Prose.
Portrait. Fcap. 8vo. 3s. 6d.

HAMILTON'S (Gen. Sir F. W.) History of the Grenadier Guards.
From Original Documents in the Rolls' Records, War Office, Regimental
Records, &c. With Illustrations. 3 Vols. 8vo. 63s.

HANNAH'S (Rev. Dr.) Divine and Human Elements in Holy
Scripture. 8vo. 10s. 6d.

HART'S ARMY LIST. (Published Quarterly and Annually.)

HAY'S (Sir J. H. Drummond) Western Barbary, its Wild Tribes
and Savage Animals. Post 8vo. 2s.

HEAD'S (Sir Francis) Royal Engineer. Illustrations. 8vo. 12s.
——— Life of Sir John Burgoyne. Post 8vo. 1s.
——— Rapid Journeys across the Pampas. Post 8vo. 2s.
——— Bubbles from the Brunnen of Nassau. Illustrations.
Post 8vo. 7s. 6d.
——— Emigrant. Fcap. 8vo. 2s. 6d.
——— Stokers and Pokers ; or, the London and North Western
Railway. Post 8vo. 2s.
——— (Sir Edmund) Shall and Will; or, Future Auxiliary
Verbs. Fcap. 8vo. 4s.

HEBER'S (Bishop) Journals in India. 2 Vols. Post 8vo. 7s.
——— Poetical Works. Portrait. Fcap. 8vo. 3s. 6d.
——— Hymns adapted to the Church Service. 16mo. 1s. 6d.

HERODOTUS. A New English Version. Edited, with Notes
and Essays, historical, ethnographical, and geographical, by Canon
Rawlinson, assisted by Sir Henry Rawlinson and Sir J. G. Wilkinson. Third Edition. Maps and Woodcuts. 4 Vols. 8vo.

HATHERLEY'S (Lord) Continuity of Scripture, as Declared
by the Testimony of our Lord and of the Evangelists and Apostles.
Fourth Edition. 8vo. 6s. Popular Edition. Post 8vo. 2s. 6d.

HOLLWAY'S (J. G.) Month in Norway. Fcap. 8vo. 2s.

HONEY BEE. By Rev. Thomas James. Fcap. 8vo. 1s.

HOOK'S (Dean) Church Dictionary. Tenth Edition. 8vo. 16s.
——— Theodore) Life. By J. G. Lockhart. Fcap. 8vo. 1s.

HOPE'S (T. C.) ARCHITECTURE OF AHMEDABAD, with Historical Sketch and Architectural Notes. With Maps, Photographs, and Woodcuts. 4to. 5*l.* 5*s.*
——— (A. J. BERESFORD) Worship in the Church of England. 8vo. 9*s.*

FOREIGN HANDBOOKS.

HAND-BOOK—TRAVEL-TALK. English, French, German, and Italian. 18mo. 3*s.* 6*d.*
——— HOLLAND,—BELGIUM, and the Rhine to Mayence. Map and Plans. Post 8vo. 6*s.*
——— NORTH GERMANY,—PRUSSIA, SAXONY, HANOVER, and the Rhine from Mayence to Switzerland. Map and Plans. Post 8vo. 6*s.*
——— SOUTH GERMANY,—Bavaria, Austria, Styria, Salzburg, the Austrian and Bavarian Alps, the Tyrol, Hungary, and the Danube, from Ulm to the Black Sea. Map. Post 8vo. 10*s.*
——— KNAPSACK GUIDE TO THE TYROL. 16mo. 6*s.*
——— PAINTING. German, Flemish, and Dutch Schools. Illustrations. 2 Vols. Post 8vo. 24*s.*
——— LIVES OF EARLY FLEMISH PAINTERS. By CROWE and CAVALCASELLE. Illustrations. Post 8vo. 10*s.* 6*d.*
——— SWITZERLAND, Alps of Savoy, and Piedmont. Maps. Post 8vo. 9*s.*
——— FRANCE, Normandy, Brittany, the French Alps, the Rivers Loire, Seine, Rhone, and Garonne. Dauphiné, Provence, and the Pyrenees. Maps. 2 Parts. Post 8vo. 12*s.*
——— ISLANDS OF THE MEDITERRANEAN—Malta, Corsica, Sardinia, and Sicily. Maps. Post 8vo.
——— ALGERIA. Map. Post 8vo. 9*s.*
——— PARIS, and its Environs. Map. 16mo. 3*s.* 6*d.*
** MURRAY'S PLAN OF PARIS, mounted on canvas. 3*s.* 6*d.*
——— SPAIN, Madrid, The Castiles, The Basque Provinces, Leon, The Asturias, Galicia, Estremadura, Andalusia, Ronda, Granada, Murcia, Valencia, Catalonia, Aragon, Navarre, The Balearic Islands, &c.&c. Maps. 2 Vols. Post 8vo. 24*s.*
——— PORTUGAL, LISBON, Porto, Cintra, Mafra, &c. Map. Post 8vo. 9*s.*
——— NORTH ITALY, Piedmont, Liguria, Venetia, Lombardy, Parma, Modena, and Romagna. Map. Post 8vo. 10*s.*
——— CENTRAL ITALY, Lucca, Tuscany, Florence, The Marches, Umbria, and the Patrimony of St. Peter's. Map. Post 8vo. 10*s.*
——— ROME AND ITS ENVIRONS. Map. Post 8vo. 10*s.*
——— SOUTH ITALY, Two Sicilies, Naples, Pompeii, Herculaneum, and Vesuvius. Map. Post 8vo. 10*s.*
——— KNAPSACK GUIDE TO ITALY. 16mo.
——— PAINTING. The Italian Schools. Illustrations. 2 Vols. Post 8vo. 30*s.*
——— LIVES OF ITALIAN PAINTERS, FROM CIMABUE to BASSANO. By Mrs. JAMESON. Portraits. Post 8vo. 12*s.*
——— RUSSIA, ST. PETERSBURG, Moscow, POLAND, and FINLAND. Maps. Post 8vo. 15*s.*
——— DENMARK. Map. Post 8vo. 6*s.*

HAND-BOOK—SWEDEN. Map. Post 8vo. 6s.
—— - NORWAY. Map. 6s.
—— GREECE, the Ionian Islands, Continental Greece, Athens, the Peloponnesus, the Islands of the Ægean Sea, Albania, Thessaly, and Macedonia. Maps. Post 8vo. 15s.
—— TURKEY IN ASIA—Constantinople, the Bosphorus, Dardanelles, Broussa, Plain of Troy, Crete, Cyprus, Smyrna, Ephesus, the Seven Churches, Coasts of the Black Sea, Armenia, Mesopotamia, &c. Maps. Post 8vo. 15s.
—— EGYPT, including Descriptions of the Course of the Nile through Egypt and Nubia, Alexandria, Cairo, and Thebes, the Suez Canal, the Pyramids, the Peninsula of Sinai, the Oases, the Fyoom, &c. Map. Post 8vo. 15s
—— HOLY LAND—Syria Palestine, Peninsula of Sinai, Edom, Syrian Desert, &c. Maps. Post 8vo.
—— - —— INDIA — Bombay and Madras. Map. 2 Vols. Post 8vo. 12s. each.

ENGLISH HANDBOOKS.

HAND-BOOK—MODERN LONDON. Map. 16mo. 3s. 6d.
—— ESSEX, CAMBRIDGE, SUFFOLK, AND NORFOLK, Chelmsford, Colchester, Maldon, Cambridge, Ely, Newmarket, Bury, Ipswich, Woodbridge, Felixstowe, Lowestoft, Norwich, Yarmouth, Cromer, &c. Map and Plans. Post 8vo. 12s.
—— CATHEDRALS of Oxford, Peterborough, Norwich, Ely, and Lincoln. With 90 Illustrations. Crown 8vo. 18s.
—— KENT AND SUSSEX, Canterbury, Dover, Ramsgate, Sheerness, Rochester, Chatham, Woolwich, Brighton, Chichester, Worthing, Hastings, Lewes, Arundel, &c. Map. Post 8vo. 10s.
—— SURREY AND HANTS, Kingston, Croydon, Reigate, Guildford, Dorking, Boxhill, Winchester, Southampton, New Forest, Portsmouth, and Isle of Wight. Maps. Post 8vo. 10s.
—— BERKS, BUCKS, AND OXON, Windsor, Eton, Reading, Aylesbury, Uxbridge, Wycombe, Henley, the City and University of Oxford, Blenheim, and the Descent of the Thames. Map. Post 8vo. 7s. 6d.
—— WILTS, DORSET, AND SOMERSET, Salisbury, Chippenham, Weymouth, Sherborne, Wells, Bath, Bristol, Taunton, &c. Map. Post 8vo. 10s.
—— DEVON AND CORNWALL, Exeter, Ilfracombe, Linton, Sidmouth, Dawlish, Teignmouth, Plymouth, Devonport, Torquay, Launceston, Truro, Penzance, Falmouth, the Lizard, Land's End, &c. Maps. Post 8vo. 12s.
—— CATHEDRALS of Winchester, Salisbury, Exeter, Wells, Chichester, Rochester, Canterbury. With 110 Illustrations. 2 Vols. Crown 8vo. 24s.
—— GLOUCESTER, HEREFORD, and WORCESTER, Cirencester, Cheltenham, Stroud, Tewkesbury, Leominster, Ross, Malvern, Kidderminster, Dudley, Bromsgrove, Evesham. Map. Post 8vo. 9s.
—— CATHEDRALS of Bristol, Gloucester, Hereford, Worcester, and Lichfield. With 50 Illustrations. Crown 8vo. 16s.
—— - -- NORTH WALES, Bangor, Carnarvon, Beaumaris, Snowdon, Llanberis, Dolgelly, Cader Idris, Conway, &c. Map. Post 8vo. 7s.
—— SOUTH WALES, Monmouth, Llandaff, Merthyr, Vale of Neath, Pembroke, Carmarthen, Tenby, Swansea, and The Wye, &c. Map. Post 8vo. 7s.

HAND-BOOK—CATHEDRALS OF BANGOR, ST. ASAPH,
Llandaff, and St. David's. With Illustrations. Post 8vo. 15s.

———— — — DERBY, NOTTS, LEICESTER, STAFFORD,
Matlock, Bakewell, Chatsworth, The Peak, Buxton, Hardwick, Dove
Dale, Ashborne. Southwell, Mansfield, Retford, Burton, Belvoir, Melton
Mowbray, Wolverhampton, Lichfield, Walsall, Tamworth. Map.
Post 8vo. 9s.

———————— SHROPSHIRE, CHESHIRE AND LANCASHIRE
—Shrewsbury, Ludlow, Bridgnorth, Oswestry, Chester, Crewe, Alderley,
Stockport, Birkenhead, Warrington, Bury, Manchester, Liverpool,
Burnley, Clitheroe, Bolton, Blackburn,† Wigan, Preston, Rochdale,
Lancaster. Southport, Blackpool, &c. Map. Post 8vo. 10s.

———————— YORKSHIRE, Doncaster, Hull, Selby, Beverley,
Scarborough, Whitby, Harrogate, Ripon, Leeds, Wakefield, Bradford,
Halifax, Huddersfield, Sheffield. Map and Plans. Post 8vo. 12s.

———————— CATHEDRALS of York, Ripon, Durham, Carlisle,
Chester, and Manchester. With 60 Illustrations. 2 Vols. Crown 8vo.
21s.

———————— DURHAM AND NORTHUMBERLAND, New-
castle, Darlington, Gateshead, Bishop Auckland, Stockton, Hartlepool,
Sunderland, Shields, Berwick-on-Tweed, Morpeth, Tynemouth, Cold-
stream, Alnwick, &c. Map. Post 8vo. 9s.

———————— WESTMORLAND AND CUMBERLAND—Lan-
caster, Furness Abbey, Ambleside, Kendal, Windermere, Coniston,
Keswick, Grasmere, Ulswater, Carlisle, Cockermouth, Penrith, Appleby,
Map. Post 8vo. 6s.
⁎ MURRAY'S MAP OF THE LAKE DISTRICT, on canvas. 3s. 6d.

———————— SCOTLAND, Edinburgh, Melrose, Kelso, Glasgow,
Dumfries, Ayr, Stirling, Arran, The Clyde, Oban, Inverary, Loch
Lomond, Loch Katrine and Trossachs, Caledonian Canal, Inverness,
Perth, Dundee, Aberdeen, Braemar, Skye, Caithness, Ross, Suther-
land, &c. Maps and Plans. Post 8vo. 9s.

———————— IRELAND, Dublin, Belfast, Donegal, Galway,
Wexford, Cork, Limerick, Waterford, Killarney, Munster, &c. Maps.
Post 8vo. 12s.

———— — — FAMILIAR QUOTATIONS. From English
Authors. Third Edition. Fcap. 8vo. 5s.

HORACE; a New Edition of the Text. Edited by DEAN MILMAN.
With 100 Woodcuts. Crown 8vo. 7s. 6d.

———— Life of. By DEAN MILMAN. Illustrations. 8vo. 9s.

HOUGHTON'S (LORD) Monographs, Personal and Social. With
Portraits. Crown 8vo. 10s. 6d.

HUME'S (The Student's) History of England, from the Invasion of Julius Cæsar to the Revolution of 1688. Corrected and continued to 1868. Woodcuts. Post 8vo. 7s. 6d.

HUTCHINSON (GEN.), on the most expeditions, certain, and
easy Method of Dog-Breaking. Fifth Edition. With 40 Illustrations.
Crown 8vo. 9s.

HUTTON'S (H. E.) Principia Græca; an Introduction to the Study
of Greek. Comprehending Grammar, Delectus, and Exercise-book,
with Vocabularies. Sixth Edition. 12mo. 3s. 6d.

IRBY AND MANGLES' Travels in Egypt, Nubia, Syria, and
the Holy Land. Post 8vo. 2s.

JACOBSON'S (BISHOP) Fragmentary Illustrations of the History
of the Book of Common Prayer; from Manuscript Sources (Bishop
SANDERSON and Bishop WREN). 8vo. 5s.

JAMES' (REV. THOMAS) Fables of Æsop. A New Translation, with
Historical Preface. With 100 Woodcuts by TENNIEL and WOLF.
Sixty-fourth Thousand. Post 8vo. 2s. 6d.

HOME AND COLONIAL LIBRARY. A Series of Works adapted for all circles and classes of Readers, having been selected for their acknowledged interest, and ability of the Authors. Post 8vo. Published at 2s. and 3s. 6d. each, and arranged under two distinctive heads as follows :—

CLASS A.

HISTORY, BIOGRAPHY, AND HISTORIC TALES.

1. SIEGE OF GIBRALTAR. By JOHN DRINKWATER. 2s.
2. THE AMBER-WITCH. By LADY DUFF GORDON. 2s.
3. CROMWELL AND BUNYAN. By ROBERT SOUTHEY. 2s.
4. LIFE OF SIR FRANCIS DRAKE. By JOHN BARROW. 2s.
5. CAMPAIGNS AT WASHINGTON. By REV. G. R. GLEIG. 2s.
6. THE FRENCH IN ALGIERS. By LADY DUFF GORDON. 2s.
7. THE FALL OF THE JESUITS. 2s.
8. LIVONIAN TALES. 2s.
9. LIFE OF CONDÉ. By LORD MAHON. 3s. 6d.
10. SALE'S BRIGADE. By REV. G. R. GLEIG. 2s.
11. THE SIEGES OF VIENNA. By LORD ELLESMERE. 2s.
12. THE WAYSIDE CROSS. By CAPT. MILMAN. 2s.
13. SKETCHES OF GERMAN LIFE. By SIR A. GORDON. 3s. 6d.
14. THE BATTLE OF WATERLOO. By REV. G. R. GLEIG. 3s. 6d.
15. AUTOBIOGRAPHY OF STEFFENS. 2s.
16. THE BRITISH POETS. By THOMAS CAMPBELL. 3s. 6d.
17. HISTORICAL ESSAYS, By LORD MAHON. 3s. 6d.
18. LIFE OF LORD CLIVE. By REV. G. R. GLEIG. 3s. 6d.
19. NORTH - WESTERN RAILWAY. By SIR F. B. HEAD. 2s.
20. LIFE OF MUNRO. By REV. G. R. GLEIG. 3s. 6d.

CLASS B.

VOYAGES, TRAVELS, AND ADVENTURES.

1. BIBLE IN SPAIN. By GEORGE BORROW. 3s. 6d.
2. GYPSIES OF SPAIN. By GEORGE BORROW. 3s. 6d.
3 & 4. JOURNALS IN INDIA. By BISHOP HEBER. 2 Vols. 7s.
5. TRAVELS IN THE HOLY LAND. By IRBY and MANGLES. 2s.
6. MOROCCO AND THE MOORS. By J. DRUMMOND HAY. 2s.
7. LETTERS FROM THE BALTIC. By a LADY. 2s.
8. NEW SOUTH WALES. By MRS. MEREDITH. 2s.
9. THE WEST INDIES. By M. G. LEWIS. 2s.
10. SKETCHES OF PERSIA. By SIR JOHN MALCOLM. 3s. 6d.
11. MEMOIRS OF FATHER RIPA. 2s.
12 & 13. TYPEE AND OMOO. By HERMANN MELVILLE. 2 Vols. 7s.
14. MISSIONARY LIFE IN CANADA. By REV. J. ABBOTT. 2s.
15. LETTERS FROM MADRAS. By a LADY. 2s.
16. HIGHLAND SPORTS. By CHARLES ST. JOHN. 3s. 6d.
17. PAMPAS JOURNEYS. By SIR F. B. HEAD. 2s.
18. GATHERINGS FROM SPAIN. By RICHARD FORD. 3s. 6d.
19. THE RIVER AMAZON. By W. H. EDWARDS. 2s.
20. MANNERS & CUSTOMS OF INDIA. By REV. C. ACLAND. 2s.
21. ADVENTURES IN MEXICO. By G. F. RUXTON. 3s. 6d.
22. PORTUGAL AND GALLICIA. By LORD CARNARVON. 3s. 6d.
23. BUSH LIFE IN AUSTRALIA. By REV. H. W. HAYGARTH. 2s.
24. THE LIBYAN DESERT. By BAYLE ST. JOHN. 2s.
25. SIERRA LEONE. By A LADY. 3s. 6d.

** Each work may be had separately.

JAMESON'S (Mrs.) Lives of the Early Italian Painters—and the Progress of Painting in Italy—Cimabue to Bassano. *New Edition.* With 50 Portraits. Post 8vo. 12s.

JENNINGS' (L. J.) Eighty Years of Republican Government in the United States. Post 8vo. 10s. 6d.

JERVIS'S (Rev. W. H.) Gallican Church, from the Concordat of Bologna, 1516, to the Revolution. With an Introduction. Portraits. 2 Vols. 8vo. 28s.

JESSE'S (Edward) Gleanings in Natural History. Fcp. 8vo. 3s. 6d.

JOHNS' (Rev. B. G.) Blind People; their Works and Ways. With Sketches of the Lives of some famous Blind Men. With Illustrations. Post 8vo. 7s. 6d.

JOHNSON'S (Dr. Samuel) Life. By James Boswell. Including the Tour to the Hebrides. Edited by Mr. Croker. *New revised Library Edition.* Portraits. 4 Vols. 8vo. [In Preparation.

—— Lives of the most eminent English Poets, with Critical Observations on their Works. Edited with Notes, Corrective and Explanatory, by Peter Cunningham. 3 vols. 8vo. 22s. 6d.

JUNIUS' Handwriting Professionally investigated. By Mr. Chabot, Expert. With Preface and Collateral Evidence, by the Hon. Edward Twisleton. With Facsimiles, Woodcuts, &c. 4to. £3 3s.

KEN'S (Bishop) Life. By a Layman. Portrait. 2 Vols. 8vo. 18s.

—— Exposition of the Apostles' Creed. 16mo. 1s. 6d.

KERR'S (Robert) GENTLEMAN'S HOUSE; or, How to Plan English Residences, from the Parsonage to the Palace. *Third Edition.* With Views and Plans. 8vo. 24s.

—— Small Country House. A Brief Practical Discourse on the Planning of a Residence from 2000l. to 5000l. With Supplementary Estimates to 7000l. Post 8vo. 3s.

—— Ancient Lights; a Book for Architects, Surveyors, Lawyers, and Landlords. 8vo. 5s. 6d.

—— (R. Malcolm) Student's Blackstone. A Systematic Abridgment of the entire Commentaries, adapted to the present state of the law. Post 8vo. 7s. 6d.

KING EDWARD VIth's Latin Grammar. *Seventeenth Edition.* 12mo. 3s. 6d.

—— First Latin Book. *Fifth Edition.* 12mo. 2s. 6d.

KING GEORGE IIIrd's CORRESPONDENCE WITH LORD NORTH, 1769-82. Edited, with Notes and Introduction, by W. Bodham Donne. 2 vols. 8vo. 32s.

KING'S (R. J.) Sketches and Studies; Historical and Descriptive. 8vo. 12s.

KIRK'S (J. Foster) History of Charles the Bold, Duke of Burgundy. Portrait. 3 Vols. 8vo. 45s.

KIRKES' Handbook of Physiology. Edited by W. Morrant Baker, F.R.C.S. *Eighth Edit.* With 240 Illustrations. Post 8vo. 12s. 6d.

KUGLER'S Handbook of Painting.—The Italian Schools. *Fourth Edition.* Revised and Remodelled from the most recent Researches. By Lady Eastlake. With 140 Illustrations. 2 Vols. Crown 8vo. 30s.

—— Handbook of Painting.—The German, Flemish, and Dutch Schools. *Third Edition.* Revised and in part re-written. By J. A. Crowe. With 60 Illustrations. 2 Vols. Crown 8vo. 24s.

LANE'S (E. W.) Account of the Manners and Customs of Modern Egyptians. *New Edition.* With Illustrations. 2 Vols. Post 8vo. 12s.

LAWRENCE'S (Sir Geo.) Reminiscences of Forty-three Years' Service in India; including Captivities in Cabul among the Affghans and among the Sikhs, and a Narrative of the Mutiny in Rajputana. Edited by W. Edwards, H.M.C.B.S. Crown 8vo. 10s. 6d.

c 2

LAYARD'S (A. H.) Nineveh and its Remains. Being a Narrative of Researches and Discoveries amidst the Ruins of Assyria. With an Account of the Chaldean Christians of Kurdistan; the Yezedis, or Devil-worshippers; and an Enquiry into the Manners and Arts of the Ancient Assyrians. *Sixth Edition.* Plates and Woodcuts. 2 Vols. 8vo. 36s.
  ** A POPULAR EDITION of the above work. With Illustrations. Post 8vo. 7s. 6d.

———— Nineveh and Babylon ; being the Narrative of Discoveries in the Ruins, with Travels in Armenia, Kurdistan and the Desert, during a Second Expedition to Assyria. With Map and Plates. 8vo. 21s.
  ** A POPULAR EDITION of the above work. With Illustrations. Post 8vo. 7s. 6d.

LEATHES' (STANLEY) Practical Hebrew Grammar. With the Hebrew Text of Genesis i.—vi., and Psalms i.—vi. Grammatical Analysis and Vocabulary. Post 8vo. 7s. 6d.

LENNEP'S (REV. H. J. VAN) Missionary Travels in Asia Minor. With Illustrations of Biblical History and Archæology. With Map and Woodcuts. 2 Vols. Post 8vo. 24s.

LESLIE'S (C. R.) Handbook for Young Painters. With Illustrations. Post 8vo. 7s. 6d.

———— Life and Works of Sir Joshua Reynolds. Portraits and Illustrations. 2 Vols. 8vo. 42s.

LETTERS FROM THE BALTIC. By a LADY. Post 8vo. 2s.

———— MADRAS. By a LADY. Post 8vo. 2s.

———— SIERRA LEONE. By a LADY. Post 8vo. 3s. 6d.

LEVI'S (LEONE) History of British Commerce; and of the Economic Progress of the Nation, from 1763 to 1870. 8vo. 16s.

LEWIS'S (M. G.) Journal of a Residence among the Negroes in the West Indies. Post 8vo. 2s.

LIDDELL'S (DEAN) Student's History of Rome, from the earliest Times to the establishment of the Empire. With Woodcuts. Post 8vo. 7s. 6d.

LINDSAY'S (LORD) Lives of the Lindsays ; Memoir of the Houses of Crawford and Balcarres. With Extracts from Official Papers and Personal Narratives. 3 Vols. 8vo. 24s.

———— Etruscan Inscriptions. Analysed, Translated, and Commented upon. 8vo. 12s.

LLOYD'S (W. WATKISS) History of Sicily to the Athenian War ; with Elucidations of the Sicilian Odes of Pindar. With Map. 8vo. 14s.

LISPINGS from LOW LATITUDES; or, the Journal of the Hon. Impulsia Gushington. Edited by LORD DUFFERIN. With 24 Plates.4to.21s.

LITTLE ARTHUR'S HISTORY OF ENGLAND. By LADY CALLCOTT. *New and Cheaper Edition, continued to 1872.* With Woodcuts. Fcap. 8vo. 1s. 6d.

LIVINGSTONE'S (DR.) Popular Account of Missionary Travels and Researches in South Africa. Illustrations. Post 8vo. 6s.

———— Narrative of an Expedition to the Zambezi and its Tributaries, with the Discovery of the Lakes Shirwa and Nyassa. Map and Illustrations. 8vo. 21s.

———— Last Journals in Central Africa, from 1865 to his Death. Continued by a Narrative of his last moments and sufferings. By Rev. HORACE WALLER. Maps and Illustrations. 2 Vols. 8vo. 28s.

LIVONIAN TALES. By the Author of "Letters from the Baltic." Post 8vo. 2s.

LOCH'S (H. B.) Personal Narrative of Events during Lord Elgin's Second Embassy to China. *Second Edition.* With Illustrations. Post 8vo. 9s.

LOCKHART'S (J. G.) Ancient Spanish Ballads. Historical and Romantic. Translated, with Notes. *New Edition*. With Portrait and Illustrations. Crown 8vo. 5s.

———— Life of Theodore Hook. Fcap. 8vo. 1s.

LONSDALE'S (BISHOP) Life. With Selections from his Writings. By E. B. DENISON. With Portrait. Crown 8vo. 10s. 6d.

LOUDON'S (MRS.) Gardening for Ladies. With Directions and Calendar of Operations for Every Month. *Eighth Edition*. Woodcuts. Fcap. 8vo. 3s. 6d.

LUCKNOW: A Lady's Diary of the Siege. Fcap. 8vo. 4s. 6d.

LYELL'S (SIR CHARLES) Principles of Geology; or, the Modern Changes of the Earth and its Inhabitants considered as illustrative of Geology. *Eleventh Edition*. With Illustrations. 2 Vols. 8vo. 32s.

———— Student's Elements of Geology. *Second Edition*. With Table of British Fossils and 600 Illustrations. Post 8vo. 9s.

———— Geological Evidences of the Antiquity of Man, including an Outline of Glacial Post-Tertiary Geology, and Remarks on the Origin of Species. *Fourth Edition*. Illustrations. 8vo. 14s.

———— (K. M.) Geographical Handbook of Ferns. With Tables to show their Distribution. Post 8vo. 7s. 6d.

LYTTELTON'S (LORD) Ephemera. 2 Vols. Post 8vo. 19s. 6d.

LYTTON'S (LORD) Memoir of Julian Fane. With Portrait. Post 8vo. 5s.

McCLINTOCK'S (SIR L.) Narrative of the Discovery of the Fate of Sir John Franklin and his Companions in the Arctic Seas. *Third Edition*. With Illustrations. Post 8vo. 7s. 6d.

MACDOUGALL'S (COL.) Modern Warfare as Influenced by Modern Artillery. With Plans. Post 8vo. 12s.

MACGREGOR'S (J.) Rob Roy on the Jordan, Nile, Red Sea, Gennesareth, &c. A Canoe Cruise in Palestine and Egypt and the Waters of Damascus. *Cheaper Edition*. With Map and 70 Illustrations. Crown 8vo. 7s. 6d

MACPHERSON'S (MAJOR) Services in India, while Political Agent at Gwalior during the Mutiny. Illustrations. 8vo. 12s.

MAETZNER'S ENGLISH GRAMMAR. A Methodical, Analytical, and Historical Treatise on the Orthography, Prosody, Inflections, and Syntax of the English Tongue. Translated from the German. By CLAIR J. GRECE, LL.D. 3 Vols. 8vo. 36s.

MAHON (LORD), see STANHOPE.

MAINE'S (SIR H. SUMNER) Ancient Law: its Connection with the Early History of Society, and its Relation to Modern Ideas. *Fifth Edition*. 8vo. 12s.

———— Village Communities in the East and West. *Second Edition*. 8vo. 9s.

———— Early History of Institutions. 8vo. 12s.

MALCOLM'S (SIR JOHN) Sketches of Persia. Post 8vo. 3s. 6d.

MANSEL'S (DEAN) Limits of Religious Thought Examined. *Fifth Edition*. Post 8vo. 8s. 6d.

———— Letters, Lectures, and Papers, including the Phrontisterion, or Oxford in the XIXth Century. Edited by H. W. CHANDLER, M.A. 8vo. 12s.

———— Gnostic Heresies of the First and Second Centuries. With a sketch of his life and character. By Lord CARNARVON. Edited by Canon LIGHTFOOT. 8vo. 10s. 6d.

MANUAL OF SCIENTIFIC ENQUIRY. For the Use of Travellers. Edited by SIR J. F. HERSCHEL & REV. R. MAIN. Post 8vo. 3s. 6d. (*Published by order of the Lords of the Admiralty.*)

MARCO POLO. The Book of Ser Marco Polo, the Venetian.
Concerning the Kingdoms and Marvels of the East. A new English
Version. Illustrated by the light of Oriental Writers and Modern
Travels. By Col. HENRY YULE. *New Edition*. Maps and Illustra-
tions. 2 Vols. Medium 8vo. 42s.

MARKHAM'S (Mrs.) History of England. From the First Inva-
sion by the Romans to 1867. Woodcuts. 12mo. 3s. 6d.
————— History of France. From the Conquest by the
Gauls to 1861. Woodcuts. 12mo. 3s. 6d.
————— History of Germany. From the Invasion by Marius
to 1867. Woodcuts. 12mo. 3s. 6d.
————— (CLEMENTS R.) Travels in Peru and India. Maps
and Illustrations. 8vo. 16s.

MARRYAT'S (JOSEPH) History of Modern and Mediæval Pottery
and Porcelain. With a Description of the Manufacture. *Third
Edition*. Plates and Woodcuts. 8vo. 42s.

MARSH'S (G. P.) Student's Manual of the English Language.
Post 8vo. 7s. 6d.

MATTHIÆ'S GREEK GRAMMAR. Abridged by BLOMFIELD,
Revised by E. S. CROOKE. 12mo. 4s.

MAUREL'S Character, Actions, and Writings of Wellington.
Fcap. 8vo. 1s. 6d.

MAYNE'S (CAPT.) Four Years in British Columbia and Van-
couver Island. Illustrations. 8vo. 16s.

MEADE'S (HON. HERBERT) Ride through the Disturbed Districts of
New Zealand, with a Cruise among the South Sea Islands. With Illustrations. Medium 8vo. 12s.

MELVILLE'S (HERMANN) Marquesas and South Sea Islands.
2 Vols. Post 8vo. 7s.

MEREDITH'S (MRS. CHARLES) Notes and Sketches of New South
Wales. Post 8vo. 2s.

MESSIAH (THE): The Life, Travels, Death, Resurrection, and
Ascension of our Blessed Lord. By A LAYMAN. Map. 8vo. 18s.

MILLINGTON'S (REV. T. S.) Signs and Wonders in the Land of
Ham, or the Ten Plagues of Egypt. with Ancient and Modern Illustrations. Woodcuts. Post 8vo. 7s. 6d.

MILLS' (REV. JOHN) Three Months' Residence at Nablus, with
an Account of the Modern Samaritans. Illustrations. Post 8vo. 10s. 6d.

MILMAN'S (DEAN) History of the Jews, from the earliest Period
down to Modern Times. *Fourth Edition*. 3 Vols. Post 8vo. 18s.
————— Early Christianity, from the Birth of Christ to the
Abolition of Paganism in the Roman Empire. *Fourth Edition*. 3 Vols.
Post 8vo. 18s.
————— Latin Christianity, including that of the Popes to
the Pontificate of Nicholas V. *Fourth Edition*. 9 Vols. Post 8vo. 54s.
————— Annals of St. Paul's Cathedral, from the Romans to
the funeral of Wellington. *Second Edition*. Portrait and Illustrations.
8vo. 18s.
————— Character and Conduct of the Apostles considered
as an Evidence of Christianity. 8vo. 10s. 6d.
————— Quinti Horatii Flacci Opera. With 100 Woodcuts.
Small 8vo. 7s. 6d.
————— Life of Quintus Horatius Flaccus. With Illustra-
tions. 8vo. 9s.
————— Poetical Works. The Fall of Jerusalem—Martyr of
Antioch—Balshazzar—Tamor—Anne Boleyn—Fazio, &c. With Por-
trait and Illustrations. 3 Vols. Fcap. 8vo. 18s.
————— Fall of Jerusalem. Fcap. 8vo. 1s.
————— (CAPT. E. A.) Wayside Cross. Post 8vo. 2s.

MICHIE'S (ALEXANDER) Siberian Overland Route from Peking
to Petersburg. Maps and Illustrations. 8vo. 16s.

MODERN DOMESTIC COOKERY. Founded on Principles of
Economy and Practical Knowledge. *New Edition*. Woodcuts. Fcap. 8vo. 5s.

MONGREDIEN'S (AUGUSTUS) Trees and Shrubs for English
Plantation. A Selection and Description of the most Ornamental
which will flourish in the open air in our climate. With Classified
Lists. With 30 Illustrations. 8vo. 16s.

MOORE & JACKMAN on the Clematis as a Garden Flower.
Descriptions of the Hardy Species and Varieties, with Directions for
their Cultivation. 8vo. 10s. 6d.

MOORE'S (THOMAS) Life and Letters of Lord Byron. *Cabinet
Edition.* With Plates. 6 Vols. Fcap. 8vo. 18s.; *Popular Edition*,
with Portraits. Royal 8vo. 7s. 6d.

MOSSMAN'S (SAMUEL) New Japan; the Land of the Rising Sun ;
its Annals and Progress during the past Twenty Years, recording the
remarkable Progress of the Japanese in Western Civilisation. With
Map. 8vo. 15s.

MOTLEY'S (J. L.) History of the United Netherlands : from the
Death of William the Silent to the Twelve Years' Truce, 1609. *Library
Edition.* Portraits. 4 Vols. 8vo. 60s. *Cabinet Edition.* 4 Vols. Post
8vo. 6s. each.

————— Life and Death of John of Barneveld,
Advocate of Holland. With a View of the Primary Causes and
Movements of the Thirty Years' War. Illustrations. 2 Vols. 8vo. 28s.

MOUHOT'S (HENRI) Siam, Cambojia, and Lao ; a Narrative of
Travels and Discoveries. Illustrations. 2 vols. 8vo.

MOZLEY'S (CANON) Treatise on Predestination. 8vo. 14s.

————— Primitive Doctrine of Baptismal Regeneration. 8vo. 7s. 6d.

MUNDY'S (GENERAL) Pen and Pencil Sketches in India.
Third Edition. Plates. Post 8vo. 7s. 6d.

MUNRO'S (GENERAL) Life and Letters. By REV. G. R. GLEIG.
Post 8vo. 3s. 6d.

MURCHISON'S (SIR RODERICK) Russia in Europe and the Ural
Mountains. With Coloured Maps, &c. 2 Vols. 4to. 5l. 5s.

————— Siluria ; or, a History of the Oldest Rocks containing Organic Remains. *Fifth Edition.* Map and Plates. 8vo. 18s.

————— Memoirs. With Notices of his Contemporaries,
and Rise and Progress of Palæozoic Geology. By ARCHIBALD GEIKIE.
Portraits. 2 Vols. 8vo.

MURRAY'S RAILWAY READING. Containing:—

WELLINGTON. By LORD ELLESMERE. 6d.	MAHON'S JOAN OF ARC. 1s.
NIMROD ON THE CHASE. 1s.	HEAD'S EMIGRANT. 2s. 6d.
MUSIC AND DRESS. 1s.	NIMROD ON THE ROAD. 1s.
MILMAN'S FALL OF JERUSALEM. 1s.	CROKER ON THE GUILLOTINE. 1s.
MAHON'S "FORTY-FIVE." 3s.	HOLLWAY'S NORWAY. 2s.
LIFE OF THEODORE HOOK. 1s.	MAUREL'S WELLINGTON. 1s. 6d.
DEEDS OF NAVAL DARING. 3s. 6d.	CAMPBELL'S LIFE OF BACON. 2s. 6d.
THE HONEY BEE. 1s.	THE FLOWER GARDEN. 1s.
ÆSOP'S FABLES. 2s. 6d.	TAYLOR'S NOTES FROM LIFE. 2s.
NIMROD ON THE TURF. 1s. 6d.	REJECTED ADDRESSES. 1s.
ART OF DINING. 1s. 6d.	PENN'S HINTS ON ANGLING. 1s.

MUSTERS' (CAPT.) Patagonians; a Year's Wanderings over
Untrodden Ground from the Straits of Magellan to the Rio Negro.
2nd Edition. Illustrations. Post 8vo. 7s. 6d.

NAPIER'S (SIR CHAS.) Life, Journals, and Letters. *Second
Edition.* Portraits. 4 Vols. Post 8vo. 48s.

————— (SIR WM.) Life and Letters. Portraits. 2 Vols.
Crown 8vo. 28s.

————— English Battles and Sieges of the Peninsular War.
Fourth Edition. Portrait. Post 8vo. 9s.

NAPOLEON AT FONTAINEBLEAU AND ELBA. A Journal of Occurrences and Notes of Conversations. By Sir Neil Campbell, C.B. With a Memoir. By Rev. A. N. C. Maclachlan, M.A. Portrait. 8vo. 15s.

NASMYTH and CARPENTER. The Moon. Considered as a Planet, a World, and a Satellite. With Illustrations from Drawings made with the aid of Powerful Telescopes, Woodcuts, &c. *Second Edition.* 4to. 30s.

NAUTICAL ALMANAC (The). (*By Authority.*) 2s. 6d.

NAVY LIST. (Monthly and Quarterly.) Post 8vo.

NEW TESTAMENT. With Short Explanatory Commentary. By Archdeacon Churton, M.A., and Archdeacon Basil Jones, M.A. With 110 authentic Views, &c. 2 Vols. Crown 8vo. 21s. bound.

NEWTH'S (Samuel) First Book of Natural Philosophy; an Introduction to the Study of Statics, Dynamics, Hydrostatics, Optics, and Acoustics, with numerous Examples. Small 8vo. 3s. 6d.

————— Elements of Mechanics, including Hydrostatics, with numerous Examples. *Fifth Edition.* Small 8vo. 8s. 6d. Cloth.

————— Mathematical Examinations. A Graduated Series of Elementary Examples in Arithmetic, Algebra, Logarithms, Trigonometry, and Mechanics. *Third Edition.* Small 8vo. 8s. 6d. each.

NICHOLLS' (Sir George) History of the English, Irish and Scotch Poor Laws. 4 Vols. 8vo.

NICOLAS' (Sir Harris) Historic Peerage of England. Exhibiting the Origin, Descent, and Present State of every Title of Peerage which has existed in this Country since the Conquest. By William Courthope. 8vo. 30s.

NIMROD, On the Chace—Turf—and Road. With Portrait and Plates. Crown 8vo. 5s. Or with Coloured Plates, 7s. 6d.

NORDHOFF'S (Chas.) Communistic Societies of the United States; including Detailed Accounts of the Shakers, The Amana, Oneida, Bethell, Aurora, Icarian and other existing Societies; with Particulars of their Religious Creeds, Industries, and Present Condition. With 40 Illustrations. 8vo. 15s.

OLD LONDON; Papers read at the Archæological Institute. By various Authors. 8vo. 12s.

ORMATHWAITE'S (Lord) Astronomy and Geology—Darwin and Buckle—Progress and Civilisation. Crown 8vo. 6s.

OWEN'S (Lieut.-Col.) Principles and Practice of Modern Artillery, including Artillery Material, Gunnery, and Organisation and Use of Artillery in Warfare. *Second Edition.* With Illustrations. 8vo. 15s.

OXENHAM'S (Rev. W.) English Notes for Latin Elegiacs; designed for early Proficients in the Art of Latin Versification, with Prefatory Rules of Composition in Elegiac Metre. *Fifth Edition.* 12mo. 3s. 6d.

PALGRAVE'S (R. H. I.) Local Taxation of Great Britain and Ireland. 8vo. 5s.

————— Notes on Banking in Great Britain and Ireland, Sweden, Denmark, and Hamburg, with some Remarks on the amount of Bills in circulation, both Inland and Foreign. 8vo. 6s.

PALLISER'S (Mrs.) Brittany and its Byeways, its Inhabitants, and Antiquities. With Illustrations. Post 8vo. 12s.

————— Mottoes for Monuments, or Epitaphs selected for General Use and Study. With Illustrations. Crown 8vo. 7s. 6d.

PARIS' (Dr.) Philosophy in Sport made Science in Earnest; or, the First Principles of Natural Philosophy inculcated by aid of the Toys and Sports of Youth. *Ninth Edition.* Woodcuts. Post 8vo. 7s. 6d.

PARKMAN'S (Francis) Discovery of the Great West; or, The Valleys of the Mississippi and the Lakes of North America. An Historical Narrative. Map. 8vo. 10s. 6d.

PARKYNS' (MANSFIELD) Three Years' Residence in Abyssinia: with Travels in that Country. *Second Edition*, with Illustrations. Post 8vo. 7s. 6d.

PEEK PRIZE ESSAYS. The Maintenance of the Church of England as an Established Church. By REV. CHARLES HOLE—REV. R. WATSON DIXON—and REV. JULIUS LLOYD. 8vo. 10s. 6d.

PEEL'S (SIR ROBERT) Memoirs. 2 Vols. Post 8vo. 15c.

PENN'S (RICHARD) Maxims and Hints for an Angler and Chess-player. Woodcuts. Fcap. 8vo. 1s.

PERCY'S (JOHN, M.D.) Metallurgy. Vol. I., Part 1. Fuel, Wood, Peat, Coal, Charcoal. Coke, Refractory Materials, Fire-Clays, &c. *Second Edition*. With Illustrations. 8vo. 24s.

———— Vol. I., Part 2. Copper, Zinc, Brass. *Second Edition*. With Illustrations. 8vo. *(In the Press.)*

———— Vol. II. Iron and Steel. *New Edition*. With Illustrations. 8vo. *(In Preparation.)*

. Vol. III. Lead, including Desilverization and Cupellation. With Illustrations. 8vo. 30s.

Vols. IV. and V. Gold, Silver, and Mercury, Platinum, Tin, Nickel, Cobalt, Antimony, Bismuth, Arsenic, and other Metals. With Illustrations. 8vo. *(In Preparation.)*

PERSIA'S (SHAH or) Diary during his Tour through Europe in 1873. Translated from the Original. By J. W. REDHOUSE. With Portrait and Coloured Title. Crown 8vo. 12s.

PHILLIPS' (JOHN) Memoirs of William Smith. 8vo. 7s. 6d.

———— Geology of Yorkshire, The Coast, and Limestone District. Plates. 4to.

———— Rivers, Mountains, and Sea Coast of Yorkshire. With Essays on the Climate, Scenery, and Ancient Inhabitants. *Second Edition*, Plates. 8vo. 15s.

———— (SAMUEL) Literary Essays from "The Times." With Portrait. 2 Vols. Fcap. 8vo. 7s.

PICK'S (DR.) Popular Etymological Dictionary of the French Language. 8vo. 7s. 6d.

POPE'S (ALEXANDER) Works. With Introductions and Notes, by REV. WHITWELL ELWIN. Vols. I., II., VI., VII., VIII. With Portraits. 8vo. 10s. 6d. each.

PORTER'S (REV. J. L.) Damascus, Palmyra, and Lebanon. With Travels among the Giant Cities of Bashan and the Hauran. *New Edition*. Map and Woodcuts. Post 8vo. 7s. 6d.

PRAYER-BOOK (ILLUSTRATED), with Borders, Initials, Vignettes, &c. Edited, with Notes, by REV. THOS. JAMES. Medium 8vo. 18s. *cloth ;* 31s. 6d. *calf ;* 36s. *morocco*.

PRINCESS CHARLOTTE OF WALES. A Brief Memoir. With Selections from her Correspondence and other unpublished Papers. By LADY ROSE WEIGALL. With Portrait. 8vo. 8s. 6d.

PUSS IN BOOTS. With 12 Illustrations. By OTTO SPECKTER. 16mo. 1s. 6d. Or coloured, 2s. 6d.

PRINCIPLES AT STAKE. Essays on Church Questions of the Day. 8vo. 12s. Contents:—

Ritualism and Uniformity.—Benjamin Shaw.	Scripture and Ritual.—Canon Bernard.
The Episcopate.—Bishop of Bath and Wells.	Church in South Africa. — Arthur Mills.
The Priesthood.—Dean of Canterbury.	Schismatical Tendency of Ritualism. – Rev. Dr. Salmon.
National Education.—Rev. Alexander R. Grant.	Revisions of the Liturgy.—Rev. W. G. Humphry.
Doctrine of the Eucharist.—Rev. G. H. Sumner.	Parties and Party Spirit.—Dean of Chester.

PRIVY COUNCIL JUDGMENTS in Ecclesiastical Cases relating to Doctrine and Discipline. With Historical Introduction, by G. C. Brodrick and W. H. Fremantle. 8vo. 10s. 6d.

QUARTERLY REVIEW (The). 8vo. 6s.

RAMBLES in the Syrian Deserts. Post 8vo. 10s. 6d.

RANKE'S (Leopold) History of the Popes of Rome during the 16th and 17th Centuries. Translated from the German by Sarah Austin. Third Edition. 3 Vols. 8vo. 30s.

RASSAM'S (Hormuzd) Narrative of the British Mission to Abyssinia. With Notices of the Countries Traversed from Massowah to Magdala. Illustrations. 2 Vols. 8vo. 28s.

RAWLINSON'S (Canon) Herodotus. A New English Version. Edited with Notes and Essays. Third Edition. Maps and Woodcut. 4 Vols. 8vo.

———— Five Great Monarchies of Chaldæa, Assyria, Media, Babylonia, and Persia. Third Edition. With Maps and Illustrations. 3 Vols. 8vo. 42s.

———— (Sir Henry) England and Russia in the East; a Series of Papers on the Political and Geographical Condition of Central Asia. Map. 8vo.

REED'S (E. J.) Shipbuilding in Iron and Steel; a Practical Treatise, giving full details of Construction, Processes of Manufacture, and Building Arrangements. With 5 Plans and 250 Woodcuts. 8vo. 30s.

———— Iron-Clad Ships; their Qualities, Performances, and Cost. With Chapters on Turret Ships, Iron-Clad Rams, &c. With Illustrations. 8vo. 12s.

REJECTED ADDRESSES (The). By James and Horace Smith. New Edition. Woodcuts. Post 8vo. 3s. 6d.; or Popular Edition, Fcap. 8vo. 1s.

RENNIE'S (D. F.) British Arms in Peking, 1860. Post 8vo. 12s.

———— Narrative of the British Embassy in China. Illustrations. 2 Vols. Post 8vo. 24s.

———— Story of Bhotan and the Dooar War. Map and Woodcut. Post 8vo. 12s.

RESIDENCE IN BULGARIA; or, Notes on the Resources and Administration of Turkey, &c. By S. G. B. St.Clair and Charles A. Brophy. 8vo. 12s.

REYNOLDS' (Sir Joshua) Life and Times. By C. R. Leslie, R.A. and Tom Taylor. Portraits. 2 Vols. 8vo.

RICARDO'S (David) Political Works. With a Notice of his Life and Writings. By J. R. M'Culloch. New Edition. 8vo. 16s.

RIPA'S (Father) Thirteen Years' Residence at the Court of Peking. Post 8vo. 2s.

ROBERTSON'S (Canon) History of the Christian Church, from the Apostolic Age to the Reformation, 1517. Library Edition. 4 Vols. 8vo. Cabinet Edition. 8 Vols. Post 8vo. 6s. each.

———— How shall we Conform to the Liturgy. 12mo. 9s.

ROME. See Liddell and Smith.

ROWLAND'S (David) Manual of the English Constitution. Its Rise, Growth, and Present State. Post 8vo. 10s. 6d.

———— Laws of Nature the Foundation of Morals. Post 8vo. 6s.

ROBSON'S (E. R.) SCHOOL ARCHITECTURE. Being Practical Remarks on the Planning, Designing, Building, and Furnishing of School-houses. With 300 Illustrations of School-buildings in all Parts of the World, drawn to scale. Medium 8vo. 31s. 6d.

RUNDELL'S (Mrs.) Modern Domestic Cookery. Fcap. 8vo. 5s.

RUXTON'S (George F.) Travels in Mexico; with Adventures among the Wild Tribes and Animals of the Prairies and Rocky Mountains. Post 8vo. 3s. 6d.

ROBINSON'S (Rev. Dr.) Biblical Researches in Palestine and the Adjacent Regions, 1838—52. *Third Edition.* Maps. 3 Vols. 8vo. 42s.

———————-- Physical Geography of the Holy Land. Post 8vo. 10s. 6d.

——————— (Wm.) Alpine Flowers for English Gardens. *New Edition.* With 70 Illustrations. Crown 8vo. [*Nearly ready.*

——————— Wild Garden; or, our Groves and Shrubberies made beautiful by the Naturalization of Hardy Exotic Plants. With Frontispiece. Small 8vo. 6s.

—— - —— Sub-Tropical Garden ; or, Beauty of Form in the Flower Garden. With Illustrations. Small 8vo. 7s. 6d.

SALE'S (Sir Robert) Brigade in Affghanistan. With an Account of the Defence of Jellalabad. By Rev. G. R. Gleig. Post 8vo. 2s.

SCHLIEMANN'S (Dr. Henry) Troy and Its Remains. A Narrative of Researches and Discoveries made on the Site of Ilium, and in the Trojan Plain. Edited by Philip Smith, B.A. With Maps, Plans, Views, and 500 Illustrations of Objects of Antiquity, &c. Medium 8vo.

SCOTT'S (Sir G. G.) Secular and Domestic Architecture, Present and Future. 8vo. 9s.

- (Dean) University Sermons. Post 8vo. 8s. 6d.

SHADOWS OF A SICK ROOM. *Second Edition.* With a Preface by Canon Liddon. 16mo. 2s. 6d.

SCROPE'S (G. P.) Geology and Extinct Volcanoes of Central France. Illustrations. Medium 8vo. 30s.

SHAW'S (T. B.) Manual of English Literature. Post 8vo. 7s. 6d.

—————— Specimens of English Literature. Selected from the Chief Writers. Post 8vo. 7s. 6d.

—————— (Robert) Visit to High Tartary, Yarkand, and Kashgar (formerly Chinese Tartary), and Return Journey over the Karakorum Pass. With Map and Illustrations. 8vo. 16s.

SHIRLEY'S (Evelyn P.) Deer and Deer Parks; or some Account of English Parks, with Notes on the Management of Deer. Illustrations. 4to. 21s.

SIERRA LEONE; Described in Letters to Friends at Home. By A Lady. Post 8vo. 3s. 6d.

SINCLAIR'S (Archdeacon) Old Times and Distant Places. A Series of Sketches. Crown 8vo.

SMILES' (Samuel) Lives of British Engineers; from the Earliest Period to the death of the Stephensons. With Portraits and Illustrations. *Cabinet Edition.* 5 Vols. Crown 8vo. 7s. 6d. each.

—————— Lives of George and Robert Stephenson. *Library Edition.* With Portraits and Illustrations. Medium 8vo. 21s.

—————— Lives of Boulton and Watt. *Library Edition.* With Portraits and Illustrations. Medium 8vo. 21s.

—————— Self-Help. With Illustrations of Conduct and Perseverance. Post 8vo. 6s. Or in French, 5s.

- Character. A Companion Volume to "Self-Help." Post 8vo. 6s.

-- -- — Industrial Biography: Iron-Workers and Tool-Makers. Post 8vo. 6s.

—————— Boy's Voyage round the World: including a Residence in Victoria, and a Journey by Rail across North America. With Illustrations. Post 8vo. 6s.

SMITH'S (Dr. Wm.) Dictionary of the Bible: its Antiquities, Biography, Geography, and Natural History. Illustrations. 3 Vols. 8vo. 105s.

———— ———— ———— Christian Antiquities. Comprising the History, Institutions, and Antiquities of the Christian Church. 2 Vols. 8vo. Vol. I. *(Nearly ready.*

———— ———— ———— Biography and Doctrines; from the Times of the Apostles to the Age of Charlemagne. 8vo. *(In Preparation.*

———— Concise Bible Dictionary. With 300 Illustrations. Medium 8vo. 21s.

———— Smaller Bible Dictionary. With Illustrations. Post 8vo. 7s. 6d.

———— Atlas of Ancient Geography—Biblical and Classical. (5 Parts.) Folio. 21s. each.

———— Greek and Roman Antiquities. With 500 Illustrations. Medium 8vo. 28s.

———— ———— Biography and Mythology. With 600 Illustrations. 3 Vols. Medium 8vo. 4l. 4s.

———— ———— Geography. 2 Vols. With 500 Illustrations. Medium 8vo. 56s.

———— Classical Dictionary of Mythology, Biography, and Geography. 1 Vol. With 750 Woodcuts. 8vo. 18s.

———— Smaller Classical Dictionary. With 200 Woodcuts. Crown 8vo. 7s. 6d.

———— Greek and Roman Antiquities. With 200 Woodcuts. Crown 8vo. 7s. 6d.

———— Latin-English Dictionary. With Tables of the Roman Calendar, Measures, Weights, and Money. Medium 8vo. 21s.

———— Smaller Latin-English Dictionary. 12mo. 7s. 6d.

———— English-Latin Dictionary. Medium 8vo. 21s.

———— Smaller English-Latin Dictionary. 12mo. 7s. 6d.

———— School Manual of English Grammar, with Copious Exercises. Post 8vo. 3s. 6d.

———— Primary English Grammar. 16mo. 1s.

———— ———— History of Britain. 12mo. 2s. 6d.

———— French Principia. Part I. A Grammar, Delectus, Exercises, and Vocabularies. 12mo. 3s. 6d.

———— Principia Latina—Part I. A Grammar, Delectus, and Exercise Book, with Vocabularies. With the ACCIDENCE arranged for the "Public School Primer." 12mo. 3s. 6d.

———— ———— Part II. A Reading-book of Mythology, Geography, Roman Antiquities, and History. With Notes and Dictionary. 12mo. 3s. 6d.

———— ———— Part III. A Latin Poetry Book. Hexameters and Pentameters; Eclog. Ovidianæ; Latin Prosody. 12mo. 3s. 6d.

———— ———— Part IV. Latin Prose Composition. Rules of Syntax, with Examples, Explanations of Synonyms, and Exercises on the Syntax. 12mo. 3s. 6d.

———— ———— Part V. Short Tales and Anecdotes for Translation into Latin. 12mo. 3s.

———— Latin-English Vocabulary and First Latin-English Dictionary for Phædrus, Cornelius Nepos, and Cæsar. 12mo. 3s. 6d.

———— Student's Latin Grammar. Post 8vo. 6s.

———— Smaller Latin Grammar. 12mo. 3s. 6d.

SMITH'S (DR. WM.) Tacitus, Germania, Agricola, &c. With English
Notes. 12mo. 3s. 6d.
———— Initia Græca, Part I. A Grammar, Delectus, and
Exercise-book. With Vocabularies. 12mo. 3s. 6d.
———— Initia Græca, Part II. A Reading Book. Containing
Short Tales, Anecdotes, Fables, Mythology, and Grecian History.
12mo. 3s. 6d.
———— Initia Græca, Part III. Greek Prose Composition. Con-
taining the Rules of Syntax, with copious Examples and Exercises.
12mo. 3s. 6d.
———— Student's Greek Grammar. By PROFESSOR CURTIUS.
Post 8vo. 6s.
———— Smaller Greek Grammar. 12mo. 3s. 6d.
—————— Greek Accidence. Extracted from the above work.
12mo. 2s. 6d.
———— Plato. The Apology of Socrates, the Crito, and Part of
the Phædo; with Notes in English from Stallbaum and Schleierma-
cher's Introductions. 12mo. 3s. 6d.
———— Smaller Scripture History. Woodcuts. 16mo.
3s. 6d.
———— Ancient History. Woodcuts. 16mo. 3s. 6d.
————— Geography. Woodcuts. 16mo. 3s. 6d.
———— Rome. Woodcuts. 16mo. 3s. 6d.
———— Greece. Woodcuts. 16mo. 3s. 6d.
———— Classical Mythology. With Translations from
the Poets. Woodcuts. 16mo. 3s. 6d.
———— History of England. Woodcuts. 16mo. 3s. 6d.
———— English Literature. 16mo. 3s. 6d.
———— Specimens of English Literature. 16mo. 3s. 6d.
———— (PHILIP) History of the Ancient World, from the
Creation to the Fall of the Roman Empire, A.D. 455. Fourth Edition.
3 Vols. 8vo. 31s. 6d.
———— (REV. A. C.) Nile and its Banks. Woodcuts. 2 Vols.
Post 8vo. 18s.
SIMMONS' (CAPT.) Constitution and Practice of Courts-Mar-
tial; with a Summary of the Law of Evidence, and some Notice
of the Criminal Law of England with reference to the Trial of Civil
Offences. Sixth Edition. 8vo. 15s.
STANLEY'S (DEAN) Sinai and Palestine, in connexion with their
History. 20th Thousand. Map. 8vo. 14s.
———— Bible in the Holy Land; Extracted from the above
Work. Second Edition. Woodcuts. Fcap. 8vo. 2s 6d.
———— History of the Eastern Church. Fourth Edition.
Plans. 8vo. 12s.
———————— Jewish Church. Fifth Edition.
8vo. 24s.
———————— Church of Scotland. 8vo. 7s. 6d.
———— Memorials of Canterbury Cathedral. Fifth Edition.
Woodcuts. Post 8vo. 7s. 6d.
——————— Westminster Abbey. Third Edition.
With Illustrations. 8vo. 21s.
———— Sermons during a Tour in the East. 8vo. 9s.
———————— on Evangelical and Apostolical Teaching.
Post 8vo. 7s. 6d.
——— - ADDRESSES AND CHARGES OF THE LATE BISHOP STANLEY.
With Memoir. 8vo. 10s. 6d.

STUDENT'S OLD TESTAMENT HISTORY ; from the Creation
to the Return of the Jews from Captivity. Maps and Woodcuts. Post
8vo. 7s. 6d.
———— NEW TESTAMENT HISTORY. With an Intro-
duction connecting the History of the Old and New Testaments. Maps
and Woodcuts. Post 8vo. 7s. 6d.
———— ANCIENT HISTORY OF THE EAST ; Egypt,
Assyria, Babylonia, Media, Persia, Asia Minor, and Phœnicia. By
PHILIP SMITH. Woodcuts. Post 8vo. 7s. 6d.
———— GEOGRAPHY. By REV. W. L. BEVAN.
Woodcuts. Post 8vo. 7s. 6d.
———— HISTORY OF GREECE ; from the Earliest
Times to the Roman Conquest. By WM. SMITH, D.C.L. Woodcuts.
Crown 8vo. 7s. 6d.
  ₊ Questions on the above Work, 12mo. 2s.
———— HISTORY OF ROME ; from the Earliest Times
to the Establishment of the Empire. By DEAN LIDDELL. Woodcuts.
Crown 8vo. 7s. 6d.
———— GIBBON'S Decline and Fall of the Roman Empire.
Woodcuts. Post 8vo. 7s. 6d.
———— HALLAM'S HISTORY OF EUROPE during the
Middle Ages. Post 8vo. 7s. 6d.
———— HUME'S History of England from the Invasion
of Julius Cæsar to the Revolution in 1688. Continued down to 1868.
Woodcuts. Post 8vo. 7s. 6d.
  ₊ Questions on the above Work. 12mo. 2s.
———— HALLAM'S HISTORY OF ENGLAND ; from the
Accession of Henry VII. to the Death of George II. Post 8vo. 7s. 6d.
———— ENGLISH LANGUAGE. By GEO. P. MARSH.
Post 8vo. 7s. 6d.
———— LITERATURE. By T. B. SHAW, M.A.
Post 8vo. 7s. 6d.
———— SPECIMENS of English Literature from the Chief
Writers. By T. B. SHAW, Post 8vo. 7s. 6d.
———— HISTORY OF FRANCE ; from the Earliest Times
to the Establishment of the Second Empire, 1852. By REV. H. W.
JERVIS. Woodcuts. Post 8vo. 7s. 6d.
———— MODERN GEOGRAPHY ; Mathematical, Physi-
cal, and Descriptive. By REV. W. L. BEVAN. Woodcuts. Post 8vo. 7s. 6d.
———— MORAL PHILOSOPHY. By WILLIAM FLEMING,
D.D. Post 8vo. 7s. 6d.
———— BLACKSTONE'S Commentaries on the Laws of
England. By R. MALCOLM KERR, LL.D. Post 8vo. 7s. 6d.
———— ECCLESIASTICAL HISTORY. A History of the
Christian Church from its Foundation to the Eve of the Protestant
Reformation. By PHILIP SMITH, B.A. Post 8vo. 7s. 6d.
SPALDING'S (CAPTAIN) Tale of Frithiof. Translated from the
Swedish of ESIAS TEGNER. Post 8vo. 7s. 6d.
STEPHEN'S (REV. W. R.) Life and Times of St. Chrysostom.
With Portrait. 8vo. 15s.
ST. JOHN'S (CHARLES) Wild Sports and Natural History of the
Highlands. Post 8vo. 3s. 6d.
———— (BAYLE) Adventures in the Libyan Desert. Post 8vo. 2s.
STORIES FOR DARLINGS. With Illustrations. 16mo. 5s.
STREET'S (G. E.) Gothic Architecture in Spain. From Personal
Observations made during several Journeys. Second Edition. With
Illustrations. Royal 8vo. 30s.
———— Gothic Architecture in Italy, chiefly in Brick and
Marble. With Notes of Tours in the North of Italy. Second Edition.
With 60 Illustrations. Royal 8vo. 26s.

STANHOPE'S (Earl) England during the Reign of Queen Anne, 1701—13. *Library Edition.* 8vo. 16s. *Cabinet Edition.* Portrait. 2 Vols. Post 8vo. 10s.

———— from the Peace of Utrecht to the Peace of Versailles, 1713-83. *Library Edition.* 7 vols. 8vo. 93s. *Cabinet Edition,* 7 vols. Post 8vo. 5s. each.

———— British India, from its Origin to 1783. 8vo. 3s. 6d.

———— History of " Forty-Five." Post 8vo. 3s.

———— Spain under Charles the Second. Post 8vo. 6s. 6d.

———— Historical and Critical Essays. Post 8vo. 3s. 6d.

———— Life of Belisarius. Post 8vo. 10s. 6d.

———— Condé. Post 8vo. 3s. 6d.

———— William Pitt. Portraits. 4 Vols. 8vo. 24s.

———— Miscellanies. 2 Vols. Post 8vo. 13s.

———— Story of Joan of Arc. Fcap. 8vo. 1s.

———— Addresses Delivered on Various Occasions. 16mo. 1s.

STYFFE'S (Knutt) Strength of Iron and Steel. Plates. 8vo. 12s.

SOMERVILLE'S (Mary) Physical Geography. *Sixth Edition,* Portrait. Post 8vo. 9s.

———— Connexion of the Physical Sciences. *Ninth Edition.* Portrait. Post 8vo. 9s.

———— Molecular and Microscopic Science. Illustrations. 2 Vols. Post 8vo. 21s.

———— Personal Recollections from Early Life to Old Age. With Selections from her Correspondence. *Fourth Edition.* Portrait. Crown 8vo. 12s.

SOUTHEY'S (Robert) Book of the Church. Post 8vo. 7s. 6d.

———— Lives of Bunyan and Cromwell. Post 8vo. 2s.

SWAINSON'S (Canon) Nicene and Apostles' Creeds; Their Literary History; together with some Account of " The Creed of St. Athanasius." 8vo.

SYBEL'S (Von) History of Europe during the French Revolution, 1789—1795. 4 Vols. 8vo. 48s.

SYMONDS' (Rev. W.) Records of the Rocks; or Notes on the Geology, Natural History, and Antiquities of North and South Wales, Siluria, Devon, and Cornwall. With Illustrations. Crown 8vo. 12s.

TAYLOR'S (Sir Henry) Notes from Life. Fcap. 8vo. 2s.

THIELMAN'S (Baron) Journey through the Caucasus to Tabreez, Kurdistan, down the Tigris and Euphrates to Nineveh and Babylon, and across the Desert to Palmyra. Translated by Chas. Heneage. 2 Vols. Post 8vo.

THOMS' (W. J.) Longevity of Man; its Facts and its Fiction. Including Observations on the more Remarkable Instances. Post 8vo. 10s. 6d.

THOMSON'S (Archbishop) Lincoln's Inn Sermons. 8vo. 10s. 6d.

———— Life in the Light of God's Word. Post 8vo. 5s.

TOCQUEVILLE'S State of Society in France before the Revolution, 1789, and on the Causes which led to that Event. Translated by Henry Reeve. 2nd Edition. 8vo. 12s.

TOMLINSON (Charles); The Sonnet; Its Origin, Structure, and Place in Poetry. With translations from Dante, Petrarch, &c. Post 8vo. 9s.

TOZER'S (Rev. H. F.) Highlands of Turkey, with Visits to Mounts Ida, Athos, Olympus, and Pelion. 2 Vols. Crown 8vo. 24s.

———— Lectures on the Geography of Greece. Map. Post 8vo. 9s.

TRISTRAM'S (CANON) Great Sahara. Illustrations. Crown 8vo. 15s.
——— Land of Moab ; Travels and Discoveries on the East
Side of the Dead Sea and the Jordan. *Second Edition.* Illustrations.
Crown 8vo. 15s.

TWISLETON (EDWARD). The Tongue not Essential to Speech,
with Illustrations of the Power of Speech in the case of the African
Confessors. Post 8vo. 6s.

TWISS' (HORACE) Life of Lord Eldon. 2 Vols. Post 8vo. 21s.

TYLOR'S (E. B.) Early History of Mankind, and Development
of Civilization. *Second Edition.* 8vo. 12s.
——— Primitive Culture ; the Development of Mythology,
Philosophy, Religion, Art, and Custom. *Second Edition.* 2 Vols. 8vo. 24s.

VAMBERY'S (ARMINIUS) Travels from Teheran across the Turko-
man Desert on the Eastern Shore of the Caspian. Illustrations. 8vo. 21s.

VAN LENNEP'S (HENRY J.) Travels in Asia Minor. With
Illustrations of Biblical Literature, and Archæology. With Woodcuts.
2 Vols. Post 8vo. 24s.

WELLINGTON'S Despatches during his Campaigns in India,
Denmark, Portugal, Spain, the Low Countries, and France. Edited
by COLONEL GURWOOD. 8 Vols. 8vo. 20s. each.
——— Supplementary Despatches, relating to India,
Ireland, Denmark, Spanish America, Spain, Portugal, France, Con-
gress of Vienna, Waterloo and Paris. Edited by his SON. 14 Vols.
8vo. 20s. each. *₄* *An Index.* 8vo. 20s.
——— Civil and Political Correspondence. Edited by
his SON. Vols. I. to V. 8vo. 20s. each.
——— Despatches (Selections from). 8vo. 18s.
——— Speeches in Parliament. 2 Vols. 8vo. 42s.

WHEELER'S (G.) Choice of a Dwelling ; a Practical Handbook of
Useful Information on Building a House. *Third Edition.* Plans. Post
8vo. 7s. 6d.

WHITE'S (HENRY) Massacre of St. Bartholomew. 8vo. 16s.

WHYMPER'S (EDWARD) Scrambles among the Alps. With the
First Ascent of the Matterhorn, and Notes on Glacial Phenomena.
Second Edition. Illustrations. 8vo. 21s.
——— (FREDERICK) Travels and Adventures in Alaska.
Illustrations. 8vo. 16s.

WILBERFORCE'S (BISHOP) Essays on Various Subjects. 2 vols.
8vo. 21s.
——— Life of William Wilberforce. Portrait. Crown
8vo. 6s.

WILKINSON'S (SIR J. G.) Popular Account of the Ancient
Egyptians. With 500 Woodcuts. 2 Vols. Post 8vo. 12s.

WOOD'S (CAPTAIN) Source of the Oxus. With the Geography
of the Valley of the Oxus. By COL. YULE. Map. 8vo. 12s.

WORDS OF HUMAN WISDOM. Collected and Arranged by
E. S. With a Preface by Canon LIDDON, D.D. Fcp. 8vo. 3s. 6d.

WORDSWORTH'S (BISHOP) Athens and Attica. Plates. 8vo. 5s.
——— Greece. Pictorial, Descriptive, and Historical.
With 600 Woodcuts. Royal 8vo.

YULE'S (COLONEL) Book of Marco Polo. Illustrated by the
Light of Oriental Writers and Modern Travels. With Maps and 80
Plates. 2 Vols. Medium 8vo. 42s.

ZINCKE'S (REV. F. B.) Winter in the United States. Post 8vo.
10s. 6d.

PRADBURY, AGNEW, & CO., PRINTERS, WHITEFRIARS.

www.ingramcontent.com/pod-product-compliance
Lightning Source LLC
Chambersburg PA
CBHW021755110726
47902CB00006B/1529